William Ernest Henley

English Lyrics

William Ernest Henley

English Lyrics

ISBN/EAN: 9783744769303

Printed in Europe, USA, Canada, Australia, Japan

Cover: Foto ©Andreas Hilbeck / pixelio.de

More available books at **www.hansebooks.com**

ENGLISH LYRICS

ENGLISH LYRICS

CHAUCER TO POE

1340-1809

SELECTED AND ARRANGED BY

WILLIAM ERNEST HENLEY

A Book of Verses underneath the Bough,
A Jug of Wine, a Loaf of Bread, and Thou
Beside me singing in the Wilderness—
O, Wilderness were Paradise enow.
Omàr Khàyyàm.

LONDON: METHUEN AND CO.

J. B. LIPPINCOTT COMPANY

PHILADELPHIA

1897

Edinburgh: T. and A. CONSTABLE, Printers to Her Majesty

PREFACE

BEGINNING with Chaucer, this book should have ended with Tennyson. As it could not end with Tennyson, it begins with the Beginner of English Poetry, and ends, by a piece of chronological good luck, with the one American I know who, thus far, can claim fellowship with the greater English Poets. Its object is to present a fairly representative collection of such among the purely lyrical treasures of our tongue as were amassed between Chaucer and Poe. Whether or not it achieves that object is not, of course, for me to say. But I may be pardoned for pointing out that it has two features which I believe to be novel. Acting on the principle that verse in English is, *ipso facto*, English verse, and realising that the English Lyric has lived in Scotland when it was moribund, or worse, in England, I have included, with the work of the aforesaid American, examples of certain old-world Scots, nameless and other: not much read, I fear, in the land which gave them birth, but, as seems to me, worth reading anywhere. Again, the Authorised Version is a monument of English Prose. But the inspiration and the effect of many parts of it are absolutely lyrical; and on those parts I have drawn for such a series of achievements in lyrism as will be found, I trust, neither the least interesting nor the least persuasive group in an anthology which pretends to set forth none but the choicest among English lyrics.

It is easy to tell a lyric when you see one. It is not so easy to say what a lyric is. 'Lyrical,' says Mr. Palgrave in his Preface to the best-read anthology in the language, has been—presumably, therefore, should be—'held to imply that each Poem shall turn on some single thought, feeling, or situation.' I would rather say that unless 'thought,' *and* 'feeling,' *and* 'situation' all are single, and are all present, and so present that in the final result 'feeling'

shall oblige us to forget the others, or at least to consider them as
chiefly essential to its triumphing expression, that result is not a lyric.
In *Ruth*, for instance, the situation may be described (perhaps) as
'single'; but the 'thought' is so full of change, the 'feeling' so
placid and so impersonal, that to make *Ruth* a lyric is to make
lyrics of most of the stories in lyrical forms we have.   Again,
both 'thought' and 'situation' are 'single' in Gray's *Ode on a
Distant Prospect of Eton College*; but, though the intention of the
thing is lyrical, it finds no place in this anthology, for the reason
that, to me at least, it lacks that quality without which no piece
of verse, whatever its appearance on the printed page, can ever be
held a lyric.   I mean the quality of emotion : or, as Mr. Palgrave
calls it, 'feeling.'   It is the absence of this quality, or its presence
in the smallest doses, and these extremely disguised, which makes
the lyrical output of the years between Rochester and Blake so
scant in quantity and so poor in kind.   And this, as I believe, is
rather due to a radical vice in the authors of that output than to
the tyranny of any literary fashions in deference to which they may
have worked.   Distinction in speech, clarity of phrase, elegance of
form, reserve in utterance—that these Augustan ideals, all essential
to good verse in any age, are compatible, however mannered and
made modish and so in a sense estranged, with true lyrism is shown
in the work of Collins, and is shown there for the fundamental
reason that Collins had what I must call the Lyrical Temperament,
and was therefore, in fact as well as in design, a Lyric Poet.
Apply this temperamental test to Marvell's *Horatian Ode* (257), or
Chaucer's *Merciless Beauty* (3), or Jonson's *Epithalamy* (161), or
Herrick's *To Daffodils* (214), or Dunbar's *Lament* (4), or Keats's
Belle Dame Sans Merci (400)—in fact to any number in this book,
as I believe—and your result will be the same.   Apply it to
anything of Addison's and Prior's and Shenstone's, and to well
nigh everything of Pope's and Thomson's and Gay's, and your
result is different.   Marvell and those others had the Lyrical
Temperament, and could be Lyrists at will ; Addison and those
others lacked it, and could not.   The nameless poet of *The Twa
Corbies* (265) had it, and *The Twa Corbies* is unmatched among
objective and impersonal lyrics.   Southey, to take an example
from the antipodes of letters—Southey had it not ; and you shall
search his dozen volumes in vain for so much as a trace of it.

There is plenty of verse in those volumes that would fain be lyrical
if it could. But it never can; for Southey was not thus gifted.
And, just as there is little or nothing in all Shelley which has not
at least the lyrical thrill, so there is never a lyric in all Southey.

As I think, then, the specific attribute, the saving and essential
virtue, of verse that is lyrical to ear and heart as distinguished
from verse that is lyrical to the eye alone, is temperamental in
origin and emotional in effect. If a poet have the Lyrical Temperament, his effect will be lyrical whenever, and in whatever form,[1]
he is moved to pass on an emotion, or a sequence of emotions,
from himself to his hearers, whether present or to be, in the terms
of art. The emotion thus distinguished may be grave, or gay, or
anything you please. It may soar to a rapture of supplication—as
in Drayton's famous quatorzain (102); of gaiety—as in *Green
Grow the Rashes* (326); of exultant vision and anticipation—as in
Spenser's *Epithalamion* (76). Or it may decline upon such a mood
of tender human feeling, half-generous and half-playful, as Congreve's *False Though She Be* (281); or on such a joyous yet
desperate recognition of the fleeting excellence of life as Jordan's
Careless Gallant (246):—

> ' Let 's eat, drink, and play, ere the worms do corrupt us,
>   For I say that *Post Mortem*
>   *Nulla Voluptas!*
> Let 's deal with our damsels, that we may from thence
> Have broods to succeed us a hundred years hence.'

---

[1] The Lyrical Temperament is above form, and is largely independent of it : for
the reason that its output, whatever shape it assume, is inevitably a Lyric. The
complexity of Chaucer, in *The Complaynt of Mars*, is bewildering, but its
effect is lyrical; so is that of the sumptuous and stately stanzas of Spenser's
two great bridal songs ; and so is that of the curious rhythms of Montgomerie's
Banks of Helicon (71). But, so too is that of what is in comparison the bell-
man's verse of *Since First I Saw Your Face* (150). Milton and Tennyson
have shown, each in his own way, that the noblest lyrical effects are to be got
out of new-created rhymeless rhythms and unrhyming heroic iambics. Then,
Crashaw's loose-hung dithyrambs (248-50) are absolutely lyrical ; but so, on the
other hand, are the elegant yet simple cadences of Ben Jonson's *Drink to Me
Only* (157) and *Queen and Huntress* (153); so is the magical blending of in-
tensity with utter sweetness, music the loveliest with perfect strength, in some
of Shakespeare's Sonnets (115-127). And, to pass to an extreme instance, what
is more lyrical in sound and substance and spirit than the passages which I
have excerpted from the English Bible (27-69)?

But (and this is my contention) the result is ever a Lyric. The emotion projected may be touched with humour—as in so much of the true Burns's best (316, 319, 325); with the mystery and the romance of Life and Death—as in *Proud Maisie* (340) ; with modish extravagance—as in *What Shall I Do* (274); with drink—as in *The Happy Trio* (316) and in *Vulcan, Contrive Me Such a Cup* (284) ; with all the agonies and the gallantries of a mystical piety—as in Crashaw (248-50); with a right feeling for 'old unhappy far-off things'—as in Jean Elliot (297) and Dunbar (4); with wonder and terror—as in *The Tiger* (312) ; with a true man's weariness— as in *We 'll Go No More A-Roving* (377); with a transforming sense of the picturesque in character and history—as in *Bonny Dundee* (347) and *Donald Caird* (345)—or of troubled and anxious happiness—as in *My Dear Mistress* (257); with an overpowering apprehension of the great inevitable processes of nature—as in the *Ode to the West Wind* (381). It may be hope, or remorse, or desire, or contemplation, or despair—any passion of which the human heart is capable. But, whatever its character and quality, there it must be, and it must be projected through a temperament. Or Lyric there is none.

A single emotion temperamentally expressed in the terms of poetry—that is a Lyric. And note that the Lyrical Temperament has nothing whatever to do with the capacity for feeling. They may co-exist in a Lyric Poet—as they do in Shakespeare and Byron and Keats. But it is in nowise necessary that they should. What English-speaking man was ever, so far as we know, the prey of a more desperate passion and a more poignant sense of the greater issues than Swift? And which of us, so far as we know, was ever more careless of those issues than Herrick? Yet Herrick was an unique lyrist, and Swift was no lyrist at all; and Swift could no more have written *Bid Me to ' Live* (212), or any song of Herrick's, than Herrick could have written *Gulliver* or the *Directions to Servants*, or any line of Swift's. It is a matter of, not genius but, gift. Fifty Herricks would not have made a Swift. But Herrick had the gift, and the greater man had not ; and Herrick is a master-lyrist, and Swift left never a lyric line. In the same way, we may take for granted that Johnson's capacity for feeling was certainly as great as, if not greater than, Milton's. Yet Johnson's essays in lyrical verse are frigid

trifles,[1] while Milton's Invocations to Sabrina (240) and to Echo
(243), with *Lycidas* (242) and the Song for Comus (239), are lyrics
whose essential quality is now as fresh, as clear, and as flawless as
when it first took shape in enchanted words.   We know nothing
which will help my argument of either the man Lyly or the man
Shirley.   But we can see for ourselves that Shirley's share of the
gift was greater than Lyly's, for Shirley could write such lyrics as
O, Fly, My Soul (222) and *Earth's Victories* (223), while Lyly's
best-known attempt at lyrism :—

> 'Cupid and my Campaspe played,' *etc.* :—

is plainly no lyric but an epigram.   I might go on exampling the
true Lyric and the false, the Lyric (that is) which is temperamental
and the Lyric which is not ; but I think that I have done enough.
And if I add that I have seen things so essentially anti-lyrical, to
me at least, as Bacon's :—

> ' The world 's a bubble, and the life of man
> Less than a span,' *etc.* :—

as Wordsworth's *Simon Lee* :—

> ' Few months of life has he in store,
>   As he to you will tell,
> For still, the more he works, the more
>   Do his weak ankles swell.
> My gentle Reader, I perceive
>   How patiently you 've waited,
> And now I fear that you expect
>   Some tale will be related ' :—

and as Wotton's beautiful and famous epitaph :—

> ' He first deceased ; She for a little tried
> To live without him, liked it not, and died ' :—

all quoted as Lyrics, I shall have said as much as I need to indicate
the lines on which this book is done.

   To insist on the paramount importance of the Lyrical Temperament is not in any sense to diminish or deny the importance of example and environment.   Both are such influences, indeed, that it is
possible to conceive a Jonson who, writing in an age of circulating

---

[1] I except the verses on Frank Levett : which should, perhaps, have found
a place in this anthology.

libraries, would put out his *Alchymists* and *Epicœnes* as novels, and a Dickens, who, the tune being set him by his time, would express the Pickwickians in the terms of drama, and send his Gamp to rival Mrs. Quickly on the boards. And that this is so the English Lyric shows as well as any form in which the literary genius of the race has ever expressed itself. A poet of immense genius, an artist unsurpassed (I take it) by any Englishman of any time, Chaucer wrote Lyrics, as he wrote everything that was writing in his time. But example and environment were against him, and, though he had the Lyrical Temperament, as (I believe) he had all the others, the forms imposed upon him were so complex, and the effects, as *The Compleynt of Mars*, he achieved in them are so remote, that I have been able to quote from him only two numbers whose intention and result are lyrical: together with a third for which he is responsible only in so far as he is author of the lovely narrative from which it is excerpted. Chaucer dead, a hush fell on the English Muse. There was Henryson in Scotland, the Master's greatest pupil, an admirable poet—but no lyrist; while in England there were only such founts of tedium as Lydgate and Gower and Hawes, and, till the coming of Dunbar, whose lyrical gift is shown, imperfectly but irresistibly, in my quotations from him (4-6), English Lyrics there were none. After Dunbar Skelton; and with Skelton, rough and ragged as his verses are, a breath of true lyrism, which makes his songs in praise of Johanna Scoope and Isabel Pennell (I wish I could quote his *Mannerly Margery*, but—!) lyrically alive unto this day. With Skelton came the turn. The age of Henry VIII. was lyrically given; and, if in the long run one think little of Wyatt, one remembers that the King himself wrote verses, and sang them, one makes the best one can of the general lyrical drift of the collection called *Tottel's Miscellany* (I shall deal with the shining exception presently), and one rejoices in the quatrain which I have quoted from the Royal MS. (19) as a true burst of temperament, a lyrical beginning which has never found its Burns. With this last I have grouped the anonymous numbers—well-meant, and more, in English; well metricised, and more, in Scots—culled from Tottel and from that precious manuscript which James Bannatyne, an Edinburgh citizen, wrote in a time of pestilence (1568), when needs must he do something to keep his mind off the grisly work that

was getting done outside. Signed or unsigned, however, there is
nothing in *The Bannatyne MS.* (with the exception of 25, as to
which see my Note) to lower the crest of Alexander Scott (14-17) :
just as in the *Miscellany* there is none so brilliant as to be in any
way comparable to the brilliancy of Surrey (9-11), 'Son of the Morning,' by whose execution such a blow was dealt to English letters
as is scarce equalled by that they met in the murder of Marlowe.
Come now the noble numbers—passionate, affecting, essentially
lyrical—from one of the two greatest books in English. They are
selected and repeated from the Authorised Version (1613), for that
achievement in art is, like so much else that is perdurable in art,
the outcome of a tradition, begun when Tyndale (*Pentateuch*,
1530; *Jonah*, 1531) and Coverdale (the Old and New Testaments,
1535) made the great body of Hebrew poetry and history and
legend an English book. Between Coverdale's Bible and the
Authorised Version some six or seven translations, all widely read
and each owing something to the others, were given to the English
people ; so it is safe to say that the Authorised Version, unknown
to Wyatt and Surrey and Scott, was known, in one or other of its
early metamorphoses, to Gascoigne and Breton and Spenser. The
rest is plain sailing in open water ; for these three stand at the
head of that unrivalled reach of lyrism which, spreading to and
shining in its utmost capacities of breadth and splendour in the
times of Jonson and Fletcher and Shakespeare, was presently
illuminated and refreshed by the concourse of such freshets and such
streams of song as Carew and Herrick and Suckling, the Milton
of *Comus* and *Samson Agonistes*, Crashaw, the Caroline Shelley,
the Dryden of the *Saint Cecilia* odes and certain parts of the *Anne
Killigrew* ; and, at its last term wofully dimmed and shrunken,
a little quickened and refreshed by the song of Sedley, Mrs.
Behn, and Rochester—this last, with his wild heart and his
broken life and his notable gift of temperament, easily first—(since
Milton is a belated sublimation of Elizabethanism)—after Dryden
among the Restoration lyrists. In the 'Augustan' atmosphere
of Addison and Pope the English Lyric all but died again—was
practically dead, in fact, but for Collins, and a stray burst from
Goldsmith, and the humble work of certain Scots, who had a sounder
tradition than the Augustans, and followed it as best they might.
It was the dark hour before the dawn ; and the dawn was Blake,

that Elizabethan, and something more, born into an age of prose, and Burns, the humourist of genius, the unrivalled artist, who so vamped the folk-song of a nation that he breathed new life into it at the same time that he made it seem his own. And the day of that dawn was Wordsworth and Sir Walter, was Landor, the protest and the restraint, and Coleridge, the universal inspiration, and Byron, in whom passion was figured, and the master-lyrist, Shelley, and Keats, besides performances the most glorious possibility in all the range of English Verse. And after Keats there is no fresh note, until we hear from over the Atlantic, the artful, subtle, irresistible song of Poe: the New Music which none that has heard it can forget, and which, if you listen for it, you will catch in much of the melody that has found utterance since Mr. Swinburne, working after Baudelaire, shocked and enchanted the world with his First Series of *Poems and Ballads*. It is with the beginnings of this New Music that my concert ends. The Coleridge-Keats School culminated in Tennyson; and I would fain have made my close an harmonious and beautiful contrast between Old and New. But this, for reasons which I need not discuss, was not to be. W. E. H.

POSTSCRIPT.—My thanks are due to Mr. F. T. Palgrave for permission to reprint his redaction of a famous Scots ballad (266); to Mr. George Wyndham for the hint that Shakespeare's theory of the quatorzain is based on the practice of—not Daniel nor Drayton but—Surrey, and the suggestion, among others, that the numbers excerpted from Chaucer's *Troilus* (2) might well be found lyrical in the true sense and to the finest purpose; to Mr. T. F. Henderson for revising and correcting the glossarial element, and to Mr. James Fitzmaurice-Kelly for compiling and redacting the bibliographical matter, in the Notes.

ENGLISH LYRICS

FIVE CENTURIES OF SONG

I

BALLADE TO HIS LADY

HIDE, Absolon, thy giltë tresses clere ;
Ester, lay thou thy meekness all a-doun ;
Hide, Ionathas, all thy friendly manére ;
Penalopee and Marcia Catoun,
Make of your wifehood no comparisoun ;
Hide ye your beauties, Isoude and Eleyne :
My lady cometh, that all this may disteyne !

Thy fairë body, let it not appere,
Lavyne ; and thou, Lucrece of Romë toun,
And Polixene, that boughten love so dere,
And Cleopatre, with all thy passioun,
Hide ye your trouthe of love and your renoun ;
And thou, Tisbe, that hast of love such peyne :
My lady cometh, that all this may disteyne !

Herró, Didó, Laudómia, all y-fere,
And Phyllis, hanging for thy Demophoun,
And Canacé, espiéd by thy chere,
Ysiphilé, betrayséd with Jasoun,
Maketh of your trouth neither boast nor soun,
Nor Ypermistre or Adriane, ye tweyne :
My lady cometh, that all this may disteyne !

Geoffrey Chaucer.

A

2

THE COMPLAINT OF TROILUS

I

Therewith when he was ware, and gan behold
How shut was every window of the place,
As frost, him thought, his hertë gan to cold ;
For which with changëd, deedlich, palë face,
With-outen word, he forth began to pace ;
And, as God would, he gan so fastë ride,
That no wight of his countenance espied.

Then said he thus :—'O palace desolate,
O house of houses whilom best y-hight,
O palace empty and disconsolate,
O thou lantérn, of which quaint is the light,
O palace, whilom day, that now art night,
Well oughtest thou to fall, and I to die,
Since she is went that wont was us to gye !

O palace, whilom crown of houses all,
Enluminéd with sun of allë bliss !
O ring fro which the ruby is out-fall !
O cause of woe, that cause hast been of lisse !
Yet, since I may no bet, fain would I kiss
Thy coldë dorës, durst I for this route— .
And farewell shrine, of which the saint is out !'

II

Fró thennësforth he rideth up and down,
And everything com him to remembrance
As he rood forth by places of the town,
In which he whilom had all his pleasance :—
'Lo, yond saw I mine owen lady dance ;
And in that temple, with her eyen clere,
Me caughtë first my rightë lady dere.

And yonder have I heard full lustily
My derë hertë laugh, and yonder play
Saw I her onës eke full blissfully.
And yonder onës to me gan she say :—
"Now goodë swetë, love me well, I pray."
And yond so goodly gan she me behold,
That to the death mine herte is to her hold.

And at that corner, in the yonder house,
Heard I mine alderlevest lady dere
So womanly, with voice melodious,
Singing so well, so goodly, and so clere,
That in my soul yet methinketh I hear
The blissful sound ; and, in that yonder place,
My lady first me took unto her grace.'

III

A song of wordës but a few,
Somewhat his woful hertë for to light.
And when he was from every mannës sight,
With softë voice he, of his lady dear,
That was absent, gan sing as ye may hear :—

'O star, of which I lost have all the light,
With hertë sore well ought I to bewail,
That ever dark in torment, night by night,
Toward my death with wind in stern I sail ;
For which the tenthë night, if that I fail
The guiding of thy bemës bright an hour,
My ship and me Carybdis will devour.'

IV

This song when he thus songen haddë, sone
He fell again into his sickness old ;
And every night, as was his wont to done,
He stood the brightë monë to behold,
And all his sorrow he to the monë told ;
And said :—'I wis, when thou art hornéd new,
I shall be glad, if all the world be true !

'I saw thine hornës old eke by the morrow,
When hennës rode my rightë lady dere,
That cause is of my torment and my sorrow ;
For which, O brightë Lúcina the clere,
For love of God, run fast about thy sphere !
For when thy hornës newë ginnë spring,
Then shall she come, that may my blissë bring !'

V

Upon the wallës fast eke would he walk,
And on the Greekës host he woldë see,
And to himself right thus he woldë talk :—

'Lo, yonder is mine owën lady free,
Or ellës yonder, there tho' tentës be !
And thennës comth this air, that is so sote
That in my soul I feel it doth me bote.

And hardëly this wind, that more and more
Thus stoundëmele increaseth in my face,
Is of my lady's depë sicknesse sore.
I prove it thus, for in no other place
Of all this town, save only in this space,
Feel I no wind that souneth so like pain.
It saith :—"Alas ! why twinnèd be we twain?"'

Geoffrey Chaucer.

3

MERCILESS BEAUTY

I. *Captivity*

YOUR eyën two will slay me suddenly :
I may the beauty of hem not sustene,
So woundeth it through-out my hertë kene.

And but your word will helen hastily
My hertës woundë, while that it is green,
  Your eyën two will slay me sodenly :
  I may the beauty of hem not sustene.

Upon my troth I say you faithfully,
That ye be of my life and death the queen,
For with my death the truthë shall be seen :
  Your eyën two will slay me sodenly :
  I may the beauty of hem not sustene,
  So woundeth it through-out my hertë kene.

II. *Rejection*

So hath your beauty from your hertë chased
Pity, that me ne availeth not to plain :
For Daunger halt your mercy in his chain.

Guiltless my death thus have ye me purchased ;
I say you sooth, me needeth not to feign :
  So hath your beauty from your hertë chased
  Pity, that me ne availeth not to plain.

Alas ! that nature hath in you compassed
So great beauty, that no man may attain
To mercy, though he servë for the pain !
    So hath your beauty from your hertë chased
    Pity, that me ne availeth not to plain ;
    For Daunger halt your mercy in his chain.

III. *Escape*

Since I from Love escapëd am so fat,
I never think to ben in his prison lean ;
Since I am free, I count him not a bean.

He may answér, and sayë this or that ;
I do no force, I spéak right as I mean :
    Since I from Love escapëd am so fat,
    I never think to ben in his prison lean.

Love hath my name y-strike out of his sclat,
And he is strike out of my bookës clean
For evermore ; there is none other mean.
    Since I from Love escapëd am so fat,
    I never think to ben in his prison lean ;
    Since I am free, I count him not a bean !

Geoffrey Chaucer.

4

DUNBAR'S LAMENT WHEN HE WAS SICK

I THAT in health was and gladness,
Am troubled now with great sickness,
And feebled with infirmity :—
    Timor Mortis conturbat me.

Our plesance here is all vain glory,
This false world is but transitóry,
The flesh is brukle, the Fiend is slee :—
    Timor Mortis conturbat me.

The state of man does change and vary,
Now sound, now sick, now blithe, now sary,
Now dansand merry, now like to dee :—
    Timor Mortis conturbat me.

No state in earth here standës sickir ;
As with the wind wavës the wickir,
So wavës this world's vanity :—
   Timor Mortis conturbat me.

Unto the dead goes all Estates,
Princes, Prelates, and Potestates,
Both rich and poor of all degree :—
   Timor Mortis conturbat me.

He takes the knights in to the field,
Enarmèd under helm and shield ;
Victor he is at all mellee :—
   Timor Mortis conturbat me.

That strong unmerciful tyrand
Takes, on the mother's breast sowkand,
The babe full of benignity :—
   Timor Mortis conturbat me.

He takes the campion in the stour,
The captain closit in the tour,
The lady in bower full of beauty :—
   Timor Mortis conturbat me.

He spares no lord for his piscence,
No clerk for his intelligence ;
His awful stroke may no man flee :—
   Timor Mortis conturbat me.

Art-magicians and astrologues,
Rethors, logicians, theologues,
Them helpës no conclusions slee :—
   Timor Mortis conturbat me.

In medicine the most practicians,
Leeches, surrigians, and physicians,
Themselves from death may not supplee :—
   Timor Mortis conturbat me.

I see that makars among the lave
Plays here their pageant, syne goes to grave ;
Sparéd is not their faculty :—
   Timor Mortis conturbat me.

He has done petuously devour
The noble Chaucer, of makars flower,
The Monk of Bury, and Gower, all three :—
    Timor Mortis conturbat me. . . .

Since he has all my brothers tane,
He will not let me live alane;
Of force I must his next prey be :—
    Timor Mortis conturbat me.

Since for the dead remeid is none,
Best is that we for death dispone,
After our death that live may we :—
    Timor Mortis conturbat me.

                     William Dunbar.

5

MEDITATION IN WINTER

In to these dirk and drumlie days,
When sabill all the hewin arrays
With misty vapours, clouds, and skies,
Nature all courage me denies
Of sangis, ballads, and of plays.

When that the night does lenthin hours,
With wind, with hail, and heavy showers,
My dulë spreit does lurk for schoir;
My heart for languor does forloir
For lack of Summer with his flowers.

I walk, I turn, sleep may I not;
I vexèd am with heavy thought;
This world all o'er I cast about,
And ay the mair I am in doubt,
The mair that I remeid have sought.

I am assailed on every side.
Despair says ay :—'In time provide,
And get some thing whereon to leif,
Or with great trouble and mischeif
Thou shall in to this court abide.'

Then Patience says :—' Be not aghast :
Hold Hope and Truth within thee fast ;
And let Fortúne work forth her rage,
When that no reason may assuage,
Till that her glass be run and past.'

And Prudence in my ear says ay :—
' Why would thou hold that will away ?
Or crave that thou may have no space,
Thou tending to another place,
A journey going every day ?'

And then says Age :—' My friend, come near,
And be not strange, I thee requeir !
Come, brother, by the hand me take :
Remember thou has compt to make
Of all thy time thou spended here.'

Syne Death casts up his yettis wide,
Saying :—' These opens shall ye abide !
Albeit that thou were never so stout,
Under this lintel shall thou lowt ;
There is none other way beside.'

For fear of this all day I drowp ;
No gold in kist, nor wine in cowp,
No lady's beauty, nor luif's bliss
May let me to remember this,
How glad that ever I dine or sowp.

Yet, when the night begins to short,
It does my spreit some part comfort,
Of thought oppressèd with the showers.
Come, lusty Summer ! with thy flowers,
That I may live in some disport !

                                    William Dunbar.

6

VANITAS VANITATUM

O WRETCH, beware !   This world will wend thee fro,
  Which has beguiléd many great estate.
Turn to thy friend, believe not in thy foe ;
  Since thou must go, be graithing to thy gait ;

Remeid in time, and rue not all-too late ;
Provide thy place, for thou away must pass
  Out of this vale of trouble and dissait :
Vanitas Vanitatum, et omnia Vanitas !

Walk forth, pilgramë, while thou has day's light ;
  Dress from desert, draw to thy dwelling-place ;
Speed home, for why? Anonë comes the night
  Which does thee follow with ane ythand chace !
  Bend up thy sail, and win thy port of grace ;
For and the death o'ertake thee in trespass,
  Then may thou say these wordis with allace !
Vanitas Vanitatum, et omnia Vanitas !

Here naught abides, here standës no thing stabill,
  For this false world ay flittës to and fro ;
Now day up bright, now night all black as sabill,
  Now ebb, now flood, now friend, now cruel foe ;
  Now glad, now sad, now well, now into woe ;
Now clad in gold, dissolvit now in ass ;
  So does this world transitory go :
Vanitas Vanitatum, et omnia Vanitas !

William Dunbar.

7

IN PRAISE OF JOHANNA SCROOPE

How shall I report
All the goodly sort
Of her features clere,
That hath no earthly pere ?
Her favour of her face
Ennewéd all with grace,
Comfort, pleasure, and solace,
Mine heart doth so embrace,
And so hath ravished me
Her to behold and see,
That in words plain
I cannot me refrain
To look on her again :
Alas ! what should I feign ?
It were a pleasant pain
With her ay to remain.

Her eyen gray and stepe
Causeth mine heart to lepe !
With her brows bent
She may well represent
Fair Lucrece, as I wene,
Or else fair Polexene,
Or else Caliope,
Or else Penolope :—
For this most goodly flower,
This blossom of fresh colóur,
So Jupiter me succóur,
She flourisheth fresh and new
In beauty and virtue !

The Indy sapphire blew
Her veins doth ennew.
The orient pearl so clere,
The witness of her lere.
The lusty ruby ruddes
Resemble the rose buddes.
Her lips soft and merry
Embloomed like the cherry,
It were an heavenly bliss
Her sugared mouth to kiss !
Her beauty to augment,
Dame Nature hath her lent
A wart upon her cheek.
Whoso list to seek
In her visage a scar,
That seemeth from afar
Like to the radiant star,
All with favour fret,
So properly it is set !
She is the violet,
The daisy delectáble,
The columbine commendáble,
The jelofer amiáble :—
For this most goodly flower,
This blossom of fresh colóur,
So Jupiter me succóur,
She flourisheth fresh and new
In beauty and virtue !

And when I perceived
Her wart, and conceived,
It cannot be denayd
But it was well convayd,

And set so womanly,
And nothing wantonly,
But right conveniently
And full congruently,
As Nature could devise,
In most goodly wise !
Whoso list behold.
It maketh lovers bold
To her to sue for grace,
Her favour to purcháse:
The scar upon her chin,
Enhatched on her fair skin,
Whiter than the swan,
It would make any man
To forget deadly sin
Her favóur to win :—
For this most goodly flower,
This blossom of fresh colóur,
So Jupiter me succóur,
She flourisheth fresh and new
In beauty and virtue !

Soft, and make no din,
For now I will begin
To have in remembrance
Her goodly dalyaunce
And her goodly pastaunce !
So sad and so demure,
Behaving her so sure,
With words of pleasúre
She would make to the lure,
And any man convert
To give her his whole hert.
She made me sore amazed
Upon her when I gazed.
Methought mine hert was crazed,
My eyen were so dazed :—
For this most goodly flower,
This blossom of fresh colóur,
So Jupiter me succóur,
She flourisheth fresh and new
In beauty and virtue !

And to amend her tale,
When she list to avail,
And with her fingers smale,

And hands soft as silk,
Whiter than the milk,
That are so quickly veined,
Wherewith my hand she strained,
Lord, how I was pained !
Unneath I me refrained,
How she me had reclaimed,
And me to her retained,
Embracing therewithall
Her goodly middle small
With sides long and straight !
To tell you what conceit
I had then in a trice,
The matter were too nice,
And yet there was no vice,
Nor yet no villainy,
But only fantasy :—
For this most goodly flower,
This blossom of fresh colóur,
So Jupiter me succóur,
She flourisheth fresh and new
In beauty and virtue !

But whereto should I note
How often did I tote
Upon her pretty fote ?
It raised mine hert-rote
To see her tread the ground
With heels short and round !
She is plainly express
Egeria, the goddéss,
And like to her imáge,
Emportured with couráge,
A lover's pilgrimage !
There is no beast saváge,
Nor no tiger so wood,
But she would change his mood,
Such relucent grace
Is forméd in her face :—
For this most goodly flower,
This blossom of fresh colóur,
So Jupiter me succóur,
She flourisheth fresh and new
In beauty and virtue !

So goodly as she dresses,
So properly she presses,
The bright golden tresses

Of her hair so fine
Like Phœbus' beams shine !
Whereto should I disclose
The gartering of her hose ?
It is for to suppose
How that she can wear
Gorgeously her gear,
Her fresh habiliments
With other implements
To serve for all entents,
Like Dame Flora, queen
Of lusty summer green :—
For this most goodly flower,
This blossom of fresh colóur,
So Jupiter me succóur,
She flourisheth fresh and new
In beauty and virtue !

    Her kirtle so goodly laced,
And under that is braced
Such pleasures that I may
Neither write nor say.
Yet though I write not with ink,
No man can let me think :
For thought hath liberty,
Thought is frank and free :
To think a merry thought
It cost me little or naught.
Would God mine homely style
Were polished with the file
Of Cicero's eloquence,
To praise her excellence !
For this most goodly flower,
This blossom of fresh colóur,
So Jupiter me succóur,
She flourisheth fresh and new
In beauty and virtue !

    My pen it is unable,
My hand it is unstable,
My reason rude and dull
To praise her at the full,
Goodly mistress Jane,
Sober, demure Diane !
Jane, this mistress hight
The lode-star of daylight,

Dame Venus of all pleasure,
The well of worldly treasure,
She doth exceed and pass
In prudence dame Pallas :—
For this most goodly flower,
This blossom of fresh colóur,
So Jupiter me succóur,
She flourisheth fresh and new
In beauty and virtue !

John Skelton.

8

IN PRAISE OF ISABEL PENNELL

By Saint Mary, my lady,
Your mammy and your daddy
Brought forth a goodly baby !

My maiden Isabell,
Reflaring rosabell,
The flagrant camamell,

The ruddy rosary,
The sovereign rosemary,
The pretty strawberry,

The columbine, the nepte,
The ieloffer well set,
The proper violet,

Ennewéd, your colour
Is like the daisy flower
After the April shower !

Star of the morrow gray,
The blossom on the spray,
The freshest flower of May ;

Maidenly demure,
Of womanhood the lure,
Wherefore I make you sure :

It were an heavenly health,
It were an endless wealth,
A life for God himself,

To hear this nightingale,
Among the birds smale,
Warbling in the vale :—

Dug, dug,
Iug, iug,
Good year and good luck,
With chuk, chuk, chuk, chuk !

John Skelton.

9

TO HIS LUTE

MY lute, awake, perform the last
Labour that thou and I shall waste,
And end that I have now begun,
And, when this song is sung and past,
My lute, be still, for I have done !

As to be heard where ear is none,
As lead to grave in marble stone,
My song may pierce her heart as soon :
Should we, then, sigh or sing or moan ?
No, no, my lute, for I have done !

The rocks do not so cruelly
Repulse the waves continually,
As she my suit and affectión :
So that I am past remedy :
Whereby my lute and I have done.

Proud of the spoil that thou hast got
Of simple hearts thorough Love's shot,
By whom unkind thou hast them won,
Think not he hath his bow forgot,
Although my lute and I have done !

Vengeance shall fall on thy disdain,
That mak'st but game of earnest pain.
Trow not alone under the sun
Unquit to cause thy lover's plain,
Although my lute and I have done.

Now cease, my lute, this is the last
Labour that thou and I shall waste,
And ended is that we begun :
Now is this song both sung and past—
My lute, be still, for I have done.

Thomas Wyatt.

10

IN HIS LADY'S PRAISE

GIVE place, ye lovers, here before
That spent your boasts and brags in vain !
My Lady's beauty passeth more
The best of yours, I dare well sayen,
Than doth the sun the candle light,
Or brightest day the darkest night.

And thereto hath a troth as just
As had Penelope the fair ;
For what she saith, ye may it trust,
As it by writing sealéd were :
And virtues hath she many moe
Than I with pen have skill to show.

I could rehearse, if that I would,
The whole effect of Nature's plaint,
When she had lost the perfect mould,
The like to whom she could not paint :
With wringing hands, how she did cry,
And what she said, I know it, I !

I know she swore with raging mind,
Her kingdom only set apart,
There was no loss, by law of kind,
That could have gone so near her heart ;
And this was chiefly all her pain :—
'She could not make the like again.'

Sith Nature thus gave her the praise,
To be the chiefest work she wrought ;
In faith, methink ! some better ways
On your behalf might well be sought
Than to compare, as ye have done,
To match the candle with the sun.

Howard, Earl of Surrey.

11

VOW TO LOVE FAITHFULLY HOWSOEVER HE BE REWARDED

SET me whereas the sun doth parch the green,
Or where his beams do not dissolve the ice ;
In temperate heat, where he is felt and seen ;
In presence prest of people, mad or wise ;
Set me in high, or yet in low degree ;
In longest night, or in the shortest day ;
In clearest sky, or where clouds thickest be ;
In lusty youth, or when my hairs are gray ;
Set me in heaven, in earth, or else in hell,
In hill, or dale, or in the foaming flood ;
Thrall or at large, alive whereso I dwell ;
Sick or in health, in evil fame or good :
　Hers will I be, and only with this thought
　Content myself, although my chance be nought !
Howard, Earl of Surrey.

12

COMPLAINT OF THE ABSENCE OF HER LOVER

GOOD ladies ! ye that have your pleasures in exile,
Step in your foot, come, take a place, and mourn with me awhile !
And such as by their lords do set but little price,
Let them sit still, it skills them not what chance come on the.
　dice.
But ye whom Love hath bound, by order of desire,
To love your lords, whose good deserts none other would require
Come ye yet once again, and set your foot by mine,
Whose woful plight, and sorrows great, no tongue may well
　define !
My love and lord, alas ! in whom consists my wealth,
Hath fortune sent to pass the seas, in hazard of his health.
Whom I was wont t'embrace with well contented mind,
Is now amid the foaming floods at pleasure of the wind,
Where God well him preserve, and soon him home me send—
Without which hope my life, alas ! were shortly at an end !
Whose absence yet, although my hope doth tell me plain,
With short return he comes anon, yet ceaseth not my pain.
The fearful dreams I have ofttimes do grieve me so,
That when I wake, I lie in doubt wh'er they be true or no.

B

Sometime the roaring seas, me seems, do grow so high,
That my dear lord, ay me ! alas ! methinks I see him die !
Another time the same doth tell me he is come,
And playing, where I shall him find, with his fair little son ;
So forth I go apace to see that liefsome sight,
And with a kiss, methinks I say :—' Welcome, my lord, my
     knight !
Welcome, my sweet, alas ! the stay of my welfáre,
Thy presence bringeth forth a truce betwixt me and my care.'
Then lively doth he look, and salueth me again,
And saith :—' My dear, how is it now that you have all this pain?'
Wherewith the heavy cares, that heap'd are in my breast,
Break forth and me dischargen clean of all my huge unrest.
But when I me awake, and find it but a dream,
The anguish of my former woe beginneth more extreme,
And me tormenteth so that unneath may I find
Some hidden place, wherein to slake the gnawing of my mind.
Thus every way you see, with absence how I burn,
And for my wound no cure I find but hope of good return,
Save when I think by sour how sweet is felt the more,
It doth abate some of my pains, that I abode before ;
And then unto myself I say :—' When we shall meet,
But little while shall seem this pain, the joy shall be so sweet !'
Ye winds, I you conjúre, in chiefest of your rage,
That ye my lord me safely send, my sorrows to assuage,
And that I may not long abide in this excess,
Do your good will to cure a wight that liveth in distress !

Howard, Earl of Surrey.

13

A TRUE LOVER

WHAT sweet relief the showers to thirsty plants we see,
What dear delight the blooms to bees, my true love is to me !
As fresh and lusty Ver foul Winter doth exceed,
As morning bright, with scarlet sky, doth pass the evening'
     weed,
As mellow pears above the crabs esteemed be :
So doth my love surmount them all, whom yet I hap to see !
The oak shall olives bear, the lamb the lion fray,
The owl shall match the nightingale in tuning of her lay,
Or I my love let slip out of mine entire heart,
So deep reposéd in my breast is she for her desart !
For many blessed gifts, O happy, happy land,
Where Mars and Pallas strive to make their glory most to stand !

Yet, land, more is thy bliss, that in this cruel age
A Venus' imp thou hast brought forth, so steadfast and so sage,
Among the Muses Nine a tenth if Jove would make,
And to the Graces Three a fourth, her would Apollo take !
Let some for honour hunt, and hoard the massy gold :
With her so I may live and die, my weal cannot be told.

Nicholas Grimald.

14

HENCE, HEART, WITH HER THAT MUST DEPART

HENCE, heart, with her that must depart,
And hald thee with thy sovereign,
For I had liever want ane heart,
Nor have the heart that does me pain.
Therefore, go, with thy love remain,
And let me leif thus unmolest,
And see that thou come not again,
But bide with her thou luvës best.

Sen she that I have servéd lang
Is to depart so suddenly,
Address thee now, for thou sall gang
And bear thy lady company.
Fra she be gone, heartless am I,
For why? thou art with her possest !
Therefore, my heart, go hence in high,
And bide with her thou luvës best.

Though this belappit body here
Be bound to servitude and thrall,
My faithful heart is free entire
And mind to serve my lady at all.
Would God that I were perigall,
Under that redolent rose to rest !
Yet at the least, my heart, thou sall
Abide with her thou luvës best.

Sen in your garth the lily white
May not remain among the laif,
Adieu the flower of whole delight !
Adieu the succour that may me saif :
Adieu the fragrant balm suaif,
And lamp of ladies lustiest !
My faithful heart so shall it haif
To bide with her it luvës best.

Deplore, ye ladies clear of hue,
Her absence, sen she must depart !
And specially, ye lovers true,
That wounded ben with Luvis' dart !
For some of you sall want ane heart
As well as I ; therefore at last
Do go with mine, with mind invart,
And bide with her thou luvës best.

Alexander Scott.

15

UP, HALESOM HEART

Up, halesom heart, thy rootës raise and loup,
Exalt and climb within my breast in stage !
Art thou not wanton, hale and in good howp,
Fermit in grace and free of all thirlage ?
Bathing in bliss and set in high courage,
Braisit in joy, no fault may thee affray,
Having thy lady's heart as heritage,
In blanch-farm for ane sallat every May :
So needs thou not now sussy, sytt, nor sorrow,
Sen thou art sure of solace even and morrow.

Thou, Cupëid, rewarded me with this,
I am thy own true liege without tressoun !
There lives no man in more ease, wealth, and bliss ;
I know no siching, sadness, nor yet soun,
Waking, thought, languor, lamentatioun,
Dolour, despair, weeping nor jealousie :
My breast is void and purgit of passoun,
I feel no pain, I have no purgatorie,
But peerless, perfect, paradisal pleasure,
With merry heart and mirthfulness but measure.

My lady, Lord, thou gave me for to herd,
Within mine arms I nourish on the night.
Kissing, I say :—' My babe, my tender bird,
Sweet mistress, lady love and lusty wight,
Steer, rule, and guider of my senses right !'
My voice surmounts the sapphire cloudës hie,
Thanking great God of that treasúre and might,
I cost her dear, but she far dearer me,
Whilk hazards honour, fame, in aventure,
Committing clean her corse to me in cure.

In oxters close we kiss, and cossis hairts !
Burnt in desire of amour's play and sport,
Meittand our lusts, sprightless we twa depairts.
Prolong with leisure, Lord, I thee exhort,
Sic time that we may both take our comfórt,
First for to sleep, syne walk without espies !
I blame the cock, I plain the night is short ;
Away I went—my wathe the cushat crys.
Wishing all lovers leal to have sic chance,
That they may have us in rememberance !

Alexander Scott.

16

DEPART, DEPART, DEPART

DEPART, depart, depart !
Alace ! I must depart
From her that has my heart,
          With heart full soir !
Against my will indeed,
And can find no remeid—
I wot the pains of deid
          Can do no moir.

Now must I go, alace !
From sight of her sweet face,
The ground of all my grace,
          And sovereign ;
What chance that may fall me
Sall I never merry be,
Unto the time I see
          My sweet again.

I go, and wot not where,
I wander here and there,
I weep and sich right sair,
          With panës smart :
Now must I pass away, away,
In wilderness and wildsome way—
Alace ! this woful day
          We should depart !

My spirit does quake for dreid,
My thirled heart does bleed,
My panës does exceed :
          What should I say ?

I, woful wight, alone,
Makand ane piteous moan ;
Alace! my heart is gone,
    For ever and ay !

Through languor of my sweet,
So thirléd is my spreit,
My days are most complete,
    Through her absence :
Christ, sen she knew my smart,
Ingraven in my heart,
Because I must depart
    From her presence !

Adieu, my own sweet thing,
My joy and comforting,
My mirth and solaceing
    Of earthly gloir !
Farewell, my lady bright,
And my remembrance right,
Farewell, and have good night—
    I say no moir.

Alexander Scott.

17

LO, WHAT IT IS TO LOVE

Lo, what it is to love,
Learn ye that list to prove,
By me, I say, that no ways may
The ground of grief remove,
But still decay both night and day :
Lo, what it is to love !

Love is ane fervent fire,
Kindled without desire,
Short pleasure, lang displeasure,
Repentance is the hire ;
Ane puir tressour, without measour ;
Love is ane fervent fire.

To love and to be wise,
To rage with good advice ;
Now thus, now than, so goes the game,
Uncertain is the dice ;
There is no man, I say, that can
Both love and to be wise.

Flee always from the snare,
Learn at me to beware;
It is ane pain, and double trane
Of endless woe and care;
For to refrain that danger plain,
Flee always from the snare.

Alexander Scott.

18

AMANTIUM IRÆ REDINTEGRATIO AMORIS

IN going to my naked bed as one that would have slept,
I heard a wife sing to her child, that long before had wept:
She sighéd sore and sang full sweet, to bring the babe to rest,
That would not cease but criéd still, in sucking at her breast.
She was full weary of her watch, and grievéd with her child,
She rockéd it and rated it, till that on her it smiled;
Then did she say:—'Now have I found this proverb true to prove,
The falling out of faithful friends renewing is of love!'

Then took I paper, pen and ink, this proverb for to write,
In register for to remain of such a worthy wight:
As she proceeded thus in song unto her little brat,
Much matter uttered she of weight, in place whereas she sat,
And provéd plain, there was no beast, nor creature bearing life,
Could well be known to live in love, without discord and strife:
Then kisséd she her little babe, and sware by God above,
The falling out of faithful friends renewing is of love.

She said that neither king, nor prince, nor lord could live aright,
Until their puissance they did prove, their manhood and their
    might.
When manhood shall be matchéd so that fear can take no place,
Then weary works make warriors each other to embrace,
And left their force that failéd them, which did consume the rout,
That might before have lived their time, and nature out:
Then did she sing as one that thought no man could her reprove,
The falling out of faithful friends renewing is of love.

She said she saw no fish nor fowl, nor beast within her haunt,
That met a stranger in their kind, but could give it a taunt:
Since flesh might not endure, but rest must wrath succeed,
And force the fight to fall to play, in pasture where they feed,
So noble nature can well end the work she hath begun,
And bridle well that will not cease, her tragedy in some:
Thus in song she oft rehearsed, as did her well behove,
The falling out of faithful friends renewing is of love.

'I marvel much pardy,' quoth she, ' for to behold the rout,
To see man, woman, boy, beast, to toss the world about:
Some kneel, some crouch, some beck, some check, and some can
    smoothly smile,
And some embrace others in arm, and there think many awhile;
Some stand aloof at cap and knee, some humble and some stout,
Yet are they never friends in deed, until they once fall out.'
Thus ended she her song, and said before she did remove,
The falling out of faithful friends renewing is of love.

Richard Edwards.

19

THE LOVER IN WINTER PLAINETH
FOR THE SPRING

O WESTERN wind when wilt thou blow
    [That] the small rain down can rain?
Christ, that my love were in my arms
    And I in my bed again!

Anonymous.

20

THAT LENGTH OF TIME CONSUMETH
ALL THINGS

WHAT harder is than stone? What more than water soft?
Yet with soft water drops hard stones be pierced oft.
    What gives so strong impulse,
    That stone we may withstand?
    What gives more weak repulse
    Than water prest with hand?
    Yet weak though water be,
    It holloweth hardest flint:
    By proof whereof we see,
    Time gives the greatest dint.

Anonymous.

21

THE LOVER REFUSED OF HIS LOVE

I SEE how she doth see,
    And yet she will be blind:
I see in helping me
    She seeks and will not find.

I see how she doth wry,
When I begin to moan:
I see when I come nigh,
How fain she would be gone.

I see—what will ye more?
She will me gladly kill:
And you shall see therefore
That she shall have her will.

I can not live with stones,
It is too hard a food:
I will be dead at once
To do my Lady good.

Anonymous.

22

WHEN FLORA HAD O'ERFRET
THE FIRTH

WHEN Flora had o'erfret the firth,
In May of every moneth queen;
When merle and mavis sings with mirth,
Sweet melling in the schawës sheen;
When all lovers rejoicéd been,
And most desirous of their prey;
I heard a lusty lover mene:—
' I love but I dare nocht assay!'

'Strong are the pains I daily prove,
But yet with patience I sustene,
I am so fettered with the love
Only of my lady sheen,
Whilk for her beauty might be queen,
Nature so craftily alway
Has done depaint that sweet serene !—
Whom I love I dare nocht assay.

' She is so bright of hyd and hue,
I love but her alone, I ween;
Is none her love that may eschew,
That blinkis of that dulce amene;
So comely clear are her twa een,
That she mae lovers does affray
Then ever of Greece did fair Helene !—
Whom I love I dare nocht assay.'

Anonymous.

23

A PRAISE OF HIS LADY

GIVE place, you Ladies, and be gone,
Boast not yourselves at all,
For here at hand approacheth one
Whose face will stain you all !

The virtue of her lively looks
Excels the precious stone :
I wish to have none other books
To read or look upon.

In each of her two crystal eyes,
Smileth a naked boy ;
It would you all in heart suffice
To see that lamp of joy.

I think Natúre hath lost the mould,
Where she her shape did take,
Or else I doubt if Nature could
So fair a creature make.

She may be well compared
Unto the Phœnix kind ;
Whose like was never seen or heard,
That any man can find.

In life she is Diana chast,
In truth Penelope,
In word and eke in deed steadfást—
What will you more we say?

If all the world were sought so far,
Who could find such a wight?
Her beauty twinkleth like a star
Within the frosty night.

Her rosial colour comes and goes,
With such a comely grace,
More redier to than doth the rose,
Within her lively face.

At Bacchus feast none shall her meet,
Ne at no wanton play,
Nor gazing in an open street,
Nor gadding as a stray.

The modest mirth that she doth use
Is mixed with shamefastness ;
All vice she doth wholly refuse,
And hateth idleness.

O Lord, it is a world to see,
How Virtue can repair,
And deck in her such honesty,
Whom Nature made so fair !

Truly she doth as far exceed
Our women nowadays
As doth the ieliflower a weed,
And more a thousand ways !

How might I do to get a graffe
Of this unspotted tree ?
For all the rest are plain but chaff,
Which seem good corn to be.

This gift alone I shall her give
When Death doth what he can :
Her honest fame shall ever live
Within the mouth of man.

Anonymous.

24

LUSTY MAY

O LUSTY May, with Flora queen !
The balmy drops from Phœbus sheen
Preluciand beams before the day :
By that Diana growis green
Through gladness of this lusty May.

Then Esperus, that is so bright,
Till woful heartës casts his light,
With banks that blooms on every brae,
And showers are shed forth of their sight,
Through gladness of this lusty May.

Birds on bewis of every birth,
Rejoicing notes makand their mirth
Right pleasantly upon the spray,
With flourishings o'er field and firth,
Through gladness of this lusty May.

All luvaris that are in care
To their ladies they do repair,
In fresh mornings before the day,
And are in mirth ay mair and mair
Through gladness of this lusty May.

Anonymous.

25

MY HEART IS HIGH ABOVE

My heart is high above, my body is full of bliss,
For I am set in love, as well as I would wiss :
I love my lady pure, and she loves me again,
I am her serviture, she is my sovereign !
She is my very heart, I am her hope and heill ;
She is my joy invart, I am her lover leal ;
I am her bond and thrall, she is at my command ;
I am perpetual her man, both foot and hand ;
The thing that may her please, my body shall fulfil ;
Whatever her disease, it does my body ill.
My bird, my bonnie ane, my tender babe venust,
My love, my life alone, my liking and my lust !
We interchange our hearts, in others armës soft,
Spriteless we two depart, usand our luvës oft.
We mourn when light day dawës, we plain the night is short,
We curse the cock that craws, that hinders our disport.
I glowffin up aghast, when I her miss on night,
And in my oxter fast I find the bowster right !
Then languor on me lies, like Morpheus the mair,
Which causes me uprise, and to my sweet repair ;
And then is all the sorrow furth of remembrance,
That ever I had a sorrow in love's observance !
Thus never I do rest, so lusty a life I lead,
When that I list to test the well of womanheid.
Lovers in pain, I pray God send you sic remeid
As I have night and day, you to defend from deid !
Therefore be ever true unto your ladies free,
And they will on you rue, as mine has done on me !

Anonymous.

26

UPON CONSIDERATION OF THE STATE OF THIS LIFE HE WISHETH DEATH

The longer life, the more offence :
The more offence, the greater pain :
The greater pain, the less defence :
The less defence, the lesser gain.

The loss of gain long ill doth try :
Wherefore come death, and let me die !
  The shorter life, less count I find :
The less account, the sooner made :
The count soon made, the merrier mind :
The merry mind doth thought evade.
Short life in truth this thing doth try :
Wherefore come death, and let me die !
  Come gentle death, the ebb of care,
The ebb of care, the flood of life,
The flood of life, the joyful fare,
The joyful fare, the end of strife.
The end of strife, that thing wish I :
Wherefore come death, and let me die.

Anonymous.

27

CANTEMUS DOMINO

I WILL sing unto the Lord, for he hath triumphed gloriously :
The horse and his rider hath he thrown into the sea.

The Lord is my strength and song,
And he is become my salvation :
He is my God, and I will prepare him an habitation :
My father's God, and I will exalt him.
The Lord is a man of war : .
The Lord is his name.
Pharaoh's chariots and his hosts hath he cast into the sea :
His chosen captains also are drowned in the Red Sea.
The depths have covered them :
They sank into the bottom as a stone.
Thy right hand, O Lord, is become glorious in power :
Thy right hand, O Lord, hath dashed in pieces the enemy,
And in the greatness of thine excellency thou hast overthrown
    them that rose up against thee :
Thou sentest forth thy wrath, which consumed them as stubble.
And with the blast of thy nostrils the waters were gathered
    together,
The floods stood upright as an heap,
And the depths were congealed in the heart of the sea.
The enemy said :—
I will pursue, I will overtake, I will divide the spoil ;
My lust shall be satisfied upon them ;
I will draw my sword, my hand shall destroy them.

Thou didst blow with thy wind, the sea covered them :
They sank as lead in the mighty waters.
Who is like unto thee, O Lord, among the gods?
Who is like thee, glorious in holiness,
Fearful in praises, doing wonders?
Thou stretchest out thy right hand,
The earth swallowed them.
Thou in thy mercy hast led forth the people which thou hast
      redeemed :
Thou hast guided them in thy strength unto thy holy habitation.
The people shall hear, and be afraid :
Sorrow shall take hold on the inhabitants of Palestina.
Then the dukes of Edom shall be amazed ;
The mighty men of Moab, trembling shall take hold upon them ;
All the inhabitants of Canaan shall melt away.
Fear and dread shall fall upon them ;
By the greatness of thine arm they shall be as still as a stone ;
Till thy people pass over, O Lord,
Till the people pass over, which thou hast purchased.
Thou shalt bring them in, and plant them in the mountain of thine
      inheritance,
In the place, O Lord, which thou hast made for thee to dwell in,
In the Sanctuary, O Lord, which thy hands have established.
The Lord shall reign for ever and ever.

Sing ye to the Lord, for he hath triumphed gloriously ;
The horse and his rider hath he thrown into the sea.

28

INCLYTI ISRAEL

THE beauty of Israel is slain upon thy high places :
How are the mighty fallen !
Tell it not in Gath,
Publish it not in the streets of Askelon ;
Lest the daughters of the Philistines rejoice,
Lest the daughters of the uncircumcised triumph.
Ye mountains of Gilboa,
Let there be no dew, neither let there be rain, upon you, nor
      fields of offerings ;
For there the shield of the mighty is vilely cast away,
The shield of Saul, as though he had not been anointed with oil.
From the blood of the slain, from the fat of the mighty,
The bow of Jonathan turned not back,
And the sword of Saul returned not empty.

Saul and Jonathan were lovely and pleasant in their lives,
And in their death they were not divided :
They were swifter than eagles,
They were stronger than lions.
Ye daughters of Israel, weep over Saul,
Who clothed you in scarlet, with other delights,
Who put on ornaments of gold on your apparel.
How are the mighty fallen in the midst of the battle !
O Jonathan, thou wast slain in thine high places.
I am distressed for thee, my brother Jonathan :
Very pleasant hast thou been unto me :
Thy love to me was wonderful,
Passing the love of women.
How are the mighty fallen,
And the weapons of war perished !

29

DOMINI EST TERRA

THE earth is the Lord's, and the fulness thereof ;
The world, and they that dwell therein.
For he hath founded it upon the seas,
And established it upon the floods.
Who shall ascend into the hill of the Lord ?
Or who shall stand in his holy place ?
He that hath clean hands, and a pure heart ;
Who hath not lifted up his soul unto vanity,
Nor sworn deceitfully.
He shall receive the blessing from the Lord,
And righteousness from the God of his salvation.
This is the generation of them that seek him,
That seek thy face, O Jacob.
Lift up your heads, O ye gates ;
And be ye lift up, ye everlasting doors ;
And the King of glory shall come in.
Who is this King of glory ?
The Lord strong and mighty,
The Lord mighty in battle.
Lift up your heads, O ye gates ;
Even lift them up, ye everlasting doors ;
And the King of glory shall come in.
Who is this King of glory ?
The Lord of hosts,
He is the King of glory.

30

AFFERTE DOMINO

GIVE unto the Lord, O ye mighty,
Give unto the Lord glory and strength.
Give unto the Lord the glory due unto his name ;
Worship the Lord in the beauty of holiness,
The voice of the Lord is upon the waters :
The God of glory thundereth :
The Lord is upon many waters.
The voice of the Lord is powerful :
The voice of the Lord is full of majesty.
The voice of the Lord breaketh the cedars ;
Yea, the Lord breaketh the cedars of Lebanon.
He maketh them also to skip like a calf ;
Lebanon and Sirion like a young unicorn.
The voice of the Lord divideth the flames of fire.
The voice of the Lord shaketh the wilderness ;
The Lord shaketh the wilderness of Kadesh.
The voice of the Lord maketh the hinds to calve,
And discovereth the forests :
And in His temple doth every one speak of His glory.
The Lord sitteth upon the flood ;
Yea, the Lord sitteth King for ever.
The Lord will give strength unto his people ;
The Lord will bless his people with peace.

31

QUEMADMODUM

As the hart panteth after the water brooks,
So panteth my soul after thee, O God.
My soul thirsteth for God, for the living God :
When shall I come and appear before God ?
My tears have been my meat day and night,
While they continually say unto me, Where is thy God ?
When I remember these things, I pour out my soul in me :
For I had gone with the multitude, I went with them to the
house of God,
With the voice of joy and praise, with a multitude that kept
holyday.

Why art thou cast down, O my soul?
And why art thou disquieted in me?
Hope thou in God: for I shall yet praise him
For the help of his countenance.
O my God, my soul is cast down within me:
Therefore will I remember thee from the land of Jordan,
And of the Hermonites, from the hill Mizar.
Deep calleth unto deep at the noise of thy waterspouts:
All thy waves and thy billows are gone over me:
Yet the Lord will command his lovingkindness in the daytime,
And in the night his song shall be with me,
And my prayer unto the God of my life.
I will say unto God my rock :—Why hast thou forgotten me?
Why go I mourning because of the oppression of the enemy?
As with a sword in my bones, mine enemies reproach me ;
While they say daily unto me :—Where is thy God?
Why art thou cast down, O my soul?
And why art thou disquieted within me?
Hope thou in God: for I shall yet praise him,
Who is the health of my countenance, and my God.

32

OMNES GENTES PLAUDITE

O, CLAP your hands, all ye people ;
Shout unto God with the voice of triumph.
For the Lord most high is terrible ;
He is a great King over all the earth.
He shall subdue the people under us,
And the nations under our feet.
He shall choose our inheritance for us,
The excellency of Jacob whom he loved.
God is gone up with a shout,
The Lord with the sound of a trumpet.
Sing praises to God, sing praises :
Sing praises unto our King, sing praises.
For God is the King of all the earth :
Sing ye praises with understanding.
God reigneth over the heathen ;
God sitteth upon the throne of his holiness.
The princes of the people are gathered together,
Even the people of the God of Abraham
For the shields of the earth belong unto God
He is greatly exalted.

33

DEUS, QUIS SIMILIS

KEEP not thou silence, O God:
Hold not thy peace, and be not still, O God.
For, lo, thine enemies make a tumult:
And they that hate thee have lifted up the head.
They have taken crafty counsel against thy people,
And consulted against thy hidden ones.
They have said:—Come, and let us cut them off from being
    a nation;
That the name of Israel may be no more in remembrance.
For they have consulted together with one consent:
They are confederate against thee.
The tabernacles of Edom, and the Ishmaelites;
Of Moab, and the Hagarenes.
Gebal, and Ammon, and Amalek;
The Philistines with the inhabitants of Tyre.
Assur also is joined with them:
They have holpen the children of Lot.
Do unto them as unto the Midianites;
As to Sisera, as to Jabin, at the brook of Kison:
Which perished at En-dor:
They became as dung for the earth.
Make their nobles like Oreb, and like Zeeb:
Yea, all their princes as Zebah, and as Zalmunna:
Who said:—Let us take to ourselves the houses of God in
    possession.
O my God, make them like a wheel;
As the stubble before the wind.
As the fire burneth a wood,
And as the flame setteth the mountains on fire,
So persecute them with thy tempest,
And make them afraid with thy storm.
Fill their faces with shame,
That they may seek thy name, O Lord.
Let them be confounded and troubled for ever;
Yea, let them be put to shame, and perish;
That men may know that thou, whose name alone is Jehovah,
Art the most high over all the earth.

34

BENEDIC, ANIMA MEA

BLESS the Lord, O my soul!
O Lord my God, thou art very great;
Thou art clothed with honour and majesty.
Who coverest thyself with light as with a garment :
Who stretchest out the heavens like a curtain.
Who layeth the beams of his chambers in the waters :
Who maketh the clouds his chariot :
Who walketh upon the wings of the wind :
Who maketh his angels spirits ;
His ministers a flaming fire ;
Who laid the foundations of the earth,
That it should not be removed for ever.
Thou coveredst it with the deep as with a garment :
The waters stood above the mountains.
At thy rebuke they fled ;
At the voice of thy thunder they hasted away.
They go up by the mountains ; they go down by the valleys
Unto the place which thou hast founded for them.
Thou hast set a bound that they may not pass over ;
That they turn not again to cover the earth.
He sendeth the springs into the valleys,
Which run among the hills.
They give drink to every beast of the field :
The wild asses quench their thirst.
By them shall the fowls of the heaven have their habitation,
Which sing among the branches.
He watereth the hills from his chambers :
The earth is satisfied with the fruit of thy works.
He causeth the grass to grow for the cattle,
And herb for the service of man :
That he may bring forth food out of the earth ;
And wine that maketh glad the heart of man,
And oil to make his face to shine,
And bread which strengtheneth man's heart.
The trees of the Lord are full of sap ;
The cedars of Lebanon, which he hath planted ;
Where the birds make their nests :
As for the stork, the fir trees are her house.
The high hills are a refuge for the wild goats,
And the rocks for the conies.
He appointed the moon for seasons :
The sun knoweth his going down.
Thou makest darkness, and it is night :

Wherein all the beasts of the forest do creep forth.
The young lions roar after their prey,
And seek their meat from God.
The sun ariseth, they gather themselves together,
And lay them down in their dens.
Man goeth forth unto his work
And to his labour until the evening.
O Lord, how manifold are thy works !
In wisdom hast thou made them all :
The earth is full of thy riches.
So is this great and wide sea,
Wherein are things creeping innumerable,
Both small and great beasts.
There go the ships :
There is that leviathan, whom thou hast made to play therein.
These wait all upon thee ;
That thou mayest give them their meat in due season.
That thou givest them they gather ;
Thou openest thine hand, they are filled with good.
Thou hidest thy face, they are troubled :
Thou takest away their breath, they die,
And return to their dust.
Thou sendest forth thy spirit, they are created :
And thou renewest the face of the earth.
The glory of the Lord shall endure for ever :
The Lord shall rejoice in his works.
He looketh on the earth, and it trembleth :
He toucheth the hills, and they smoke.
I will sing unto the Lord as long as I live :
I will sing praise to my God while I have my being.
My meditation of him shall be sweet :
I will be glad in the Lord.
Let the sinners be consumed out of the earth,
And let the wicked be no more.
Bless thou the Lord, O my soul !
Praise ye the Lord.

35

IN CONVERTENDO

WHEN the Lord turned again the captivity of Zion,
We were like them that dream.
Then was our mouth filled with laughter,
And our tongue with singing :
Then said they among the heathen :—

The Lord hath done great things for them.
The Lord hath done great things for us,
Whereof we are glad.
Turn again our captivity, O Lord,
As the streams in the south.
They that sow in tears shall reap in joy.
He that goeth forth and weepeth, bearing precious seed,
Shall doubtless come again with rejoicing, bringing his sheaves
    with him.

36

SUPER FLUMINA

By the rivers of Babylon,
There we sat down, yea, we wept,
When we remembered Zion.
We hanged our harps
Upon the willows in the midst thereof.
For there they that carried us away captive required of us a song;
And they that wasted us required of us mirth, saying:—
Sing us one of the songs of Zion.
How shall we sing the Lord's song
In a strange land?
If I forget thee, O Jerusalem,
Let my right hand forget her cunning.
If I do not remember thee,
Let my tongue cleave to the roof of my mouth:
If I prefer not Jerusalem
Above my chief joy.
Remember, O Lord, the children of Edom
In the day of Jerusalem; who said:—Rase it, rase it,
Even to the foundation thereof.
O daughter of Babylon, who art to be destroyed,
Happy shall he be, that rewardeth thee
As thou hast served us!
Happy shall he be, that taketh and dasheth thy little ones
Against the stones.

37

DOMINE PROBASTI

O LORD, thou hast searched me, and known me.
Thou knowest my downsitting and mine uprising,
Thou understandest my thought afar off.
Thou compassest my path and my lying down,
And art acquainted with all my ways.

For there is not a word in my tongue,
But, lo, O Lord, thou knowest it altogether !
Thou hast beset me behind and before,
And laid thine hand upon me.
Such knowledge is too wonderful for me ;
It is high, I cannot attain unto it.
Whither shall I go from thy spirit?
Or whither shall I flee from thy presence?
If I ascend up into heaven, thou art there :
If I make my bed in hell, behold thou art there.
If I take the wings of the morning,
And dwell in the uttermost parts of the sea,
Even there shall thy hand lead me,
And thy right hand shall hold me.
If I say, Surely the darkness shall cover me ;
Even the night shall be light about me.
Yea, the darkness hideth not from thee ;
But the night shineth as the day :
The darkness and the light are both alike to thee.
For thou hast possessed my reins :
Thou hast covered me in my mother's womb.
I will praise thee ; for I am fearfully and wonderfully made :
Marvellous are thy works ;
And that my soul knoweth right well.
My substance was not hid from thee,
When I was made in secret,
And curiously wrought in the lowest parts of the earth.
Thine eyes did see my substance, yet being unperfect ;
And in thy book all my members were written,
Which in continuance were fashioned,
When as yet there was none of them !
How precious also are thy thoughts unto me, O God !
How great is the sum of them !
If I should count them, they are more in number than the sand.
When I awake, I am still with thee.
Surely thou wilt slay the wicked, O God :
Depart from me therefore, ye bloody men !
For they speak against thee wickedly,
And thine enemies take thy name in vain.
Do not I hate them, O Lord, that hate thee?
And am not I grieved with those that rise up against thee?
I hate them with perfect hatred :
I count them mine enemies.
Search me, O God, and know my heart :
Try me, and know my thoughts :
And see if there be any wicked way in me,
And lead me in the way everlasting !

38

LAUDATE DOMINUM

PRAISE ye the Lord.
Praise ye the Lord from the heavens:
Praise him in the heights.
Praise ye him, all his angels:
Praise ye him, all his hosts.
Praise ye him, sun and moon:
Praise him, all ye stars of light.
Praise him, ye heavens of heavens,
And ye waters that be above the heavens.
Let them praise the name of the Lord:
For he commanded, and they were created.
He hath also stablished them for ever and ever:
He hath made a decree which shall not pass.
Praise the Lord from the earth,
Ye dragons, and all deeps:
Fire, and hail; snow, and vapours;
Stormy wind fulfilling his word;
Mountains, and all hills;
Fruitful trees, and all cedars; ·
Beasts, and all cattle;
Creeping things, and flying fowl.
Kings of the earth, and all people;
Princes, and all judges of the earth;
Both young men, and maidens;
Old men, and children:
Let them praise the name of the Lord:
For his name alone is excellent;
His glory is above the earth and heaven.
He also exalteth the horn of his people,
The praise of all his saints;
Even of the children of Israel, a people near unto him.
Praise ye the Lord.

39

PEREAT DIES

LET the day perish wherein I was born,
And the night in which it was said:—There is a man child conceived.
Let that day be darkness;
Let not God regard it from above,
Neither let the light shine upon it.

Let darkness and the shadow of death stain it ;
Let a cloud dwell upon it ;
Let the blackness of the day terrify it.
As for that night, let darkness seize upon it ;
Let it not be joined unto the days of the year,
Let it not come into the number of the months.
Lo, let that night be solitary,
Let no joyful voice come therein.
Let them curse it that curse the day,
Who are ready to raise up their mourning.
Let the stars of the twilight thereof be dark ;
Let it look for light, but have none ;
Neither let it see the dawning of the day :
Because it shut not up the doors of my mother's womb,
Nor hid sorrow from mine eyes.
Why died I not from the womb ?
Why did I not give up the ghost when I came out of the belly ?
Why did the knees prevent me ?
Or why the breasts that I should suck ?
For now should I have lain still and been quiet,
I should have slept : then had I been at rest,
With kings and counsellors of the earth,
Which built desolate places for themselves ;
Or with princes that had gold,
Who filled their houses with silver :
Or as an hidden untimely birth I had not been ;
As infants which never saw light.
There the wicked cease from troubling ;
And there the weary be at rest.
There the prisoners rest together ;
They hear not the voice of the oppressor.
The small and great are there ;
And the servant is free from his master.
Wherefore is light given to him that is in misery,
And life unto the bitter in soul :
Which long for death, but it cometh not ;
And dig for it more than for hid treasures ;
Which rejoice exceedingly,
And are glad, when they can find the grave ?
Why is light given to a man whose way is hid,
And whom God hath hedged in ?
For my sighing cometh before I eat,
And my roarings are poured out like the waters.
For the thing which I greatly feared is come upon me,
And that which I was afraid of is come unto me.
I was not in safety, neither had I rest, neither was I quiet ;
Yet trouble came.

40

ECCE DOMISTI

BEHOLD, thou hast instructed many,
And thou hast strengthened the weak hands.
Thy words have upholden him that was falling,
And thou hast strengthened the feeble knees.
But now it is come upon thee, and thou faintest;
It toucheth thee, and thou art troubled.
Is not this thy fear, thy confidence,
Thy hope, and the uprightness of thy ways?
Remember, I pray thee, who ever perished, being innocer
Or where were the righteous cut off?
Even as I have seen, they that plow iniquity,
And sow wickedness, reap the same.
By the blast of God they perish,
And by the breath of his nostrils are they consumed.
The roaring of the lion, and the voice of the fierce lion,
And the teeth of the young lions, are broken.
The old lion perisheth for lack of prey,
And the stout lion's whelps are scattered abroad.
Now a thing was secretly brought to me,
And mine ear received a little thereof.
In thoughts from the visions of the night,
When deep sleep falleth on men,
Fear came upon me, and trembling,
Which made all my bones to shake.
Then a spirit passed before my face;
The hair of my flesh stood up:
It stood still, but I could not discern the form thereof:
An image was before mine eyes,
There was silence, and I heard a voice, saying:—
Shall mortal man be more just than God?
Shall a man be more pure than his maker?
Behold, he put no trust in his servants;
And his angels he charged with folly:
How much less in them that dwell in houses of clay,
Whose foundation is in the dust,
Which are crushed before the moth!
They are destroyed from morning to evening:
They perish for ever without any regarding it.
Doth not their excellency which is in them go away?
They die, even without wisdom.

41

VERE SCIO

I KNOW it is so of a truth :
But how should man be just with God ?
If he will contend with him,
He cannot answer him one of a thousand.
He is wise in heart, and mighty in strength :
Who hath hardened himself against him, and hath prospered ?
Which removeth the mountains, and they know not :
Which overturneth them in his anger.
Which shaketh the earth out of her place,
And the pillars thereof tremble.
Which commandeth the sun, and it riseth not ;
And sealeth up the stars.
Which alone spreadeth out the heavens,
And treadeth upon the waves of the sea.
Which maketh Arcturus, Orion, and Pleiades,
And the chambers of the south.
Which doeth great things past finding out ;
Yea, and wonders without number ?
Lo, he goeth by me, and I see him not :
He passeth on also, but I perceive him not.
Behold, he taketh away, who can hinder him ?
Who will say unto him :—What doest thou ?
If God will not withdraw his anger,
The proud helpers do stoop under him.
How much less shall I answer him,
And choose out my words to reason with him !
Whom, though I were righteous, yet would I not answer,
But I would make supplication to my judge.
If I had called, and he had answered me ;
Yet would I not believe that he had hearkened unto my voice :
For he breaketh me with a tempest,
And multiplieth my wounds without cause.
He will not suffer me to take my breath,
But filleth me with bitterness.
If I speak of strength, lo, he is strong :
And if of judgment, who shall set me a time to plead ?
If I justify myself, mine own mouth shall condemn me :
If I say :—I am perfect, it shall also prove me perverse.
Though I were perfect, yet would I not know my soul :
I would despise my life.
This is one thing, therefore I said it,
He destroyeth the perfect and the wicked.

If the scourge slay suddenly,
He will laugh at the trial of the innocent.
The earth is given into the hand of the wicked:
He covereth the faces of the judges thereof;
If not, where, and who is he?
Now my days are swifter than a post:
They flee away, they see no good.
They are passed away as the swift ships:
As the eagle that hasteth to the prey.
If I say :—I will forget my complaint,
I will leave off my heaviness, and comfort myself;
I am afraid of all my sorrows,
I know that thou wilt not hold me innocent.
If I be wicked,
Why then labour I in vain?
If I wash myself with snow water,
And make my hands never so clean;
Yet shalt thou plunge me in the ditch,
And mine own clothes shall abhor me.
For he is not a man, as I am, that I should answer him,
And we should come together in judgment.
Neither is there any daysman betwixt us,
That might lay his hand upon us both.
Let him take his rod away from me,
And let not his fear terrify me:
Then would I speak, and not fear him;
But it is not so with me.
My soul is weary of my life;
I will leave my complaint upon myself;
I will speak in the bitterness of my soul.
I will say unto God :—Do not condemn me:
Show me wherefore thou contendest with me.
Is it good unto thee that thou shouldest oppress,
That thou shouldest despise the work of thine hands,
And shine upon the counsel of the wicked?
Hast thou eyes of flesh?
Or seest thou as man seeth?
Are thy days as the days of man?
Are thy years as man's days,
That thou enquirest after mine iniquity,
And searchest after my sin?
Thou knowest that I am not wicked;
And there is none that can deliver out of thine hand.
Thine hands have made me and fashioned me,
Together round about; yet thou dost destroy me.
Remember, I beseech thee, that thou hast made me as the clay;
And wilt thou bring me into dust again?

Hast thou not poured me out as milk,
And curdled me like cheese?
Thou hast clothed me with skin and flesh,
And hast fenced me with bones and sinews.
Thou hast granted me life and favour,
And thy visitation hath preserved my spirit.
And these things hast thou hid in thine heart :
I know that this is with thee.
If I sin, then thou markest me,
And thou wilt not acquit me from mine iniquity.
If I be wicked, woe unto me ;
And if I be righteous, yet will I not lift up my head.
I am full of confusion ;
Therefore see thou mine affliction ; for it increaseth.
Thou huntest me as a fierce lion :
And again thou showest thyself marvellous upon me.
Thou renewest thy witnesses against me,
And increasest thine indignation upon me ;
Changes and war are against me.
Wherefore then hast thou brought me forth out of the womb ?
O, that I had given up the ghost, and no eye had seen me !
I should have been as though I had not been ;
I should have been carried from the womb to the grave.
Are not my days few?   Cease then,
And let me alone, that I may take comfort a little :
Before I go whence I shall not return,
Even to the land of darkness and the shadow of death ;
A land of darkness, as darkness itself ;
And of the shadow of death, without any order,
And where the light is as darkness.

42

HOMO NATUS DE MULIERE

MAN that is born of a woman
Is of few days, and full of trouble.
He cometh forth like a flower, and is cut down :
He fleeth also as a shadow, and continueth not.
And dost thou open thine eyes upon such an one,
And bringest me into judgment with thee?
Who can bring a clean thing out of an unclean? Not one.
Seeing his days are determined, the number of his months are
    with thee,
Thou hast appointed his bounds that he cannot pass ;

Turn from him, that he may rest,
Till he shall accomplish, as an hireling, his day.
For there is hope of a tree, if it be cut down, that it will sprout again,
And that the tender branch thereof will not cease.
Though the root thereof wax old in the earth,
And the stock thereof die in the ground,
Yet through the scent of water it will bud,
And bring forth boughs like a plant.
But man dieth, and wasteth away:
Yea, man giveth up the ghost, and where is he?
As the waters fail from the sea,
And the flood decayeth and drieth up:
So man lieth down, and riseth not.
Till the heavens be no more, they shall not awake,
Nor be raised out of their sleep.
O, that thou wouldest hide me in the grave,
That thou wouldest keep me secret, until thy wrath be past,
That thou wouldest appoint me a set time, and remember me!
If a man die, shall he live again?
All the days of my appointed time will I wait,
Till my change come.
Thou shalt call, and I will answer thee:
Thou wilt have a desire to the work of thine hands.
For now thou numberest my steps:
Dost thou not watch over my sin?
My transgression is sealed up in a bag,
And thou sewest up mine iniquity.
And surely the mountain falling cometh to nought,
And the rock is removed out of his place.
The waters wear the stones:
Thou washest away the things which grow out of the dust of the earth:
And thou destroyest the hope of man.
Thou prevailest for ever against him, and he passeth:
Thou changest his countenance, and sendest him away.
His sons come to honour, and he knoweth it not;
And they are brought low, but he perceiveth it not of them.
But his flesh upon him shall have pain,
And his soul within him shall mourn.

43

CUJUS ADJUTOR ES

How hast thou helped him that is without power?
How savest thou the arm that hath no strength?
How hast thou counselled him that hath no wisdom?

And how hast thou plentifully declared the thing as it is?
To whom hast thou uttered words?
And whose spirit came from thee?
Dead things are formed
From under the waters, and the inhabitants thereof.
Hell is naked before him,
And destruction hath no covering.
He stretcheth out the north over the empty place,
And hangeth the earth upon nothing.
He bindeth up the waters in his thick clouds;
And the cloud is not rent under them.
He holdeth back the face of his throne,
And spreadeth his cloud upon it.
He hath compassed the waters with bounds,
Until the day and night come to an end.
The pillars of heaven tremble
And are astonished at his reproof.
He divideth the sea with his power,
And by his understanding he smiteth through the proud.
By his spirit he hath garnished the heavens;
His hand hath formed the crooked serpent.
Lo, these are parts of his ways:
But how little a portion is heard of him?
But the thunder of his power who can understand?

44

QUIS EST ISTE

WHO is this that darkeneth counsel
By words without knowledge?
Gird up now thy loins like a man;
For I will demand of thee, and answer thou me.
Where wast thou when I laid the foundations of the earth?
Declare, if thou hast understanding.
Who hath laid the measures thereof, if thou knowest?
Or who hath stretched the line upon it?
Whereupon are the foundations thereof fastened?
Or who laid the corner stone thereof,
When the morning stars sang together,
And all the sons of God shouted for joy?
Or who shut up the sea with doors,
When it brake forth, as if it had issued out of the womb?
When I made the cloud the garment thereof,
And thick darkness a swaddling band for it,
And brake up for it my decreed place,

And set bars and doors,
And said :—Hitherto shalt thou come, but no further:
And here shall thy proud waves be stayed?
Hast thou commanded the morning since thy days,
And caused the dayspring to know his place;
That it might take hold of the ends of the earth,
That the wicked might be shaken out of it?
It is turned as clay to the seal;
And they stand as a garment.
And from the wicked their light is withholden,
And the high arm shall be broken.
Hast thou entered into the springs of the sea?
Or hast thou walked in the search of the depth?
Have the gates of death been opened unto thee?
Or hast thou seen the doors of the shadow of death?
Hast thou perceived the breadth of the earth?
Declare if thou knowest it all.
Where is the way where light dwelleth?
And as for darkness, where is the place thereof,
That thou shouldest take it to the bound thereof,
And that thou shouldest know the paths to the house thereof?
Knowest thou it, because thou wast then born?
Or because the number of thy days is great?
Hast thou entered into the treasures of the snow?
Or hast thou seen the treasures of the hail,
Which I have reserved against the time of trouble,
Against the day of battle and war?
By what way is the light parted,
Which scattereth the east wind upon the earth?
Who hath divided a water-course for the overflowing of waters,
Or a way for the lightning of thunder;
To cause it to rain on the earth, where no man is;
On the wilderness, wherein there is no man;
To satisfy the desolate and waste ground;
And to cause the bud of the tender herb to spring forth?
Hath the rain a father?
Or who hath begotten the drops of dew?
Out of whose womb came the ice?
And the hoary frost of heaven, who hath gendered it?
The waters are hid as with a stone,
And the face of the deep is frozen.
Canst thou bind the sweet influences of Pleiades,
Or loose the bonds of Orion?
Canst thou bring forth Mazzaroth in his season?
Or canst thou guide Arcturus with his sons?
Knowest thou the ordinances of heaven?
Canst thou set the dominion thereof in the earth?

Canst thou lift up thy voice to the clouds,
That abundance of waters may cover thee?
Canst thou send lightnings, that they may go,
And say unto thee :—Here we are?
Who hath put wisdom in the inward parts?
Or who hath given understanding to the heart?
Who can number the clouds in wisdom?
Or who can stay the bottles of heaven,
When the dust groweth into hardness,
And the clods cleave fast together?
Wilt thou hunt the prey for the lion?
Or fill the appetite of the young lions,
When they couch in their dens,
And abide in the covert to lie in wait?
Who provideth for the raven his food?
When his young ones cry unto God,
They wander for lack of meat.
Knowest thou the time when the wild goats of the rock bring forth?
Or canst thou mark when the hinds do calve?
Canst thou number the months that they fulfil?
Or knowest thou the time when they bring forth?
They bow themselves, they bring forth their young ones,
They cast out their sorrows.
Their young ones are in good liking, they grow up with corn;
They go forth, and return not unto them.
Who hath sent out the wild ass free?
Or who hath loosed the bands of the wild ass?
Whose house I have made the wilderness,
And the barren land his dwellings?
He scorneth the multitude of the city,
Neither regardeth he the crying of the driver.
The range of the mountains is his pasture,
And he searcheth after every green thing.
Will the unicorn be willing to serve thee,
Or abide by the crib?
Canst thou bind the unicorn with his band in the furrow?
Or will he harrow the valleys after thee?
Wilt thou trust him, because his strength is great?
Or wilt thou leave thy labour to him?
Wilt thou believe him, that he will bring home thy seed,
And gather it into thy barn?
Gavest thou the goodly wings unto the peacocks?
Or wings and feathers unto the ostrich?
Which leaveth her eggs in the earth,
And warmeth them in dust,
And forgetteth that the foot may crush them,
Or that the wild beast may break them?

She is hardened against her young ones, as though they were not hers:
Her labour is in vain without fear:
Because God hath deprived her of wisdom,
Neither hath he imparted to her understanding.
What time she lifteth up herself on high,
She scorneth the horse and his rider.
Hast thou given the horse strength?
Hast thou clothed his neck with thunder?
Canst thou make him afraid as a grasshopper?
The glory of his nostrils is terrible.
He paweth in the valley, and rejoiceth in his strength:
He goeth on to meet the armed men.
He mocketh at fear, and is not affrighted;
Neither turneth he back from the sword.
The quiver rattleth against him,
The glittering spear and the shield.
He swalloweth the ground with fierceness and rage:
Neither believeth he that it is the sound of the trumpet.
He saith among the trumpets, Ha, ha;
And he smelleth the battle afar off,
The thunder of the captains, and the shouting.
Doth the hawk fly by thy wisdom,
And stretch her wings towards the south?
Doth the eagle mount up at thy command,
And make her nest on high?
She dwelleth and abideth on the rock,
Upon the crag of the rock, and the strong place.
From thence she seeketh the prey,
And her eyes behold afar off.
Her young ones also suck up blood:
And where the slain are, there is she.

45

ACCINGE SICUT

GIRD up thy loins now like a man:
I will demand of thee, and declare thou unto me.
Wilt thou also disannul my judgment?
Wilt thou condemn me, that thou mayest be righteous?
Hast thou an arm like God?
Or canst thou thunder with a voice like him?
Deck thyself now with majesty and excellency;
And array thyself with glory and beauty.
Cast abroad the rage of thy wrath:
And behold every one that is proud, and abase him.

D

Look on every one that is proud, and bring him low;
And tread down the wicked in their place.
Hide them in the dust together;
And bind their faces in secret.
Then will I also confess unto thee
That thine own right hand can save thee.
Behold now behemoth, which I made with thee;
He eateth grass as an ox.
Lo now, his strength is in his loins,
And his force is in the navel of his belly.
He moveth his tail like a cedar:
The sinews of his stones are wrapped together.
His bones are as strong pieces of brass;
His bones are like bars of iron.
He is the chief of the ways of God:
He that made him can make his sword to approach unto him.
Surely the mountains bring him forth food,
Where all the beasts of the field play.
He lieth under the shady trees,
In the covert of the reeds, and fens.
The shady trees cover him with their shadow;
The willows of the brook compass him about.
Behold he drinketh up a river, and hasteth not:
He trusteth that he can draw up Jordan into his mouth.
He taketh it with his eyes:
His nose pierceth through snares.
Canst thou draw out leviathan with a hook?
Or his tongue with a cord which thou lettest down?
Canst thou put an hook into his nose?
Or bore his jaw through with a thorn?
Will he make many supplications unto thee?
Will he speak soft words unto thee?
Will he make a covenant with thee?
Wilt thou take him for a servant for ever?
Wilt thou play with him as with a bird?
Or wilt thou bind him for thy maidens?
Shall the companions make a banquet of him?
Shall they part him among the merchants?
Canst thou fill his skin with barbed irons?
Or his head with fish spears?
Lay thine hand upon him,
Remember the battle, do no more.
Behold, the hope of him is in vain:
Shall not one be cast down even at the sight of him?
None is so fierce that dare stir him up:
Who then is able to stand before me?
Who hath prevented me, that I should repay him?

Whatsoever is under the whole heaven is mine.
I will not conceal his parts,
Nor his power, nor his comely proportion.
Who can discover the face of his garment?
Or who can come to him with his double bridle?
Who can open the doors of his face?
His teeth are terrible round about.
His scales are his pride,
Shut up together as with a close seal.
One is so near to another,
That no air can come between them.
They are joined one to another,
They stick together, that they cannot be sundered.
By his neesings a light doth shine,
And his eyes are like the eyelids of the morning.
Out of his mouth go burning lamps,
And sparks of fire leap out.
Out of his nostrils goeth smoke,
As out of a seething pot or caldron.
His breath kindleth coals,
And a flame goeth out of his mouth.
In his neck remaineth strength,
And sorrow is turned into joy before him.
The flakes of his flesh are joined together :
They are firm in themselves ; they cannot be moved.
His heart is as firm as a stone ;
Yea, as hard as a piece of the nether millstone.
When he raiseth up himself, the mighty are afraid ;
By reason of breakings they purify themselves.
The sword of him that layeth at him cannot hold :
The spear, the dart, nor the habergeon.
He esteemeth iron as straw,
And brass as rotten wood.
The arrow cannot make him flee :
Slingstones are turned with him into stubble.
Darts are counted as stubble :
He laugheth at the shaking of a spear.
Sharp stones are under him :
He spreadeth sharp pointed things upon the mire.
He maketh the deep to boil like a pot :
He maketh the sea like a pot of ointment.
He maketh a path to shine after him ;
One would think the deep to be hoary.
Upon earth there is not his like,
Who is made without fear.
He beholdeth all high things :
He is a king over all the children of pride.

46

FILI MI, CUSTODI

My son, keep my words,
And lay up my commandments with thee.
Keep my commandments, and live ;
And my law as the apple of thine eye.
Bind them upon thy fingers,
Write them upon the table of thine heart.
Say unto wisdom :—Thou art my sister ;
And call understanding thy kinswoman :
That they may keep thee from the strange woman,
From the stranger which flattereth with her words.
For at the window of my house
I looked through my casement,
And behold, among the simple ones,
I discerned among the youths,
A young man void of understanding,
Passing through the street near her corner ;
And he went the way to her house,
In the twilight, in the evening,
In the black and dark night ;
And, behold, there met him a woman
With the attire of an harlot, and subtile of heart.
She is loud and stubborn ;
Her feet abide not in her house :
Now is she without, now in the streets,
And lieth in wait at every corner.
So she caught him, and kissed him,
And with an impudent face said unto him :—
' I have peace offerings with me ;
This day have I paid my vows :
Therefore came I forth to meet thee,
Diligently to seek thy face, and I have found thee.
I have decked my bed with coverings of tapestry,
With carved works,
With fine linen of Egypt.
I have perfumed my bed
With myrrh, aloes, and cinnamon.
Come, let us take our fill of love until the morning ;
Let us solace ourselves with loves :
For the goodman is not at home,
He is gone a long journey :
He hath taken a bag of money with him,
And will come home at the day appointed.'

With her much fair speech she caused him to yield,
With the flattering of her lips she forced him.
He goeth after her straightway,
As an ox goeth to the slaughter,
Or as a fool to the correction of the stocks :
Till a dart strike through his liver ;
As a bird hasteth to the snare,
And knoweth not that it is for his life.
Hearken unto me now therefore, O ye children,
And attend to the words of my mouth !
Let not thine heart decline to her ways,
Go not astray in her paths :·
For she hath cast down many wounded ;
Yea, many strong men have been slain by her.
Her house is the way to hell,
Going down to the chambers of death.

47

MULIEREM FORTEM

WHO can find a virtuous woman ? ·
For her price is far above rubies.
The heart of her husband doth safely trust in her,
So that he shall have no need of spoil.
She will do him good and not evil
All the days of her life.
She seeketh wool, and flax,
And worketh willingly with her hands.
She is like the merchants' ships ;
She bringeth her food from afar.
She riseth also while it is yet night,
And giveth meat to her household,
And a portion to her maidens.
She considereth a field, and buyeth it :
With the fruit of her hands she planteth a vineyard.
She girdeth her loins with strength,
And strengtheneth her arms.
She perceiveth that her merchandise is good ;
Her candle goeth not out by night.
She layeth her hands to the spindle,
And her hands hold the distaff.
She stretcheth out her hand to the poor ;
Yea, she reacheth forth her hands to the needy.

She is not afraid of the snow for her household :
For all her household are clothed with scarlet.
She maketh herself coverings of tapestry ;
Her clothing is silk and purple.
Her husband is known in the gates,
When he sitteth among the elders of the land.
She maketh fine linen, and selleth it ;
And delivereth girdles unto the merchants.
Strength and honour are her clothing ;
And she shall rejoice in time to come.
She openeth her mouth with wisdom ;
And in her tongue is the law of kindness.
She looketh well to the ways of her household,
And eateth not the bread of idleness.
Her children arise up, and call her blessed ;
Her husband also, and he praiseth her.
Many daughters have done virtuously,
But thou excellest them all.
Favour is deceitful, and beauty is vain :
But a woman that feareth the Lord, she shall be praised.
Give her of the fruit of her hands ;
And let her own works praise her in the gates.

48

VANITAS VANITATUM

Vanity of vanities, saith the Preacher,
Vanity of vanities ; all is vanity.
What profit hath a man of all his labour which he taketh
    under the sun ?
One generation passeth away, and another generation cometh :
But the earth abideth for ever.
The sun also ariseth, and the sun goeth down,
And hasteth to his place where he arose.
The wind goeth toward the south,
And turneth about unto the north ;
It whirleth about continually,
And the wind returneth again according to his circuits.
All the rivers run into the sea,
Yet the sea is not full ;
Unto the place from whence the rivers come,
Thither they return again.
All things are full of labour ;

Man cannot utter it :
The eye is not satisfied with seeing,
Nor the ear filled with hearing.
The thing that hath been, it is that which shall be ;
And that which is done is that which shall be done :
And there is no new thing under the sun.
Is there any thing whereof it may be said :—See, this is new?
It hath been already of old time, which was before us.
There is no remembrance of former things ;
Neither shall there be any remembrance of things that are to come
    with those that shall come after.
I the Preacher was king over Israel in Jerusalem.
And I gave my heart to seek and search out by wisdom concerning
    all things that are done under heaven :
This sore travail hath God given to the sons of man to be exercised
    therewith.
I have seen all the works that are done under the sun ;
And, behold, all is vanity and vexation of spirit.
That which is crooked cannot be made straight :
And that which is wanting cannot be numbered.
I communed with mine own heart, saying :—
Lo, I am come to great estate,
And have gotten more wisdom than all they that have been before
    me in Jerusalem :
Yea, my heart had great experience of wisdom and knowledge.
And I gave my heart to know wisdom,
And to know madness and folly :
I perceived that this also is vexation of spirit.
For in much wisdom is much grief :
And he that increaseth knowledge increaseth sorrow.

49

OMNIA HAEC

FOR all this I considered in my heart even to declare all this,
That the righteous, and the wise, and their works, are in the hand
    of God :
No man knoweth either love or hatred by all that is before them.
All things come alike to all :
There is one event to the righteous, and to the wicked ;
To the good and to the clean, and to the unclean ;
To him that sacrificeth, and to him that sacrificeth not :
As is the good, so is the sinner ;
And he that sweareth, as he that feareth an oath.

This is an evil among all things that are done under the sun,
That there is one event unto all.
Yea, also the heart of the sons of men is full of evil,
And madness is in their heart while they live,
And after that they go to the dead.
For to him that is joined to all the living there is hope :
For a living dog is better than a dead lion.
For the living know that they shall die :
But the dead know not any thing,
Neither have they any more a reward ;
For the memory of them is forgotten.
Also their love, and their hatred, and their envy, is now perished ;
Neither have they any more a portion for ever in any thing that is
    done under the sun.
Go thy way, eat thy bread with joy,
And drink thy wine with a merry heart ;
For God now accepteth thy works.
Let thy garments be always white ;
And let thy head lack no ointment.
Live joyfully with the wife whom thou lovest all the days of the
    life of thy vanity,
Which he hath given thee under the sun, all the days of thy vanity :
For that is thy portion in this life,
And in thy labour which thou takest under the sun.
Whatsoever thy hand findeth to do, do it with thy might ;
For there is no work, nor device, nor knowledge, nor wisdom, in
    the grave, whither thou goest.
I returned, and saw under the sun,
That the race is not to the swift,
Nor the battle to the strong,
Neither yet bread to the wise,
Nor yet riches to men of understanding,
Nor yet favour to men of skill ;
But time and chance happeneth to them all.

50

MEMENTO CREATORIS TUI

REMEMBER now thy Creator in the days of thy youth,
While the evil days come not, nor the years draw nigh,
When thou shalt say :—I have no pleasure in them ;
While the sun, or the light, or the moon, or the stars, be
    not darkened,

Nor the clouds return after the rain :
In the day when the keepers of the house shall tremble,
And the strong men shall bow themselves,
And the grinders cease because they are few,
And those that look out of the windows be darkened,
And the doors shall be shut in the streets, when the sound
    of the grinding is low,
And he shall rise up at the voice of the bird,
And all the daughters of music shall be brought low ;
Also when they shall be afraid of that which is high,
And fears shall be in the way,
And the almond tree shall flourish,
And the grasshopper shall be a burden,
And desire shall fail :
Because man goeth to his long home,
And the mourners go about the streets :
Or ever the silver cord be loosed,
Or the golden bowl be broken,
Or the pitcher be broken at the fountain,
Or the wheel broken at the cistern.
Then shall the dust return to the earth as it was :
And the spirit shall return unto God who gave it.

51

OSCULETUR ME

Let him kiss me with the kisses of his mouth :
For thy love is better than wine.
Because of the savour of thy good ointments,
Thy name is as ointment poured forth,
Therefore do the virgins love thee.
Draw me, we will run after thee.
The King hath brought me into his chambers :
We will be glad and rejoice in thee ;
We will remember thy love more than wine :
The upright love thee.
I am black, but comely,
O ye daughters of Jerusalem,
As the tents of Kedar,
As the curtains of Solomon !
Look not upon me, because I am black,
Because the sun hath looked upon me :
My mother's children were angry with me ;

They made me the keeper of the vineyards:
But mine own vineyard have I not kept.
Tell me, O thou whom my soul loveth,
Where thou feedest, where thou makest thy flock to rest at
    noon :
For why should I be as one that turneth aside
By the flocks of thy companions?
If thou know not, O thou fairest among women,
Go thy way forth by the footsteps of the flock,
And feed thy kids beside the shepherds' tents.
I have compared thee, O my love,
To a company of horses in Pharaoh's chariots.
Thy cheeks are comely with rows of jewels,
Thy neck with chains of gold.
We will make thee borders of gold,
With studs of silver.
While the king sitteth at his table,
My spikenard sendeth forth the smell thereof.
A bundle of myrrh is my well-beloved unto me ;
He shall lie all night betwixt my breasts.
My beloved is unto me as a cluster of camphire
In the vineyards of En-gedi.
Behold, thou art fair, my love ; behold, thou art fair ;
Thou hast doves' eyes.
Behold, thou art fair, my beloved, yea, pleasant ;
Also our bed is green.
The beams of our house are cedar,
And our rafters of fir.

52

EGO FLOS CAMPI

I AM the rose of Sharon,
And the lily of the valleys.
As the lily among thorns,
So is my love among the daughters.
As the apple-tree among the trees of the wood,
So is my beloved among the sons.
I sat down under his shadow with great delight,
And his fruit was sweet to my taste.
He brought me to the banqueting-house,
And his banner over me was love.
Stay me with flagons, comfort me with apples:
For I am sick of love.

His left hand is under my head,
And his right hand doth embrace me.
I charge you, O ye daughters of Jerusalem,
By the roes, and by the hinds of the field,
That ye stir not up, nor awake my love, till he please.
The voice of my beloved ! behold he cometh
Leaping upon the mountains, skipping upon the hills.
My beloved is like a roe, or a young hart :
Behold, he standeth behind our wall,
He looketh forth at the windows,
Shewing himself through the lattice.
My beloved spake, and said unto me :—
' Rise up, my love, my fair one, and come away.
For, lo, the winter is past,
The rain is over and gone ;
The flowers appear on the earth ;
The time of the singing of birds is come,
And the voice of the turtle is heard in our land ;
The fig-tree putteth forth her green figs,
And the vines with the tender grapes give a good smell.
Arise, my love, my fair one, and come away.
O my dove, that art in the clefts of the rock, in the secret
    places of the stairs,
Let me see thy countenance,
Let me hear thy voice ;
For sweet is thy voice, and thy countenance is comely.'
Take us the foxes, the little foxes, that spoil the vines :
For our vines have tender grapes.
My beloved is mine, and I am his ;
He feedeth among the lilies.
Until the day break, and the shadows flee away,
Turn, my beloved, and be thou like a roe or a young hart
Upon the mountains of Bether.
By night on my bed I sought him whom my soul loveth ;
I sought him, but I found him not.
I will rise now, and go about the city
In the streets, and in the broad ways
I will seek him whom my soul loveth :
I sought him, but I found him not.
The watchmen that go about the city found me :
To whom I said :—Saw ye him whom my soul loveth ?
It was but a little that I passed from them,
But I found him whom my soul loveth :
I held him, and would not let him go,
Until I had brought him into my mother's house,
And into the chamber of her that conceived me.
I charge you, O ye daughters of Jerusalem,

By the roes, and by the hinds of the field,
That ye stir not up, nor awake my love, till he please.
Who is this that cometh out of the wilderness like pillars of
    smoke,
Perfumed with myrrh and frankincense,
With all powders of the merchants?
Behold his bed, which is Solomon's;
Threescore valiant men are about it,
Of the valiant of Israel.
They all hold swords, being expert in war:
Every man hath his sword upon his thigh,
Because of fear in the night.
King Solomon made himself a chariot
Of the wood of Lebanon.
He made the pillars thereof of silver,
The bottom thereof of gold, the covering of it of purple;
The midst thereof being paved with love,
For the daughters of Jerusalem.
Go forth, O ye daughters of Zion, and behold king Solomon
With the crown wherewith his mother crowned him in the
    day of his espousals,
And in the day of the gladness of his heart.

53

QUAM PULCHRA

BEHOLD, thou art fair, my love;
Behold, thou art fair;
Thou hast doves' eyes within thy locks:
Thy hair is as a flock of goats,
That appear from mount Gilead.
Thy teeth are like a flock of sheep that are even shorn,
Which came up from the washing;
Whereof every one bears twins,
And none is barren among them.
Thy lips are like a thread of scarlet,
And thy speech is comely:
Thy temples are like a piece of a pomegranate
Within thy locks.
Thy neck is like the tower of David, builded for an armoury,
Whereon there hang a thousand bucklers,
All shields of mighty men.

Thy two breasts are like two young roes that are twins,
Which feed among the lilies.
Until the day break, and the shadows flee away,
I will get me to the mountain of myrrh,
And to the hill of frankincense.
Thou art all fair, my love;
There is no spot in thee.
Come with me from Lebanon, my spouse,
With me from Lebanon:
Look from the top of Amana,
From the top of Shenir and Hermon,
From the lions' dens,
From the mountains of the leopards.
Thou hast ravished my heart, my sister, my spouse;
Thou hast ravished my heart with one of thine eyes,
With one chain of thy neck.
How fair is thy love, my sister, my spouse!
How much better is thy love than wine!
And the smell of thine ointments than all spices!
Thy lips, O my spouse, drop as the honeycomb:
Honey and milk are under thy tongue;
And the smell of thy garments is like the smell of Lebanon.
A garden inclosed is my sister, my spouse;
A spring shut up, a fountain sealed.
Thy plants are an orchard of pomegranates, with pleasant fruits;
Camphire with spikenard;
Spikenard and saffron;
Calamus and cinnamon, with all trees of frankincense;
Myrrh and aloes, with all the chief spices:
A fountain of gardens,
A well of living waters,
And streams from Lebanon.
Awake, O north wind; and come, thou south!
Blow upon my garden, that the spices thereof may flow out.
Let my beloved come into his garden,
And eat his pleasant fruits.

54

VENI IN HORTUM

I AM come into my garden, my sister, my spouse:
I have gathered my myrrh with my spice;
I have eaten my honeycomb with my honey;

I have drunk my wine with my milk:
Eat, O friends;
Drink, yea, drink abundantly, O beloved!
I sleep, but my heart waketh:
It is the voice of my beloved that knocketh, saying :—
'Open to me, my sister, my love, my dove, my undefiled:
For my head is filled with dew,
And my locks with the drops of the night.'
I have put off my coat; how shall I put it on?
I have washed my feet; how shall I defile them?
My beloved put in his hand by the hole of the door,
And my bowels were moved for him.
I rose up to open to my beloved;
And my hands dropped with myrrh,
And my fingers with sweet smelling myrrh,
Upon the handles of the lock.
I opened to my beloved;
But my beloved had withdrawn himself, and was gone:
My soul failed when he spake:
I sought him, but I could not find him;
I called him, but he gave me no answer.
The watchmen that went about the city found me,
They smote me, they wounded me;
The keepers of the walls took away my veil from me.
I charge you, O daughters of Jerusalem, if ye find my beloved,
That ye tell him, that I am sick of love.
What is thy beloved more than another beloved,
O thou fairest among women?
What is thy beloved more than another beloved,
That thou dost so charge us?
My beloved is white and ruddy,
The chiefest among ten thousand.
His head is as the most fine gold;
His locks are bushy, and black as a raven:
His eyes are as the eyes of doves by the rivers of waters,
Washed with milk, and fitly set:
His cheeks are as a bed of spices, as sweet flowers;
His lips like lilies, dropping sweet-smelling myrrh:
His hands are as gold rings set with the beryl;
His belly is as bright ivory overlaid with sapphires:
His legs are as pillars of marble set upon sockets of fine gold;
His countenance is as Lebanon, excellent as the cedars:
His mouth is most sweet; yea, he is altogether lovely.
This is my beloved, and this is my friend,
O daughters of Jerusalem.

55

QUAM PULCHRI

How beautiful are thy feet with shoes, O prince's daughter !
The joints of thy thighs are like jewels,
The work of the hands of a cunning workman :
Thy navel is like a round goblet,
Which wanteth not liquor ;
Thy belly is like an heap of wheat
Set about with lilies :
Thy two breasts are like two young roes that are twins :
Thy neck is as a tower of ivory ;
Thine eyes like the fish pools in Heshbon, by the gate of Bath-
    rabbim ;
Thy nose is as the tower of Lebanon,
Which looketh toward Damascus :
Thine head upon thee is like Carmel,
And the hair of thine head like purple :
The king is held in the galleries.
How fair and how pleasant art thou,
O love, for delights !
This thy stature is like to a palm-tree,
And thy breasts to clusters of grapes.
I said, I will go up to the palm-tree,
I will take hold of the boughs thereof:
Now also thy breasts shall be as clusters of the vine,
And the smell of thy nose like apples ;
And the roof of thy mouth like the best wine for my beloved,
That goeth down sweetly,
Causing the lips of those that are asleep to speak.
I am my beloved's,
And his desire is toward me.
Come, my beloved, let us go forth into the field ;
Let us lodge in the villages.
Let us get up early to the vineyards ;
Let us see if the vine flourish, whether the tender grape appear,
And the pomegranates bud forth :
There will I give thee my loves.
The mandrakes give a smell,
And at our gates are all manner of pleasant fruits, new and old,
Which I have laid up for thee, O my beloved.

56

LEVATE SIGNUM

LIFT ye up a banner upon the high mountain,
Exalt the voice unto them, shake the hand,
That they may go into the gates of the nobles.
I have commanded my sanctified ones,
I have also called my mighty ones for mine anger,
Even them that rejoice in my highness.
The noise of a multitude in the mountains, like as of a great people :
A tumultuous noise of the kingdoms of nations gathered together :
The lord of hosts mustereth the host of the battle.
They come from a far country, from the end of heaven,
Even the Lord, and the weapons of his indignation,
To destroy the whole land.
Howl ye ; for the day of the Lord is at hand ;
It shall come as a destruction from the Almighty.
Therefore shall all hands be faint,
And every man's heart shall melt,
And they shall be afraid :
Pangs and sorrow shall take hold of them ;
They shall be in pain as a woman that travaileth :
They shall be amazed one at another ;
Their faces shall be as flames.
Behold, the day of the Lord cometh,
Cruel both with wrath and fierce anger,
To lay the land desolate :
And he shall destroy the sinners thereof out of it.
For the stars of heaven and the constellations thereof shall not give
    their light :
The sun shall be darkened in his going forth,
And the moon shall not cause her light to shine.
And I will punish the world for their evil, and the wicked for their
    iniquity ;
And I will cause the arrogancy of the proud to cease,
And will lay low the haughtiness of the terrible.
I will make a man more precious than fine gold ;
Even a man than the golden wedge of Ophir.
Therefore I will shake the heavens,
And the earth shall remove out of her place,
In the wrath of the Lord of hosts, and in the day of his fierce
    anger.
And it shall be as the chased roe, and as a sheep that no man
    taketh up

They shall every man turn to his own people,
And flee every one into his own land.
Every one that is found shall be thrust through ;
And every one that is joined unto them shall fall by the sword.
Their children also shall be dashed to pieces before their eyes ;
Their houses shall be spoiled, and their wives ravished.
Behold, I will stir up the Medes against them, which shall not
    regard silver ;
And as for gold, they shall not delight in it.
Their bows also shall dash the young men to pieces ;
And they shall have no pity on the fruit of the womb ;
Their eye shall not spare children.
And Babylon, the glory of kingdoms, the beauty of the Chaldees'
    excellency,
Shall be as when God overthrew Sodom and Gomorrah.
It shall never be inhabited,
Neither shall it be dwelt in from generation to generation :
Neither shall the Arabian pitch tent there ;
Neither shall the shepherds make their fold there.
But wild beasts of the desert shall lie there ;
And their houses shall be full of doleful creatures ;
And owls shall dwell there, and satyrs shall dance there.
And the wild beasts of the islands shall cry in their desolate
    houses,
And dragons in their pleasant palaces :
And her time is near to come, and her days shall not be prolonged.

57

QUIA NOCTE

BECAUSE in the night Ar of Moab is laid waste, and brought to
    silence ;
Because in the night Kir of Moab is laid waste, and brought to
    silence ;
He is gone up to Bajith, and to Dibon, the high places, to weep :
Moab shall howl over Nebo, and over Medeba :
On all their heads shall be baldness, and every beard cut off.
In their streets they shall gird themselves with sackcloth :
On the tops of their houses, and in their streets,
Every one shall howl, weeping abundantly.
And Heshbon shall cry, and Elealeh :
Their voice shall be heard even unto Jahaz :
Therefore the armed soldiers of Moab shall cry out ;
His life shall be grievous unto him.

E

My heart shall cry out for Moab ;
His fugitives shall flee unto Zoar, an heifer of three years old :
For by the mounting up of Luhith with weeping shall they go
    it up ;
For in the way of Horonaim they shall raise up a cry of destruction.
For the waters of Nimrim shall be desolate :
For the hay is withered away, the grass faileth, there is no green
    thing.
Therefore the abundance they have gotten, and that which they
    have laid up,
Shall they carry away to the brook of the willows.
For the cry is gone round the borders of Moab ;
The howling thereof unto Eglaim,
And the howling thereof unto Beer-elim.
For the waters of Dimon shall be full of blood :
For I will bring more upon Dimon,
Lions upon him that escapeth of Moab, and upon the remnant of
    the land.

58

ULULATE NAVES

HOWL, ye ships of Tarshish ;
For it is laid waste, so that there is no house, no entering in :
From the land of Chittim it is revealed to them.
Be still, ye inhabitants of the isle ;
Thou whom the merchants of Zidon, that pass over the sea, have
    replenished.
And by great waters the seed of Sihor, the harvest of the river, is
    her revenue ;
And she is a mart of nations.
Be thou ashamed, O Zidon :
For the sea hath spoken, even the strength of the sea,
Saying, I travail not, nor bring forth children,
Neither do I nourish up young men, nor bring up virgins.
As at the report concerning Egypt,
So shall they be sorely pained at the report of Tyre.
Pass ye over to Tarshish ;
Howl, ye inhabitants of the isle.
Is this your joyous city, whose antiquity is of ancient days ?
Her own feet shall carry her afar off to sojourn.
Who hath taken this counsel against Tyre, the crowning city,
Whose merchants are princes, whose traffickers are the honourable
    of the earth ?

The Lord of hosts hath purposed it, to stain the pride of all glory,
And to bring into contempt all the honourable of the earth.
Pass through thy land as a river, O daughter of Tarshish :
There is no more strength.
He stretched out his hand over the sea, he shook the kingdoms :
The Lord hath given a commandment against the merchant city,
      to destroy the strong holds thereof.
And he said, Thou shalt no more rejoice, O thou oppressed virgin,
      daughter of Zidon :
Arise, pass over to Chittim ;
There also shalt thou have no rest.
Behold the land of the Chaldeans ;
This people was not, till the Assyrian founded it for them that
      dwell in the wilderness :
They set up the towers thereof, they raised up the palaces thereof ;
And he brought it to ruin.
Howl, ye ships of Tarshish :
For your strength is laid waste.
And it shall come to pass in that day, that Tyre shall be forgotten
      seventy years,
According to the days of one king :
After the end of seventy years shall Tyre sing as an harlot.
Take an harp, go about the city, thou harlot that hast been forgotten ;
Make sweet melody, sing many songs, that thou mayest be
      remembered.
And it shall come to pass after the end of seventy years, that the
      Lord will visit Tyre,
And she shall turn to her hire,
And shall commit fornication with all the kingdoms of the world
      upon the face of the earth.
And her merchandise and her hire shall be holiness to the Lord :
It shall not be treasured nor laid up ;
For her merchandise shall be for them that dwell before the Lord,
To eat sufficiently, and for durable clothing.

59

REQUIRITE IN LIBRO

SEEK ye out of the book of the Lord, and read :
No one of these shall fail, none shall want her mate :
For my mouth it hath commanded,
And his spirit it hath gathered them.
And he hath cast the lot for them,
And his hand hath divided it unto them by line :

They shall possess it for ever,
From generation to generation shall they dwell therein.
The wilderness and the solitary place shall be glad for them ;
And the desert shall rejoice, and blossom as the rose.
It shall blossom abundantly, and rejoice even with joy and singing :
The glory of Lebanon shall be given unto it,
The excellency of Carmel and Sharon,
They shall see the glory of the Lord, and the excellency of our God.
Strengthen ye the weak hands, and confirm the feeble knees.
Say to them that are of a fearful heart, Be strong, fear not :
Behold, your God will come with vengeance, even God with a
    recompence ;
He will come and save you.
Then the eyes of the blind shall be opened,
And the ears of the deaf shall be unstopped.
Then shall the lame man leap as an hart, and the tongue of the
    dumb sing :
For in the wilderness shall waters break out, and streams in the
    desert.
And the parched ground shall become a pool, and the thirsty land
    springs of water :
In the habitation of dragons, where each lay, shall be grass with
    reeds and rushes.
And an highway shall be there, and a way,
And it shall be called The way of holiness ;
The unclean shall not pass over it ;
But it shall be for those :
The wayfaring men, though fools, shall not err therein.
No lions shall be there,
Nor any ravenous beast shall go up thereon,
It shall not be found there ;
But the redeemed shall walk there :
And the ransomed of the Lord shall return,
And come to Zion with songs and everlasting joy upon their heads ;
They shall obtain joy and gladness, and sorrow and sighing shall
    flee away.

60

IN DIMIDIO DIERUM

I SAID in the cutting off of my days, I shall go to the gates of the
    grave :
I am deprived of the residue of my years.
I said, I shall not see the Lord, even the Lord in the land of the
    living :

I shall behold man no more with the inhabitants of the
    world.
Mine age is departed, and is removed from me as a shepherd's
    tent :
I have cut off like a weaver my life :
He will cut me off with pining sickness :
From day even till night wilt thou make an end of me.
I reckoned till morning, that, as a lion, so will he break all my
    bones :
From day even to night wilt thou make an end of me.
Like a crane or a swallow, so did I chatter :
I did mourn as a dove :
Mine eyes fail with looking upward :
O Lord, I am oppressed ;
Undertake for me.
What shall I say ?
He hath both spoken unto me, and himself hath done it.
I shall go softly all my years in the bitterness of my soul.
O Lord, by these things men live,
And in all these things is the life of my spirit :
So wilt thou recover me, and make me to live.
Behold, for peace I had great bitterness :
But thou hast in love to my soul delivered it from the pit of
    corruption :
For thou hast cast all my sins behind thy back.
For the grave cannot praise thee,
Death cannot celebrate thee,
They that go down into the pit cannot hope for thy truth.
The living, the living, he shall praise thee, as I do this day :
The father to the children shall make known thy truth.
The Lord was ready to save me :
Therefore we will sing my songs to the stringed instruments all
    the days of our life in the house of the Lord.

61

CONSURGE, CONSURGE

AWAKE, awake ;
Put on thy strength, O Zion ;
Put on thy beautiful garments, O Jerusalem, the holy city :
For henceforth there shall no more come into thee the uncircumcised
    and the unclean.
Shake thyself from the dust ;
Arise, and sit down, O Jerusalem :

Loose thyself from the bands of thy neck, O captive daughter of
    Zion.
For thus saith the Lord,
Ye have sold yourselves for nought ;
And ye shall be redeemed without money.
For thus saith the Lord God,
My people went down aforetime into Egypt to sojourn there ;
And the Assyrian oppressed them without cause.
Now therefore, what have I here, saith the Lord,
That my people is taken away for nought?
They that rule over them make them to howl, saith the Lord ;
And my name continually every day is blasphemed.
Therefore my people shall know my name :
Therefore they shall know in that day that I am he that doth
    speak :
Behold, it is I.
How beautiful upon the mountains are the feet of him that bring-
    eth good tidings, that publisheth peace ;
That bringeth good tidings of good, that publisheth salvation ;
That saith unto Zion, Thy God reigneth.
Thy watchmen shall lift up the voice ;
With the voice together shall they sing :
For they shall see eye to eye, when the Lord shall bring again
    Zion.
Break forth into joy, sing together, ye waste places of Jerusalem :
For the Lord hath comforted his people, he hath redeemed
    Jerusalem.
The Lord hath made bare his holy arm in the eyes of all the
    nations :
And all the ends of the earth shall see the salvation of our God.
Depart ye, depart ye, go ye out from thence, touch no unclean
    thing ;
Go ye out of the midst of her ;
Be ye clean, that bear the vessels of the Lord.
For ye shall not go out with haste, nor go by flight :
For the Lord will go before you ;
And the God of Israel will be your rereward.

62

SURGE, ILLUMINARE

ARISE, shine ; for thy light is come,
And the glory of the Lord is risen upon thee.
For, behold, the darkness shall cover the earth, and gross darkness
    the people :

But the Lord shall arise upon thee,
And his glory shall be seen upon thee.
And the Gentiles shall come to thy light,
And kings to the brightness of thy rising.
Lift up thine eyes round about, and see :
All they gather themselves together, they come to thee :
Thy sons shall come from far,
And thy daughters shall be nursed at thy side.
Then thou shalt see, and flow together,
And thine heart shall fear, and be enlarged ;
Because the abundance of the sea shall be converted unto thee,
The forces of the Gentiles shall come unto thee.
The multitude of camels shall cover thee,
The dromedaries of Midian and Ephah ;
All they from Sheba shall come :
They shall bring gold and incense ;
And they shall shew forth the praises of the Lord.
All the flocks of Kedar shall be gathered unto thee,
The rams of Nebaioth shall minister unto thee :
They shall come up with acceptance on mine altar,
And I will glorify the house of my glory.
Who are these that fly as a cloud, and as the doves to their
    windows?
Surely the isles shall wait for me,
And the ships of Tarshish first,
To bring thy sons from far,
Their silver and their gold with them,
Unto the name of the Lord thy God, and to the Holy One of
    Israel,
Because he hath glorified thee.
And the sons of strangers shall build up thy walls,
And their kings shall minister unto thee :
For in my wrath I smote thee, but in my favour have I mercy
    on thee.
Therefore thy gates shall be open continually ;
They shall not be shut day nor night ;
That men may bring unto thee the forces of the Gentiles,
And that their kings may be brought.
For the nation and kingdom that will not serve thee shall
    perish ;
Yea, those nations shall be utterly wasted.
The glory of Lebanon shall come unto thee,
The fir tree, the pine tree, and the box together,
To beautify the place of my sanctuary ;
And I will make the place of my feet glorious.
The sons also of them that afflicted thee shall come bending unto
    thee ;

And all they that despised thee shall bow themselves down
　　　at the soles of thy feet;
And they shall call thee, The city of the Lord,
The Zion of the Holy One of Israel.
Whereas thou hast been forsaken and hated,
So that no man went through thee,
I will make thee an eternal excellency,
A joy of many generations.
Thou shalt also suck the milk of the Gentiles,
And shalt suck the breast of kings:
And thou shalt know that I the Lord am thy Saviour and
　　　thy Redeemer,
The mighty One of Jacob.
For brass I will bring gold, and for iron I will bring silver,
And for wood brass, and for stones iron:
I will also make thy officers peace,
And thine exactors righteousness.
Violence shall no more be heard in thy land,
Wasting nor destruction within thy borders;
But thou shalt call thy walls Salvation, and thy gates Praise.
The sun shall be no more thy light by day;
Neither for brightness shall the moon give light unto thee:
But the Lord shall be unto thee an everlasting light,
And thy God thy glory.
Thy sun shall no more go down:
Neither shall thy moon withdraw itself:
For the Lord shall be thine everlasting light,
And the days of thy mourning shall be ended.
Thy people also shall be all righteous:
They shall inherit the land for ever,
The branch of my planting, the work of my hands,
That I may be glorified.
A little one shall become a thousand,
And a small one a strong nation:
I the Lord will hasten it in his time.

63

PRAEPARATE SCUTUM

ORDER ye the buckler and shield, and draw near to battle.
Harness the horses;
And get up, ye horsemen, and stand forth with your
　　　helmets;
Furbish the spears, and put on the brigandines.

Wherefore have I seen them dismayed and turned away back?
And their mighty ones are beaten down, and are fled apace, and
    look not back:
For fear was round about, saith the Lord.
Let not the swift flee away, nor the mighty man escape;
They shall stumble, and fall toward the north by the river
    Euphrates.
Who is this that cometh up as a flood,
Whose waters are moved as the rivers?
Egypt riseth up like a flood,
And his waters are moved like the rivers;
And he saith, I will go up, and will cover the earth;
I will destroy the city and the inhabitants thereof.
Come up, ye horses;
And rage, ye chariots;
And let the mighty men come forth;
The Ethiopians and the Libyans, that handle the shield;
And the Lydians, that handle and bend the bow.
For this is the day of the Lord God of hosts, a day of vengeance,
That he may avenge him of his adversaries:
And the sword shall devour,
And it shall be satiate and made drunk with their blood:
For the Lord God of hosts hath a sacrifice in the north country by
    the river Euphrates.
Go up into Gilead, and take balm, O virgin, the daughter of
    Egypt:
In vain shalt thou use many medicines;
For thou shalt not be cured.
The nations have heard of thy shame,
And thy cry hath filled the land:
For the mighty man hath stumbled against the mighty,
And they are fallen both together.

64

QUOMODO SEDET

How doth the city sit solitary, that was full of people!
How is she become as a widow!
She that was great among the nations, and princess among the
    provinces,
How is she become tributary!
She weepeth sore in the night, and her tears are on her cheeks:
Among all her lovers she hath none to comfort her:

All her friends have dealt treacherously with her,
They are become her enemies.
Judah is gone into captivity because of affliction, and because of
    great servitude :
She dwelleth among the heathen, she findeth no rest :
All her persecutors overtook her between the straits.
The ways of Zion do mourn, because none come to the solemn
    feasts :
All her gates are desolate :
Her priests sigh, her virgins are afflicted,
And she is in bitterness.
Her adversaries are the chief, her enemies prosper ;
For the Lord hath afflicted her for the multitude of her trans-
    gressions :
Her children are gone into captivity before the enemy.
And from the daughter of Zion all her beauty is departed :
Her princes are become like harts that find no pasture,
And they are gone without strength before the pursuer.
Jerusalem remembered in the days of her affliction and of her
    miseries all her pleasant things that she had in the days of
    old,
When her people fell into the hand of the enemy,
And none did help her :
The adversaries saw her, and did mock at her Sabbaths.
Jerusalem had grievously sinned ;
Therefore she is removed :
All that honoured her despise her,
Because they have seen her nakedness :
Yea, she sigheth, and turneth backward.
Her filthiness is in her skirts ;
She remembereth not her last end ;
Therefore she came down wonderfully :
She had no comforter.
O Lord, behold my affliction :
For the enemy hath magnified himself.
The adversary hath spread out his hand upon all her pleasant
    things.
For she hath seen that the heathen entered into her sanctuary,
Whom thou didst command that they should not enter into thy
    congregation.
All her people sigh, they seek bread ;
They have given their pleasant things for meat to relieve the soul :
See, O Lord, and consider ;
For I am become vile.
Is it nothing to you,
All ye that pass by ?
Behold, and see if there be any sorrow like unto my sorrow,

Which is done unto me,
Wherewith the Lord hath afflicted me in the day of his fierce anger.
From above hath he sent fire into my bones,
And it prevaileth against them :
He hath spread a net for my feet,
He hath turned me back :
He hath made me desolate and faint all the day.
The yoke of my transgressions is bound by his hand :
They are wreathed, and come up upon my neck :
He hath made my strength to fall,
The Lord hath delivered me into their hands,
From whom I am not able to rise up.
The Lord hath trodden under foot all my mighty men in the midst
    of me :
He hath called an assembly against me to crush my young men :
The Lord hath trodden the virgin, the daughter of Judah, as in a
    winepress.
For these things I weep ;
Mine eye, mine eye runneth down with water,
Because the comforter that should relieve my soul is far from me :
My children are desolate, because the enemy prevailed.
Zion spreadeth forth her hands, and there is none to comfort her :
The Lord hath commanded concerning Jacob, that his adversaries
    should be round about him :
Jerusalem is as a menstruous woman among them.
The Lord is righteous ;
For I have rebelled against his commandment :
Hear, I pray you, all people, and behold my sorrow :
My virgins and my young men are gone into captivity.
I called for my lovers, but they deceived me :
My priests and mine elders gave up the ghost in the city,
While they sought their meat to relieve their souls.
Behold, O Lord ; for I am in distress :
My bowels are troubled ;
Mine heart is turned within me ;
For I have grievously rebelled :
Abroad the sword bereaveth, at home there is as death.
They have heard that I sigh :
There is none to comfort me :
All mine enemies have heard of my trouble ;
They are glad that thou hast done it :
Thou wilt bring the day that thou hast called,
And they shall be like unto me.
Let all their wickedness come before thee ;
And do unto them, as thou hast done unto me for all my trans-
    gressions :
For my sighs are many, and my heart is faint.

65

FINIS VENIT

AN end, the end is come upon the four corners of the land.
Now is the end come upon thee,
And I will send mine anger upon thee,
And will judge thee according to thy ways,
And will recompense upon thee all thine abominations.
And mine eye shall not spare thee, neither will I have pity :
But I will recompense thy ways upon thee,
And thine abominations shall be in the midst of thee :
And ye shall know that I am the Lord.
An evil, an only evil, behold, is come.
An end is come, the end is come :
It watcheth for thee ;
Behold, it is come.
The morning is come unto thee, O thou that dwellest in the land :
The time is come, the day of trouble is near,
And not the sounding again of the mountains.
Now will I shortly pour out my fury upon thee,
And accomplish mine anger upon thee :
And I will judge thee according to thy ways,
And will recompense thee for all thine abominations.
And mine eye shall not spare, neither will I have pity :
I will recompense thee according to thy ways and thine abomina-
    tions that are in the midst of thee ;
And ye shall know that I am the Lord that smiteth.
Behold the day, behold, it is come :
The morning is gone forth ;
The rod hath blossomed,
Pride hath budded.
Violence is risen up into a rod of wickedness :
None of them shall remain, nor of their multitude, nor of any of
    theirs :
Neither shall there be wailing for them.
The time is come, the day draweth near :
Let not the buyer rejoice, nor the seller mourn :
For wrath is upon all the multitude thereof.
For the seller shall not return to that which is sold, although they
    were yet alive :
For the vision is touching the whole multitude thereof, which
    shall not return ;
Neither shall any strengthen himself in the iniquity of his life.
They have blown the trumpet, even to make all ready ;
But none goeth to the battle :
For my wrath is upon all the multitude thereof.

The sword is without, and the pestilence and the famine within :
He that is in the field shall die with the sword ;
And he that is in the city, famine and pestilence shall devour him.
But they that escape of them shall escape,
And shall be on the mountains like doves of the valleys,
All of them mourning, every one for his iniquity.
All hands shall be feeble,
And all knees shall be weak as water.
They shall also gird themselves with sackcloth, and horror shall
    cover them ;
And shame shall be upon all faces, and baldness upon all their
    heads.
They shall cast their silver in the streets, and their gold shall be
    removed :
Their silver and their gold shall not be able to deliver them in the
    day of the wrath of the Lord :
They shall not satisfy their souls, neither fill their bowels :
Because it is the stumblingblock of their iniquity.
As for the beauty of his ornament, he set it in majesty :
But they made the images of their abominations and of their
    detestable things therein :
Therefore have I set it far from them.
And I will give it into the hands of the strangers for a prey, and
    to the wicked of the earth for a spoil ;
And they shall pollute it.
My face will I turn also from them, and they shall pollute my
    secret place :
For the robbers shall enter into it, and defile it.
Make a chain :
For the land is full of bloody crimes, and the city is full of violence.
Wherefore I will bring the worst of the heathen, and they shall
    possess their houses :
I will also make the pomp of the strong to cease ;
And their holy places shall be defiled.
Destruction cometh ;
And they shall seek peace, and there shall be none.
Mischief shall come upon mischief, and rumour shall be upon
    rumour ;
Then shall they seek a vision of the prophet ;
But the law shall perish from the priest, and counsel from the
    ancients.
The king shall mourn, and the prince shall be clothed with
    desolation,
And the hands of the people of the land shall be troubled :
I will do unto them after their way,
And according to their deserts will I judge them ;
And they shall know that I am the Lord.

66

QUARE MATER

WHAT is thy mother?
A lioness:
She lay down among lions, she nourished her whelps among young
    lions.
And she brought up one of her whelps:
It became a young lion, and it learned to catch the prey;
It devoured men.
The nations also heard of him;
He was taken in their pit, and they brought him with chains unto
    the land of Egypt.
Now when she saw that she had waited, and her hope was lost,
Then she took another of her whelps, and made him a young
    lion.
And he went up and down among the lions,
He became a young lion,
And learned to catch the prey, and devoured men.
And he knew their desolate palaces, and he laid waste their cities;
And the land was desolate, and the fulness thereof, by the noise of
    his roaring.
Then the nations set against him on every side from the provinces,
    and spread their net over him:
He was taken in their pit.
And they put him in ward in chains, and brought him to the king
    of Babylon:
They brought him into holds, that his voice should no more be
    heard upon the mountains of Israel.
Thy mother is like a vine in thy blood, planted by the waters:
She was fruitful and full of branches by reason of many waters.
And she had strong rods for the sceptres of them that bare rule,
And her stature was exalted among the thick branches,
And she appeared in her height with the multitude of her branches.
But she was plucked up in fury,
She was cast down to the ground,
And the east wind dried up her fruit:
Her strong rods were broken and withered;
The fire consumed them.
And now she is planted in the wilderness, in a dry and thirsty
    ground.
And fire is gone out of a rod of her branches, which hath devoured
    her fruit,
So that she hath no strong rod to be a sceptre to rule.
This is a lamentation, and shall be for a lamentation.

67

CANITE TUBA

BLOW ye the trumpet in Zion, and sound an alarm in my holy
    mountain :
Let all the inhabitants of the land tremble :
For the day of the Lord cometh, for it is nigh at hand ;
A day of darkness and of gloominess,
A day of clouds and of thick darkness,
As the morning spread upon the mountains :
A great people and a strong ;
There hath not been ever the like,
Neither shall be any more after it,
Even to the years of many generations.
A fire devoureth before them ;
And behind them a flame burneth :
The land is as the garden of Eden before them, and behind them
    a desolate wilderness ;
Yea, and nothing shall escape them.
The appearance of them is as the appearance of horses ;
And as horsemen, so shall they run.
Like the noise of chariots on the tops of mountains shall they leap,
Like the noise of a flame of fire that devoureth the stubble,
As a strong people set in battle array.
Before their face the people shall be much pained :
All faces shall gather blackness.
They shall run like mighty men ;
They shall climb the wall like men of war ;
And they shall march every one on his ways,
And they shall not break their ranks :
Neither shall one thrust another ;
They shall walk every one in his path :
And when they fall upon the sword, they shall not be wounded.
They shall run to and fro in the city ;
They shall run upon the wall,
They shall climb up upon the houses ;
They shall enter in at the windows like a thief.
The earth shall quake before them ;
The heavens shall tremble :
The sun and the moon shall be dark,
And the stars shall withdraw their shining :
And the Lord shall utter his voice before his army :
For his camp is very great :
For he is strong that executeth his word :
For the day of the Lord is great and very terrible ;
And who can abide it ?

68

QUAERITE ME

SEEK ye me, and ye shall live:
But seek not Beth-el, nor enter into Gilgal, and pass not to
 Beersheba:
For Gilgal shall surely go into captivity,
And Beth-el shall come to nought.
Seek the Lord, and ye shall live;
Lest he break out like fire in the house of Joseph, and
 devour it,
And there be none to quench it in Beth-el.
Ye who turn judgment to wormwood,
And leave off righteousness in the earth,
Seek him that maketh the seven stars and Orion,
And turneth the shadow of death into the morning,
And maketh the day dark with night:
That calleth for the waters of the sea,
And poureth them out upon the face of the earth:
The Lord is his name:
That strengtheneth the spoiled against the strong,
So that the spoiled shall come against the fortress.

69

DOMINE, AUDIVI

O LORD, I have heard thy speech, and was afraid:
O Lord, revive thy work in the midst of the years,
In the midst of the years make known;
In wrath remember mercy.
God came from Teman,
And the Holy One from mount Paran.
His glory covered the heavens,
And the earth was full of his praise.
And his brightness was as the light;
He had horns coming out of his hand:
And there was the hiding of his power.
Before him went the pestilence,
And burning coals went forth at his feet.

He stood, and measured the earth:
He beheld, and drove asunder the nations;
And the everlasting mountains were scattered,
The perpetual hills did bow:
His ways are everlasting.
I saw the tents of Cushan in affliction:
And the curtains of the land of Midian did tremble.
Was the Lord displeased against the rivers?
Was thine anger against the rivers?
Was thy wrath against the sea,
That thou didst ride upon thine horses,
And thy chariots of salvation?
Thy bow was made quite naked,
According to the oaths of the tribes, even thy word.
Thou didst cleave the earth with rivers.
The mountains saw thee, and they trembled;
The overflowing of the water passed by:
The deep uttered his voice,
And lifted up his hands on high.
The sun and moon stood still in their habitation:
At the light of thine arrows they went,
And at the shining of thy glittering spear.
Thou didst march through the land in indignation,
Thou didst thresh the heathen in anger.
Thou wentest forth for the salvation of thy people,
Even for salvation with thine anointed;
Thou woundedst the head out of the house of the wicked,
By discovering the foundation unto the neck.
Thou didst strike through with his staves the head of
      his villages;
They came out as a whirlwind to scatter me:
Their rejoicing was as to devour the poor secretly.
Thou didst walk through the sea with thine horses,
Through the heap of great waters.
When I heard, my belly trembled;
My lips quivered at the voice:
Rottenness entered into my bones, and I trembled in
      myself,
That I might rest in the day of trouble:
When he cometh up unto the people, he will invade
      them with his troops.
Although the fig-tree shall not blossom,
Neither shall fruit be in the vines;
The labour of the olive shall fail,
And the fields shall yield no meat;
The flock shall be cut off from the fold,
And there shall be no herd in the stalls:

F

Yet I will rejoice in the Lord,
I will joy in the God of my salvation.
The Lord God is my strength,
And he will make my feet like hinds' feet,
And he will make me to walk upon mine high places.

70

A LOVER'S LULLABY

SING lullaby, as women do,
  Wherewith they bring their babes to rest ;
And lullaby can I sing too,
  As womanly as can the best.
With lullaby they still the child,
And, if I be not much beguiled,
Full many a wanton babe have I,
Which must be stilled with lullaby.

First, lullaby my youthful years !
  It is now time to go to bed,
For crooked age and hoary hairs
  Have won the haven within my head.
With lullaby then, youth, be still,
With lullaby content thy will.
Since courage quails and comes behind,
Go sleep, and so beguile thy mind !

Next, lullaby my gazing eyes,
  Which wonted were to glance apace,
For every glass may now suffice
  To show the furrows in my face !
With lullaby then wink awhile ;
With lullaby your looks beguile ;
Let no fair face, nor beauty bright,
Entice you eft with vain delight.

And lullaby my wanton will !
  Let reason's rule now rein thy thought;
Since all too late I find by skill
  How dear I have thy fancies bought.
With lullaby now take thine ease,
With lullaby thy doubts appease.
For trust to this, if thou be still,
My body shall obey thy will.

Eke lullaby my loving boy—
  My little robin, take thy rest !
Since age is cold and nothing coy,
  Keep close thy coin, for so is best.
With lullaby be thou content,
With lullaby thy lusts relent !
Let others pay which have more pence :
Thou art too poor for such expense.

Thus lullaby my youth, mine eyes,
  My will, my ware, and all that was !
I can no more delays devise ;
  But welcome pain, let pleasure pass !
With lullaby now take your leave,
With lullaby your dreams deceive,
And when you rise with waking eye,
Remember then this lullaby.
George Gascoyne.

71

A FAREWELL

Adieu, O daisy of delight !
Adieu, most pleasant and perfyt ;
  Adieu, and have good night !
Adieu, thou lustiest of lyve ;
Adieu, sweet thing superlatyve ;
  Adieu, my lamp of light !
Like as the lizard does indeed
  Live by the manis' face,
Thy beauty likewise should me feed,
  If we had time and space.
    Adieu now ; be true now,
      Sen that we must depart.
    Forget not, and set not
      At light my constant heart.

Albeit my body be absent,
My faithful heart is vigilent
  To do you service true ;
But, when I hant into the place
Where I was wont to see that face,
  My dolour does renew.
Then all my pleasure is but pain,
  My cares they do increase ;

Until I see your face again,
  I live in heaviness.
     Sore weeping, but sleeping,
      The nights I overdrive ;
     Whiles mourning, whiles turning,
      With thoughtis pensitive.

Sometime Good Hope did me comfort,
Saying, the time should be but short
  Of absence to endure.
Then Courage quickens so my spreit,
When I think on my lady sweet,
  I hald my service sure.
I cannot plaint of my estate,
  I thank the gods above ;
For I am first in her consait,
   Whom both I serve and love.
     Her friends aye weinds
      To cause her to revoke ;
     She bides, and slides
      No more than does a rock.

O lady, for thy constancy
A faithful servant sall I be,
  Thine honour to defend ;
And I sall surely, for thy saik,
As doth the turtle for her maik,
  Love to my lyfis end.
No pain nor travail, fear nor dreid,
  Shall cause me to desist.
Then, aye when ye this letter read,
  Remember how we kissed :
     Embracing, with lacing,
      With others tearis sweet !
     Sic blissing in kissing
      I quit till we two meet.

               Alexander Montgomerie.

72

AUBADE

Hey ! now the day daws ;
The jolly cock craws ;
Now shroudës the shaws,
  Through Nature anon.

The thissell-cock cries
On lovers who lies.
Now skails the skies :
    The night is near gone.

The feilds overflows
With gowans that grows,
Where lilies like lowes,
    As red as the rone.
The turtle that true is,
With notes that renews,
Her pairty pursues :
    The night is near gone.

Now hairtës with hinds,
Conform to their kinds,
Hie tosses their tynds,
    On ground where they grone.
Now hurchons, with hairs,
Aye passes in pairs,
Which duly declares
    The night is near gone.

The season excells
Through sweetness that smells ;
Now Cupid compels
    Our heartës echone
On Venus, who waiks,
To muse on our maiks,
Syne sing for their saiks :—
    'The night is near gone !'

All courageous knichts
Aganes the day dichts
The breast plate that bright is,
    To fight with their fone.
The stoned steed stamps
Through courage, and cramps,
Syne on the land lamps :
    The night is near gone.

The freikës on feilds
That wight wapins weilds
With shining bright shields
    As Titan in trone,

Stiff speirs, in reists
Over corsers' crests,
Are broke on their breists :
    The night is near gone.

So hard are their hitts,
Some sways, some sitts,
And some perforce flitts
    On ground while they groan.
Some groomës that gay is,
On blonkës that brays,
With swordës assays :
    The night is near gone.

Alexander Montgomerie.

73

COME, LITTLE BABE

COME, little babe, come, silly soul,
Thy father's shame, thy mother's grief,
Born as I doubt to all our dole,
And to thyself unhappy chief :
    Sing lullaby and lap it warm,
    Poor soul that thinks no creature harm.

Thou little think'st, and less dost know
The cause of this thy mother's moan.
Thou want'st the wit to wail her woe,
And I myself am all alone.
    Why dost thou weep? why dost thou wail?
    And know'st not yet what thou dost ail.

Come, little wretch! Ah! silly heart,
Mine only joy, what can I more?
If there be any wrong thy smart,
That may the destinies implore,
    'Twas I, I say, against my will—
    I wail the time, but be thou still.

And dost thou smile? O thy sweet face !
Would God Himself He might thee see !
No doubt thou soon wouldst purchase grace,
I know right well, for thee and me.
    But come to mother, babe, and play,
    For father false is fled away.

Sweet boy, if it by fortune chance
Thy father home again to send,
If Death do strike me with his lance,
Yet may'st thou me to him commend :
    If any ask thy mother's name,
    Tell how by love she purchased blame.

Then will his gentle heart soon yield :
I know him of a noble mind :
Although a lion in the field,
A lamb in town thou shalt him find :
    Ask blessing, babe, be not afraid !
    His sugared words hath me betrayed.

Then may'st thou joy and be right glad,
Although in woe I seem to moan.
Thy father is no rascal lad :
A noble youth of blood and bone,
    His glancing looks, if he once smile,
    Right honest women may beguile.

Come, little boy, and rock a-sleep !
Sing lullaby, and be thou still !
I, that can do naught else but weep,
Will sit by thee and wail my fill :
    God bless my babe, and lullaby
    From this thy father's quality.

Nicholas Breton.

74

SONG

LOVELY kind and kindly loving,
Such a mind were worth the moving :
Truly fair and fairly true—
Where are all these but in you?

Wisely kind and kindly wise,
Blessèd life, where such love lies !
Wise, and kind, and fair, and true—
Lovely live all these in you.

Sweetly dear and dearly sweet,
Blessèd where these blessings meet !
Sweet, fair, wise, kind, blessèd, true—
Blessèd be all these in you !

Nicholas Breton.

75

PASTORAL

IN the merry month of May,
On a morn by break of day,
Forth I walk'd by the wood-side,
Whereas May was in her pride :
There I spied all alone
Phillida and Corydon.
Much ado there was, God wot !
He would love and she would not.
She said, Never man was true ;
He said, None was false to you.
He said, He had loved her long ;
She said, Love should have no wrong.
Corydon would kiss her then ;
She said, Maids must kiss no men
Till they did for good and all ;
Then she made the shepherd call
All the heavens to witness truth
Never loved a truer youth.
Thus with many a pretty oath,
Yea and nay, faith and troth,
Such as seely shepherds use
When they will not love abuse,
Love, which had been long deluded,
Was with kisses sweet concluded ;
And Phillida with garlands gay
Was made the Lady of the May.

Nicholas Breton.

76

EPITHALAMION

YE learned Sisters, which have oftentimes
Been to the aiding, others to adorn,
Whom ye thought worthy of your graceful rhymes,
That even the greatest did not greatly scorn
To hear their names sung in your simple lays,
But joyed in their praise ;
And when ye list your own mishaps to mourn,
Which death, or love, or fortune's wreck did raise,
Your string could soon to sadder tenor turn,
And teach the woods and waters to lament
Your doleful dreriment :

Now lay those sorrowful complaints aside ;
And having all your heads with garlands crowned,
Help me mine own love's praises to resound ;
Ne let the same of any be envíed :
So Orpheus did for his own bride,
So I unto myself alone will sing ;
The woods shall to me answer, and my echo ring.

Early, before the world's light-giving lamp
His golden beam upon the hills doth spread,
Having dispersed the night's uncheerful damp,
Do ye awake ; and with fresh lusty head
Go to the bower of my beloved love,
My truest turtle dove :
Bid her awake ; for Hymen is awake,
And long since ready forth his mask to move,
With his bright Tead that flames with many a flake,
And many a bachelor to wait on him,
In their fresh garments trim.
Bid her awake therefore, and soon her dight,
For lo ! the wished day is come at last,
That shall for all the pains and sorrows past
Pay to her usury of long delight :
And, whilst she doth her dight,
Do ye to her of joy and solace sing,
That all the woods may answer, and your echo ring.

Bring with you all the Nymphs that you can hear,
Both of the rivers and the forests green
And of the sea that neighbours to her near,
All with gay garlands goodly well beseen.
And let them also with them bring in hand
Another gay garlánd,
For my fair love, of lilies and of roses,
Bound truelove wise, with a blue silk ribánd.
And let them make great store of bridal poses,
And let them eke bring store of other flowers,
To deck the bridal bowers.
And let the ground whereas her foot shall tread,
For fear the stones her tender foot should wrong,
Be strewed with fragrant flowers all along,
And diapred like the discoloured mead.
Which done, do at her chamber door await,
For she will waken straight,
The whiles do ye this song unto her sing,
The woods shall to you answer, and your echo ring.

Ye Nymphs of Mulla, which with careful heed
The silver-scaly trouts do tend full well,
And greedy pikes which use therein to feed
(Those trouts and pikes all others do excel),
And ye likewise, which keep the rushy lake
Where none do fishes take,
Bind up the locks the which hang scattered light,
And in his waters, which your mirror make,
Behold your faces as the crystal bright,
That when you come whereas my love doth lie,
No blemish she may spy.
And eke, ye lightfoot maids, which keep the door,
That on the hoary mountain used to tower,
And the wild wolves, which seek them to devour,
With your steel darts do chase from coming near,
Be also present here,
To help to deck her, and to help to sing,
That all the woods may answer, and your echo ring.

Wake now, my love, awake! for it is time:
The rosy Morn long since left Tithon's bed,
All ready to her silver couch to climb,
And Phœbus gins to show his glorious head.
Hark! how the cheerful birds do chant their lays,
And carol of love's praise.
The merry lark her matins sings aloft;
The thrush replies; the mavis descant plays;
The ouzel shrills; the ruddock warbles soft:
So goodly all agree with sweet consent
To this day's merriment.
Ah! my dear love, why do ye sleep thus long,
When meeter were that ye should now awake,
To await the coming of your joyous make,
And hearken to the bird's lovelearned song
The dewy leaves among?
For they of joy and pleasance to you sing,
That all the woods them answer, and their echo ring.

My love is now awake out of her dreams,
And her fair eyes, like stars that dimmed were
With darksome cloud, now show their goodly beams
More bright than Hesperus his head doth rear.
Come now, ye Damsels, daughters of delight,
Help quickly her to dight!
But first come, ye fair Hours, which were begot,
In Jove's sweet paradise, of Day and Night;
Which do the seasons of the year allot,

And all that ever in this world is fair
Do make and still repair :
And ye three handmaids of the Cyprian Queen,
The which do still adorn her beauty's pride, ˜ .
Help to adorn my beautifulest bride ;
And, as ye her array, still throw between
Some graces to be seen ;
And, as ye use to Venus, to her sing,
The whiles the woods shall answer, and your echo ring.

Now is my love all ready forth to come :
Let all the virgins therefore well await ;
And ye, fresh Boys, that tend upon her groom,
Prepare yourselves, for he is coming straight.
Set all your things in seemly good array,
Fit for so joyful day :
The joyful'st day that ever Sun did see.
Fair Sun ! show forth thy favourable ray,
And let thy lifull heat not fervent be,
For fear of burning her sunshiny face,
Her beauty to disgrace.
O fairest Phœbus ! father of the Muse !
If ever I did honour thee aright,
Or sing the thing that mote thy mind delight,
Do not thy servant's simple boon refuse ;
But let this day, let this one day, be mine ;
Let all the rest be thine :
Then I thy sovereign praises loud will sing,
That all the woods shall answer, and their echo ring.

Hark ! how the Minstrels gin to shrill aloud
Their merry Music that resounds from far,
The pipe, the tabor, and the trembling crowd,
That well agree withouten breach or jar.
But most of all the Damsels do delight,
When they their timbrels smite,
And thereunto do dance and carol sweet,
That all the senses they do ravish quite ;
The whiles the Boys run up and down the street,
Crying aloud with strong confused noise,
As if it were one voice,
Hymen ! ïo Hymen ! Hymen they do shout ;
That even to the heavens their shouting shrill
Doth reach, and all the firmament doth fill :
To which the people standing all about,
As in approvance, do thereto applaud,
And loud advance her laud ;

And evermore they Hymen, Hymen! sing,
That all the woods them answer, and their echo ring.

Lo! where she comes along with portly pace,
Like Phœbe, from her chamber of the East,
Arising forth to run her mighty race,
Clad all in white, that seems a virgin best.
So well it her beseems, that ye would ween
Some Angel she had been.
Her long loose yellow locks, like golden wire
Sprinkled with pearl, and pearling flowers atween,
Do like a golden mantle her attire;
And being crowned with a garland green,
Seem like some maiden Queen.
Her modest eyes, abashéd to behold
So many gazers as on her do stare,
Upon the lowly ground affixed are;
Ne dare lift up her countenance too bold,
But blush to hear her praises sung so loud,
So far from being proud.
Nathless, do ye still loud her praises sing,
That all the woods may answer, and your echo ring.

Tell me, ye Merchants' Daughters, did ye see
So fair a creature in your town before,
So sweet, so lovely, and so mild as she,
Adorned with beauty's grace and virtue's store?
Her goodly eyes like sapphires shining bright,
Her forehead ivory white,
Her cheeks like apples which the sun hath rudded,
Her lips like cherries charming men to bite,
Her breast like to a bowl of cream uncrudded,
Her paps like lilies budded,
Her snowy neck like to a marble tower;
And all her body like a palace fair,
Ascending up, with many a stately stair,
To honour's seat and chastity's sweet bower!
Why stand ye still, ye Virgins, in amaze
Upon her so to gaze,
Whiles ye forget your former lay to sing,
To which the woods did answer, and your echo ring.

But if ye saw that which no eyes can see,
The inward beauty of her lively spright,
Garnished with heavenly gifts of high decree,
Much more then would ye wonder at that sight,

And stand astonished like to those which read
Medusæ's mazeful head.
There dwells sweet love, and constant chastity,
Unspotted faith, and comely womanhood,
Regard of honour, and mild modesty.
There virtue reigns as Queen in royal throne,
And giveth laws alone,
The which the base affections do obey,
And yield their services unto her will.
Ne thought of things uncomely ever may
Thereto approach to tempt her mind to ill.
Had ye once seen these her celestial treasures
And unrevealed pleasures,
Then would ye wonder, and her praises sing,
That all the woods should answer, and your echo ring.

Open the temple gates unto my love !
Open them wide that she may enter in,
And all the posts adorn as doth behove,
And all the pillars deck with garlands trim,
For to receive this Saint with honour due
That cometh in to you !
With trembling steps and humble reverence,
She cometh in before the Almighty's view :
Of her, ye virgins, learn obedience,
When so ye come into those holy places,
To humble your proud faces !
Bring her up to the high altar, that she may
The sacred ceremonies there partake,
The which do endless matrimony make ;
And let the roaring organs loudly play
The praises of the Lord in lively notes ;
The whiles, with hollow throats,
The Choristers the joyous anthem sing,
That all the woods may answer, and their echo ring.

Behold, whiles she before the altar stands,
Hearing the holy priest that to her speaks,
And blesseth her with his two happy hands,
How the red roses flush up in her cheeks,
And the pure snow, with goodly vermil stain,
Like crimson dyed in grain !
That even the Angels, which continually
About the sacred altar do remain,
Forget their service, and about her fly,
Oft peeping in her face, that seems more fair
The more they on it stare.

But her sad eyes, still fastened on the ground,
Are governéd with goodly modesty,
That suffers not one look to glance awry,
Which may let in a little thought unsound.
Why blush ye, love, to give to me your hand
The pledge of all our band?
Sing, ye sweet Angels, alleluia sing,
That all the woods may answer, and your echo ring.

Now all is done: bring home the Bride again!
Bring home the triumph of our victory!
Bring home with you the glory of her gain,
With joyance bring her and with jollity!
Never had man more joyful day than this,
Whom heaven would heap with bliss.
Make feast therefore now all this livelong day;
This day for ever to me holy is.
Pour out the wine without restraint or stay,
Pour not by cups but by the bellyful!
Pour out to all that wull,
And sprinkle all the posts and walls with wine,
That they may sweat, and drunken be withal!
Crown ye God Bacchus with a coronal,
And Hymen also crown with wreaths of vine;
And let the Graces dance unto the rest,
For they can do it best:
The whiles the maidens do their carol sing,
To which the woods shall answer, and their echo ring.

Ring ye the bells, ye Young Men of the town,
And leave your wonted labours for this day:
This day is holy; do ye write it down,
That ye for ever it remember may.
This day the sun is in his chiefest height,
With Barnaby the bright,
From whence declining daily by degrees,
He somewhat loseth of his heat and light,
When once the Crab behind his back he sees.
But for this time it ill ordained was,
To choose the longest day in all the year,
And shortest night, when longest fitter were:
Yet never day so long but late would pass!
Ring ye the bells, to make it wear away,
And bonfires make all day;
And dance about them, and about them sing,
That all the woods may answer, and your echo ring!

Ah ! when will this long weary day have end,
And lend me leave to come unto my love?
How slowly do the hours their numbers spend ;
How slowly does sad Time his feathers move !
Haste thee, O fairest Planet ! to thy home
Within the Western foam :
Thy tiréd steeds long since have need of rest !
Long though it be, at last I see it gloom,
And the bright evening star with golden crest
Appear out of the East.
Fair child of beauty ! glorious lamp of love !
That all the host of heaven in ranks dost lead,
And guidest lovers through the night's sad dread,
How cheerfully thou lookest from above,
And seem'st to laugh atween thy twinkling light,
As joying in the sight
Of these glad many, which for joy do sing,
That all the woods them answer, and their echo ring !

Now cease, ye Damsels, your delights forepast !
Enough is it that all the day was yours :
Now day is done, and night is nighing fast,
Now bring the Bride into the bridal bowers.
The night is come, now soon her disarray,
And in her bed her lay ;
Lay her in lilies and in violets,
And silken curtains over her display,
And odoured sheets, and Arras coverlets.
Behold how goodly my fair love does lie
In proud humility !
Like unto Maia, when as Jove her took
In Tempe, lying on the flowery grass
'Twixt sleep and wake, after she weary was
With bathing in the Acidalian brook !
Now it is night, ye Damsels may be gone ;
And leave my love alone ;
And leave likewise your former lay to sing :
The woods no more shall answer, nor your echo ring.

Now welcome, Night ! thou Night so long expected,
That long day's labour dost at last defray,
And all my cares, which cruel love collected,
Hast summed in one, and cancelléd for aye !
Spread thy broad wing over my love and me,
That no man may us see ;
And in thy sable mantle us enwrap,
From fear of peril and foul horror free.

Let no false treason seek us to entrap,
Nor any dread disquiet once annoy
The safety of our joy ; .
But let the night be calm and quietsome,
Without tempestuous storms or sad affray :
Like as when Jove with fair Alcmena lay,
When he begot the great Tirynthian groom :
Or like as when he with thyself did lie,
And begot Majesty.
And let the maids and young men cease to sing ;
Ne let the woods them answer, nor their echo ring.

Let no lamenting cries nor doleful tears
Be heard all night within, nor yet without ;
Ne let false whispers, breeding hidden fears,
Break gentle sleep with misconceived doubt.
Let no deluding dreams, nor dreadful sights,
Make sudden sad affrights,
Ne let housefires, nor lightning's helpless harms ;
Ne let the Pouke, nor other evil sprites,
Ne let mischievous witches with their charms,
Ne let hobgoblins, names whose sense we see not,
Fray us with things that be not !
Let not the shriek-owl, nor the stork, be heard ;
Nor the night raven, that still deadly yells ;
Nor damnèd ghosts, called up with mighty spells,
Nor grisly vultures make us once affeared !
Ne let the unpleasant choir of frogs still croaking
Make us to wish their choking !
Let none of these their dreary accents sing ;
Ne let the woods them answer, nor their echo ring.

But let still Silence true night-watches keep,
That sacred peace may in assurance reign,
And timely Sleep, when it is time to sleep,
May pour his limbs forth on your pleasant plain ;
The whiles an hundred little winged Loves,
Like divers feathered doves,
Shall fly and flutter round about the bed,
And in the secret dark, that none reproves,
Their pretty stealths shall work, and snares shall spread
To filch away sweet snatches of delight,
Concealed through covert night.
Ye sons of Venus, play your sports at will ;
For greedy Pleasure, careless of your toys,
Thinks more upon her paradise of joys,
Then what ye do, albeit good or ill !

All night therefore attend your merry play,
For it will soon be day:
Now none doth hinder you, that say or sing;
Ne will the woods now answer, nor your echo ring.

Who is the same, which at my window peeps,
Or whose is that fair face that shines so bright?
Is it not Cynthia, she that never sleeps,
But walks about high heaven all the night?
O fairest goddess! do thou not envý
My love with me to spy;
For thou likewise didst love, though now unthought,
And for a fleece of wool, which privily
The Latmian shepherd once unto thee brought,
His pleasures with thee wrought!
Therefore to us be favourable now;
And sith of women's labours thou hast charge,
And generation goodly dost enlarge,
Incline thy will t' effect our wishful vow,
And the chaste womb inform with timely seed,
That may our comfort breed:
Till which we cease our hopeful hap to sing,
Ne let the woods us answer, nor our echo ring.

And thou, great Juno, which with awful might
The laws of wedlock still dost patronise,
And the religion of the faith first plight
With sacred rights hast taught to solemnise,
And eke for comfort often calléd art
Of women in their smart:
Eternally bind thou this lovely band,
And all thy blessings unto us impart!
And thou, glad Genius, in whose gentle hand
The bridal bower and genial bed remain
Without blemish or stain,
And the sweet pleasures of their love's delight
With secret aid dost succour and supply,
Till they bring forth the fruitful progeny:
Send us the timely fruit of this same night!
And thou, fair Hebe, and thou, Hymen free,
Grant that it may so be!
Till which we cease your further praise to sing,
Ne any woods shall answer, nor your echo ring.

And ye high Heavens, the temple of the Gods,
In which a thousand torches flaming bright
Do burn, that to us wretched earthly clods
In dreadful darkness lend desired light;

G

And all ye Powers which in the same remain,
More than we men can feign :
Pour out your blessing on us plenteously,
And happy influence upon us rain,
That we may raise a large posterity,
Which from the earth, which they may long possess
With lasting happiness,
Up to your haughty palaces may mount :
And, for the guerdon, of their glorious merit,
May heavenly tabernacles there inherit,
Of blessed Saints, for to increase the count !
So let us rest, sweet love, in hope of this,
And cease till then our timely joys to sing—
The woods no more us answer, nor our echo ring.

Song! made in lieu of many ornaments,
With which my love should duly have been decked,
Which cutting off through hasty accidents,
Ye would not stay your due time to expect,
But promised both to recompense :
Be unto her a goodly ornament,
And for short time an endless monument.

Edmund Spenser.

77

PROTHALAMION

CALM was the day, and through the trembling air
Sweet breathing Zephyrus did softly play,
A gentle spirit that lightly did delay
Hot Titan's beams, which then did glister fair ;
When I, whom sullen care,
Through discontent of my long fruitless stay
In Prince's court, and expectation vain
Of idle hopes, which still do fly away
Like empty shadows, did afflict my brain,
Walked forth to ease my pain
Along the shore of silver-streaming Thames ;
Whose rutty bank, the which his river hems,
Was painted all with variable flowers,
And all the meads adorned with dainty gems
Fit to deck maidens' bowers,
And crown their paramours
Against the bridal day, which is not long :
  Sweet Thames ! run softly, till I end my song.

There, in a meadow by the river's side,
A flock of Nymphs I chancéd to espy,
All lovely daughters of the Flood thereby,
With goodly greenish locks, all loose untied,
As each had been a bride ;
And each one had a little wicker basket,
Made of fine twigs, entrailéd curiously,
In which they gathered flowers to fill their flasket,
And with fine fingers cropped full featously
The tender stalks on high.
Of every sort which in that meadow grew
They gathered some : the violet, pallid blue,
The little daisy that at evening closes,
The virgin lily, and the primrose true,
With store of vermeil roses,
To deck their bridegrooms' posies
Against the bridal day, which was not long :
   Sweet Thames ! run softly, till I end my song.

With that I saw two swans of goodly hue
Come softly swimming down along the lea ;
Two fairer birds I yet did never see :
The snow, which doth the top of Pindus strew,
Did never whiter shew,
Nor Jove himself, when he a swan would be
For love of Leda, whiter did appear ;
Yet Leda was, they say, as white as he,
Yet not so white as these, nor nothing near :
So purely white they were,
That even the gentle stream, the which them bare,
Seemed foul to them, and bade his billows spare
To wet their silken feathers, lest they might
Soil their fair plumes with water not so fair,
And mar their beauties bright,
That shone as heaven's light
Against their bridal day, which was not long ;
   Sweet Thames ! run softly, till I end my song.

Eftsoons the Nymphs, which now had flowers their fill,
Ran all in haste to see that silver brood,
As they came floating on the crystal flood ;
Whom when they saw, they stood amazéd still,
Their wond'ring eyes to fill :
Them seemed they never saw a sight so fair,
Of fowls so lovely that they sure did deem
Them heavenly born, or to be that same pair
Which through the sky draw Venus' silver team ;

For sure they did not seem
To be begot of any earthly seed,
But rather angels, or of angels' breed ;
Yet were they bred of summer's heat, they say,
In sweetest season, when each flower and weed
The earth did fresh array ;
So fresh they seemed as day,
Even as their bridal day, which was not long :
   Sweet Thames ! run softly, till I end my song.

Then forth they all out of their baskets drew
Great store of flowers, the honour of the field,
That to the sense did fragrant odours yield,
All which upon those goodly birds they threw,
And all the waves did strew,
That like old Peneus' waters they did seem,
When, down along by pleasant Tempe's shore,
Scattered with flowers through Thessaly they stream,
That they appear, through lilies' plenteous store,
Like a bride's chamber floor.
Two of those Nymphs, meanwhile, two garlands bound
Of freshest flowers which in that mead they found,
The which presenting all in trim array,
Their snowy foreheads therewithal they crowned,
Whilst one did sing this lay,
Prepared against that day,
Against their bridal day, which was not long
   (Sweet Thames ! run softly, till I end my song !):—

' Ye gentle birds, the world's fair ornament,
And heaven's glory, whom this happy hour
Doth lead unto your lovers' blissful bower,
Joy may you have, and gentle hearts content
Of your love's couplement !
And let fair Venus, that is queen of love,
With her heart-quelling son upon you smile :
Whose smile, they say, hath virtue to remove
All love's dislike, and friendship's faulty guile
For ever to assoil !
Let endless peace your steadfast hearts accord,
And blessed plenty wait upon your board ;
And let your bed with pleasures chaste abound,
That fruitful issue may to you afford,
Which may your foes confound,
And make your joys redound
Upon your bridal day, which is not long :
   Sweet Thames ! run softly, till I end my song.'

So ended she ; and all the rest around
To her redoubled that her undersong,
Which said, their bridal day should not be long :
And gentle Echo from the neighbour ground
Their accents did resound.
So forth those joyous birds did pass along
Adown the Lee, that to them murmured low,
As he would speak, but that he lacked a tongue,
Yet did by signs his glad affection show,
Making his stream run slow ;
And all the fowl which in his flood did dwell
'Gan flock about these twain, that did excel
The rest, so far as Cynthia doth shend
The lesser stars. So they, enrangéd well,
Did on those two attend,
And their best service lend
Against their wedding day, which was not long :
  Sweet Thames ! run softly, till I end my song.

At length they all to merry London came,
To merry London, my most kindly nurse,
That to me gave this life's first native source,
Though from another place I take my name,
An house of ancient fame !
There when they came, whereas those bricky towers
The which on Thames' broad, agéd back do ride,
Where now the studious lawyers have their bowers ;
There whilom wont the Templar Knights to bide,
Till they decayed through pride ;
Next whereunto there stands a stately place,
Where oft I gainéd gifts and goodly grace
Of that great lord, which therein wont to dwell ;
Whose want too well now feels my friendless case ;
But ah ! here fits not well
Old woes, but joys, to tell
Against the bridal day, which is not long :
  Sweet Thames ! run softly, till I end my song.

Yet therein now doth lodge a noble peer,
Great England's glory and the world's wide wonder,
Whose dreadful name late through all Spain did thunder,
And Hercules' two pillars standing near
Did make to quake and fear.
Fair branch of honour, flower of chivalry,
That fillest England with thy triumph's fame,
Joy have thou of thy noble victory,
And endless happiness of thine own name

That promiseth the same !
That, through thy prowess and victorious arms,
Thy country may be freed from foreign harms,
And great Elisa's glorious name may ring
Through all the world, filled with thy wide alarms,
Which some brave muse may sing
To ages following,
Upon the bridal day, which is not long :
   Sweet Thames ! run softly, till I end my song.

From those high towers this noble lord issúing,
Like radiant Hesper, when his golden hair
In the ocean billows he hath bathéd fair,
Descended to the river's open viewing,
With a great train ensuing.
Above the rest were goodly to be seen
Two gentle knights of lovely face and feature,
Beseeming well the bower of any queen,
With gifts of wit and ornaments of nature
Fit for so goodly stature
That like the twins of Jove they seemed in sight,
Which deck the bauldrick of the heavens bright :
They two, forth pacing to the river's side,
Received those two fair brides, their love's delight ;
Which at th' appointed tide,
Each one did make his bride
Against their bridal day, which is not long :
   Sweet Thames ! run softly, till I end my song.

Edmund Spenser.

78

FAIN WOULD I, BUT I DARE NOT

FAIN would I, but I dare not ; I dare, and yet I may not ;
I may, although I care not, for pleasure when I play not.
You laugh because you like not ; I jest whenas I joy not ;
You pierce, although you strike not ; I strike and yet annoy
   not.

I spy, whenas I speak not ; for oft I speak and speed not ;
But of my wounds you reck not, because you see they bleed
   not ;
Yet bleed they where you see not, but you the pain endure not ;
Of noble mind they be not, that ever kill and cure not.

I see, whenas I view not; I wish, although I crave not;
I serve, and yet I sue not; I hope for that I have not;
I catch, although I hold not; I burn, although I flame not;
I seem, whenas I would not; and when I seem, I am not.

Yours am I, though I seem not, and will be, though I show not;
Mine outward deeds then deem not, when mine intent you know
    not;
But if my serving prove not most sure, although I sue not,
Withdraw your mind and love not, nor of my ruin rue not.

                                    Walter Raleigh.

79

THE SILENT LOVER

Passions are likened best to floods and streams :
The shallow murmur but the deep are dumb ;
So, when affections yield discourse, it seems
   The bottom is but shallow whence they come.
They that are rich in words, in words discover
That they are poor in that which makes a lover.

WRONG not, sweet empress of my heart,
   The merit of true passion,
With thinking that he feels no smart,
   That sues for no compassion;

Since, if my plaints serve not to approve
   The conquest of thy beauty,
It comes not from defect of love,
   But from excess of duty.

For, knowing that I sue to serve
   A saint of such perfection,
As all desire, but none deserve,
   A place in her affection :

I rather choose to want relief
   Than venture the revealing.
Where glory recommends the grief,
   Despair distrusts the healing !

Thus those desires that aim too high
  For any mortal lover,
When reason cannot make them die,
  Discretion doth them cover.

Yet, when discretion doth bereave
  The plaints that they should utter,
Then thy discretion may perceive
  That silence is a suitor.

Silence in love bewrays more woe
  Than words, though ne'er so witty ;
A beggar that is dumb, you know,
  May challenge double pity.

Then wrong not, dearest to my heart,
  My true, though secret, passion :
He smarteth most that hides his smart,
  And sues for no compassion.

                 Walter Raleigh.

80

TO COLIN CLOUT

BEAUTY sat bathing by a spring,
  Where fairest shades did hide her.
The winds blew calm, the birds did sing,
  The cool streams ran beside her.
My wanton thoughts enticed mine eye
  To see what was forbidden :
But better memory said, Fie,
  So vain desire was chidden—
  Hey, nonnie, nonnie !

Into a slumber then I fell,
  When fond imagination
Seeméd to see but could not tell
  Her feature or her fashion.
But, even as babes in dreams do smile
  And sometimes fall a weeping,
So I awaked, as wise this while,
  As when I fell a sleeping—
  Hey, nonnie, nonnie !

                 Anthony Munday.

81

ONLY JOY

ONLY Joy, now here you are
Fit to hear and ease my care,
Let my whispering voice obtain
Sweet reward for sharpest pain;
Take me to thee, and thee to me—
' No, no, no, no, my Dear, let be !'

Night hath closed all in her cloak,
Twinkling stars love-thoughts provoke,
Danger hence, good care doth keep,
Jealousy himself doth sleep;
Take me to thee, and thee to me—
' No, no, no, no, my Dear, let be !'

Better place no wit can find
Cupid's knot to loose or bind;
These sweet flowers our fine bed too,
Us in their best language woo;
Take me to thee, and thee to me—
' No, no, no, no, my Dear, let be !'

This small light the moon bestows
Serves thy beams but to disclose;
So to raise my hap more high,
Fear not else, none can us spy;
Take me to thee, and thee to me—
' No, no, no, no, my Dear, let be !'

That you heard was but a mouse,
Dumb Sleep holdeth all the house:
Yet asleep, methinks they say,
' Young fools take time while you may !'
Take me to thee, and thee to me—
' No, no, no, no, my Dear, let be !'

Niggard Time threats, if we miss
This large offer of our bliss,
Long stay, ere he grant the same.
Sweet, then, while each thing doth frame,
Take me to thee, and thee to me—
' No, no, no, no, my Dear, let be !'

Your fair mother is a-bed,
Candles out and curtains spread ;
She thinks you do letters write ;
Write, but first let me indite :
Take me to thee, and thee to me—
'No, no, no, no, my Dear, let be !'

Sweet, alas, why strive you thus ?
Concord better fitteth us.
Leave to Mars the force of hands,
Your power in your beauty stands.
Take thee to me, and me to thee—
'No, no, no, no, my Dear, let be !'

Woe to me ! and do you swear
Me to hate ? but I forbear !
Cursed be my destinies all,
That brought me so high to fall !
Soon with my death I will please thee—
'No, no, no, no, my Dear, let be !'

Philip Sidney.

82

THOSE LOOKS WHOSE BEAMS BE JOY

THOSE looks, whose beams be joy, whose motion is delight ;
That face, whose lecture shows what perfect beauty is ;
That presence, which doth give dark hearts a living light ;
That grace, which Venus weeps that she herself doth miss ;
That hand, which without touch holds more than Atlas might ;
Those lips, which make death's pay a mean price for a kiss ;
That skin, whose past-praise hue scorns this poor term of white ;
Those words, which do sublime the quintessence of bliss ;
That voice, which makes the soul plant himself in the ears ;
That conversation sweet, where such high comforts be,
As, constered in true speech, the name of heaven it bears—
Makes me in my best thoughts and quietest judgments see
That in no more but these I might be fully blest :
Yet, ah ! my maiden Muse doth blush to tell the best !

Philip Sidney.

83

WITH HOW SAD STEPS

WITH how sad steps, O Moon, thou clim'st the skies !
How silently, and with how wan a face !
What, may it be that even in heav'nly place
That busy archer his sharp arrows tries ?
Sure, if that long-with-love-acquainted eyes
Can judge of love, thou feel'st a lover's case :
I read it in thy looks ; thy languished grace
To me, that feel the like, thy state descries.
Then, ev'n of fellowship, O Moon, tell me,
Is constant love deem'd there but want of wit ?
Are beauties there as proud as here they be ?
Do they above love to be lov'd, and yet
Those lovers scorn whom that love doth possess ?
Do they call virtue there ungratefulness ?

Philip Sidney.

84

I MIGHT

I MIGHT !—unhappy word—O me, I might,
And then would not, or could not, see my bliss,
Till now wrapt in a most infernal night,
I find how heav'nly day, wretch ! I did miss !
Heart, rend thyself—thou dost thyself but right !
No lovely Paris made thy Helen his ;
No force, no fraud robbed thee of thy delight ;
Nor Fortune of thy fortune author is ;
But to myself myself did give the blow,
While too much wit, forsooth, so troubled me,
That I respects for both our sakes must show :
And yet could not, by rising morn, foresee
How fair a day was near. O punished eyes,
That I had been more foolish, or more wise !

Philip Sidney.

85

SONG

WHO hath his fancy pleaséd
With fruits of happy sight,
Let here his eyes be raiséd
On Nature's sweetest light :

A light which doth dissever,
And yet unite the eyes ;
    A light which, dying never,
Is cause the looker dies.

    She never dies, but lasteth
In life of lover's heart ;
    He ever dies that wasteth
In love his chiefest part :
    Thus is her life still guarded
In never-dying faith ;
    Thus is his death rewarded,
Since she lives in his death.

    Look, then, and die.   The pleasure
Doth answer well the pain ;
    Small loss of mortal treasure,
Who may immortal gain !
    Immortal be her graces,
Immortal is her mind :
    They fit for heavenly places,
This heaven in it doth bind.

    But eyes these beauties see not,
Nor sense that grace descries ;
    Yet eyes deprivéd be not
From sight of her fair eyes,
    Which, as of inward glory
They are the outward seal,
    So may they live still sorry,
Which die not in that weal.

    But who hath fancies pleaséd
With fruits of happy sight,
    Let here his eyes be raiséd
On Nature's sweetest light !

                    Philip Sidney.

86

MY TRUE LOVE HATH MY HEART

My true love hath my heart, and I have his,
    By just exchange one for another given :
I hold his dear, and mine he cannot miss,
    There never was a better bargain driven :
        My true love hath my heart, and I have his.

His heart in me keeps him and me in one,
  My heart in him his thoughts and senses guides :
He loves my heart, for once it was his own,
  I cherish his because in me it bides :
      My true love hath my heart, and I have his.

Philip Sidney.

87

SONG

THE Nightingale, as soon as April bringeth
Unto her rested sense a perfect waking,
While late-bare Earth, proud of new clothing, springeth,
Sings out her woes, a thorn her song-book making ;
And, mournfully bewailing,
Her throat in tunes expresseth
What grief her breast oppresseth
For Tereus' force on her chaste will prevailing.
O Philomela fair ! O take some gladness
That here is juster cause of plaintful sadness !
Thine earth now springs, mine fadeth ;
Thy thorn without, my thorn my heart invadeth.

Alas ! she hath no other cause of anguish
But Tereus' love, on her by strong hand wroken ;
Wherein she suffering, all her spirits languish,
Full womanlike complains her will was broken.
But I, who, daily craving,
Cannot have to content me,
Have more cause to lament me,
Since wanting is more woe than too much having.
O Philomela fair ! O take some gladness
That here is juster cause of plaintful sadness !
Thine earth now springs, mine fadeth ;
Thy thorn without, my thorn my heart invadeth.

Philip Sidney.

88

SPLENDIDIS LONGUM VALEDICO NUGIS

LEAVE me, O Love, which reachest but to dust,
And thou, my mind, aspire to higher things !
Grow rich in that which never taketh rust :
Whatever fades, but fading pleasure brings.

Draw in thy beams, and humble all thy might
To that sweet yoke where lasting freedoms be ;
Which breaks the clouds, and opens forth the light,
That doth both shine, and give us sight to see.
O, take fast hold ! let that light be thy guide
In this small course which birth draws out to death,
And think how evil becometh him to slide,
Who seeketh heaven, and comes of heavenly breath.
Then farewell, world ; thy uttermost I see :
Eternal Love, maintain thy life in me.

Philip Sidney.

89

WHAT BIRD SO SINGS

WHAT bird so sings, yet so does wail ?
O, 'tis the ravished nightingale !
'Jug, jug, jug, jug, tereu,' she cries,
And still her woes at midnight rise.
Brave prick-song ! who is't now we hear ?
None but the lark so shrill and clear ;
Now at heaven's gates she claps her wings,
The morn not waking till she sings,
Hark, hark, with what a pretty throat,
Poor robin redbreast tunes his note ;
Hark how the jolly cuckoos sing
Cuckoo to welcome in the spring !
Cuckoo to welcome in the spring !

John Lyly.

90

ROSALIND'S SONG

LOVE in my bosom like a bee
  Doth suck his sweet :
Now with his wings he plays with me,
  Now with his feet.
Within mine eyes he makes his nest,
His bed amidst my tender breast ;
My kisses are his daily feast ;
And yet he robs me of my rest.
  Ah wanton, will ye ?

And if I sleep, then percheth he
  With pretty flight,
And makes his pillow of my knee
  The livelong night.
Strike I my lute, he tunes the string ;
He music plays, if so I sing ;
He lends me every lovely thing :
Yet cruel he my heart doth sting.
  Whist, wanton, still ye !

Else I with roses every day
  Will whip you hence,
And bind you, when you long to play,
  For your offence.
I 'll shut mine eyes to keep you in,
I 'll make you fast it for your sin,
I 'll count your power not worth a pin . . .
Alas, what hereby shall I win,
  If he gainsay me?

What if I beat the wanton boy
  With many a rod ?
He will repay me with annoy,
  Because a god.
Then sit thou safely on my knee,
Then let thy bower my bosom be ;
Lurk in mine eyes, I like of thee !
O Cupid, so thou pity me,
  Spare not, but play thee !

Thomas Lodge.

91

A LOVER'S VOW

FIRST shall the heavens want starry light,
The seas be robbéd of their waves,
The day want sun, the sun want bright,
The night want shade, the dead men graves,
    The April flowers and leaf and tree,
    Before I false my faith to thee !

First shall the tops of highest hills
By humble plains be overpried,

And poets scorn the Muses' quills,
And fish forsake the water-glide,
    And Iris lose her coloured weed,
    Before I fail thee at thy need !

First direful Hate shall turn to peace,
And Love relent in deep disdain,
And Death his fatal stroke shall cease,
And Envy pity every pain,
    And Pleasure mourn, and Sorrow smile,
    Before I talk of any guile !

First Time shall stay his stayless race,
And Winter bless his boughs with corn,
And snow bemoisten July's face,
And Winter Spring and Summer mourn,
    Before my pen by help of fame
    Cease to recite thy sacred name !

Thomas Lodge.

92

A PRAISE OF ROSALIND

Of all chaste birds the Phœnix doth excel,
Of all strong beasts the lion bears the bell,
Of all sweet flowers the rose doth sweetest smell,
Of all fair maids my Rosalind is fairest.

Of all pure metals gold is sole purest,
Of all high trees the pine hath highest crest,
Of all soft sweets I like my mistress' breast,
Of all chaste thoughts my mistress' thoughts are rarest.

Of all proud birds the eagle pleaseth Jove,
Of pretty fowls kind Venus likes the dove,
Of trees Minerva doth the olive love,
Of all sweet nymphs I honour Rosalind.

Of all her gifts her wisdom pleaseth most,
Of all her graces virtue she doth boast :
For all these gifts my life and joy is lost,
If Rosalind prove cruel and unkind.

Thomas Lodge.

93

AN OLD SOLDIER

His golden locks Time hath to silver turned—
O Time too swift, O swiftness never ceasing!
His youth 'gainst time and age hath ever spurned,
But spurned in vain; youth waneth by increasing!
Beauty, strength, youth, are flowers but fading seen;
Duty, faith, love, are roots, and ever green.

His helmet now shall make an hive for bees,
And, lovers' sonnets turned to holy psalms,
A man-at-arms must now serve on his knees,
And feed on prayers, which are Old Age his alms:
But, though from court to cottage he depart,
His saint is sure of his unspotted heart.

And when he saddest sits in homely cell,
He'll teach his swains this carol for a song:—
'Blessed be the hearts that wish my sovereign well,
Curséd be souls that think her any wrong!'
Goddess, allow this aged man his right,
To be your bedesman now that was your knight!

George Peele.

94

SAMELA

Like to Diana in her summer-weed,
Girt with a crimson robe of brightest dye
                    Goes fair Samela

Whiter than be the flocks that straggling feed,
When washed by Arethusa's Fount they lie,
                    Is fair Samela.

As fair Aurora in her morning-grey,
Decked with the ruddy glister of her love,
                    Is fair Samela.

Like lovely Thetis on a calméd day,
Whenas her brightness Neptune's fancy move,
                    Shines fair Samela.

H

Her tresses gold, her eyes like glassy streams,
Her teeth are pearl, the breasts are ivory
                    Of fair Samela !

Her cheeks, like rose and lily, yield forth gleams,
Her brows bright arches framed of ebony,
                    Thus fair Samela

Passeth fair Venus in her bravest hue,
And Juno in the show of majesty
                    (For she's Samela !),

Pallas in wit !   All three, if you well view,
For beauty, wit, and matchless dignity
                    Yield to Samela.

                                    Robert Greene.

95

WEEP NOT, MY WANTON

WEEP not, my wanton, smile upon my knee ;
When thou art old there's grief enough for thee !
    Mother's wag, pretty boy,
    Father's sorrow, father's joy,
    When thy father first did see
    Such a boy by him and me,
    He was glad, I was woe :
    Fortune changéd made him so,
    When he left his pretty boy,
    Last his sorrow, first his joy.

Weep not, my wanton, smile upon my knee ;
When thou art old there's grief enough for thee !
    Streaming tears that never stint,
    Like pearl-drops from a flint,
    Fell by course from his eyes,
    That one another's place supplies.
    Thus he grieved in every part :
    Tears of blood fell from his heart,
    When he left his pretty boy,
    Father's sorrow, father's joy.

Weep not, my wanton, smile upon my knee ;
When thou art old there's grief enough for thee !
    The wanton smiled, father wept,
    Mother cried, baby leapt ;

More he crowed, more we cried,
Nature could not sorrow hide :
He must go, he must kiss
Child and mother, baby bliss,
For he left his pretty boy,
Father's sorrow, father's joy.
Weep not, my wanton, smile upon my knee ;
When thou art old there 's grief enough for thee !

Robert Greene.

96

LOVE IN ARCADY

Ah, what is love?   It is a pretty thing,
As sweet unto a shepherd as a king,
     And sweeter too ;
For kings have cares that wait upon a crown,
And cares can make the sweetest love to frown :
     Ah then ! ah then !
If country loves such sweet desires do gain,
What lady would not love a shepherd swain?

His flocks are folded, he comes home at night,
As merry as a king in his delight,
     And merrier too ;
For kings bethink them what the state require,
Where shepherds careless carol by the fire :
     Ah then ! ah then !
If country loves such sweet desires do gain,
What lady would not love a shepherd swain?

He kisseth first, then sits as blithe to eat
His cream and curds as doth the king his meat,
     And blither too ;
For kings have often fears when they do sup,
Where shepherds dread no poison in their cup :
     Ah then ! ah then !
If country loves such sweet desires do gain,
What lady would not love a shepherd swain?

To bed he goes, as wanton then, I ween,
As is a king in dalliance with a queen,
     More wanton too ;
For kings have many grief's effects to move,

Where shepherds have no greater grief than love :
  Ah then ! ah then!
If country loves such sweet desires do gain,
What lady would not love a shepherd swain ?

Upon his couch of straw he sleeps as sound,
As doth the king upon his beds of down,
  More sounder too ;
For cares cause kings full oft their sleep to spill,
Where weary shepherds lie and snort their fill :
  Ah then ! ah then !
If country loves such sweet desires do gain,
What lady would not love a shepherd swain ?

Thus with his wife he spends the year, as blithe
As doth the king at every tide or sithe,
  And blither too ;
For kings have wars and broils to take in hand,
Where shepherds laugh and love upon the land :
  Ah then! ah then !
If country loves such sweet desires do gain,
What lady would not love a shepherd swain ?

          Robert Greene.

97

THE BURNING BABE

As I in hoary winter's night
 Stood shivering in the snow,
Surprised I was with sudden heat,
 Which made my heart to glow ;
And lifting up a fearful eye
 To view what fire was near,
A pretty Babe all burning bright,
 Did in the air appear :
Who, scorchéd with excessive heat,
 Such floods of tears did shed,
As though his floods should quench his flames,
 Which with his tears were bred.
' Alas !' quoth he, ' but newly born,
 In fiery heats I fry,
Yet none approach to warm their hearts
 Or feel my fire, but I.

My faultless breast the furnace is,
    The fuel wounding thorns;
Love is the fire, and sighs the smoke,
    The ashes shames and scorns;
The fuel Justice layeth on,
    And Mercy blows the coals;
The metal in this furnace wrought
    Are men's defiléd souls:
For which, as now on fire I am
    To work them to their good,
So will I melt into a bath,
    To wash them in my blood!'
With this he vanished out of sight,
    And swiftly shrunk away,
And straight I called unto my mind
    That it was Christmas Day.

Robert Southwell.

98

A SUPPLICATION

Look, Delia, how we esteem the half-blown rose,
The image of thy blush, and summer's honour,
Whilst yet her tender bud doth undisclose
That full of beauty Time bestows upon her!
No sooner spreads her glory in the air,
But straight her wide-blown pomp comes to decline.
She then is scorn'd, that late adorn'd the fair:
So fade the roses of those cheeks of thine!
No April can revive thy wither'd flow'rs,
Whose springing grace adorns the glory now:
Swift speedy Time, feather'd with flying hours,
Dissolves the beauty of the fairest brow!
Then do not thou such treasure waste in vain,
But love now, whilst thou may'st be lov'd again.

But love whilst that thou may'st be lov'd again,
Now whilst thy May hath fill'd thy lap with flowers!
Now, whilst thy beauty bears without a stain,
Now use the summer smiles, ere winter lowers!
And whilst thou spread'st unto the rising sun
The fairest flower that ever saw the light,
Now joy thy time before thy sweet be done,
And, Delia, think thy morning must have night,

And that thy brightness sets at length to west,
When thou wilt close up that which now thou show'st,
And think the same becomes thy fading best,
Which then shall most inveil, and shadow most !
Men do not weigh the stalk for that it was,
When once they find her flow'r, her glory, pass.

When men shall find thy flow'r, thy glory, pass,
And thou, with careful brow, sitting alone,
Receivéd hast this message from thy glass,
That tells the truth, and says that all is gone ;
Fresh shalt thou see in me the wounds thou mad'st,
Though spent thy flame, in me the heat remaining :
I that have lov'd thee thus before thou fad'st,
My faith shall wax, when thou art in thy waning.
The world shall find this miracle in me,
That fire can burn when all the matter 's spent !
Then what my faith hath been thyself shall see,
And that thou wast unkind thou may'st repent—
Thou may'st repent that thou hast scorn'd my tears,
When winter snows upon thy sable hairs !

Samuel Daniel.

99

LOVE

LOVE is a sickness full of woes,
    All remedies refusing ;
A plant that with most cutting grows,
    Most barren with best using.
                Why so ?
More we enjoy it, more it dies ;
If not enjoyed, it sighing cries
            Heigh ho !

Love is a torment of the mind,
    A tempest everlasting ;
And Jove hath made it of a kind
    Not well, nor full, nor fasting.
                Why so ?
More we enjoy it, more it dies ;
If not enjoyed, it sighing cries
            Heigh ho !

Samuel Daniel.

100

A REMONSTRANCE

WHY should your fair eyes with such sov'reign grace
Disperse their rays on ev'ry vulgar spirit,
Whilst I in darkness, in the self-same place,
Get not one glance to recompense my merit?
So doth the ploughman gaze the wand'ring star,
And only rest contented with the light
That never learn'd what constellations are,
Beyond the bent of his unknowing sight.
O, why should beauty (custom to obey)
To their gross sense apply herself so ill?
Would God I were as ignorant as they,
When I am made unhappy by my skill,
Only compell'd on this poor good to boast,
Heav'ns are not kind to them that know them most!

Michael Drayton.

101

TO HIS COY LOVE

I PRAY thee leave, love me no more,
    Call home the heart you gave me!
I but in vain that saint adore,
    That can but will not save me.
These poor half-kisses kill me quite—
    Was ever man thus servéd?
Amidst an ocean of delight
    For pleasure to be stervéd?

Show me no more those snowy breasts,
    With azure rivers branchéd,
Where, whilst mine eye with plenty feasts,
    Yet is my thirst not stanchéd.
O Tantalus, thy pains ne'er tell!
    By me thou art prevented:
'Tis nothing to be plagued in Hell,
    But thus in Heaven tormented.

Clip me no more in those dear arms,
    Nor thy life's comfort call me.
O, these are but too powerful charms,
    And do but more enthral me!

But see how patient I am grown,
In all this coil about thee :
Come, nice thing, let thy heart alone,
I cannot live without thee !

Michael Drayton.

102

VALEDICTION

Since there 's no help, come let us kiss and part !
Nay, I have done, you get no more of me,
And I am glad, yea glad with all my heart,
That thus so cleanly I myself can free !
Shake hands for ever, cancel all our vows,
And, when we meet at any time again,
Be it not seen in either of our brows
That we one jot of former love retain.
Now at the last gasp of Love's latest breath,
When, his pulse failing, Passion speechless lies,
When Faith is kneeling by his bed of death,
And Innocence is closing up his eyes,
Now if thou wouldst, when all have given him over,
From death to life thou might'st him yet recover !

Michael Drayton.

103

THE SHEPHERD PLEADS

Come live with me and be my love,
And we will all the pleasures prove
That hills and valleys, dale and field,
And all the craggy mountains yield !

There will we sit upon the rocks
And see the shepherds feed their flocks,
By shallow rivers, to whose falls
Melodious birds sing madrigals.

There will I make thee beds of roses
And a thousand fragrant posies ;
A cap of flowers, and a kirtle
Embroider'd all with leaves of myrtle ;

A gown made of the finest wool,
Which from our pretty lambs we pull ;
Fair-linéd slippers for the cold,
With buckles of the purest gold ;

A belt of straw and ivy buds
With coral clasps and amber studs :
And if these pleasures may thee move, ·
Come live with me and be my love !

Thy silver dishes, for thy meat
As precious as the gods do eat,
Shall on an ivory table be
Prepared each day for thee and me.

The shepherd swains shall dance and sing
For thy delight each May-morning.
If these delights thy mind may move,
Then live with me and be my love !

Christopher Marlowe.

104

THE SHEPHERDESS REPLIES

IF all the world and love were young,
And truth in every shepherd's tongue,
These pretty pleasures might me move
To live with thee and be thy love.

But time drives flocks from field to fold,
When rivers rage and rocks grow cold ;
And Philomel becometh dumb ;
The rest complains of cares to come.

The flowers do fade, and wanton fields
To wayward winter reckoning yields ;
A honey tongue, a heart of gall,
Is fancy's spring, but sorrow's fall.

Thy gowns, thy shoes, thy beds of roses,
Thy cap, thy kirtle, and thy posies,
Soon break, soon wither, soon forgotten—
In folly ripe, in reason rotten !

Thy belt of straw and ivy buds,
Thy coral clasps and amber studs—
All those in me no means can move
To come to thee and be thy love.

But could youth last, and love still breed ;
Had joys no date, nor age no need ;
Then those delights my mind might move
To live with thee and be thy love.

Walter Raleigh.

105

ON A DAY

ON a day, alack the day !
Love, whose month is ever May,
Spied a blossom passing fair
Playing in the wanton air :
Through the velvet leaves the wind
All unseen 'gan passage find,
That the lover, sick to death,
Wish'd himself the heaven's breath.
' Air,' quoth he, ' thy cheeks may blow ;
Air, would I might triumph so !
But, alack, my hand is sworn
Ne'er to pluck thee from thy thorn :
Vow, alack, for youth unmeet—
Youth so apt to pluck a sweet !
Do not call it sin in me
That I am forsworn for thee :
Thou for whom e'en Jove would swear
Juno but an Ethiope were,
And deny himself for Jove,
Turning mortal for thy love.'

William Shakespeare.

106

WHO IS SILVIA

WHO is Silvia? what is she,
    That all our swains commend her?—
Holy, fair, and wise is she ;
    The heaven such grace did lend her,
That she might admired be.

Is she kind as she is fair,
  For beauty lives with kindness?—
Love doth to her eyes repair,
  To help him of his blindness;
And, being helped, inhabits there.

Then to Silvia let us sing,
  That Silvia is excelling;
She excels each mortal thing,
  Upon the dull earth dwelling:
To her let us garlands bring.

                    William Shakespeare.

107

'HIEMS, WINTER . . . VER, THE SPRING'

I

WHEN daisies pied, and violets blue,
  And lady-smocks all silver-white,
And cuckoo-buds of yellow hue
  Do paint the meadows with delight,
The cuckoo then on every tree
Mocks married men, for thus sings he :—
          Cuckoo!
Cuckoo, cuckoo—O word of fear,
Unpleasing to a married ear!

When shepherds pipe on oaten straws,
  And merry larks are ploughmen's clocks,
When turtles tread, and rooks, and daws,
  And maidens bleach their summer smocks,
The cuckoo then on every tree
Mocks married men, for thus sings he :—
          Cuckoo!
Cuckoo, cuckoo—O word of fear,
Unpleasing to a married ear!

II

When icicles hang by the wall,
  And Dick the shepherd blows his nail,
And Tom bears logs into the hall,
  And milk comes frozen home in pail,
When blood is nipped, and ways be foul,
Then nightly sings the staring owl :—

To-whit !
To-who !—a merry note,
While greasy Joan doth keel the pot.

When all around the wind doth blow,
  And coughing drowns the parson's saw,
And birds sit brooding in the snow,
  And Marian's nose looks red and raw,
When roasted crabs hiss in the bowl,
Then nightly sings the staring owl :—
          To-whit !
      To-who !—a merry note,
While greasy Joan doth keel the pot.

William Shakespeare.

108

UNDER THE GREENWOOD TREE

UNDER the greenwood tree,
Who loves to lie with me,
And turn his merry note
Unto the sweet bird's throat,
Come hither, come hither, come hither !
    Here shall he see
    No enemy
But winter and rough weather.

Who doth ambition shun,
And loves to live i' the sun,
Seeking the food he eats,
And pleased with what he gets,
Come hither, come hither, come hither !
    Here shall he see
    No enemy
But winter and rough weather.

William Shakespeare.

109

BLOW, BLOW THOU WINTER WIND

BLOW, blow, thou winter wind,
Thou art not so unkind
    As man's ingratitude ;

Thy tooth is not so keen,
Because thou art not seen,
    Although thy breath be rude.
Heigh ho ! sing, heigh ho ! unto the green holly ;
Most friendship is feigning, most loving mere folly ;
    Then, heigh ho, the holly !
    This life is most jolly.

Freeze, freeze, thou bitter sky,
That dost not bite so nigh
    As benefits forgot ;
Though thou the waters warp,
Thy sting is not so sharp
    As friend remembered not.
Heigh ho ! sing heigh ho !

William Shakespeare.

110

TAKE, O, TAKE THOSE LIPS AWAY

TAKE, O, take those lips away,
    That so sweetly were forsworn,
And those eyes, the break of day,
    Lights that do mislead the morn !
But my kisses bring again,
Seals of love but sealed in vain.

William Shakespeare.

111

HARK, HARK, THE LARK

HARK ! hark ! the lark at heaven's gate sings,
    And Phœbus 'gins arise,
His steeds to water at those springs
    On chaliced flowers that lies ;
And winking Mary-buds begin
    To ope their golden eyes ;
With everything that pretty bin,
    My lady sweet, arise !

William Shakespeare.

112

FEAR NO MORE

FEAR no more the heat o' the sun
Nor the furious winter's rages !
Thou thy worldly task hast done,
Home art gone, and ta'en thy wages :
Golden lads and girls all must,
As chimney-sweepers, come to dust.

Fear no more the frown o' the great,
Thou art past the tyrant's stroke !
Care no more to clothe, and eat ;
To thee the reed is as the oak :
The sceptre, learning, physic, must
All follow this, and come to dust.

Fear no more the lightning flash,
Nor the all-dreaded thunder-stone !
Fear not slander, censure rash ;
Thou hast finished joy and moan :
All lovers young, all lovers must
Consign to thee, and come to dust.

William Shakespeare.

113

A DIRGE

FULL fathom five thy father lies ;
  Of his bones are coral made ;
Those are pearls that were his eyes ;
  Nothing of him that doth fade
But doth suffer a sea-change
Into something rich and strange.
Sea-nymphs hourly ring his knell ;
Hark ! now I hear them,—ding-dong, bell !

William Shakespeare.

114

WHERE THE BEE SUCKS

WHERE the bee sucks, there suck I ;
In a cowslip's bell I lie ;
There I couch when owls do cry ;
On the bat's back I do fly
After summer merrily ;
Merrily, merrily, shall I live now
Under the blossom that hangs on the bough.

William Shakespeare.

115

WHEN, IN DISGRACE

WHEN, in disgrace with fortune and men's eyes,
I all alone beweep my outcast state,
And trouble deaf heaven with my bootless cries,
And look upon myself, and curse my fate :
Wishing me like to one more rich in hope,
Featured like him, like him with friends possess'd,
Desiring this man's art and that man's scope,
With what I most enjoy contented least :
Yet in these thoughts myself almost despising,
Haply I think on thee, and then my state,
Like to the lark at break of day arising
From sullen earth, sings hymns at heaven's gate :
For thy sweet love rememb'red such wealth brings
That then I scorn to change my state with kings.

William Shakespeare.

116

WHEN TO THE SESSIONS

WHEN to the sessions of sweet silent thought
I summon up remembrance of things past,
I sigh the lack of many a thing I sought,
And with old woes new wail my dear time's waste :
Then can I drown an eye, unused to flow,
For precious friends hid in death's dateless night,

And weep afresh love's long since cancell'd woe,
And moan the expense of many a vanish'd sight ;
Then can I grieve at grievances foregone,
And heavily from woe to woe tell o'er
The sad account of fore-bemoaned moan,
Which I new pay as if not paid before :
But if the while I think on thee, dear friend,
All losses are restored and sorrows end.

William Shakespeare.

117

WHAT IS YOUR SUBSTANCE?

WHAT is your substance? whereof are you made,
That millions of strange shadows on you tend?
Since every one hath, every one, one shade,
And you, but one, can every shadow lend !
Describe Adonis, and the counterfeit
Is poorly imitated after you ;
On Helen's cheek all art of beauty set,
And you in Grecian tires are painted new ;
Speak of the spring and foison of the year,
The one doth shadow of your beauty show,
The other as your bounty doth appear ;
And you in every blessèd shape we know.
In all external grace you have some part,
But you like none, none you, for constant heart.

William Shakespeare.

118

NO LONGER MOURN

No longer mourn for me when I am dead
Than you shall hear the surly sullen bell
Give warning to the world that I am fled
From this vile world, with vilest worms to dwell.
Nay, if you read this line, remember not
The hand that writ it ; for I love you so,
That I in your sweet thoughts would be forgot,
If thinking on me then should make you woe.
O, if, I say, you look upon this verse
When I perhaps compounded am with clay,

Do not so much as my poor name rehearse,
But let your love even with my life decay !
Lest the wise world should look into your moan,
And mock you with me after I am gone.
                              William Shakespeare.

119

THAT TIME OF YEAR

THAT time of year thou may'st in me behold
When yellow leaves, or none, or few, do hang
Upon those boughs which shake against the cold,
Bare ruin'd choirs, where late the sweet birds sang.
In me thou see'st the twilight of such day
As after sunset fadeth in the west ;
Which by and by black night doth take away,
Death's second self, that seals up all in rest.
In me thou see'st the glowing of such fire,
That on the ashes of his youth doth lie,
As the death-bed whereon it must expire,
Consumed with that which it was nourish'd by.
This thou perceiv'st, which makes thy love more strong
To love that well which thou must leave ere long.
                              William Shakespeare.

120

THEN HATE ME

THEN hate me when thou wilt ; if ever, now !
Now, while the world is bent my deeds to cross,
Join with the spite of fortune, make me bow,
And do not drop in for an after-loss :
Ah, do not, when my heart hath 'scaped this sorrow,
Come in the rearward of a conquer'd woe ;
Give not a windy night a rainy morrow,
To linger out a purposed overthrow.
If thou wilt leave me, do not leave me last,
When other petty griefs have done their spite,
But in the onset come : so shall I taste
At first the very worst of fortune's might ;
And other strains of woe, which now seem woe,
Compared with loss of thee will not seem so.
                              William Shakespeare.

I

121

HOW LIKE A WINTER

How like a winter hath my absence been
From thee, the pleasure of the fleeting year !
What freezings have I felt, what dark days seen'!
What old December's bareness every where !
And yet this time removed was summer's time ;
The teeming autumn, big with rich increase,
Bearing the wanton burthen of the prime,
Like widow'd wombs after their lords' decease :
Yet this abundant issue seem'd to me
But hope of orphans and unfather'd fruit ;
For summer and his pleasures wait on thee,
And, thou away, the very birds are mute :
Or, if they sing, 'tis with so dull a cheer
That leaves look pale, dreading the winter's near.

William Shakespeare.

122

MY LOVE IS STRENGTHEN'D

My love is strengthen'd, though more weak in seeming ;
I love not less, though less the show appear :
That love is merchandised whose rich esteeming
The owner's tongue doth publish every where.
Our love was new, and then but in the spring,
When I was wont to greet it with my lays ;
As Philomel in summer's front doth sing,
And stops her pipe in growth of riper days.
Not that the summer is less pleasant now
Than when her mournful hymns did hush the night,
But that wild music burthens every bough,
And sweets grown common lose their dear delight.
Therefore, like her, I sometime hold my tongue,
Because I would not dull you with my song.

William Shakespeare.

123

TO ME, FAIR FRIEND

To me, fair friend, you never can be old,
For as you were when first your eye I eyed,
Such seems your beauty still.   Three winters cold

Have from the forests shook three summers' pride,
Three beauteous springs to yellow autumn turn'd
In process of the seasons have I seen,
Three April perfumes in three hot Junes burn'd,
Since first I saw you fresh, which yet are green.
Ah, yet doth beauty, like a dial-hand,
Steal from his figure, and no pace perceived ;
So your sweet hue, which methinks still doth stand,
Hath motion, and mine eye may be deceived :
For fear of which, hear this, thou age unbred :
Ere you were born was beauty's summer dead.

William Shakespeare.

124

WHEN IN THE CHRONICLE

WHEN in the chronicle of wasted time
I see descriptions of the fairest wights,
And beauty making beautiful old rhyme
In praise of ladies dead and lovely knights,
Then, in the blazon of sweet beauty's best,
Of hand, of foot, of lip, of eye, of brow,
I see their antique pen would have express'd
Even such a beauty as you master now.
So all their praises are but prophecies
Of this our time, all you prefiguring ;
And, for they look'd but with divining eyes,
They had not skill enough your worth to sing :
For we, which now behold these present days,
Have eyes to wonder, but lack tongues to praise.

William Shakespeare.

125

O, NEVER SAY

O, NEVER say that I was false of heart,
Though absence seem'd my flame to qualify !
As easy might I from myself depart
As from my soul, which in thy breast doth lie.
That is my home of love : if I have ranged,
Like him that travels, I return again ;

Just to the time, not with the time exchanged,
So that myself bring water for my stain.
Never believe, though in my nature reign'd
All frailties that besiege all kinds of blood,
That it could so preposterously be stain'd,
To leave for nothing all thy sum of good ;
For nothing this wide universe I call,
Save thou, my rose ; in it thou art my all.

William Shakespeare.

126

THE MARRIAGE OF TRUE MINDS

LET me not to the marriage of true minds
Admit impediments.   Love is not love
Which alters when it alteration finds,
Or bends with the remover to remove :
O, no ! it is an ever-fixéd mark,
That looks on tempests and is never shaken ;
It is the star to every wandering bark,
Whose worth 's unknown, although his height be taken.
Love's not Time's fool, though rosy lips and cheeks
Within his bending sickle's compass come ;
Love alters not with his brief hours and weeks,
But bears it out even to the edge of doom.
If this be error and upon me proved,
I never writ, nor no man ever loved.

William Shakespeare.

127

POOR SOUL

POOR soul, the centre of my sinful earth,
My sinful earth these rebel powers array,
Why dost thou pine within and suffer dearth,
Painting thy outward walls so costly gay ?
Why so large cost, having so short a lease,
Dost thou upon thy fading mansion spend ?
Shall worms, inheritors of this excess,
Eat up thy charge ?   Is this thy body's end ?
Then, soul, live thou upon thy servant's loss,
And let that pine to aggravate thy store ;

Buy terms divine in selling hours of dross;
Within be fed, without be rich no more:
So shalt thou feed on Death, that feeds on men,
And, Death once dead, there's no more dying then.
William Shakespeare.

128

LULLABY

UPON my lap my sovereign sits
And sucks upon my breast;
Meantime his love maintains my life
And gives my sense her rest.
    Sing lullaby, my little boy,
    Sing lullaby, mine only joy!

When thou hast taken thy repast,
Repose, my babe, on me;
So may thy mother and thy nurse
Thy cradle also be.
    Sing lullaby, my little boy,
    Sing lullaby, mine only joy!

I grieve that duty doth not work
All that my wishing would,
Because I would not be to thee
But in the best I should.
    Sing lullaby, my little boy,
    Sing lullaby, mine only joy!

Yet as I am, and as I may,
I must and will be thine,
Though all too little for thy self
Vouchsafing to be mine.
    Sing lullaby, my little boy,
    Sing lullaby, mine only joy!
Richard Rowlands.

129

FOLLOW YOUR SAINT

FOLLOW your saint, follow with accents sweet!
Haste you, sad notes, fall at her flying feet!
There, wrapped in cloud of sorrow, pity move,
And tell the ravisher of my soul I perish for her love:
But, if she scorns my never ceasing pain,
Then burst with sighing in her sight, and ne'er return again.

All that I sang still to her praise did tend,
Still she was first, still she my songs did end ;
Yet she my love and music doth both fly,
The music that her echo is and beauty's sympathy :
Then let my notes pursue her scornful flight !
It shall suffice that they were breathed and died for her delight.

Thomas Campion.

130

COME, O, COME

COME, O, come, my life's delight !
  Let me not in languor pine !
Love loves no delay ; thy sight
  The more enjoyed, the more divine !
O, come, and take from me
The pain of being deprived of thee !

Thou all sweetness dost enclose,
  Like a little world of bliss ;
Beauty guards thy looks, the rose
  In them pure and eternal is :
Come, then, and make thy flight
  As swift to me as heavenly light !

Thomas Campion.

131

LOVE ME OR NOT

LOVE me or not, love her I must or die,
Leave me or not, follow her needs must I.
O, that her grace would my wished comforts give !
How rich in her, how happy I should live !

All my desire, all my delight should be
Her to enjoy, her to unite to me ;
Envy should cease, her would I love alone :
Who loves by looks is seldom true to one.

Could I enchant, and that it lawful were,
Her would I charm softly that none should hear ;
But love enforced rarely yields firm content :
So would I love that neither should repent.

Thomas Campion.

132

THERE IS A GARDEN

THERE is a garden in her face
Where roses and white lilies grow ;
A heavenly paradise is that place
Wherein all pleasant fruits do flow.
     There cherries grow which none may buy,
     Till 'Cherry Ripe' themselves do cry.

Those cherries fairly do enclose
Of orient pearl a double row,
Which when her lovely laughter shows,
They look like rose-buds filled with snow ;
     Yet them nor peer nor prince can buy,
     Till 'Cherry Ripe' themselves do cry.

Her eyes like angels watch them still,
Her brows like bended bows do stand,
Threatening with piercing frowns to kill
All that attempt with eye or hand
     Those sacred cherries to come nigh,
     ·Till 'Cherry Ripe' themselves do cry.

Thomas Campion.

133

O SWEET DELIGHT

O SWEET delight, O more than human bliss,
With her to live that ever loving is !
To hear her speak whose words are so well placed
That she by them, as they in her are graced !
Those looks to view that feast the viewer's eye,
How blest is he that may so live and die !

Such love as this the Golden Times did know,
When all did reap, yet none took care to sow ;
Such love as this an endless summer makes,
And all distaste from frail affection takes.
So loved, so blest in my beloved am I :
Which till their eyes do ache, let iron men envý !

Thomas Campion.

134

WHEN THOU MUST HOME

WHEN thou must home to shades of underground,
And, there arrived, a new admiréd guest,
The beauteous spirits do engirt thee round,
White Iope, blithe Helen, and the rest,
To hear the stories of thy finished love
From that smooth tongue whose music hell can move;

Then wilt thou speak of banqueting delights,
Of masques and revels which sweet youth did make,
Of tourneys and great challenges of knights,
And all these triumphs for thy beauty's sake:
When thou hast told these honours done to thee,
Then tell, O, tell, how thou didst murder me.

Thomas Campion.

135

NEVER WEATHER-BEATEN SAIL

NEVER weather-beaten sail more willing bent to shore,
Never tiréd pilgrim's limbs affected slumber more,
Than my wearied sprite now longs to fly out of my troubled
    breast—
O, come quickly, sweetest Lord, and take my soul to rest!

Ever blooming are the joys of heaven's high Paradise,
Cold age deafs not there our ears, nor vapour dims our eyes:
Glory there the sun outshines; whose beams the Blessed only see—
O, come quickly, glorious Lord, and raise my sprite to Thee!

Thomas Campion.

136

SPRING, THE SWEET SPRING

SPRING, the sweet Spring, is the year's pleasant king!
Then blooms each thing, then maids dance in a ring,
Cold doth not sting, the pretty birds do sing :—
Cuckoo, jug, jug, pu we, to witta woo!

The palm and may make country houses gay,
Lambs frisk and play, the shepherds pipe all day,
And we hear ay birds tune this merry lay :—
Cuckoo, jug, jug, pu we, to witta woo !

The fields breathe sweet, the daisies kiss our feet,
Young lovers meet, old wives a·sunning sit,
In every street these tunes our ears do greet :—
Cuckoo, jug, jug, pu we, to witta woo !

Thomas Nashe.

137

IN TIME OF PESTILENCE

ADIEU !   Farewell earth's bliss !
This world uncertain is ;
Fond are life's lustful joys,
Death proves them all but toys.
None from his darts can fly ;
I am sick, I must die.
            Lord have mercy on us !

Rich men, trust not in wealth :
Gold cannot buy you health ;
Physic himself must fade ;
All things to end are made ;
The plague full swift goes by ;
I am sick, I must die.
            Lord have mercy on us !

Beauty is but a flower,
Which wrinkles will devour ;
Brightness falls from the air ;
Queens have died young and fair ;
Dust hath closed Helen's eye ;
I am sick, I must die.
            Lord have mercy on us !

Strength stoops unto the grave :
Worms feed on Hector brave ;
Swords may not fight with fate ;
Earth still holds ope her gate ;
' Come, come,' the bells do cry.
I am sick, I must die.
            Lord have mercy on us !

Wit with his wantonness,
Tasteth death's bitterness.
Hell's executioner
Hath no ears for to hear
What vain art can reply.
I am sick, I must die.
           Lord have mercy on us !

Haste, therefore, each degree,
To welcome destiny !
Heaven is our heritage,
Earth but a player's stage.
Mount we unto the sky !
I am sick, I must die.
           Lord have mercy on us !

Thomas Nashe.

138

TO HIS MISTRESS, THE QUEEN OF BOHEMIA

You meaner beauties of the night,
    That poorly satisfy our eyes
More by your number than your light,
    You common people of the skies,
    What are you when the moon shall rise?

You curious chanters of the wood,
    That warble forth Dame Nature's lays,
Thinking your passions understood
    By your weak accents, what's your praise
When Philomel her voice shall raise?

You violets that first appear,
    By your pure purple mantles known
Like the proud virgins of the year,
    As if the spring were all your own,
    What are you when the rose is blown?

So when my mistress shall be seen
    In form and beauty of her mind,
By virtue first, then choice, a Queen,
    Tell me if she were not designed
    The eclipse and glory of her kind?

Henry Wotton.

139

THE SHEPHERD TO THE FLOWERS

SWEET violets, Love's Paradise, that spread
Your gracious odours, which you couchéd bear
Within your paly faces,
Upon the gentle wing of some calm breathing wind
That plays amidst the plain !
If by the favour of propitious stars you gain
Such grace as in my lady's bosom place to find,
Be proud to touch those places ;
And when her warmth your moisture forth doth wear,
Whereby her dainty parts are sweetly fed,
Your honours of the flowery meads I pray,
You pretty daughters of the earth and sun,
With mild and seemly breathing straight display
My bitter sighs that have my heart undone.

Vermilion roses, that with new day's rise
Display your crimson folds fresh-looking fair,
Whose radiant bright disgraces
The rich adornéd rays of roseate rising morn,
Ah ! if her virgin's hand
Do pluck your pure, ere Phœbus view the land,
And vail your gracious pomp in lovely Nature's scorn,
If chance my mistress traces
Fast by your flowers to take the summer's air,
Then, woful blushing, tempt her glorious eyes
To spread their tears, Adonis' death reporting,
And tell love's torments, sorrowing for her friend,
Whose drops of blood, within your leaves consorting,
Report fair Venus' moans to have no end.
Then may Remorse in pitying of my smart,
Dry up my tears, and dwell within her heart.

Anonymous.

140

TO NIGHT

O NIGHT, O jealous Night, repugnant to my measures !
  O Night so long desired, yet cross to my content !
There 's none but only thou that can perform my pleasures,
  Yet none but only thou that hindereth my intent.

Thy beams, thy spiteful beams, thy lamps that burn too brightly,
   Discover all my trains, and naked lay my drifts,
That night by night I hope, yet fail my purpose nightly,
   Thy envious, glaring gleam defeateth so my shifts.

Sweet Night, withhold thy beams, withhold them till to-morrow,
   Whose joys in lack so long a hell of torment breeds !
Sweet Night, sweet gentle Night, do not prolong my sorrow :
   Desire is guide to me, and love no lodestar needs.

Let sailors gaze on stars and moon so freshly shining ;
   Let them that miss the way be guided by the light ;
I know my Lady's bower, there needs no more divining :
   Affection sees in dark, and Love hath eyes by night.

Dame Cynthia, couch awhile ! hold in thy horns for shining,
   And glad not low'ring Night with thy too glorious rays ;
But be she dim and dark, tempestuous and repining,
   That in her spite my sport may work thy endless praise !

And when my will is wrought, then, Cynthia, shine, good lady,
   All other nights and days in honour of that night,
That happy heavenly night, that night so dark and shady,
   Wherein my Love had eyes that lighted my delight !

Anonymous.

141

MADRIGAL

My Love in her attire doth show her wit,
   It doth so well become her :
For every season she hath dressings fit,
   For Winter, Spring, and Summer.
     No beauty she doth miss,
       When all her robes are on :
     For Beauty's self she is,
       When all her robes are gone.

Anonymous.

142

DISPRAISE OF LOVE

If love be life, I long to die,
   Live they that list for me :
And he that gains the most thereby
   A fool, at least, shall be.

But he that feels the sorest fits
'Scapes with no less than loss of wits :
    Unhappy life they gain,
    Which love do entertain.

In day by feigned looks they live,
    By lying dreams in night ;
Each frown a deadly wound doth give,
    Each smile a false delight.
If 't hap their lady pleasant seem,
It is for other's love they deem ;
    If void she seem of joy,
    Disdain doth make her coy.

Such is the peace that lovers find,
    Such is the life they lead,
Blown here and there with every wind,
    Like flowers in the mead.
Now war, now peace, then war again,
Desire, despair, delight, disdain :
    Though dead, in midst of life,
    In peace, and yet at strife !

Anonymous.

143

WEEP YOU NO MORE

WEEP you no more, sad fountains !
    What need you flow so fast ?
Look how the snowy mountains
    Heaven's sun doth gently waste !
But my sun's heavenly eyes
    View not your weeping,
    ·That now lies sleeping
Softly, now softly lies
            Sleeping.

Sleep is a reconciling,
    A rest that peace begets :
Doth not the sun rise smiling
    When fair at ev'n he sets ?
Rest you then, rest, sad eyes !
    Melt not in weeping,
    While she lies sleeping
Softly, now softly lies
            Sleeping.

Anonymous.

144

ARISE, MY THOUGHTS

ARISE, my Thoughts, and mount you with the sun,
Call all the winds to make you speedy wings,
And to my fairest Maya see you run,
And weep your last while wantonly she sings ;
Then if you cannot move her heart to pity,
Let *O, alas, ay me* be all your ditty.

Arise, my Thoughts, no more, if you return
Denied of grace which only you desire,
But let the sun your wings to ashes burn
And melt your passions in his quenchless fire ;
Yet if you move fair Maya's heart to pity,
Let smiles and love and kisses be your ditty.

Arise, my Thoughts, beyond the highest star
And gently rest you in fair Maya's eye,
For that is fairer than the brightest are ;
But, if she frown to see you climb so high,
Couch in her lap, and with a moving ditty,
Of smiles and love and kisses beg for pity.

Anonymous.

145

MADRIGAL

I SAW my Lady weep,
And Sorrow proud to be advanced so
In those fair eyes where all perfections keep.
Her face was full of woe,
But such a woe (believe me) as wins more hearts
Than Mirth can do with her enticing parts.

Sorrow was there made fair,
And Passion wise ; Tears a delightful thing ;
Silence beyond all speech ; a Wisdom rare
She made her sighs to sing,
And all things with so sweet a sadness move
As made my heart at once both grieve and love.

O fairer than aught else
The world can show, leave off in time to grieve !
Enough, enough !   Your joyful look excels ;
Tears kill the heart, believe !
O, strive not to be excellent in woe,
Which only breeds your beauty's overthrow !

Anonymous.

146

ANOTHER

THOU art but young, thou say'st,
    And love's delight thou weigh'st not ;
O, take time while thou may'st,
    Lest when thou would'st thou may'st not !

If love shall then assail thee,
    A double anguish will torment thee ;
And thou wilt wish (but wishes all will fail thee),
    ' O me ! that I were young again ! ' and so repent
        thee.

Anonymous.

147

MY LOVE

MY Love is neither young nor old,
Not fiery-hot nor frozen-cold,
But fresh and fair as springing-briar
Blooming the fruit of love's desire ;
Not snowy-white nor rosy-red,
But fair enough for shepherd's bed ;
And such a love was never seen
On hill or dale or country-green.

Anonymous.

148

DEAR, IF YOU CHANGE

DEAR, if you change, I 'll never choose again ;
Sweet, if you shrink, I 'll never think of love ;
Fair, if you fail, I 'll judge all beauty vain ;
Wise, if too weak, more wits I 'll never prove.

Dear, sweet, fair, wise ! change, shrink, nor be not weak,
And, on my faith, my faith shall never break !

Earth with her flowers shall sooner heaven adorn ;
Heaven her bright stars through earth's dim globe shall move ;
Fire heat shall lose, and frosts of flames be born ;
Air, made to shine, as black as hell shall prove ;
Earth, heaven, fire, air, the world transformed shall view,
Ere I prove false to faith or strange to you !

Anonymous.

149

MADRIGAL

LOVE not me for comely grace,
For my pleasing eye or face,
Nor for any outward part,
No, nor for a constant heart !
For these may fail or turn to ill—
　　So thou and I shall sever.
Keep, therefore, a true woman's eye,
And love me still, but know not why !
So hast thou the same reason still
　　To dote upon me ever.

Anonymous.

150

SINCE FIRST I SAW YOUR FACE

SINCE first I saw your face I resolved to honour and renown ye ;
If now I be disdained, I wish my heart had never known ye.
What ? I that loved and you that liked, shall we begin to wrangle ?
No, no, no, my heart is fast, and cannot disentangle.

If I admire or praise too much, that fault you may forgive me ;
Or if my hands had strayed a touch, then justly might you leave me.
I asked you leave, you bade me love ; is 't now a time to chide me ?
No, no, no, I 'll love you still, what fortune e'er betide me.

The sun, whose beams most glorious are, rejecteth no beholder,
And your sweet beauty past compare made my poor eyes the
　　bolder.
Where beauty moves, and wit delights, and signs of kindness bind
　　me,
There, O, there ! where'er I go I 'll leave my heart behind me.

Anonymous.

151

COME, SHEPHERD SWAINS

COME, shepherd swains, that wont to hear me sing,
    Now sigh and groan !
Dead is my Love, my Hope, my Joy, my Spring ;
    Dead, dead, and gone !

O, She that was your Summer's Queen,
    Your days' delight,
Is gone and will no more be seen ;
    O cruel spite !

Break all your pipes that wont to sound
    With pleasant cheer,
And cast yourselves upon the ground
    To wail my Dear !

Come, shepherd swains, come, nymphs, and all a-row
    To help me cry ;
Dead is my Love, and, seeing She is so,
    Lo, now I die !

Anonymous.

152

SISTER, AWAKE

SISTER, awake ! close not your eyes
    The Day her light discloses,
And the bright Morning doth arise
    Out of her bed of roses.

See, the clear Sun, the world's bright eye,
    In at our window peeping :
Lo ! how he blusheth to espy
    Us idle wenches sleeping.

Therefore, awake ! make haste, I say,
    And let us, without staying,
All in our gowns of green so gay,
    Into the park a-maying !

Anonymous.

K

153

TO DIANA

Queen and huntress, chaste and fair,
Now the sun is laid to sleep,
Seated in thy silver chair,
State in wonted manner keep :
Hesperus entreats thy light,
Goddess excellently bright.

Earth, let not thy envious shade
Dare itself to interpose !
Cynthia's shining orb was made
Heaven to clear when day did close :
Bless us then with wished sight,
Goddess excellently bright.

Lay thy bow of pearl apart,
And thy crystal-shining quiver :
Give unto the flying hart
Space to breathe, how short soever ;
Thou that makest a day of night,
Goddess excellently bright.

Ben Jonson.

154

CHARIS

See the chariot at hand here of Love,
Wherein my Lady rideth !
Each that draws is a swan or a dove,
And well the car Love guideth.
As she goes, all hearts do duty
Unto her beauty ;
And enamoured do wish, so they might
But enjoy such a sight,
That they still were to run by her side,
Through swords, through seas, whither she would glide.

Do but look on her eyes—they do light
All that Love's world compriseth !
Do but look on her hair—it is bright
As Love's star when it riseth !

Do but mark—her forehead 's smoother
Than words that soothe her,
And from her arched brows such a grace
Sheds itself through the face,
As alone there triumphs to the life
All the gain, all the good of the elements' strife !

Have you seen but a bright lily grow,
Before rude hands have touched it ?
Have you marked but the fall of the snow,
Before the soil hath smutched it ?
Have you felt the wool of the beaver,
Or swan's down ever?
Or have smelt o' the bud of the brier,
Or the nard in the fire ?
Or have tasted the bag of the bee ?—
O, so white, O, so soft, O, so sweet is she !

Ben Jonson.

155

KISS ME, SWEET

KISS me, sweet : the wary lover
Can your favours keep, and cover,
When the common courting jay
All your bounties will betray.
Kiss again : no creature comes.
Kiss, and score up wealthy sums
On my lips, thus hardly sundred
While you breathe.   First give a hundred.
Then a thousand, then another
Hundred, then unto the other
Add a thousand, and so more :
Till you equal with the store,
All the grass that Rumney yields,
Or the sands in Chelsea fields,
Or the drops in silver Thames,
Or the stars that gild his streams,
In the silent summer-nights,
When youths ply their stolen delights :
That the curious may not know
How to tell 'em as they flow,
And the envious, when they find
What their number is, be pined.

Ben Jonson.

156

FOLLOW A SHADOW

FOLLOW a shadow, it still flies you,
Seem to fly it, it will pursue:
So court a mistress, she denies you;
Let her alone, she will court you.
Say are not women truly, then,
Styled but the shadows of us men?

At morn and even shades are longest;
At noon they are or short or none:
So men at weakest, they are strongest,
But grant us perfect, they're not known.
Say are not women truly, then,
Styled but the shadows of us men?

Ben Jonson.

157

TO CELIA

DRINK to me only with thine eyes,
  And I will pledge with mine;
Or leave a kiss but in the cup,
  And I'll not look for wine.
The thirst that from the soul doth rise,
  Doth ask a drink divine:
But might I of Jove's nectar sup,
  I would not change for thine.

I sent thee late a rosy wreath,
  Not so much honouring thee,
As giving it a hope, that there
  It could not withered be;
But thou thereon didst only breathe,
· And sent'st it back to me:
Since when it grows, and smells, I swear,
  Not of itself, but thee.

Ben Jonson.

158

THE KISS

O, THAT joy so soon should waste!
Or so sweet a bliss
As a kiss

Might not for ever last !
So sugared, so melting, so soft, so delicious,
The dew that lies on roses,
When the morn herself discloses,
Is not so precious.
O, rather than I would it smother,
Were I to taste such another,
It should be my wishing
That I might die kissing !

Ben Jonson.

159

BEGGING ANOTHER

For Love's sake, kiss me once again !
I long, and should not beg in vain.
Here 's none to spy or see ;
Why do you doubt or stay?
I 'll taste as lightly as the bee,
That doth but touch his flower, and flies away.

Once more, and, faith, I will be gone—
Can he that loves ask less than one?
Nay, you may err in this,
And all your bounty wrong :
This could be called but half a kiss ;
What we 're but once to do, we should do long.

I will but mend the last, and tell
Where, how, it would have relished well ;
Join lip to lip, and try :
Each suck the other's breath,
And whilst our tongues perplexéd lie,
Let who will think us dead, or wish our death !

Ben Jonson.

160

A NYMPH'S PASSION

I love, and he loves me again,
Yet dare I not tell who ;
For if the nymphs should know my swain,
I fear they 'd love him too ;

Yet if it be not known,
The pleasure is as good as none,
For that's a narrow joy is but our own.

I'll tell, that if they be not glad,
They yet may envy me ;
But then, if I grow jealous mad,
And of them pitied be,
It were a plague 'bove scorn ;
And yet it cannot be forborne,
Unless my heart would, as my thought, be torn.

He is, if they can find him, fair,
And fresh and fragrant too,
As summer's sky, or purgéd air,
And looks as lilies do
That are this morning blown :
Yet, yet I doubt he is not known,
And fear much more, that more of him be shown !

But he hath eyes so round and bright
As make away my doubt,
Where Love may all his torches light
Though hate had put them out :
But then, t' increase my fears,
What nymph soe'er his voice but hears,
Will be my rival, though she have but ears !

I'll tell no more, and yet I love,
And he loves me ; yet no
One unbecoming thought doth move
From either heart, I know ;
But so exempt from blame,
As it would be to each a fame,
If love or fear would let me tell his name.

Ben Jonson.

161

EPITHALAMY

UP! youths and virgins ! up, and praise
The god whose nights outshine his days !
Hymen, whose hallowed rites
Could never boast of brighter lights,
Whose bands pass liberty !

Two of your troop, that with the morn were free,
Are now waged to his war ;
And what they are,
If you 'll perfection see,
Yourselves must be.
Shine, Hesperus ! shine forth, thou wishéd star !

What joy or honours can compare
With holy nuptials when they are
Made out of equal parts
Of years, of states, of hands, of hearts?
When in the happy choice
The spouse and spouséd have the foremost voice,
Such, glad of Hymen's war,
Live what they are
And long perfection see :
And such ours be.
Shine, Hesperus ! shine forth, thou wishéd star !

The solemn state of this one night
Were fit to last an age's light ;
But there are rites behind
Have less of state and more of kind :
Love's wealthy crop of kisses,
And fruitful harvest of his mother's blisses.
Sound then to Hymen's war !
That what these are,
Who will perfection see
May haste to be.
Shine, Hesperus ! shine forth, thou wishéd star !

Love's Commonwealth consists of toys ;
His Council are those antic boys,
Games, Laughter, Sports, Delights,
That triumph with him on these nights :
To whom we must give way,
For now their reign begins, and lasts till day.
They sweeten Hymen's war,
And in that jar
Make all that married be
Perfection see.
Shine, Hesperus ! shine forth, thou wishéd star !

Why stays the bridegroom to invade
Her that would be a matron made?
Good-night ! whilst yet we may
Good-night to you a virgin say.

To-morrow rise the same
Your mother is, and use a nobler name !
Speed well in Hymen's war,
That what you are,
By your perfection, we
And all may see !
Shine, Hesperus ! shine forth, thou wishéd star !

To-night is Venus' vigil kept,
This night no bridegroom ever slept ;
And if the fair bride do,
The married say 'tis his fault too.
Wake then, and let your lights
Wake too, for they 'll tell nothing of your nights,
But that in Hymen's war
You perfect are ;
And such perfection we
Do pray should be—
Shine, Hesperus ! shine forth, thou wishéd star !—

That, ere the rosy-fingered Morn
Behold nine moons, there may be born
A babe to uphold the fame
Of Radcliffe's blood and Ramsay's name,
That may, in his great seed,
Wear the long honours of his father's deed !
Such fruits of Hymen's war
Most perfect are :
And all perfection we
Wish you should see.
Shine, Hesperus ! shine forth, thou wishéd star !

Ben Jonson.

162

O, DO NOT WANTON

O, DO not wanton with those eyes,
    Lest I be sick with seeing ;
Nor cast them down, but let them rise,
    Lest shame destroy their being.

O, be not angry with those fires,
    For then their threats will kill me ;
Nor look too kind on my desires,
    For then my hopes will spill me.

O, do not steep them in thy tears,
　For so will sorrow slay me ;
Nor spread them as distraught with fears—
　Mine own enough betray me !

Ben Jonson.

163

GO AND CATCH

Go and catch a falling star,
　Get with child a mandrake root,
Tell me where all times past are,
　Or who cleft the Devil's foot,
Teach me to hear mermaids singing,
Or to keep off envy's stinging ;
　　　And find,
　　　What wind
Serves to advance an honest mind !

If thou be'st born to strange sights,
　Things invisible go see ;
Ride ten thousand days and nights,
　Till age snow white hairs on thee ;
Thou, when thou return'st, wilt tell me
All strange wonders that befell thee ;
　　　And swear
　　　No where
Lives a woman true and fair !

If thou find'st one let me know,
　Such a pilgrimage were sweet ;
Yet do not, I would not go,
　Though at next door we might meet :
Though she were true when you met her,
And last, till you write your letter ;
　　　Yet she
　　　Will be
False, ere I come, to two or three !

John Donne.

164

BREAK OF DAY

STAY, O sweet, and do not rise !
The light, that shines, comes from thine eyes.

The day breaks not : it is my heart,
Because that you and I must part.
Stay, or else my joys will die,
And perish in their infancy.

'Tis true, 'tis day : what though it be?
O, wilt thou therefore rise from me?
Why should we rise, because 'tis light?
Did we lie down, because 'twas night?
Love, which in spite of darkness brought us hither,
Should in despite of light keep us together.

Light hath no tongue, but is all eye.
If it could speak as well as spy,
This were the worst that it could say :—
That, being well, I fain would stay,
And that I lov'd my heart and honour so,
That I would not from her, that had them, go.

Must business thee from hence remove?
O, that's the worst disease of love !
The poor, the foul, the false, love can
Admit, but not the busied man.
He, which hath business, and makes love, doth do
Such wrong, as when a married man doth woo.

John Donne.

165

THE MESSAGE

SEND home my long-strayed eyes to me,
Which, O ! too long have dwelt on thee.
But if they there have learn'd such ill,
Such forced fashions
And false passions,
That they be
Made by thee
Fit for no good sight, keep them still.

Send home my harmless heart again,
Which no unworthy thought could stain !
But, if it be taught by thine
To make jestings
Of protestings,
And break both
Word and oath,
Keep it still—'tis none of mine.

Yet send me back my heart and eyes,
That I may know and see thy lies,
And may laugh and joy, when thou
Art in anguish,
And dost languish
For some one,
That will none,
Or prove as false as thou dost now.

John Donne.

166

AS IT FELL UPON A DAY

As it fell upon a day
In the merry month of May;
Sitting in a pleasant shade
Which a grove of myrtles made,
Beasts did leap, and birds did sing,
Trees did grow, and plants did spring;
Everything did banish moan,
Save the Nightingale alone.
She, poor bird, as all-forlorn,
Lean'd her breast up-till a thorn,
And there sung the dolefull'st ditty,
That to hear it was great pity.
'Fie, fie, fie,' now would she cry;
'Teru, teru!' by and by;
That to hear her so complain,
Scarce from tears I could refrain;
For her griefs, so lively shown,
Made me think upon mine own.
'Ah,' thought I, 'thou mourn'st in vain!
None takes pity on thy pain:
Senseless trees, they cannot hear thee;
Ruthless beasts, they will not cheer thee:
King Pandion he is dead;
All thy friends are lapp'd in lead;
All thy fellow birds do sing,
Careless of thy sorrowing.
(Even so, poor bird, like thee—
None alive will pity me)—
Whilst as fickle Fortune smiled,
Thou and I were both beguiled.'

Every one that flatters thee
Is no friend in misery.

Words are easy, like the wind;
Faithful friends are hard to find.
Every man will be thy friend
Whilst thou hast wherewith to spend;
But if store of crowns be scant,
No man will supply thy want.
If that one be prodigal,
Bountiful they will him call,
And with such-like flattering,
' Pity but he were a king' !
If he be addict to vice,
Quickly him they will entice.
If to women he be bent,
They have at commandment.
But if Fortune once do frown,
Then farewell his great renown !
They that fawn'd on him before
Use his company no more.

He that is thy friend indeed,
He will help thee in thy need :
If thou sorrow, he will weep ;
If thou wake, he cannot sleep ;
Thus of every grief in heart
He with thee doth bear a part.
These are certain signs to know
Faithful friend from flattering foe.

Richard Barnfield.

167

ANTHEM

LORD, what am I? A worm, dust, vapour, nothing !
What is my life? A dream, a daily dying !
What is my flesh? My soul's uneasy clothing !
What is my time? A minute ever flying :
My time, my flesh, my life, and I ;
What are we, Lord, but vanity?

Where am I, Lord? down in a vale of death :
What is my trade? sin, my dear God offending ;
My sport sin too, my stay a puff of breath :
What end of sin? Hell's horror never ending:
My way, my trade, sport, stay, and place
Help to make up my doleful case.

Lord, what art thou? pure life, power, beauty, bliss:
Where dwell'st thou? up above in perfect light:
What is Thy time? eternity it is:
What state? attendance of each glorious sprite:
Thyself, thy place, thy days, thy state
Pass all the thoughts of powers create.

How shall I reach thee, Lord? O, soar above,
Ambitious soul! But which way should I fly?
Thou, Lord, art way and end: what wings have I?
Aspiring thoughts, of faith, of hope, of love—
O, let these wings, that way alone
Present me to thy blissful throne!

Joseph Hall.

168

MADRIGAL

LOVE in thy youth, fair maid; be wise,
  Old Time will make thee colder,
And though each morning new arise
  Yet we each day grow older.

Thou as heaven art fair and young,
  Thine eyes like twin stars shining;
But ere another day be sprung,
  All these will be declining.

Then winter comes with all his fears,
  And all thy sweets shall borrow;
Too late then wilt thou shower thy tears,
  And I too late shall sorrow.

Anonymous.

169

O SWEET CONTENT

ART thou poor, yet hast thou golden slumbers?
        O sweet content!
Art thou rich, yet is thy mind perplexéd?
        O punishment!
Dost thou laugh to see how fools are vexéd
To add to golden numbers golden numbers?
        O sweet content!

Canst drink the waters of the crispéd spring?
　　　O sweet content!
Swim'st thou in wealth, yet sink'st in thine own tears?
　　　O punishment!
Then he that patiently want's burden bears,
No burden bears, but is a king, a king!
　　　O sweet content!

Work apace, apace, apace, apace;
Honest labour bears a lovely face;
Then hey noney, noney, hey noney, noney!

　　　　　　　　　　　　　　　Thomas Dekker.

170

BEAUTY, ARISE

BEAUTY, arise, show forth thy glorious shining!
Thine eyes feed Love, for them he standeth pining.
Honour and youth attend to do their duty
To thee, their only sovereign beauty.
Beauty, arise, whilst we, thy servants, sing
Io to Hymen, wedlock's jocund king:
Io to Hymen, Io, Io, sing!
Of wedlock, love, and youth, is Hymen king.

Beauty, arise, thy glorious lights display,
Whilst we sing Io, glad to see this day.
Io to Hymen, Io, Io, sing!
Of wedlock, love, and youth, is Hymen king.

　　　　　　　　　　　　　　　Thomas Dekker.

171

YE LITTLE BIRDS

YE little birds that sit and sing
　　Amidst the shady valleys,
And see how Phillis sweetly walks
　　Within her garden-alleys:
Go, pretty birds, about her bower;
Sing, pretty birds, she may not lower;
Ah, me! methinks I see her frown!
　　Ye pretty wantons, warble.

Go, tell her through your chirping bills,
    As you by me are bidden,
To her is only known my love,
    Which from the world is hidden.
Go, pretty birds, and tell her so ;
See that your notes strain not too low ;
For still, methinks, I see her frown—
    Ye pretty wantons, warble.

Go tune your voices' harmony,
    And sing, I am her lover ;
Strain loud and sweet, that every note
    With sweet content may move her.
And she that hath the sweetest voice,
Tell her I will not change my choice ;
Yet still, methinks, I see her frown !
    Ye pretty wantons, warble.

O, fly ! make haste ! see, see, she falls
    Into a pretty slumber.
Sing round about her rosy bed,
    That, waking, she may wonder.
Say to her, 'tis her lover true
That sendeth love to you, to you ;
And when you hear her kind reply,
    Return with pleasant warblings.

                    Thomas Heywood.

172

PACK, CLOUDS, AWAY

PACK, clouds, away, and welcome, day !
With night we banish sorrow.
Sweet air, blow soft ; mount, lark, aloft
To give my love good morrow !
Wings from the wind to please her mind,
Notes from the lark I 'll borrow :
Bird, prune thy wing, nightingale, sing,
To give my love good morrow !
To give my love good morrow,
Notes from them all I 'll borrow.

Wake from thy nest, robin redbreast !
Sing, birds, in every furrow,
And from each bill let music shrill
Give my fair love good morrow !

Blackbird and thrush in every bush,
Stare, linnet, and cocksparrow,
You pretty elves, amongst yourselves
Sing my fair love good morrow !
To give my love good morrow,
Sing, birds, in every furrow !

Thomas Heywood.

173

ASPATIA'S SONG

LAY a garland on my hearse
    Of the dismal yew.
Maidens, willow branches bear—
    Say I died true.

My love was false, but I was firm
    From my hour of birth.
Upon my buried body lie
    Lightly, gentle earth !

John Fletcher

174

AWAY, DELIGHTS

AWAY, delights ! go seek some other dwelling,
For I must die.
Farewell, false love ! thy tongue is ever telling
Lie after lie.
For ever let me rest now from thy smarts ;
Alas, for pity, go,
And fire their hearts
That have been hard to thee ! Mine was not so.

Never again deluding love shall know me,
For I will die ;
And all those griefs that think to overgrow me,
Shall be as I.
For ever will I sleep, while poor maids cry :—
' Alas, for pity, stay,
And let us die
With thee ! men cannot mock us in the clay.'

John Fletcher.

175

COME HITHER, YOU THAT LOVE

COME hither, you that love, and hear me sing
    Of joys still growing,
Green, fresh, and lusty as the pride of spring,
    And ever blowing !
Come hither, youths, that blush, and dare not know
    What is desire,
And old men, worse than you, that cannot blow
    One spark of fire !
And with the power of my enchanting song,
Boys shall be able men, and old men young.

Come hither, you that hope, and you that cry,
    Leave off complaining !
Youth, strength, and beauty, that shall never die,
    Are here remaining.
Come hither, fools, and blush you stay so long
    From being blessed,
And mad men, worse than you, that suffer wrong,
    Yet seek no rest'!
And in an hour, with my enchanting song,
You shall be ever pleased, and young maids long.

John Fletcher.

176

NOW THE LUSTY SPRING

Now the lusty Spring is seen !
    Golden yellow, gaudy blue,
    Daintily invite the view.
Everywhere on every green,
Roses blushing as they blow,
    And enticing men to pull,
Lilies whiter than the snow,
    Woodbines of sweet honey full :
All love's emblems, and all cry :—
' Ladies, if not plucked, we die.'

Yet the lusty Spring hath stayed !
    Blushing red and purest white
    Daintily to love invite
Every woman, every maid.

L

Cherries kissing as they grow,
  And inviting men to taste,
Apples even right below,
  Winding gently to the waist :
All love's emblems, and all cry :—
'Ladies, if not plucked, we die.'

John Fletcher.

177

HEAR, YE LADIES

HEAR, ye ladies that despise,
  What the mighty Love has done !
Fear examples, and be wise :
  Fair Calisto was a nun ;
Leda, sailing on the stream
  To deceive the hopes of man,
Love accounting but a dream,
  Doted on a silver swan ;
    Danaë, in a brazen tower,
    Where no love was, loved a shower.

Hear, ye ladies that are coy,
  What the mighty Love can do !
Fear the fierceness of the boy :
  The chaste moon he makes to woo ;
Vesta, kindling holy fires,
  Circled round about with spies,
Never dreaming loose desires,
  Doting at the altar dies ;
    Ilion in a short hour higher
    He can build, and once more fire.

John Fletcher.

178

DEAREST, DO NOT

DEAREST, do not you delay me,
Since thou knowest, I must be gone !
Wind and tide, 'tis thought, doth stay me,
But 'tis wind that must be blown

From that breath, whose native smell
Indian odours far excel.

O, then speak, thou fairest fair!
Kill not him that vows to serve thee,
But perfume this neighbouring air,
Else dull silence, sure, will sterve me!
'Tis a word that's quickly spoken,
Which being restrained, a heart is broken.

John Fletcher.

179

A SONG OF BRIDAL

ROSES, their sharp spines being gone,
Not royal in their smells alone
   But in their hue;
Maiden pinks, of odour faint;
Daisies smell-less, yet most quaint;
   And sweet thyme true;

Primrose, firstborn child of Ver,
Merry springtime's harbinger,
   With her bells dim;
Oxlips in their cradles growing;
Marigolds on deathbeds blowing;
   Larks'-heels trim:

All dear Nature's children sweet
Lie 'fore bride and bridegroom's feet,
   Blessing their sense!
Not an angel of the air,
Bird melodious or bird fair,
   Be absent hence!

The crow, the slanderous cuckoo, nor
The boding raven, nor chough hoar,
   Nor chattering pie,
May on our bride-house perch or sing,
Or with them any discord bring,
   But from it fly!

John Fletcher.

180

IN PRAISE OF MELANCHOLY

HENCE, all you vain delights,
As short as are the nights
   Wherein you spent your folly !
There's nought in this life sweet,
If man were wise to see't,
   But only Melancholy,
   O sweetest Melancholy !
Welcome, folded arms, and fixed eyes,
A sight that piercing mortifies,
A look that's fastened to the ground,
A tongue chained up without a sound !

Fountain-heads and pathless groves,
 Places which pale passion loves ;
Moonlight walks, when all the fowls
Are warmly housed, save bats and owls ;
A midnight bell, a parting groan—
These are the sounds we feed upon,
Then stretch our bones in a still gloomy valley . . .
Nothing's so dainty sweet as lovely melancholy !

John Fletcher.

181

INVOCATION

WHY art thou slow, thou rest of trouble, Death,
  To stop a wretch's breath,
That calls on thee, and offers her sad heart
  A prey unto thy dart ?
I am nor young nor fair ; be, therefore, bold :
  Sorrow hath made me old,
Deformed, and wrinkled ; all that I can crave
  Is quiet in my grave.
Such as live happy, hold long life a jewel ;
  But to me thou art cruel,
If thou end not my tedious misery
  And I soon cease to be.
Strike, and strike home, then !   Pity unto me,
In one short hour's delay, is tyranny.

Philip Massinger.

182

MEDITATION

(On the Tombs in Westminster Abbey)

MORTALITY, behold and fear!
What a change of flesh is here!
Think how many royal bones
Sleep within this heap of stones;
Here they lie had realms and lands,
Who now want strength to stir their hands;
Where from their pulpits seal'd with dust
They preach :—' In greatness is no trust.'
Here 's an acre sown indeed
With the richest royall'st seed
That the earth did e'er suck in,
Since the first man died for sin!
Here the bones of birth have cried :—
' Though gods they were, as men they died.'
Here are sands, ignoble things,
Dropt from the ruin'd sides of kings.
Here 's a world of pomp and state,
Buried in dust, once dead by fate.

Francis Beaumont.

183

PHOEBUS, ARISE

PHOEBUS, arise,
And paint the sable skies
With azure, white, and red!
Rouse Memnon's mother from her Tython's bed,
That she thy carrier may with roses spread;
The nightingales thy coming each where sing;
Make an eternal spring,
Give life to this dark world which lieth dead;
Spread forth thy golden hair
In larger locks than thou wast wont before,
And, emperor-like, decore
With diadem of pearl thy temples fair;
Chase hence the ugly Night,
Which serves but to make dear thy glorious light.
This is that happy morn
That day, long-wishéd day,
Of all my life so dark

(If cruel stars have not my ruin sworn,
And Fates not hope betray),
Which, only white, deserves
A diamond for ever should it mark :
This is the morn should bring unto this grove
My love, to hear and recompense my love.
Fair king, who all preserves,
But show thy blushing beams
And thou two sweeter eyes
Shalt see than those which by Peneus' streams
Did once thy heart surprise :
Nay, suns, which shine as clear
As thou when two thou did to Rome appear !
Now, Flora, deck thyself in fairest guise ;
If that ye, Winds, would hear
A voice surpassing far Amphion's lyre,
Your stormy chiding stay ;
Let Zephyr only breathe,
And with her tresses play,
Kissing sometimes these purple ports of death !
The winds all silent are,
And Phœbus in his chair,
Ensaffroning sea and air,
Makes vanish every star :
Night like a drunkard reels
Beyond the hills to shun his flaming wheels ;
The fields with flow'rs are deck'd in every hue ;
The clouds bespangle with bright gold their blue ;
Here is the pleasant place,
And ev'ry thing, save her, who all should grace.

William Drummond.

184

MADRIGAL

My thoughts hold mortal strife :
I do detest my life,
And, with lamenting cries,
Peace to my soul to bring
Oft call that prince which here doth monarchise.
But he, grim-grinning king,
Who caitives scorns, and doth the blest surprise,
Late having decked with beauty's rose his tomb,
Disdains to crop a weed, and will not come.

William Drummond.

185

WOOING SONG

LOVE is the blossom where there blows
Everything that lives or grows :
Love doth make the Heav'ns to move,
And the Sun doth burn in love :
Love the strong and weak doth yoke,
And makes the ivy climb the oak,
Under whose shadows lions wild,
Soften'd by love, grow tame and mild.
Love no med'cine can appease,
He burns the fishes in the seas.
Not all the skill his wounds can stench,
Not all the sea his fire can quench.
Love did make the bloody spear
Once a leafy coat to wear,
While in his leaves there shrouded lay
Sweet birds, for love, that sing and play.
And of all love's joyful flame,
I the bud and blossom am.
Only bend thy knee to me,
Thy wooing shall thy winning be !

See, see the flowers that below
Now as fresh as morning blow,
And of all the virgin rose
That as bright Aurora shows,
How they all unleaved die,
Losing their virginity !
Like unto a summer-shade,
But now born, and now they fade.
Every thing doth pass away.
There is danger in delay.
Come, come gather then the rose,
Gather it, or it you lose !
All the sand of Tagus' shore
Into my bosom casts his ore :
All the valleys' swimming corn
To my house is yearly borne :
Every grape of every vine
Is gladly bruis'd to make me wine,
While ten thousand kings, as proud,
To carry up my train have bow'd,

And a world of ladies send me
In my chambers to attend me:
All the stars in heaven that shine,
And ten thousand more, are mine:
Only bend thy knee to me,
Thy wooing shall thy winning be!

Giles Fletcher.

186

A BROKEN HEART

GLORIES, pleasures, pomps, delights and ease,
Can but please
Outward senses, when the mind
Is untroubled, or by peace refin'd.
Crowns may flourish and decay,
Beauties shine, but fade away.
Youth may revel, yet it must
Lie down in a bed of dust.
Earthly honours flow and waste,
Time alone doth change and last.
Sorrows mingled with contents prepare
Rest for care.
Love only reigns in death; though art
Can find no comfort for a Broken Heart.

John Ford.

187

SHALL I TELL YOU WHOM I LOVE

SHALL I tell you whom I love?
Hearken then a while to me,
And if such a woman move
As I now shall versify,
Be assured, 'tis she, or none
That I love, and love alone.

Nature did her so much right,
As she scorns the help of art.
In as many virtues dight
As e'er yet embraced a heart,
So much good so truly tried
Some for less were deified.

William Browne.

188

A LOVER'S GREETING

Welcome, welcome do I sing,
  Far more welcome than the spring !
He that parteth from you never
  Shall enjoy a spring for ever.

LOVE, that to the voice is near
  Breaking from your ivory pale,
Need not walk abroad to hear
  The delightful nightingale.

Love, that looks still on your eyes,
  Tho' the winter have begun
To benumb our arteries,
  Shall not want the summer's sun.

Love, that still may see your cheeks,
  Where all rareness still reposes,
Is a fool if ere he seeks
  Other lilies, other roses.

Love, to whom your soft lip yields,
  And perceives your breath in kissing,
All the odours of the fields
  Never, never shall be missing.

Love, that question would anew
  What fair Eden was of old,
Let him rightly study you,
  And a brief of that behold !

    Welcome, welcome then I sing,
    Far more welcome than the spring !
    He that parteth from you never
    Shall enjoy a spring for ever.
                    William Browne.

189

LOVE'S ERRAND

Go, thou gentle whispering Wind,
Bear this Sigh ! and if thou find
Where my cruel fair doth rest,
Cast it in her snowy breast :

So, inflam'd by my desire,
It may set her heart on fire.

 Those sweet kisses thou shalt gain,
Will reward thee for thy pain.
Boldly light upon her lip,
There suck odours, and thence skip
To her bosom. Lastly fall
Down, and wander over all.

 Range about those ivory hills,
From whose every part distils
Amber dew. There spices grow,
There pure streams of nectar flow :
There perfume thyself, and bring
All those sweets upon thy wing.

 As thou return'st, change by thy power
Every weed into a flower,
Turn every thistle to a vine,
Make the bramble eglantine :
For so rich a booty made,
Do but this, and I am paid.

 Thou canst with thy powerful blast
Heat apace, and cool as fast ;
Thou canst kindle hidden flame,
And again destroy the same :
Then, for pity, either stir
Up the Fire of Love in her,
That alike both flames may shine,
Or else quite extinguish mine.

      Thomas Carew.

190

GIVE ME MORE LOVE

GIVE me more love or more disdain !
The torrid or the frozen zone
Bring equal ease unto my pain :
The temperate affords me none.
Either extreme, of love or hate,
Is sweeter than a calm estate.

Give me a storm : if it be love,
Like Danaë in that golden shower,
I swim in pleasure ; if it prove
Disdain, that torrent will devour
My vulture-hopes ; and he 's possessed
Of Heaven, that 's but from Hell released.

Then crown my joys, or cure my pain :
Give me more love or more disdain !

Thomas Carew.

191

WHEN THOU, POOR EXCOMMUNICATE

WHEN thou, poor Excommunicate
    From all the joys of love, shalt see
The full reward and glorious fate
    Which my strong faith shall purchase me,
    Then curse thine own inconstancy !

A fairer hand than thine shall cure
    That heart, which thy false oaths did wound ;
And to my soul a soul more pure
    Than thine shall by Love's hand be bound,
    And both with equal glory crown'd.

Then shalt thou weep, entreat, complain
    To Love, as I did once to thee ;
When all thy tears shall be as vain
    As mine were then : for thou shalt be
    Damn'd for thy false apostacy.

Thomas Carew.

192

ASK ME NO MORE

ASK me no more where Jove bestows,
When June is past, the fading rose :
For in your beauty's orient deep
These flowers, as in their causes, sleep.

Ask me no more, whither do stray
The golden atoms of the day :
For in pure love heaven did prepare
Those powders to enrich your hair.

Ask me no more, whither doth haste
The Nightingale, when May is past :
For in your sweet dividing throat
She winters, and keeps warm her note.

Ask me no more, where those stars 'light,
That downwards fall in dead of night :
For in your eyes they sit, and there
Fixéd become, as in their sphere.

Ask me no more, if east or west
The Phœnix build her spicy nest :
For unto you at last she flies,
And in your fragrant bosom dies.

Thomas Carew.

193

THE LOVER AND THE BELOVÉD

E'EN like two little bank-dividing brooks
That wash the pebbles with their wanton streams,
And, having ranged and searched a thousand nooks,
Meet both at length in silver-breasted Thames,
Where in a greater current they conjoin :
So I my Best-Belovéd's am ; so He is mine.

E'en so we met ; and after long pursuit,
E'en so we join'd ; we both became entire ;
No need for either to renew a suit,
For I was flax and he was flames of fire :
Our firm-united souls did more than twine ;
So I my Best-Belovéd's am ; so He is mine.

If all those glittering Monarchs that command
The servile quarters of this earthly ball,
Should tender, in exchange, their shares of land,
I would not change my fortunes for them all :
Their wealth is but a counter to my coin ;
The world 's but theirs ; but my Belovéd 's mine.

Francis Quarles.

194

HAVE YOU A DESIRE

HAVE you a desire to see
The glorious Heaven's epitome?
Or an abstract of the Spring?
Adonis' garden? or a Thing
    Fuller of wonder?   Nature's shop displayed,
    Hung with the choicest pieces she has made?—
    Here behold it open laid.

Or else would you bless your eyes
With a type of Paradise?
Or behold how poets feign
Jove to sit amidst his train?
    Or see (what made Actæon rue)
    Diana 'mongst her virgin crew?—
    Lift up your eyes and view.

Peter Hausted.

195

EASTER

I

RISE, heart; thy Lord is risen.   Sing his praise
Without delays,
Who takes thee by the hand, that thou likewise
With him may'st rise,
That, as his death calcinéd thee to dust,
His life may make thee gold, and much more just.

Awake, my lute, and struggle for thy part
With all thy art.
The Cross taught all wood to resound his name,
Who bore the same.
His stretchéd sinews taught all strings, what key
Is best to celebrate this most high day.

Consort both heart and lute, and twist a song
Pleasant and long;
Or, since all music is but three parts vied
And multiplied,
O, let thy blessed Spirit bear a part,
And make up our defects with his sweet art!

II

I got me flowers to strew thy way,
I got me boughs off many a tree:
But thou wast up by break of day,
And brought'st thy sweets along with thee.

The Sun arising in the East,
Though he give light, and th' East perfume,
If they should offer to contest
With thy arising, they presume.

Can there be any day but this,
Though many suns to shine endeavour?
We count three hundred, but we miss:
There is but one, and that one ever.

George Herbert.

196

THE QUIP

THE merry World did on a day
  With his train-bands and mates agree
To meet together, where I lay,
  And all in sport to jeer at me.

First, Beauty crept into a rose,
  Which when I plucked not, 'Sir,' said she,
'Tell me, I pray, whose hands are those?'—
  But Thou shalt answer, Lord, for me.

Then Money came, and chinking still,
  'What tune is this, poor man?' said he:
'I heard in Music you had skill.'
  But Thou shalt answer, Lord, for me.

Then came brave Glory puffing by
  In silks that whistled—who but he?
He scarce allowed me half an eye—
  But Thou shalt answer, Lord, for me.

Then came quick Wit and Conversation,
  And he would needs a comfort be,
And, to be short, make an oration—
  But Thou shalt answer, Lord, for me.

Yet when the hour of Thy design
  To answer these fine things shall come,
Speak not at large, say, I am Thine,
  And then they have their answer home.

George Herbert.

197

VIRTUE

SWEET day, so cool, so calm, so bright,
  The bridal of the earth and sky :
The dew shall weep thy fall to-night,
      For thou must die.

Sweet rose, whose hue angry and brave
  Bids the rash gazer wipe his eye :
Thy root is ever in its grave,
      And thou must die.

Sweet spring, full of sweet days and roses,
  A box where sweets compacted lie :
My music shows ye have your closes,
      And all must die.

Only a sweet and virtuous soul,
  Like seasoned timber, never gives,
But though the whole world turn to coal,
      Then chiefly lives.

George Herbert.

198

THE CALL

COME, my Way, my Truth, my Life :
  Such a Way as gives us breath,
Such a Truth as ends all strife,
  And such a Life as killeth death !

Come, my Light, my Feast, my Strength :
  Such a Light as shows a feast,
Such a Feast as mends in length,
  Such a Strength as makes his guest !

Come, my Joy, my Love, my Heart:
 Such a Joy as none can move,
Such a Love as none can part,
 Such a Heart as joys in love!

       George Herbert.

199

CHERRY-RIPE

CHERRY-RIPE, ripe, ripe, I cry!
Full and fair ones! Come and buy!
If so be you ask me where
They do grow, I answer:—'There,
Where my Julia's lips do smile;
There 's the land, or cherry-isle,
Whose plantations fully show
All the year where cherries grow.'

       Robert Herrick.

200

TO HIS MISTRESS

. CHOOSE me your valentine,
 Next let us marry—
Love to the death will pine
 If we long tarry.

Promise, and keep your vows,
 Or vow ye never:
Love's doctrine disallows
 Troth-breakers ever.

You have broke promise twice,
 Dear, to undo me!
If you prove faithless thrice,
 None then will woo ye.

       Robert Herrick.

201

TO MYRRHA, HARD-HEARTED

FOLD now thine arms, and hang the head
Like to a lily witheréd;

Next look thou like a sickly moon,
Or like Jocasta in a swoon ;
Then weep, and sigh, and softly go
Like to a widow drown'd in woe,
Or like a virgin full of ruth
For the lost sweetheart of her youth :
And all because, fair maid, thou art
Insensible of all my smart,
And of those evil days that be
Now posting on to punish thee !
The gods are easy, and condemn
All such as are not soft like them.

                              Robert Herrick.

202

TO DIANEME

SWEET, be not proud of those two eyes
Which, starlike, sparkle in their skies ;
Nor be you proud that you can see
All hearts your captives, yours yet free ;
Be you not proud of that rich hair
Which wantons with the love-sick air :
Whenas that ruby, which you wear
Sunk from the tip of your soft ear,
Will last to be a precious stone
When all your world of beauty's gone.

                              Robert Herrick.

203

TO CORINNA GOING A-MAYING

GET up, get up for shame !   The blooming Morn
Upon her wings presents the God unshorn.
    .See how Aurora throws her fair,
    Fresh-quilted colours through the air :
    Get up, sweet slug-a-bed, and see
    The dew bespangle herb and tree !
Each flower has wept and bow'd toward the east
Above an hour since : yet you not dress'd ?
    Nay ! not so much as out of bed ?
    When all the birds have matins said

M

And sung their thankful hymns, 'tis sin,
  Nay ! profanation to keep in,
Whereas a thousand virgins on this day
Spring sooner than the lark to fetch in May.

Rise and put on your foliage, and be seen
To come forth, like the spring-time, fresh and green
    And sweet as Flora.   Take no care
    For jewels for your gown or hair :
    Fear not ; the leaves will strew
    Gems in abundance upon you :
Besides, the childhood of the day has kept,
Against you come, some orient pearls unwept !
    Come and receive them while the light
    Hangs on the dew-locks of the Night :
    And Titan on the eastern hill
    Retires himself, or else stands still.
    You come forth.   Wash, dress, be brief in praying :
Few beads are best when once we go a-Maying.

Come, my Corinna, come ; and, coming, mark
How each field turns a street, each street a park
    Made green and trimm'd with trees ; see how
    Devotion gives each house a bough
    Or branch : each porch, each door ere this
    An ark, a tabernacle is,
Made up of white-thorn neatly interwove,
As if here were those cooler shades of love !
    Can such delights be in the street
    And open fields, and we not see 't ?
    Come, we 'll abroad ; and let's obey
    The proclamation made for May,
And sin no more, as we have done, by staying,
But, my Corinna, come, let's go a-Maying !

There 's not a budding boy or girl this day
But is got up, and gone to bring in May.
    A deal of youth ere this is come
    Back, and with white-thorn laden home.
    Some have despatch'd their cakes and cream
    Before that we have left to dream :
And some have wept, and woo'd, and plighted troth,
And chose their priest ere we can cast off sloth : ·
    Many a green-gown has been given,
    Many a kiss, both odd and even !
    Many a glance, too, has been sent
    From out the eye, love's firmament !

Many a jest told of the keys' betraying
This night, and locks pick'd, yet we're not a-Maying!

Come, let us go, while we are in our prime,
And take the harmless folly of the time.
    We shall grow old apace, and die
    Before we know our liberty.
    Our life is short, and our days run
    As fast away as does the sun.
And, as a vapour or a drop of rain,
Once lost, can ne'er be found again,
    So when or you or I are made
    A fable, song, or fleeting shade,
    All love, all liking, all delight
    Lies drowned with us in endless night.
Then while time serves, and we are but decaying,
Come, my Corinna, come, let's go a-Maying.

Robert Herrick.

204

TO LIVE MERRILY AND TO TRUST TO GOOD VERSES

    Now is the time for mirth,
      Nor cheek or tongue be dumb;
    For, with the flowery earth,
      The golden pomp is come.

    The golden pomp is come;
      For now each tree does wear,
    Made of her pap and gum,
      Rich beads of amber here.

    Now rains the rose, and now
      The Arabian dew besmears
    My uncontrolléd brow
      And my retorted hairs.

    Homer, this health to thee,
      In sack of such a kind
    That it would make thee see
      Though thou wert ne'er so blind!

HERRICK

Next, Virgil I'll call forth
  To pledge this second health
In wine, whose each cup's worth
  An Indian commonwealth.

A goblet next I'll drink
  To Ovid, and suppose,
Made he the pledge, he'd think
  The world had all one nose.

Then this immensive cup
  Of aromatic wine,
Catullus, I quaff up
  To that terse muse of thine!

Wild I am now with heat:
  O Bacchus, cool thy rays,
Or, frantic, I shall eat
  Thy thyrse, and bite the bays!

Round, round the roof does run,
  And, being ravish'd thus,
Come, I will drink a tun
  To my Propertius.

Now, to Tibullus, next,
  This flood I drink to thee!
But stay, I see a text
  That this presents to me :—

' Behold, Tibullus lies
  Here burnt, whose small return
Of ashes scarce suffice
  To fill a little urn.'

Trust to good verses then :
  They only will aspire
When pyramids, as men,
  Are lost i' the funeral fire ;

And when all bodies meet
  In Lethe to be drown'd,
Then only numbers sweet
  With endless life are crown'd.

Robert Herrick.

205

TO VIOLETS

WELCOME, maids-of-honour !
    You do bring
    In the Spring,
And wait upon her.

She has virgins many,
        Fresh and fair ;
        Yet you are
More sweet than any.

You 're the maiden posies,
        And so grac'd
        To be plac'd
'Fore damask roses.

Yet, though thus respected,
        By-and-by
        Ye do lie,
Poor girls, neglected !

                        Robert Herrick.

206

TO THE VIRGINS, TO MAKE MUCH
OF TIME

GATHER ye rosebuds while ye may :
    Old Time is still a-flying,
And this same flower that smiles to-day
    To-morrow will be dying.

The glorious lamp of heaven, the sun,
    The higher he 's a-getting,
The sooner will his race be run,
    And nearer he 's to setting.

That age is best which is the first,
    When youth and blood are warmer ;
But, being spent, the worse, and worst
    Times still succeed the former.

Then be not coy, but use your time,
　And while ye may, go marry :
For, having lost but once your prime,
　You may for ever tarry.

Robert Herrick.

207

A MEDITATION FOR HIS MISTRESS

YOU are a tulip seen to-day :
But, dearest, of so short a stay
That where you grew scarce man can say.

You are a lovely July-flower :
Yet one rude wind or ruffling shower
Will force you hence, and in an hour.

You are a sparkling rose i' th' bud :
Yet lost ere that chaste flesh and blood
Can show where you or grew or stood.

You are a full-spread, fair-set vine,
And can with tendrils love entwine,
Yet dried ere you distil your wine.

You are like balm enclosed well
In amber, or some crystal shell,
Yet lost ere you transfuse your smell.

You are a dainty violet,
Yet wither'd ere you can be set
Within the virgin's coronet.

You are the queen all flowers among :
But die you must, fair maid, ere long,
As he, the maker of this song.

Robert Herrick.

208

TO MUSIC, TO BECALM HIS FEVER

CHARM me asleep and melt me so
　With thy delicious numbers,
That, being ravished, hence I go
　Away in easy slumbers.

Ease my sick head
And make my bed,
Thou Power that canst sever
From me this ill,
And quickly still,
Though thou not kill
My fever.

Thou sweetly canst convert the same
From a consuming fire
Into a gentle-licking flame,
And make it thus expire.
Then make me weep
My pains asleep,
And give me such reposes
That I, poor I,
May think thereby
I live and die
'Mongst roses.

Fall on me like a silent dew,
Or like those maiden showers
Which, by the peep of day, do strew
A baptism o'er the flowers !
Melt, melt my pains
With thy soft strains,
That, having ease me given,
With full delight
I leave this light,
And take my flight
For heaven !

                                   Robert Herrick.

209

TO THE ROSE: A SONG

Go, happy Rose, and, interwove
With other flowers, bind my love.
Tell her, too, she must not be
Longer flowing, longer free,
That so oft has fetter'd me.

Say, if she 's fretful, I have bands
Of pearl and gold to bind her hands.
Tell her, if she struggle still,
I have myrtle rods (at will)
For to tame, though not to kill.

Take thou my blessing thus, and go
And tell her this—but do not so :
Lest a handsome anger fly
Like a lightning from her eye,
And burn thee up as well as I !

Robert Herrick.

210

TO PRIMROSES FILLED WITH MORNING DEW

WHY do ye weep, sweet babes ? can tears
Speak grief in you,
Who were but born
Just as the modest morn
Teem'd her refreshing dew ?
Alas ! you have not known that shower
That mars a flower ;
Nor felt th' unkind
Breath of a blasting wind ;
Nor are ye worn with years, .
Or wrapp'd as we,
Who think it strange to see
Such pretty flowers, such like to orphans young,
To speak by tears before ye have a tongue.

Speak, whimp'ring younglings, and make known
The reason why
Ye droop and weep.
Is it for want of sleep
Or childish lullaby ?
Or that ye have not seen as yet
The violet ?
Or brought a kiss
From that sweetheart to this ?
No, no, this sorrow shown
By your tears shed
Would have this lecture read :
That things of greatest, so of meanest worth,
Conceiv'd with grief are, and with tears brought forth.

Robert Herrick.

211

TO THE WILLOW TREE

THOU art to all lost love the best,
   The only true plant found,
Wherewith young men and maids, distress'd
   And left of love, are crown'd.

When once the lover's rose is dead
   Or laid aside forlorn,
Then willow-garlands 'bout the head
   Bedew'd with tears are worn.

When with neglect, the lovers' bane,
   Poor maids rewarded be,
For their love lost, their only gain
   Is but a wreath from thee.

And underneath thy cooling shade,
   When weary of the light,
The love-spent youth and love-sick maid
   Come to weep out the night.

Robert Herrick.

212

TO ANTHEA, WHO MAY COMMAND HIM
ANYTHING

BID me to live, and I will live
   Thy Protestant to be;
Or bid me love, and I will give
   A loving heart to thee.

A heart as soft, a heart as kind,
   A heart as sound and free
As in the whole world thou canst find,
   That heart I'll give to thee.

Bid that heart stay, and it will stay
   To honour thy decree;
Or bid it languish quite away,
   And 't shall do so for thee.

Bid me to weep, and I will weep
  While I have eyes to see ;
And, having none, yet I will keep
  A heart to weep for thee.

Bid me despair, and I'll despair
  Under that cypress-tree ;
Or bid me die, and I will dare
  E'en death to die for thee.

Thou art my life, my love, my heart,
  The very eyes of me,
And hast command of every part
  To live and die for thee.

Robert Herrick.

213

TO MEADOWS

YE have been fresh and green,
  Ye have been fill'd with flowers,
And ye the walks have been
  Where maids have spent their hours.

You have beheld how they
  With wicker arks did come
To kiss and bear away
  The richer cowslips home.

You 've heard them sweetly sing,
  And seen them in a round :
Each virgin like a spring,
  With honeysuckles crown'd.

But now we see none here
  Whose silvery feet did tread,
And with dishevell'd hair
  Adorn'd this smoother mead.

Like unthrifts, having spent
  Your stock and needy grown,
Y' are left here to lament
  Your poor estates, alone.

Robert Herrick.

214

TO DAFFODILS

FAIR daffodils, we weep to see
  You haste away so soon :
As yet the early-rising sun
  Has not attain'd his noon.
      Stay, stay,
    Until the hasting day
        Has run
    But to the evensong,
And, having prayed together, we
  Will go with you along.

We have short time to stay as you,
  We have as short a spring,
As quick a growth to meet decay,
  As you, or anything.
      We die,
    As your hours do, and dry
        Away,
    Like to the summer's rain,
Or as the pearls of morning's dew,
  Ne'er to be found again.

Robert Herrick.

215

THE MAD MAID'S SONG

GOOD-morrow to the day so fair,
  Good-morning, sir, to you ;
Good-morrow to mine own torn hair,
  Bedabbled with the dew.

Good-morning to this primrose too,
  Good-morrow to each maid
That will with flowers the tomb bestrew
  Wherein my love is laid.

Ah ! woe is me, woe, woe is me !
  Alack and well-a-day !
For pity, sir, find out that bee
  Which bore my love away.

I'll seek him in your bonnet brave,
   I'll seek him in your eyes ;
Nay, now I think they've made his grave
   I' th' bed of strawberries.

I'll seek him there : I know ere this
   The cold, cold earth doth shake him,
But I will go, or send a kiss
   By you, sir, to awake him.

Pray, hurt him not though he be dead !
   He knows well who do love him,
And who with green turfs rear his head,
   And who do rudely move him.

He's soft and tender (pray take heed !).
   With bands of cowslips bind him,
And bring him home !　But 'tis decreed
   That I shall never find him.
              Robert Herrick.

216

TO DAISIES, NOT TO SHUT SO SOON

SHUT not so soon : the dull-ey'd night
   Has not as yet begun
To make a seizure on the light,
   Or to seal up the sun.

No marigolds yet closéd are,
   No shadows great appear,
Nor doth the early shepherd's star
   Shine like a spangle here.

O, stay but till my Julia close
   Her life-begetting eye,
And let the whole world then dispose
   Itself to live or die !
              Robert Herrick.

217

TO OENONE

WHAT conscience, say, is it in thee,
   When I a heart had one,
To take away that heart from me,
   And to retain thy own?

For shame or pity now incline
  To play a loving part :
Either to send me kindly thine,
  Or give me back my heart.

Covet not both ; but if thou dost
  Resolve to part with neither,
Why ! yet to show that thou art just,
  Take me and mine together.

Robert Herrick.

218

TO THE WATER NYMPHS DRINKING
AT THE FOUNTAIN

REACH, with your whiter hands, to me
  Some crystal of the spring,
And I about the cup shall see
  Fresh lilies flourishing.

Or else, sweet nymphs, do you but this :
  To the glass your lips incline,
And I shall see by that one kiss
  The water turn'd to wine.

Robert Herrick.

219

THE PRIMROSE

ASK me why I send you here
This sweet Infanta of the year?
Ask me why I send to you
This primrose, thus bepearl'd with dew?
I will whisper to your ears :—
The sweets of love are mix'd with tears.

Ask me why this flower does show
So yellow-green, and sickly too?
Ask me why the stalk is weak
And bending (yet it doth not break)?
I will answer :—These discover
What fainting hopes are in a lover.

Robert Herrick.

220

THE NIGHT PIECE: TO JULIA

HER eyes the glow-worm lend thee,
The shooting stars attend thee,
    And the elves also,
    Whose little eyes glow
Like the sparks of fire, befriend thee !

No Will-o'-th'-Wisp mislight thee,
Nor snake nor slow-worm bite thee ;
    But on, on thy way
    Not making a stay,
Since ghost there 's none to affright thee !

Let not the dark thee cumber :
What though the moon does slumber ?
    The stars of the night
    Will lend thee their light,
Like tapers clear without number.

Then, Julia, let me woo thee,
Thus, thus to come unto me !
    And when I shall meet
    Thy silv'ry feet,
My soul I 'll pour into thee.

Robert Herrick.

221

TO ELECTRA

I DARE not ask a kiss,
    I dare not beg a smile,
Lest, having that or this,
    I might grow proud the while.

No, no, the utmost share
    Of my desire shall be
Only to kiss that air
    That lately kisséd thee.

Robert Herrick.

222

A HYMN

O, FLY, my soul ! What hangs upon
Thy drooping wings,
And weighs them down
With love of gaudy mortal things?

The Sun is now i' the east : each shade,
As he doth rise,
Is shorter made,
That earth may lessen to our eyes.

O, be not careless then and play
Until the star of peace
Hide all his beams in dark recess !
Poor pilgrims needs must lose their way,
When all the shadows do increase.

James Shirley.

223

EARTH'S VICTORIES

THE glories of our blood and state
  Are shadows, not substantial things ;
There is no armour against Fate ;
  Death lays his icy hand on kings :
      Sceptre and crown
      Must tumble down,
And in the dust be equal made
With the poor crooked scythe and spade.

Some men with swords may reap the field,
  And plant fresh laurels where they kill ;
But their strong nerves at last must yield—
  They tame but one another still :
      Early or late,
      They stoop to fate,
And must give up their murmuring breath,
When they, pale captives, creep to death.

The garlands wither on your brow,
  Then boast no more your mighty deeds !
Upon Death's purple altar now,
  See where the victor-victim bleeds !

Your heads must come
To the cold tomb;
Only the actions of the just
Smell sweet and blossom in their dust.

James Shirley.

224

DIRGE

HARK! now everything is still,
The screech-owl and the whistler shrill
Call upon our dame aloud,
And bid her quickly don her shroud.
Much you had of land and rent;
Your length in clay's now competent.
A long war disturbed your mind;
Here your perfect peace is signed.
Of what is 't fools make such vain keeping?
Sin their conception, their birth weeping,
Their life a general mist of error,
Their death a hideous storm of terror!
Strew your hair with powders sweet,
Don clean linen, bathe your feet,
And (the foul fiend more to check)
A crucifix let bless your neck:
'Tis now full tide 'tween night and day;
End your groan, and come away.

John Webster.

225

OF TIME

TIME is the feathered thing,
And, whilst I praise
The sparklings of thy looks and call them rays,
Takes wing,
Leaving behind him as he flies
An unperceivéd dimness in thine eyes.
His minutes, whilst they are told,
Do make us old;
And every sand of his fleet glass,
Increasing age as it doth pass,
Insensibly sows wrinkles there
Where flowers and roses do appear.

Whilst we do speak, our fire
Doth into ice expire,
Flames turn to frost ;
And, ere we can
Know how our crow turns swan,
Or how a silver snow
Springs there where jet did grow,
Our fading spring is in dull winter lost'!

Since then the Night hath hurled
Darkness, love's shade,
Over its enemy, the Day, and made
The world
Just such a blind and shapeless thing
As 'twas before light did from darkness spring,
Let us employ its treasure
And make shade pleasure :
Let's number out the hours by blisses,
And count the minutes by our kisses ;
Let the heavens new motions feel
And by our embraces wheel ;
And whilst we try the way
By which Love doth convey
Soul into soul,
And, mingling, so
Makes them such raptures know
As makes them entrancéd lie
In mutual ecstasy,
Let the harmonious spheres in music roll !

Jasper Mayne.

226

THE LARK NOW LEAVES

THE lark now leaves his wat'ry nest,
And, climbing, shakes his dewy wings.
He takes this window for the east,
And to implore your light, he sings :—
'Awake, awake ! the morn will never rise,
Till she can dress her beauty at your eyes.'

The merchant bows unto the seaman's star,
The ploughman from the sun his season takes ;
But still the lover wonders what they are,
Who look for day before his mistress wakes.

N

Awake, awake ! break thro' your veils of lawn !
Then draw your curtains, and begin the dawn.

William Davenant.

227

THE SOLDIER GOING TO THE WARS

PRESERVE thy sighs, unthrifty girl,
  To purify the air !
Thy tears to thread, instead of pearl,
  On bracelets of thy hair !

The trumpet makes the echo hoarse,
  And wakes the louder drum ;
Expense of grief gains no remorse,
  When sorrow should be dumb.

For I must go where lazy Peace
  Will hide her drowsy head,
And, for the sport of kings, increase
  The number of the dead.

But first I'll chide thy cruel theft !
  Can I in war delight,
Who, being of my heart bereft,
  Can have no heart to fight ?

Thou know'st the sacred laws of old
  Ordain'd a thief should pay,
To quit him of his theft, sevenfold
  What he had stolen away ?

Thy payment shall but double be :
  O, then with speed resign
My own seducéd heart to me,
  Accompanied with thine.

William Davenant.

228

WAKE, ALL THE DEAD

WAKE, all the dead ! What ho ! what ho !
How soundly they sleep whose pillows lie low !
They mind not poor lovers, who walk above
On the decks of the world in storms of love.

No whisper now nor glance shall pass
Through wickets or through panes of glass,
For our windows and doors are shut and barred.
Lie close in the church, and in the churchyard !
In every grave make room, make room !
The world 's at an end, and we come, we come !

The State is now Love's foe, Love's foe :
'T has seized on his arms, his quiver and bow,
Has pinioned his wings, and fettered his feet,
Because he made way for lovers to meet.
But, O sad chance, his judge was old !
Hearts cruel grow, when blood grows cold.
No man being young his process would draw.
O heavens, that love should be subject to law !
Lovers go woo the dead, the dead !
Lie two in a grave, and to bed, to bed !

William Davenant.

229

TO ROSES IN THE BOSOM OF CASTARA

YE blushing virgins happy are
In the chaste nunn'ry of her breasts,
For he 'd profane so chaste a fair,
Who ere should call them Cupid's nests.

Transplanted thus how bright ye grow !
How rich a perfume do ye yield !
In some close garden, cowslips so
Are sweeter than i 'th' open field.

In those white cloisters live secure
From the rude blasts of wanton breath,
Each hour more innocent and pure,
Till you shall wither into death.

Then that which living gave you room,
Your glorious sepulchre shall be.
There wants no marble for a tomb,
Whose breast hath marble been to me.

William Habington.

230

GO, LOVELY ROSE

Go, lovely Rose—
Tell her, that wastes her time and me,
    That now she knows,
When I resemble her to thee,
How sweet and fair she seems to be.

    Tell her, that's young
And shuns to have her graces spied,
    That, hadst thou sprung
In deserts where no men abide,
Thou must have uncommended died.

    Small is the worth
Of beauty from the light retired :
    Bid her come forth,
Suffer herself to be desired,
And not blush so to be admired.

    Then die—that she
The common fate of all things rare
    May read in thee :
How small a part of time they share
That are so wondrous sweet and fair.

Edmund Waller.

231

ON A GIRDLE

THAT which her slender waist confined
Shall now my joyful temples bind :
No monarch but would give his crown
His arms might do what this has done.

It was my Heaven's extremest sphere,
The pale which held that lovely deer :
My joy, my grief, my hope, my love
Did all within this circle move.

A narrow compass !   And yet there
Dwelt all that's good, and all that's fair !
Give me but what this ribband bound,
Take all the rest the Sun goes round.

Edmund Waller.

232

THE ART OF LOVE

HONEST lover whosoever,
If in all thy love there ever
Was one wav'ring thought, if thy flame
Were not still ever, still the same :
      Know this,
      Thou lov'st amiss ;
      And to love true,
Thou must begin again, and love anew.

If when she appears i' th' room,
Thou dost not quake, and art struck dumb,
And in striving this to cover
Dost not speak thy words twice over :
      Know this,
      Thou lov'st amiss ;
      And to love true,
Thou must begin again, and love anew.

If fondly thou dost not mistake,
And all defects for graces take ;
Persuad'st thy self that jests are broken,
When she hath little or nothing spoken :
      Know this,
      Thou lov'st amiss ;
      And to love true,
Thou must begin again, and love anew.

If when thou appear'st to be within,
Thou lett'st not men ask and ask again ;
And when thou answer'st, if it be
To what was ask'd thee properly :
      Know this,
      Thou lov'st amiss ;
      And to love true,
Thou must begin again, and love anew.

If when thy stomach calls to eat,
Thou cutt'st not fingers 'stead of meat,
And with much gazing on her face
Dost not rise hungry from the place :
      Know this,
      Thou lov'st amiss ;
      And to love true,
Thou must begin again, and love anew.

If by this thou dost discover
That thou art no perfect lover,
And desiring to love true,
Thou dost begin to love anew :
          Know this,
          Thou lov'st amiss ;
          And to love true,
Thou must begin again, and love anew.

John Suckling.

233

OUT UPON IT! I HAVE LOVED

OUT upon it ! I have loved
   Three whole days together,
And am like to love three more,
   If it prove fair weather !

Time shall moult away his wings,
   Ere he shall discover
In the whole wide world again
   Such a constant lover.

But the spite on 't is, no praise
   Is due at all to me :
Love with me had made no stays,
   Had it any been but she.

Had it any been but she,
   And that very face,
There had been at least e'er this
   A dozen dozen in her place !

John Suckling.

234

I PRITHEE, SEND ME BACK MY HEART

I PRITHEE, send me back my heart,
   Since I cannot have thine :
For if from yours you will not part,
   Why then shouldst thou have mine ?

Yet now I think on 't—let it lie!
  To find it were in vain:
For thou 'st a thief in either eye
  Would steal it back again.

Why should two hearts in one breast lie,
  And yet not lodge together?
O Love, where is thy sympathy,
  If thus our breasts thou sever?

But love is such a mystery
  I cannot find it out;
For when I think I 'm best resolved,
  I then am in most doubt.

Then farewell care, and farewell woe!
  I will no longer pine:
For I 'll believe I have her heart,
  As much as she has mine.
John Suckling.

235

WHEN, DEAREST, I BUT THINK OF THEE

WHEN, dearest, I but think of thee,
Methinks all things that lovely be
  Are present, and my soul delighted;
For beauties that from worth arise
Are like the grace of deities,
  Still present with us, tho' unsighted.

Thus, whilst I sit, and sigh the day
With all his borrow'd lights away,
  Till night's black wings do overtake me,
Thinking on thee, thy beauties then,
As sudden lights do sleepy men,
  So they by their bright rays awake me.

Thus absence dies, and dying proves
No absence can subsist with loves
  That do partake of fair perfection:
Since in the darkest night they may,
By love's quick motion, find a way
  To see each other by reflection.

The waving sea can with each flood
Bathe some high promont, that has stood
    Far from the main up in the river :
O, think not then but love can do
As much, for that's an ocean too,
    Which flows, not every day but, ever !

John Suckling.

236

HYMN ON THE MORNING OF CHRIST'S NATIVITY

IT was the winter wild,
    While the heaven-born child
All meanly wrapt in the rude manger lies ;
    Nature, in awe to him,
    Had doffed her gaudy trim,
With her great Master so to sympathise :
It was no season then for her
To wanton with the Sun, her lusty paramour.

    Only with speeches fair
    She woos the gentle air
To hide her guilty front with innocent snow,
    And on her naked shame,
    Pollute with sinful blame,
The saintly veil of maiden white to throw ;
Confounded, that her Maker's eyes
Should look so near upon her foul deformities.

    But He, her fears to cease,
    Sent down the meek-eyed Peace :
She, crowned with olive green, came softly sliding
    Down through the turning sphere,
    His ready harbinger,
With turtle wing the amorous clouds dividing ;
And, waving wide her myrtle wand,
She strikes a universal peace through sea and land.

    No war, or battle's sound,
    Was heard the world around ;
The idle spear and shield were high uphung ;
    The hookéd chariot stood
    Unstained with hostile blood ;
The trumpet spake not to the arméd throng ;

And kings sat still with awful eye,
As if they surely knew their sovran Lord was by.

But peaceful was the night
Wherein the Prince of Light
His reign of peace upon the earth began.
The winds, with wonder whist,
Smoothly the waters kissed,
Whispering new joys to the mild Oceán,
Who now hath quite forgot to rave,
While birds of calm sit brooding on the charmèd wave.

The stars, with deep amaze,
Stand fixed in steadfast gaze,
Bending one way their precious influence,
And will not take their flight
For all the morning light,
Or Lucifer that often warned them thence ;
But in their glimmering orbs did glow,
Until their Lord himself bespake, and bid them go.

And, though the shady Gloom
Had given Day her room,
The Sun himself withheld his wonted speed,
And hid his head for shame,
As his inferior flame
The new-enlightened world no more should need :
He saw a greater Sun appear
Than his bright throne or burning axletree could bear.

The shepherds on the lawn,
Or ere the point of dawn,
Sat simply chatting in a rustic row :
Full little thought they than
That the mighty Pan
Was kindly come to live with them below :
Perhaps their loves, or else their sheep,
Was all that did their silly thoughts so busy keep.

When such music sweet
Their hearts and ears did greet
As never was by mortal finger strook,
Divinely-warbled voice
Answering the stringed noise,
As all their souls in blissful rapture took :
The air, such pleasure loth to lose,
With thousand echoes still prolongs each heavenly close.

Nature, that heard such sound
Beneath the hollow round
Of Cynthia's seat the Airy region thrilling,
Now was almost won
To think her part was done,
And that her reign had here its last fulfilling :
She knew such harmony alone
Could hold all Heaven and Earth in happier union.

At last surrounds their sight
A globe of circular light,
That with long beams the shamefaced Night arrayed ;
The helméd Cherubim
And sworded Seraphim
Are seen in glittering ranks with wings displayed,
Harping in loud and solemn quire,
With unexpressive notes, to Heaven's new-born Heir.

Such music (as 'tis said)
Before was never made
But when of old the Sons of Morning sung,
While the Creator great
His constellations set,
And the well-balanced World on hinges hung,
And cast the dark foundations deep,
And bid the weltering waves their oozy channel keep.

Ring out, ye crystal spheres !
Once bless our human ears,
If ye have power to touch our senses so ;
And let your silver chime
Move in melodious time ;
And let the bass of heaven's deep organ blow ;
And with your ninefold harmony
Make up full consort to the angelic symphony.

For, if such holy song
Enwrap our fancy long,
Time will run back and fetch the Age of Gold ;
And speckled Vanity
Will sicken soon and die ;
And leprous Sin will melt from earthly mould ;
And Hell itself will pass away,
And leave her dolorous mansions to the peering day.

Yea, Truth and Justice then
Will down return to men,
Orbed in a rainbow ; and, like glories wearing,

Mercy will sit between,
Throned in celestial sheen,
With radiant feet the tissued clouds down steering;
And Heaven, as at some festival,
Will open wide the gates of her high palace-hall.

But wisest Fate says :—No,
This must not yet be so;
The Babe yet lies in smiling infancy
That on the bitter cross
Must redeem our loss,
So both himself and us to glorify :
Yet first, to those ychained in sleep,
The wakeful trump of doom must thunder through the deep,

With such a horrid clang
As on Mount Sinai rang,
While the red fire and smouldering clouds outbrake :
The aged Earth, aghast,
With terror of that blast,
Shall from the surface to the centre shake,
When, at the world's last sessión,
The dreadful Judge in middle air shall spread his throne.

And then at last our bliss
Full and perfect is,
But now begins; for from this happy day
The Old Dragon under ground,
In straiter limits bound,
Not half so far casts his usurpéd sway,
And, wroth to see his kingdom fail,
Swinges the scaly horror of his folded tail.

The Oracles are dumb;
No voice or hideous hum
Runs through the archéd roof in words deceiving.
Apollo from his shrine
Can no more divine,
With hollow shriek the steep of Delphos leaving.
No nightly trance, or breathéd spell,
Inspires the pale-eyed priest from the prophetic cell.

The lonely mountains o'er,
And the resounding shore,
A voice of weeping heard and loud lament;
From haunted spring, and dale
Edged with poplar pale,
The parting Genius is with sighing sent;

With flower-inwoven tresses torn
The Nymphs in twilight shade of tangled thickets mourn.

    In consecrated earth,
    And on the holy hearth,
The Lars and Lemures moan with midnight plaint ;
    In urns, and altars round,
    A drear and dying sound
Affrights the flamens at their service quaint ;
And the chill marble seems to sweat,
While each peculiar Power forgoes his wonted seat.

    Peor and Baälim
    Forsake their temples dim,
With that twice-battered God of Palestine ;
    And moonéd Ashtaroth,
    Heaven's queen and mother both,
Now sits not girt with tapers' holy shine ;
The Libyc Hammon shrinks his horn ;
In vain the Tyrian maids their wounded Thammuz mourn.

    And sullen Moloch, fled,
    Hath left in shadows dread
His burning idol all of blackest hue :
    In vain with cymbal's ring
    They call the grisly king,
In dismal dance about the furnace blue ;
The brutish gods of Nile as fast,
Isis, and Orus, and the dog Anubis, haste.

    Nor is Osiris seen
    In Memphian grove or green,
Trampling the unshowered grass with lowings loud :
    Nor can he be at rest
    Within his sacred chest ;
Nought but profoundest Hell can be his shroud ;
In vain, with timbrelled anthems dark,
The sable-stoléd sorcerers bear his worshipped ark.

    He feels from Juda's land
    The dreaded Infant's hand ;
The rays of Bethlehem blind his dusky eye ;
    Nor all the gods beside
    Longer dare abide,
Not Typhon huge ending in snaky twine :
Our Babe, to show his Godhead true,
Can in his swaddling bands control the damnéd crew.

So, when the sun in bed,
Curtained with cloudy red,
Pillows his chin upon an orient wave,
The flocking shadows pale
Troop to the infernal jail,
Each fettered ghost slips to his several grave,
And the yellow-skirted fays
Fly after the night-steeds, leaving their moon-loved maze.

But see ! the Virgin blest
Hath laid her Babe to rest.
Time is our tedious song should here have ending :
Heaven's youngest-teeméd star
Hath fixed her polished car,
Her sleeping Lord with handmaid lamp attending ;
And all about the courtly stable
Bright-harnessed Angels sit in order serviceable.

John Milton.

237

AT A SOLEMN MUSIC

BLEST pair of Sirens, pledges of Heaven's joy,
Sphere-born harmonious sisters, Voice and Verse,
Wed your divine sounds, and mixed power employ,
Dead things with inbreathed sense able to pierce ;
And to our high-raised phantasy present
That undisturbéd song of pure concent
Aye sung before the sapphire-coloured throne
To Him that sits thereon,
With saintly shout and solemn jubilee :
Where the bright Seraphim in burning row
Their loud uplifted angel-trumpets blow,
And the Cherubic host in thousand quires
Touch their immortal harps of golden wires,
With those just Spirits, that wear victorious palms,
Hymns devout and holy psalms
Singing everlastingly :
That we on Earth, with undiscording voice,
May rightly answer that melodious noise ;
As once we did, till disproportioned sin
Jarred against nature's chime, and with harsh din
Broke the fair music that all creatures made
To their great Lord, whose love their motion swayed
In perfect diapason, whilst they stood
In first obedience, and their state of good.

O, may we soon again renew that song,
And keep in tune with Heaven, till God ere long
To His celestial consort us unite,
To live with Him, and sing in endless morn of light !

John Milton.

238

ON TIME

FLY, envious Time, till thou run out thy race :
Call on the lazy leaden-stepping Hours,
Whose speed is but the heavy plummet's pace :
And glut thyself with what thy womb devours,
Which is no more than what is false and vain,
And merely mortal dross ;
So little is our loss,
So little is thy gain !
For, when as each thing bad thou hast entombed,
And, last of all, thy greedy self consumed,
Then long Eternity shall greet our bliss
With an individual kiss,
And joy shall overtake us as a flood ;
When every thing that is sincerely good
And perfectly divine,
With Truth, and Peace, and Love, shall ever shine
About the supreme throne
Of Him, to whose happy-making sight alone
When once our heavenly-guided soul shall climb,
Then, all this earthly grossness quit,
Attired with stars we shall for ever sit,
Triumphing over Death, and Chance, and thee, O Time !

John Milton.

239

THE SONG OF COMUS

THE star that bids the shepherd fold
Now the top of heaven doth hold,
And the gilded car of day
His glowing axle doth allay
In the steep Atlantic stream,
And the slope sun his upward beam
Shoots against the dusky pole,

Pacing toward the other goal
Of his chamber in the east.
Meanwhile welcome joy and feast,
Midnight shout and revelry,
Tipsy dance and jollity !
Braid your locks with rosy twine,
Dropping odours, dropping wine !
Rigour now has gone to bed ;
And Advice with scrupulous head,
Strict Age, and sour Severity,
With their grave saws, in slumber lie.
We, that are of purer fire,
Imitate the starry quire,
Who, in their nightly watchful spheres,
Lead in swift round the months and years.
The sounds and seas, with all their finny drove,
Now to the moon in wavering morrice move ;
And, on the tawny sands and shelves,
Trip the pert faeries and the dapper elves.
By dimpled brook and fountain-brim
The wood nymphs, decked with daisies trim,
Their merry wakes and pastimes keep—
What hath night to do with sleep?
Night hath better sweets to prove :
Venus now wakes, and wakens Love.
Come, let us our rites begin
—'Tis only daylight that makes sin—
Which these dun shades will ne'er report.

Hail, Goddess of nocturnal sport,
Dark-veiled Cotytto, to whom the secret flame
Of midnight torches burns !   Mysterious dame,
That ne'er art called but when the dragon-womb
Of Stygian darkness spets her thickest gloom,
And makes one blot of all the air,
Stay thy cloudy ebon chair,
Wherein thou ridest with Hecate, and befriend
Us thy vowed priests, till utmost end
Of all thy dues be done, and none left out :
Ere the blabbing eastern scout,
The nice Morn, on the Indian steep,
From her cabined loophole peep,
And to the tell-tale Sun descry
Our concealed solemnity !
Come, knit hands, and beat the ground
In a light fantastic round !

John Milton.

240

THE INVOCATION TO SABRINA

SABRINA fair,
Listen, where thou art sitting
Under the glassy, cool, translucent wave,
In twisted braid of lilies knitting
The loose train of thy amber-dropping hair !
Listen for dear honour's sake,
Goddess of the silver lake,
Listen, and save !
Listen and appear to us,
In name of great Oceanus ;
By the earth-shaking Neptune's mace,
And Tethys' grave majestic pace ;
By hoary Nereus' wrinkled look,
And the Carpathian wizard's hook ;
By scaly Triton's winding shell,
And old soothsaying Glaucus' spell ;
By Leucothea's lovely hands,
And her son that rules the strands ;
By Thetis' tinsel-slippered feet,
And the songs of Sirens sweet ;
By dead Parthenope's dear tomb,
And fair Ligeia's golden comb,
Wherewith she sits on diamond-rocks,
Sleeking her soft alluring locks ;
By all the nymphs that nightly dance
Upon thy streams with wily glance :
Rise, rise, and heave thy rosy head
From thy coral-paven bed,
And bridle in thy headlong wave,
Till thou our summons answered have !
Listen, and save !

John Milton.

241

THE SPIRIT EPILOGUISES

To the ocean now I fly,
And those happy climes that lie
Where day never shuts his eye,
Up in the broad fields of the sky !

There I suck the liquid air,
All amidst the gardens fair
Of Hesperus, and his daughters three
That sing about the golden tree.
Along the crispéd shades and bowers
Revels the spruce and jocund Spring;
The Graces, and the rosy-bosomed Hours,
Thither all their bounties bring.
There eternal summer dwells,
And west-winds with musky wing
About the cedarn alleys fling
Nard and cassia's balmy smells.
Iris there with humid bow
Waters the odorous banks, that blow
Flowers of more mingled hue
Than her purfled scarf can show,
And drenches with Elysian dew
—List, mortals, if your ears be true!—
Beds of hyacinth and roses,
Where young Adonis oft reposes,
Waxing well of his deep wound,
In slumber soft; and on the ground
Sadly sits the Assyrian queen.
But far above, in spangled sheen,
Celestial Cupid her famed son advanced
Holds his dear Psyche, sweet entranced
After her wandering labours long,
Till free consent the gods among
Makes her his eternal bride;
And from her fair unspotted side
Two blissful twins are to be born,
Youth and Joy—so Jove hath sworn!

But now my task is smoothly done:
I can fly or I can run
Quickly to the green earth's end,
Where the bowed welkin slow doth bend,
And from thence can soar as soon
To the corners of the moon.

John Milton.

242

LYCIDAS

YET once more, O ye laurels, and once more,
Ye myrtles brown, with ivy never sere,

O

I come to pluck your berries harsh and crude,
And with forced fingers rude
Shatter your leaves before the mellowing year !
Bitter constraint and sad occasion dear
Compels me to disturb your season due ;
For Lycidas is dead, dead ere his prime,
Young Lycidas, and hath not left his peer !
Who would not sing for Lycidas ? he knew
Himself to sing, and build the lofty rhyme.
He must not float upon his watery bier
Unwept, and welter to the parching wind,
Without the meed of some melodious tear.

   Begin, then, Sisters of the sacred well
That from beneath the seat of Jove doth spring ;
Begin, and somewhat loudly sweep the string.
Hence with denial vain and coy excuse :
So may some gentle Muse
With lucky words favour my destined urn,
And, as he passes, turn
And bid fair peace be to my sable shroud !

   For we were nursed upon the self-same hill,
Fed the same flock, by fountain, shade, and rill ;
Together both, ere the high lawns appeared
Under the opening eyelids of the Morn,
We drove a-field, and both together heard
What time the grey-fly winds her sultry horn,
Battening our flocks with the fresh dews of night,
Oft till the star that rose at evening bright
Toward heaven's descent had sloped his westering wheel.
Meanwhile the rural ditties were not mute :
Tempered to the oaten flute,
Rough Satyrs danced, and Fauns with cloven heel
From the glad sound would not be absent long ;
And old Damœtas loved to hear our song.

   But, O ! the heavy change, now thou art gone,
Now thou art gone and never must return !
Thee, Shepherd, thee the woods and desert caves,
With wild thyme and the gadding vine o'ergrown,
And all their echoes, mourn.   .
The willows, and the hazel copses green,
Shall now no more be seen
Fanning their joyous leaves to thy soft lays.
As killing as the canker to the rose,
Or taint-worm to the weanling herds that graze,

Or frost to flowers, that their gay wardrobe wear,
When first the white-thorn blows :
Such, Lycidas, thy loss to shepherd's ear.

   Where were ye, Nymphs, when the remorseless deep
Closed o'er the head of your loved Lycidas?
For neither were ye playing on the steep
Where your old bards, the famous Druids, lie,
Nor on the shaggy top of Mona high,
Nor yet where Deva spreads her wizard stream.
Ay me ! I fondly dream
' Had ye been there ' . . . for what could that have done ?
What could the Muse herself that Orpheus bore,
The Muse herself, for her enchanting son,
Whom universal nature did lament,
When by the rout that made the hideous roar,
His gory visage down the stream was sent,
Down the swift Hebrus to the Lesbian shore ?

   Alas ! what boots it with incessant care
To tend the homely, slighted, shepherd's trade,
And strictly meditate the thankless Muse?
Were it not better done, as others use,
To sport with Amaryllis in the shade,
Or with the tangles of Neæra's hair ?
Fame is the spur that the clear spirit doth raise
(That last infirmity of noble mind)
To scorn delights and live laborious days ;
But, the fair guerdon when we hope to find,
And think to burst out into sudden blaze,
Comes the blind Fury with the abhorréd shears,
And slits the thin-spun life.   ' But not the praise,'
Phœbus replied, and touched my trembling ears :
' Fame is no plant that grows on mortal soil,
Nor in the glistering foil
Set off to the world, nor in broad rumour lies,
But lives and spreads aloft by those pure eyes
And perfect witness of all-judging Jove ;
As he pronounces lastly on each deed,
Of so much fame in heaven expect thy meed.'

   O fountain Arethuse, and thou honoured flood,
Smooth-sliding Mincius, crowned with vocal reeds,
That strain I heard was of a higher mood.
But now my oat proceeds,
And listens to the Herald of the Sea,
That came in Neptune's plea.

He asked the waves, and asked the felon winds,
What hard mishap hath doomed this gentle swain?
And questioned every gust of rugged wings
That blows from off each beakéd promontory.
They knew not of his story;
And sage Hippotades their answer brings,
That not a blast was from his dungeon strayed:
The air was calm, and on the level brine
Sleek Panope with all her sisters played.
It was that fatal and perfidious bark,
Built in the eclipse and rigged with curses dark,
That sunk so low that sacred head of thine.

Next, Camus, reverend sire, went footing slow,
His mantle hairy, and his bonnet sedge,
Inwrought with figures dim, and on the edge
Like to that sanguine flower inscribed with woe.
'Ah! who hath reft,' quoth he, 'my dearest pledge?'
Last came, and last did go,
The Pilot of the Galilean Lake;
Two massy keys he bore of metals twain
(The golden opes, the iron shuts amain).
He shook his mitred locks, and stern bespake :—
'How well could I have spared for thee, young swain,
Enow of such as, for their bellies' sake,
Creep, and intrude, and climb into the fold!
Of other care they little reckoning make
Than how to scramble at the shearers' feast,
And shove away the worthy bidden guest.
Blind mouths! that scarce themselves know how to hold
A sheep-hook, or have learnt aught else the least
That to the faithful herdman's art belongs!
What recks it them? What need they? They are sped;
And, when they list, their lean and flashy songs
Grate on their scrannel pipes of wretched straw;
The hungry sheep look up, and are not fed,
But, swoln with wind and the rank mist they draw,
Rot inwardly, and foul contagion spread;
Besides what the grim wolf with privy paw
Daily devours apace, and nothing said.
But that two-handed engine at the door
Stands ready to smite once, and smite no more.'

Return, Alpheus; the dread voice is past
That shrunk thy streams! Return, Sicilian Muse,
And call the vales, and bid them hither cast
Their bells and flowerets of a thousand hues!

Ye valleys low, where the mild whispers use
Of shades, and wanton winds, and gushing brooks,
On whose fresh lap the swart star sparely looks,
Throw hither all your quaint enamelled eyes,
That on the green turf suck the honeyed showers,
And purple all the ground with vernal flowers.
Bring the rathe primrose that forsaken dies,
The tufted crow-toe, and pale jessamine,
The white pink, and the pansy freaked with jet,
The glowing violet,
The musk-rose, and the well-attired woodbine,
With cowslips wan that hang the pensive head,
And every flower that sad embroidery wears;
Bid amaranthus all his beauty shed,
And daffadillies fill their cups with tears,
To strew the laureate hearse where Lycid lies.
For so, to interpose a little ease,
Let our frail thoughts dally with false surmise,
Ay me! whilst thee the shores and sounding seas
Wash far away, where'er thy bones are hurled:
Whether beyond the stormy Hebrides,
Where thou perhaps under the whelming tide
Visit'st the bottom of the monstrous world;
Or whether thou, to our moist vows denied,
Sleep'st by the fable of Bellerus old,
Where the great Vision of the guarded mount
Looks toward Namancos and Bayona's hold.
Look homeward, Angel, now, and melt with ruth:
And, O ye dolphins, waft the hapless youth!

Weep no more, woful shepherds, weep no more,
For Lycidas, your sorrow, is not dead,
Sunk though he be beneath the watery floor!
So sinks the day-star in the ocean bed,
And yet anon repairs his drooping head,
And tricks his beams, and with new-spangled ore
Flames in the forehead of the morning sky;
So Lycidas sunk low, but mounted high,
Through the dear might of Him that walked the waves,
Where, other groves and other streams along,
With nectar pure his oozy locks he laves,
And hears the unexpressive nuptial song,
In the blest kingdoms meek of joy and love.
There entertain him all the Saints above,
In solemn troops, and sweet societies,
That sing, and singing in their glory move,
And wipe the tears for ever from his eyes.

Now, Lycidas, the shepherds weep no more ;
Henceforth thou art the Genius of the shore,
In thy large recompense, and shalt be good
To all that wander in that perilous flood.

    Thus sang the uncouth swain to the oaks and rills,
While the still morn went out with sandals grey :
He touched the tender stops of various quills,
With eager thought warbling his Doric lay :
And now the sun had stretched out all the hills,
And now was dropt into the western bay.
At last he rose, and twitched his mantle blue :
To-morrow to fresh woods, and pastures new.

                    John Milton.

243

SWEET ECHO

SWEET Echo, sweetest Nymph, that liv'st unseen
Within thy airy shell
By slow Meander's margent green,
And in the violet-embroidered vale
Where the love-lorn Nightingale
Nightly to thee her sad song mourneth well :
Canst thou not tell me of a gentle pair
That likest thy Narcissus are ?
O, if thou have
Hid them in some flowery cave,
Tell me but where,
Sweet Queen of Parley, Daughter of the Sphere !
So may'st thou be translated to the skies,
And give resounding grace to all Heaven's harmonies !

                    John Milton.

244

OUT OF ADVERSITY

O, HOW comely it is, and how reviving
To the spirits of just men long oppressed,
When God into the hands of their deliverer

Puts invincible might
To quell the mighty of the earth, the oppressor,
The brute and boisterous force of violent men,
Hardy and industrious to support
Tyrannic power, but raging to pursue
The righteous and all such as honour truth !
He all their ammunition
And feats of war defeats,
With plain heroic magnitude of mind
And celestial vigour armed ;
Their armouries and magazines contemns,
Renders them useless, while
With wingèd expedition
Swift as the lightning glance he executes
His errand on the wicked, who, surprised,
Lose their defence, distracted and amazed.

John Milton.

245

BID ME NOT GO

BID me not go where neither suns nor showers
Do make or cherish flowers ;
Where discontented things in sadness lie,
And Nature grieves as I !
When I am parted from those eyes,
From which my better day doth rise,
Though some propitious power
Should plant me in a bower,
Where amongst happy lovers I might see
How showers and sunbeams bring
One everlasting spring,
Nor would those fall, nor these shine forth to me.
Nature herself to him is lost,
Who loseth her he honours most !
Then, fairest, to my parting view display
Your graces all in one full day,
Whose blessed shapes I 'll snatch and keep, till when
I do return and view again :
So by this art fancy shall fortune cross,
And lovers live by thinking on their loss !

William Cartwright.

246

THE CARELESS GALLANT

Let us sing and be merry, dance, joke, and rejoice,
With claret and sherry, theorbo and voice !
The changeable world to our joy is unjust,
    All treasure 's uncertain,
    Then down with your dust :
In frolicks dispose your pounds, shillings, and pence,
For we shall be nothing a hundred years hence.

We 'll sport and be free, with Frank, Betty, and Dolly,
Have lobsters and oysters to cure melancholy :
Fish-dinners will make a man spring like a flea,
    Dame Venus, love's lady,
    Was born of the sea :
With her and with Bacchus we 'll tickle the sense,
For we shall be past it a hundred years hence.

Your most beautiful bit, who hath all eyes upon her,
That her honesty sells for a hogo of honour,
Whose lightness and brightness doth cast such a splendeur
    That none but the stars
    Are thought fit to attend her,
Though now she seems pleasant and sweet to the sense,
Will be damnable mouldy a hundred years hence.

Then why should we turmoil in cares and in fears,
And turn our tranquillity to sighs and tears ?
Let 's eat, drink, and play, ere the worms do corrupt us,
    For I say, that *Post mortem*
    Nulla voluptas !
Let 's deal with our damsels, that we may from thence
Have broods to succeed us a hundred years hence !

                        Thomas Jordan.

247

MY DEAR AND ONLY LOVE

My dear and only love, I pray
    That little world of thee
Be governed by no other sway
    But purest monarchy ;
For if confusion have a part,
    Which virtuous souls abhor,
And hold a synod in thy heart,
    I 'll never love thee more.

Like Alexander I will reign,
   And I will reign alone:
My thoughts did evermore disdain
   A rival on my throne.
He either fears his fate too much,
   Or his deserts are small,
Who dares not put it to the touch,
   To gain or lose it all.

But, if thou wilt prove faithful then
   And constant of thy word,
I 'll make thee glorious by my pen,
   And famous by my sword ;
I 'll serve thee in such noble ways
   Was never heard before ;
I 'll crown and deck thee all with bays,
   And love thee more and more.

         James Graham, Marquis of Montrose.

248

ON A PRAYER-BOOK SENT TO MRS. M. R.

Lo, here a little volume, but great book !
A nest of new-born sweets,
Whose native pages, disdaining
To be thus folded and complaining
Of these ignoble sheets,
Affect more comely bands,
Fair one, from thy kind hands,
And confidently look
To find the rest
Of a rich binding in your breast !

It is in one choice handful, Heaven ; and all
Heaven's royal hosts encamp'd, thus small
To prove that true schools use to tell,
A thousand angels in one point can dwell.

It is love's great artillery,
Which here contracts itself, and comes to lie
Close couch'd in their white bosom ; and from thence,
As from a snowy fortress of defence,
Against their ghostly foe to take their part,
And fortify the hold of your chaste heart.

It is an armoury of light ;
Let constant use but keep it bright,
You 'll find it yields
To holy hands and humble hearts
More swords and shields
Than sin hath snares, or hell hath darts.

Only be sure
The hands be pure
That hold these weapons, and the eyes
Those of turtles, chaste, and true,
Wakeful, and wise,
Here 's a friend shall fight for you.
Hold but this book before your heart,
Let Prayer alone to play his part !

But, O I the heart
That studies this high art
Must be a sure housekeeper,
And yet no sleeper.
Dear soul, be strong,
Mercy will come ere long,
And bring her bosom full of blessings,
Flowers of never-fading graces
To make immortal dressings
For worthy souls, whose wise embraces
Store up themselves for Him who is alone
The spouse of virgins, and the Virgin's Son !

But if the noble bridegroom when He comes
Shall find the wand'ring heart from home,
Leaving her chaste abode
To gad abroad,
Amongst the gay mates of the God of Flies
To take her pleasure, and to play
And keep the Devil's holy day ;
To dance in the sunshine of some smiling,
But beguiling

Spheres of sweet and sugar'd lies,
Some slippery pair
Of false, perhaps, as fair,
Flattering but forswearing eyes :

Doubtless some other heart
Will get the start
Meanwhile, and, stepping in before,
Will take possession of that sacred store

Of hidden sweets and holy joys ;
Words which are not heard with ears—
These tumultuous shops of noise ;
Effectual whispers, whose still voice
The soul itself more feels than hears ;

Amorous languishments, luminous trances,
Sights which are not seen with eyes ;
Spiritual and soul-piercing glances,
Whose pure and subtle lightning flies
Home to the heart, and sets the house on fire,
And melts it down in sweet desire,
Yet does not stay
To ask the windows leave to pass that way :

Delicious deaths, soft exhalations
Of soul ; dear and divine annihilations ;
A thousand unknown rites
Of joys, and rarified delights ;

A hundred thousand goods, glories, and graces,
And many a mystic thing,
Which the divine embraces
Of the dear Spouse of Spirits with them will bring,
For which it is no shame
That dull mortality must not know a name :

Of all this store
Of blessings, and ten thousand more,
If when He come
He find the heart from home,
Doubtless He will unload
Himself some otherwhere,
And pour abroad
His precious sweets,
On the fair soul whom first he meets.

O fair ! O fortunate ! O rich ! O dear !
O happy, and thrice happy she,
Dear silver-breasted dove
Whoe'er she be,
Whose early love,
With wingéd vows,
Makes haste to meet her morning spouse,
And close with his immortal kisses !
Happy, indeed, who never misses

To improve that precious hour,
And every day
Seize her sweet prey,
All fresh and fragrant as he rises,
Dropping with a balmy shower,
A delicious dew of spices !

O, let the blessful heart hold fast
Her heavenly armful, she shall taste
At once ten thousand paradises !
She shall have power
To rifle and deflower
The rich and roseal spring of those rare sweets,
Which with a swelling bosom there she meets,
Boundless and infinite, bottomless treasures
Of pure inebriating pleasures !
Happy proof she shall discover,
What joy, what bliss,
How many heavens at once it is,
To have a God become her lover !

Richard Crashaw.

249

ON THE GLORIOUS ASSUMPTION OF THE BLESSED VIRGIN

HARK ! she is call'd, the parting hour is come ;
Take thy farewell, poor world, Heaven must go home.
A piece of heavenly light, purer and brighter
Than the chaste stars, whose choice lamps come to light her,
While through the crystal orbs, clearer than they,
She climbs, and makes a far more milky way.
She's call'd again ; hark l how th' immortal Dove
Sighs to his silver mate :—' Rise up, my love,
Rise up, my fair, my spotless one !
The winter 's past, the rain is gone :
The spring is come, the flowers appear,
No sweets, since thou are wanting here.
Come away, my love ;
Come away, my dove ;
Cast off delay :
The court of heav'n is come,
To wait upon thee home ;
Come away, come away ! '

She's call'd again, and will she go?
When Heav'n bids come, who can say no?
Heav'n calls her, and she must away;
Heav'n will not, and she cannot stay.
Go then, go, glorious, on the golden wings
Of the bright youth of heaven, that sings
Under so sweet a burden: go,
Since thy great Son will have it so:
And while thou go'st, our song and we
Will, as we may, reach after thee :—
' Hail ! holy queen of humble hearts,
We in thy praise will have our parts;
And though thy dearest looks must now be light
To none but the blest heavens, whose bright
Beholders, lost in sweet delight,
Feed for ever their fair sight
With those divinest eyes, which we
And our dark world no more shall see;
Though our poor joys are parted so,
Yet shall our lips never let go
Thy gracious name, but to the last
Our loving song shall hold it fast.

Thy sacred name shall be
Thyself to us, and we
With holy cares will keep it by us;
We to the last
Will hold it fast,
And no assumption shall deny us.
All sweetest showers
Of fairest flowers
We 'll strew upon it :
Though our sweetness cannot make
It sweeter, they may take
Themselves new sweetness from it.

Maria, men and angels sing,
Maria, mother of our King.
Live, rarest princess, and may the bright
Crown of a most incomparable light
Embrace thy radiant brows ! O, may the best
Of everlasting joys bathe thy white breast !
Live our chaste love, the holy mirth
Of heaven, and humble pride of earth :
Live crown of women, queen of men :
Live mistress of our song; and when
Our weak desires have done their best,
Sweet angels come, and sing the rest ! '

Richard Crashaw.

250

ON THE NAME ABOVE EVERY NAME

I SING the name which none can say
But touch'd with an interior ray;
The name of our new peace; our good:
Our bliss, and supernatural blood:
The name of all our lives and loves.
Hearken, and help, ye holy doves!
The high-born brood of day; you bright
Candidates of blissful light,
The heirs elect of love; whose names belong
Unto the everlasting life of song;
All ye wise souls, who in the wealthy breast
Of this unbounded name build your warm nest.
Awake, my glory, Soul, if such thou be,
And that fair word at all refer to thee,
Awake and sing,
And be all wing;
Bring hither thy whole self; and let me see
What of thy parent heav'n yet speaks in thee!
O, thou art poor
Of noble pow'rs, I see,
And full of nothing else but empty me;
Narrow, and low, and infinitely less
Than this great morning's mighty business!
One little world or two,
Alas! will never do;
We must have store.
Go, Soul, out of thyself, and seek for more;
Go and request
Great Nature for the key of her huge chest
Of Heav'ns, the self-involving set of spheres,
Which dull mortality more feels than hears;
Then rouse the nest
Of nimble art, and traverse round
The airy shop of soul-appeasing sound:
And beat a summons in the same
All-sovereign name,
To warn each several kind
And shape of sweetness—be they such
As sigh with supple wind
Or answer artful touch—
That they convene and come away

To wait at the love-crownéd doors of that
Illustrious day.
Shall we dare this, my Soul? We 'll do 't, and bring
No other note for 't, but the Name we sing.
Wake, lute and harp,
And every sweet-lipp'd thing
That talks with tuneful string;
Start into life, and leap with me
Into a hasty fit-tuned harmony.
Nor must you think it much
T' obey my bolder touch;
I have authority in Love's name to take you
And to the work of love this morning wake you.
Wake, in the name
Of Him who never sleeps, all things that are;
Or what's the same,
Are musical;
Answer my call
And come along;
Help me to meditate mine immortal song!
Come, ye soft ministers of sweet sad mirth,
Bring all your household-stuff of heav'n on earth:
O you, my Soul's most certain wings,
Complaining pipes, and prattling strings,
Bring all the store
Of sweets you have, and murmur that you have no more.
Come, ne'er to part,
Nature and art!
Come, and come strong,
To the conspiracy of our spacious song.
Bring all the pow'rs of praise
Your provinces of well-united worlds can raise;
Bring all your lutes and harps of heav'n and earth;
Whate'er co-operates to the common mirth;
Vessels of vocal joys,
Or you, more noble architects of intellectual noise,
Cymbals of heav'n, or human spheres,
Solicitors of souls or ears;
And when you are come, with all
That you can bring, or we can call,
O, may you fix
For ever here, and mix
Yourselves into the long
And everlasting series of a deathless song!
Mix all your many worlds above,
And loose them into one of love!
Cheer thee, my heart!

For thou, too, hast thy part
And place in the great throng
Of this unbounded, all-embracing song.
Pow'rs of my soul, be proud !
And speak loud
To all the dear-bought nations this redeeming name ;
And in the wealth of one rich word proclaim
New smiles to nature.
May it be no wrong,
Blest Heav'ns, to you, and your superior song,
That we dark sons of dust and sorrow
Awhile dare borrow
The name of your delights, and our desires,
And fit it to so far inferior lyres !
Our murmurs have their music, too,
Ye mighty orbs, as well as you,
Nor yields the noblest nest
Of warbling seraphim to the ears of love,
A choicer lesson than the joyful breast
Of a poor panting turtle-dove ;
And we, low worms, have leave to do
The same bright business, ye third Heav'ns, with you.
Gentle spirits, do not complain,
We will have care
To keep it fair,
And send it back to you again.
Come, lovely name ! appear from forth the bright
Regions of peaceful light ;
Look from Thine own illustrious home,
Fair king of names, and come :
Leave all thy native glories in their gorgeous nest,
And give thyself awhile the gracious guest
Of humble souls, that seek to find
The hidden sweets
Which man's heart meets
When Thou art master of the mind.
Come, lovely name ! life of our hope !
Lo, we hold our hearts wide ope !
Unlock thy cabinet of day,
Dearest sweet, and come away.
Lo. how the thirsty lands
Gasp for thy golden showers with long-stretch'd hands !
Lo, how the labouring earth,
That hopes to be
All heaven by thee,
Leaps at thy birth !
Th' attending world, to wait thy rise,

First turn'd to eyes,
And then, not knowing what to do,
Turn'd them to tears, and spent them, too.
Come, royal name! and pay th' expense
Of all this precious patience;
O, come away,
And kill the death of this delay!
O, see so many worlds of barren years
Melted and measured out in seas of tears!
O, see the weary lids of wakeful hope,
Love's eastern windows, all wide ope,
With curtains drawn,
To catch the day-break of thy dawn!
O, dawn, at last, long-look'd for day!
Take thine own wings and come away.
Lo, where aloft it comes!   It comes, among
The conduct of adoring spirits, that throng,
Like diligent bees, and swarm about it.
O, they are wise,
And know what sweets are suck'd from out it!
It is the hive
By which they thrive,
Where all their hoard of honey lies.
Lo, where it comes, upon the snowy dove's
Soft back, and brings a bosom big with loves!
Welcome to our dark world, thou womb of day!
Unfold thy fair conceptions, and display
The birth of our bright joys.
O thou compacted
Body of blessings! spirit of souls extracted!
O, dissipate thy spicy pow'rs,
Cloud of condensèd sweets, and break upon us
In balmy show'rs!
O, fill our senses, and take from us
All force of so profane a fallacy
To think aught sweet but that which smells of thee!
Fair, flow'ry name, in none but thee
And thy nectareal fragrancy
Hourly there meets
An universal synod of all sweets;
By whom it is definèd thus
That no perfume
For ever shall presume
To pass for odoriferous,
But such alone whose sacred pedigree
Can prove itself some kin, sweet name, to thee!
Sweet name, in thy each syllable

P

A thousand blest Arabias dwell :
A thousand hills of frankincense,
Mountains of myrrh, and beds of spices,
And ten thousand paradises,
The soul that tastes thee takes from thence.
How many unknown worlds there are
Of comforts, which thou hast in keeping !
How many thousand mercies there
In Pity's soft lap lie a-sleeping !
Happy he who has the art
To awake them,
And to take them
Home, and lodge them in his heart !
O, that it were as it was wont to be,
When thy old friends of fire, all full of thee,
Fought against frowns with smiles ; gave glorious chase
To persecutions ; and against the face
Of death and fiercest dangers durst, with brave
And sober pace, march on to meet a grave !
On their bold breasts about the world they bore thee,
And to the teeth of hell stood up to teach thee ;
In centre of their inmost souls they wore thee,
Where racks and torments strived in vain to reach thee.
Little, alas ! thought they
Who tore the fair breasts of thy friends,
Their fury but made way
For thee, and served them in thy glorious ends.
What did their weapons, but with wider pores
Enlarge thy flaming-breasted lovers,
More freely to transpire
That impatient fire,
The heart that hides thee hardly covers !
What did their weapons, but set wide the doors
For thee : fair purple doors, of Love's devising,
The ruby windows which enrich'd the east
Of thy so oft-repeated rising !
Each wound of theirs was thy new morning,
And re-enthroned thee in thy rosy nest,
With blush of thine own blood thy day adorning !
It was the wit of love o'erflow'd the bounds
Of wrath, and made the way through all these wounds.
Welcome, dear, all-adoréd name,
For sure there is no knee
That knows not thee !
Or, if there be such sons of shame,
Alas ! what will they do
When stubborn rocks shall bow,

And hills hang down their heav'n-saluting heads
To seek for humble beds
Of dust, where, in the bashful shades of night,
Next to their own low nothing they may lie,
And couch before the dazzling light of thy dread Majesty !
They that by Love's mild dictate now
Will not adore thee,
Shall then, with just confusion, bow
And break before thee.

Richard Crashaw.

251

TO LUCASTA GOING BEYOND THE SEAS

IF to be absent were to be
Away from thee ;
Or that when I am gone,
You or I were alone ;
Then, my Lucasta, might I crave
Pity from blust'ring wind or swallowing wave.

But I 'll not sigh one blast or gale
To swell my sail,
Or pay a tear to suage
The foaming blue-god's rage ;
For, whether he will let me pass
Or no, I 'm still as happy as I was.

Though seas and land betwixt us both,
Our faith and troth,
Like separated souls,
All time and space controls.
Above the highest sphere we meet,
Unseen, unknown, and greet as angels greet.

So then we do anticipate
Our after-fate,
And are alive i' th' skies,
If thus our lips and eyes
Can speak like spirits unconfined
In heaven, their earthy bodies left behind.

Richard Lovelace.

252

TO LUCASTA GOING TO THE WARS

TELL me not, sweet, I am unkind,
  That from the nunnery
Of thy chaste breast and quiet mind
  To war and arms I flie.

True, a new mistress now I chase,
  The first foe in the field,
And with a stronger faith embrace
  A sword, a horse, a shield.

Yet this inconstancy is such
  As you, too, shall adore:
I could not love thee, dear, so much,
  Loved I not honour more.

Richard Lovelace.

253

TO ALTHEA FROM PRISON

WHEN Love with unconfinéd wings
  Hovers within my gates,
And my divine Althea brings
  To whisper at the grates;
When I lie tangled in her hair,
  And fettered to her eye,
The gods that wanton in the air
  Know no such liberty.

When flowing cups run swiftly round
  With no allaying Thames,
Our careless heads with roses bound,
  Our hearts with loyal flames;
When thirsty grief in wine we steep,
  When healths and draughts go free,
Fishes that tipple in the deep
  Know no such liberty.

When, like committed linnets, I
  With shriller throat shall sing
The sweetness, mercy, majesty,
  And glories of my King;

When I shall voice aloud how good
    He is, how great should be,
Enlargéd winds that curl the flood
    Know no such liberty.

Stone walls do not a prison make,
    Nor iron bars a cage ;
Minds innocent and quiet take
    That for an hermitage :
If I have freedom in my love,
    And in my soul am free,
Angels alone that soar above
    Enjoy such liberty.

Richard Lovelace.

254

AWAKE, AWAKE, MY LYRE

AWAKE, awake, my Lyre,
And tell thy silent master's humble tale
In sounds that may prevail,
Sounds that gentle thoughts inspire !
Though so exalted she
And I so lowly be,
Tell her, such different notes make all thy harmony.

Hark ! how the strings awake,
And, though the moving hand approach not near,
Themselves with awful fear
A kind of numerous trembling make !
Now all thy forces try ;
Now all thy charms apply ;
Revenge upon her ear the conquests of her eye.

Weak Lyre ! thy virtue sure
Is useless here, since thou art only found
To cure, but not to wound,
And she to wound, but not to cure !
Too weak too wilt thou prove
My passion to remove :
Physic to other ills, thou 'rt nourishment to love.

Sleep, sleep again, my Lyre !
For thou canst never tell my humble tale
In sounds that will prevail,
Nor gentle thoughts in her inspire ;

All thy vain mirth lay by ;
Bid thy strings silent lie ;
Sleep, sleep again, my Lyre, and let thy master die.

Abraham Cowley

255

A MOCK SONG

'TIS true, I never was in love :
  But now I mean to be,
For there 's no art can shield a heart
  From love's supremacy.

Though in my nonage I have seen
  A world of taking faces,
I had not age or wit to ken
  Their several hidden graces.

Those virtues which, though thinly set,
  In others are admired,
In thee are altogether met,
  Which make thee so desired

That, though I never was in love,
  Nor never meant to be,
Thyself and parts above my arts
  Have drawn my heart to thee.

Alexander Brome.

256

B E R M U D A S

Where the remote Bermudas ride
In the Ocean's bosom unespied,
From a small boat that rowed along
The listening winds received this song :—
  ' What should we do but sing his praise
That led us through the watery maze,
Where he the huge sea-monsters wracks
That lift the deep upon their backs,
Unto an isle so long unknown,
And yet far kinder than our own ?

He lands us on a grassy stage,
Safe from the storms' and prelates' rage :
He gave us this eternal spring
Which here enamels everything,
And sends the fowls to us in care
On daily visits through the air.
He hangs in shades the orange bright
Like golden lamps in a green night,
And does in the pomegranates close
Jewels more rich than Ormus shows :
He makes the figs our mouths to meet,
And throws the melons at our feet ;
But apples plants of such a price,
No tree could ever bear them twice.
With cedars chosen by his hand
From Lebanon he stores the land,
And makes the hollow seas that roar
Proclaim the ambergrease on shore. .
He cast (of which we rather boast)
The Gospel's pearl upon our coast,
And in these rocks for us did frame
A temple where to sound his name.
O let our voice his praise exalt
Till it arrive at heaven's vault,
Which, thence (perhaps) rebounding, may
Echo beyond the Mexique Bay !'
    Thus sang they in the English boat
A holy and a cheerful note :
And all the way, to guide their chime,
With falling oars they kept the time.

                              Andrew Marvell.

257

AN HORATIAN ODE

THE forward youth that would appear
Must now forsake his Muses dear,
      Nor in the shadows sing
      His numbers languishing.

'Tis time to leave the books in dust,
And oil the unuséd armour's rust,
      Removing from the wall
      The corselet of the hall.

So restless Cromwell could not cease
In the inglorious arts of peace,
    But through adventurous war
    Urgèd his active star ;

And, like the three-forked lightning, first
Breaking the clouds where it was nurst,
    Did thorough his own side
    His fiery way divide :

For 'tis all one to courage high,
The emulous or enemy,
    And with such to inclose
    Is more than to oppose !

Then burning through the air he went,
And palaces and temples rent ;
    And Cæsar's head at last
    Did through his laurels blast.

'Tis madness to resist or blame
The face of angry Heaven's flame ;
    And if we would speak true,
    Much to the man is due,

Who from his private gardens, where
He lived reservéd and austere,
    As if his highest plot
    To plant the bergamot,

Could by industrious valour climb
To ruin the great work of Time,
    And cast the kingdoms old
    Into another mould.

Though Justice against Fate complain,
And plead the ancient rights in vain
    (But those do hold or break,
    As men are strong or weak),

Nature, that hated emptiness,
Allows of penetration less,
    And therefore must make room
    Where greater spirits come.

What field of all the civil war,
Where his were not the deepest scar?

And Hampton shows what part
He had of wiser art,

Where, twining subtile fears with hope,
He wove a net of such a scope
    That Charles himself might chase
    To Carisbrook's narrow case,

That thence the royal actor borne
The tragic scaffold might adorn :
    While round the arméd bands
    Did clap their bloody hands.

He nothing common did or mean
Upon that memorable scene,
    But with his keener eye
    The axe's edge did try ;

Nor called the gods with vulgar spite
To vindicate his helpless right,
    But bowed his comely head
    Down, as upon a bed.

This was that memorable hour
Which first assured the forcéd power :
    So, when they did design
    The Capitol's first line,

A bleeding head, where they begun,
Did fright the architects to run ;
    And yet in that the State
    Foresaw its happy fate !

And now the Irish are ashamed
To see themselves in one year tamed :
    So much one man can do
    That doth both act and know :

They can affirm his praises best,
And have, though overcome, confessed
    How good he is, how just,
    And fit for highest trust.

Nor yet grown stiffer with command,
But still in the Republic's hand
    (How fit he is to sway,
    That can so well obey !),

He to the Commons' feet presents
A kingdom for his first year's rents,
    And (what he may) forbears
    His fame to make it theirs,

And has his sword and spoils ungirt
To lay them at the public's skirt.
    So when the falcon high
    Falls heavy from the sky,

She, having killed, no more doth search
But on the next green bough to perch,
    Where, when he first does lure,
    The falconer has her sure.

What may not then our isle presume,
While victory his crest does plume?
    What may not others fear,
    If thus he crowns each year?

As Cæsar he, ere long, to Gaul,
To Italy an Hannibal,
    And to all states not free
    Shall climacteric be.

The Pict no shelter now shall find
Within his party-coloured mind,
    But from this valour sad
    Shrink underneath the plaid :

Happy if in the tufted brake
The English hunter him mistake,
    Nor lay his hounds in near
    The Caledonian deer.

But thou, the war's and fortune's son,
March indefatigably on,
    And for the last effect,
    Still keep the sword erect !

Besides the force it has to fright
The spirits of the shady night,
    The same arts that did gain
    A power must it maintain.

Andrew Marvell.

258

O, LET ME CLIMB

O, LET me climb
When I lie down! The pious soul by night
Is like a clouded star, whose beams, though said
To shed their light
Under some cloud,
Yet are above,
And shine and move
Beyond that misty shroud.
So in my bed,
—That curtain'd grave—though sleep, like ashes, hide
My lamp and life, both shall in Thee abide.

Henry Vaughan.

259

THE REVIVAL

UNFOLD! unfold! Take in His light,
Who makes thy cares more short than night.
The joys which with His day-star rise
He deals to all but drowsy eyes;
And, what the men of this world miss,
Some drops and dews of future bliss.

Hark! how the winds have changed their note,
And with warm whispers call thee out!
The frosts are past, the storms are gone,
And backward life at last comes on;
The lofty groves in express joys
Reply unto the turtle's voice;
And here in dust and dirt, O here,
The lilies of His love appear!

Henry Vaughan.

260

THE WREATH

SINCE I in storms used most to be,
    And seldom yielded flowers,
How shall I get a wreath for Thee
    From those rude, barren hours?

The softer dressings of the Spring
    Or Summer's later store
I will not for Thy temples bring,
    Which thorns, not roses, wore.

But a twined wreath of grief and praise,
    Praise soil'd with tears, and tears again
Shining with joy, like dewy days,
    This day I bring for all Thy pain—
Thy causeless pain !—and, sad as death,
    Which sadness breeds in the most vain,
—O, not in vain !—now beg Thy breath,
Thy quickening breath, which gladly bears
    Through saddest clouds to that glad place,
Where cloudless quires sing without tears,
    Sing Thy just praise, and see Thy face.

Henry Vaughan.

261

PEACE

My Soul, there is a country
    Far beyond the stars,
Where stands a wingèd sentry
    All skilful in the wars :

There above noise, and danger,
    Sweet Peace sits crown'd with smiles,
And One born in a manger
    Commands the beauteous files.

He is thy gracious Friend,
    And—O my Soul, awake !—
Did in pure love descend
    To die here for thy sake.

If thou canst get but thither,
    There grows the flower of Peace,
The Rose that cannot wither,
    Thy fortress, and thy ease.

Leave then thy foolish ranges,
    For none can thee secure
But One, Who never changes,
    Thy God, thy life, thy cure.

Henry Vaughan.

262

THE DAY OF JUDGMENT

O DAY of life, of light, of love !
The only day dealt from above !
A day so fresh, so bright, so brave,
'Twill show us each forgotten grave,
And make the dead, like flowers, arise
Youthful and fair to see new skies !
All other days, compared to thee,
Are but Light's weak minority?
They are but veils and cypress drawn
Like clouds, before thy glorious dawn.
O, come ! arise ! shine ! do not stay,
Dearly loved Day !
The fields are long since white, and I
With earnest groans for freedom cry.
My fellow-creatures too say :—Come !
And stones, though speechless, are not dumb.
When shall we hear that glorious voice
Of life and joys ?
That voice which to each secret bed
Of my Lord's dead
Shall bring true day, and make dust see
The way to immortality?
When shall those first white pilgrims rise,
Whose holy, happy histories,
—Because they sleep so long—some men
Count but the blots of a vain pen ?
Dear Lord ! make haste !

Henry Vaughan.

263

O, WALY WALY UP THE BANK

O, WALY waly up the bank,
  And waly waly down the brae,
And waly waly yon burn-side
  Where I and my Love wont to gae !
I leant my back against an aik,
  I thought it was a trusty tree ;
But first it bow'd, and syne it brak—
  Sae my true Love did lichtly me.

O, waly waly, but love is bonny
  A little time while it is new ;
But when 'tis auld, it waxeth cauld
  And fades awa' like morning dew.
O, wherefore should I busk my head ?
  Or wherefore should I kame my hair ?
For my true Love has me forsook,
  And says he 'll never loe me mair.

Now Arthur's-Seat sall be my bed :
  The sheets sall ne'er be prest by me.
Saint Anton's Well sall be my drink,
  Since my true Love has forsaken me.
Marti'mas wind, when wilt thou blaw
  And shake the green leaves aff the tree ?
O gentle Death, when wilt thou come ?
  For of my life I am wearie.

'Tis not the frost, that freezes fell,
  Nor blawing snaw's inclemencie,
'Tis not sic cauld that makes me cry ;
  But my Love's heart grown cauld to me.
When we came in by Glasgow town
  We were a comely sight to see :
My Love was clad in the black velvét,
  And I mysell in cramasie.

But had I wist, before I kist,
  That love had been sae ill to win,
I had lockt my heart in a case of gowd
  And pinn'd it with a siller pin.
And, O ! if my young babe were born,
  And set upon the nurse's knee,
And I mysell were dead and gane,
  And the green grass growing over me !

Anonymous.

264

HELEN OF KIRCONNELL

I WISH I were where Helen lies ;
Night and day on me she cries :
O, that I were where Helen lies
  On fair Kirconnell lea !

Curst be the heart that thought the thought,
And curst the hand that fired the shot,
When in my arms burd Helen dropt,
    And died to succour me !

O, think na but my heart was sair
When my Love dropt down and spak nae mair !
I laid her down wi' meikle care
    On fair Kirconnell lea.

As I went down the water-side,   .
None but my foe to be my guide,
None but my foe to be my guide,
    On fair Kirconnell lea :

I lighted down my sword to draw,
I hackèd him in pieces sma',
I hackèd him in pieces sma'
    For her sake that died for mc.

O Helen fair beyond compare !
I 'll make a garland of thy hair
Shall bind my heart for evermair
    Until the day I die.

O, that I were where Helen lies !
Night and day on me she cries :
Out of my bed she bids me rise,
    Says :—' Haste and come to me ! '

O Helen fair ! O Helen chaste !
If I were with thee, I were blest,
Where thou lies low and takes thy rest
    On fair Kirconnell lea.

I wish my grave were growing green,
A winding-sheet drawn ower my een,
And I in Helen's arms lying,
    On fair Kirconnell lea.

I wish I were where Helen lies ;
Night and day on me she cries ;
And I am weary of the skies,
    Since my Love died for me.

Anonymous.

265

THE TWA CORBIES

As I was walking all alane,
I heard twa corbies making a mane,
The tane unto the tither say :—
' Where sall we gang and dine to-day ? '

'—In behint yon auld fail dyke,
I wat there lies a new slain Knight ;
And naebody kens that he lies there
But his hawk, his hound, and lady fair.

' His hound is to the hunting gane,
His hawk to fetch the wild-fowl hame,
His lady's ta'en another mate,
So we may mak our dinner sweet.

' Ye 'll sit on his white hause-bane,
And I 'll pick out his bonnie blue een.
Wi' ae lock o' his gowden hair
We 'll theek our nest when it grows bare.

' Mony a one for him maks mane,
But nane sall ken where he is gane !
O'er his white banes, where they are bare,
The wind sall blaw for evermair.'

Anonymous.

266

WILLIE DROWNED IN YARROW

Down in yon garden sweet and gay
  Where bonnie grows the lily,
I heard a fair maid sighing say :—
  ' My wish be wi' sweet Willie !

' Willie 's rare, and Willie 's fair,
  And Willie 's wondrous bonny ;
And Willie hecht to marry me,
  Gin e'er he married ony.

' O gentle wind, that bloweth south
  From where my Love repaireth,
Convey a kiss frae his dear mouth,
  And tell me how he fareth !

' O, tell sweet Willie to come doun
  And hear the mavis singing,
And see the birds on ilka bush
  And leaves around them hinging :

' The lav'rock there, wi' her white breast
  And gentle throat sae narrow !
There 's sport eneuch for gentlemen
  On Leader haughs and Yarrow.

' O, Leader haughs are wide and braid,
  And Yarrow haughs are bonny ;
There Willie hecht to marry me,
  If ere he married ony.

' But Willie 's gone, whom I thought on,
  And does not hear the weeping
Draws many a tear frae 's true love's e'c,
  When other maids are sleeping.

' Yestreen I made my bed fu' braid,
  The night I 'll mak' it narrow,
For a' the lee-lang winter night
  I lie twined o' my marrow.

' O, came ye by yon water-side ?
  Pu'd you the rose or lily ?
Or came you by yon meadow green,
  Or saw you my sweet Willie ? '

She sought him up, she sought him down,
  She sought him braid and narrow ;
Syne, in the cleaving of a crag,
  She found him drown'd in Yarrow.

Anonymous.

267

O, FAIN WOULD I

O, FAIN would I, before I die,
Bequeath to thee a legacy,
That thou may'st say, when I am gone,
None had my heart but thee alone !
Had I as many hearts as hairs,
As many lives as lovers' fears,
As many lives as years have hours,
They all and only should be yours !

Q

Dearest, before you condescend
To entertain a bosom-friend,
Be sure you know your servant well
Before your liberty you sell :
For love's a fire in young and old,
'Tis sometimes hot and sometimes cold,
And now you know that, when they please,
They can be sick of love's disease.

Then wisely choose a friend that may
Last for an age, and not a day,
Who loves thee not for lip or eye,
But for thy mutual sympathy !
Let such a friend thy heart engage,
For he will comfort thee in age,
And kiss thy wrinkled, furrowed brow
With as much joy as I do now.

Anonymous.

268

THE RELAPSE

O, TURN away those cruel eyes,
  The stars of my undoing ;
Or death in such a bright disguise
  May tempt a second wooing.

Punish their blind and impious pride,
  Who dare contemn thy glory !
It was my fall that deified
  Thy name, and scaled thy story.

Yet no new sufferings can prepare
  A higher praise to crown thee :
Though my first death proclaim thee fair,
  My second will unthrone thee.

Lovers will doubt thou canst entice
  No other for thy fuel,
And if thou burn one victim twice,
  Both think thee poor and cruel.

Thomas Stanley.

269

A SONG FOR SAINT CECILIA'S DAY

FROM harmony, from heavenly harmony
This universal frame began :
When Nature underneath a heap
Of jarring atoms lay,
And could not heave her head,
The tuneful voice was heard from high :—
' Arise, ye more than dead ! '
Then cold, and hot, and moist, and dry,
In order to their stations leap,
And music's power obey.
From harmony, from heavenly harmony,
This universal frame began :
From harmony to harmony
Through all the compass of the notes it ran,
The diapason closing full in man.

What passion cannot Music raise and quell ?
When Jubal struck the chorded shell,
His listening brethren stood around,
And, wond'ring, on their faces fell
To worship that celestial sound.
Less than a God they thought there could not dwell
Within the hollow of that shell,
That spoke so sweetly and so well.
What passion cannot Music raise and quell ?

The trumpet's loud clangor
Excites us to arms,
With shrill notes of anger
And mortal alarms.
The double double double beat
Of the thundering drum
Cries :—' Hark ! the foes come !
Charge, charge, 'tis too late to retreat.'

The soft complaining flute
In dying notes discovers
The woes of hopeless lovers,
Whose dirge is whisper'd by the warbling lute.

Sharp violins proclaim
Their jealous pangs, and desperation,
Fury, frantic indignation,
Depth of pains, and height of passion
For the fair, disdainful dame.

But, O ! what art can teach,
What human voice can reach,
The sacred organ's praise?
Notes inspiring holy love,
Notes that wing their heavenly ways
To mend the choirs above !

Orpheus could lead the savage race,
And trees uprooted left their place,
Sequacious of the lyre.
But bright Cecilia rais'd the wonder higher,
When to her organ vocal breath was given,
And angels heard, and straight appear'd,
Mistaking Earth for Heaven.

Grand Chorus.

As from the power of sacred lays,
The spheres began to move,
And sung the great Creator's praise
To all the bless'd above :
So when the last and dreadful hour
This crumbling pageant shall devour,
The trumpet shall be heard on high,
The dead shall live, the living die,
And music shall untune the sky.

John Dryden.

270

FAIR, SWEET, AND YOUNG

FAIR, sweet, and young, receive a prize
Reserv'd for your victorious eyes :
From crowds, whom at your feet you see,
O, pity and distinguish me !
As I from thousand beauties more
Distinguish you, and only you adore.

Your face for conquest was design'd,
Your every motion charms my mind !
Angels, when you your silence break,
Forget their hymns, to hear you speak,
But when at once they hear and view,
Are loth to mount, and long to stay with you.

No graces can your form improve,
But all are lost, unless you love ;
While that sweet passion you disdain,
Your veil and beauty are in vain :
In pity then prevent my fate,
For after dying all reprieve 's too late.

John Dryden.

271

NO, NO, POOR SUFFERING HEART

No, no, poor suffering heart, no change endeavour,
Choose to sustain the smart, rather than leave her !
My ravished eyes behold such charms about her,
I can die with her, but not live without her.
One tender sigh of hers to see me languish,
Will more than pay the price of my past anguish.
Beware, O cruel fair, how you smile on me !
'Twas a kind look of yours that has undone me.

Love has in store for me one happy minute,
And she will end my pain, who did begin it :
Then, no day void of bliss or pleasure leaving,
Ages shall slide away without perceiving ;
Cupid shall guard the door, the more to please us,
And keep out Time and Death, when they would seize us ;
Time and Death shall depart, and say, in flying,
Love has found out a way to live by dying.

John Dryden.

272

AH, HOW SWEET IT IS TO LOVE

AH, how sweet it is to love !
Ah, how gay is young Desire !
And what pleasing pains we prove
When we first approach Love's fire !
　　Pains of love be sweeter far
　　Than all other pleasures are.

Sighs which are from lovers blown
Do but gently heave the heart:
E'en the tears they shed alone
Cure, like trickling balm, their smart.
  Lovers, when they lose their breath,
  Bleed away in easy death.

Love and Time with reverence use:
Treat them like a parting friend,
Nor the golden gifts refuse
Which in youth sincere they send,
  For each year their price is more
  And they less simple than before.

Love, like spring-tides full and high,
Swells in every youthful vein;
But each tide does less supply,
Till they quite shrink in again:
  If a flow in age appear,
  'Tis but rain, and runs not clear.

John Dryden.

273

I FEED A FLAME

I FEED a flame within, which so torments me
That it both pains my heart, and yet contents me:
'Tis such a pleasing smart, and I so love it,
That I had rather die than once remove it.

Yet he, for whom I grieve, shall never know it;
My tongue does not betray, nor my eyes show it.
Not a sigh, not a tear, my pain discloses,
But they fall silently, like dew on roses.

Thus, to prevent my love from being cruel,
My heart's the sacrifice, as 'tis the fuel;
And while I suffer this to give him quiet,
My faith rewards my love, though he deny it.

On his eyes will I gaze, and there delight me;
While I conceal my love no frown can fright me.
To be more happy I dare not aspire,
Nor can I fall more low, mounting no higher.

John Dryden.

274

THE MAGNIFICENT LOVER

WHAT shall I do to show how much I love her?
How many millions of sighs can suffice?
That which wins other hearts never can move her—
Such feeble offerings of love she'll despise!
I will love more than man e'er loved before me,
  Gaze on her all the day, melt all the night,
Till for her own sake at last she'll implore me
  To love her less to preserve our delight.

Since Gods themselves could not ever be living,
  Men must have breathing recruits for new joys:
I would my soul could be ever improving,
  Tho' eager love more than sorrow destroys!
In fair Aurelia's arms leave me expiring!
  To be embalmed with the sweets of her breath,
To the last moment I'll still be desiring—
  Never had hero so glorious a death!

                                    Thomas Betterton.

275

THE DESPERATE LOVER

I

O MIGHTY King of Terrors, come,
Command thy slave to his long home!
Great Sanctuary, Grave! to thee
In throngs the miserable flee;
Encircled in thy frozen arms,
They bid defiance to their harms,
Regardless of those pond'rous little things,
That discompose the uneasy heads of Kings.

II

In the cold earth the prisoner lies
Ransom'd from all his miseries;
Himself forgotten, he forgets
His cruel creditors and debts;
And there in everlasting peace
Contentions with their authors cease:
A turf of grass or monument of stone
Umpires the petty competitión.

III

The disappointed lover there,
Breathes not a sigh, nor sheds a tear ;
With us (fond fools) he never shares
In sad perplexities and cares ;
The willow near his tomb that grows
Revives his memory, not his woes ;
Or rain or shine, he is advanc'd above
Th' affronts of Heaven and stratagems of Love.

IV

Then, mighty King of Terrors, come,
Command thy slave to his long home !
And thou, my friend, that lov'st me best,
Seal up these eyes that break my rest ;
Put out the lights, bespeak my knell,
And then eternally farewell !
'Tis all th' amends our wretched Fates can give,
That none can force a desperate man to live.

Thomas Flatman.

276

O, THE SAD DAY

O, the sad day !
When friends shall shake their heads, and say
Of miserable me :—
' Hark, how he groans !
Look, how he pants for breath !
See how he struggles with the pangs of death ! '
When they shall say of these dear eyes :—
' How hollow, O, how dim they be !
Mark how his breast doth rise and swell
Against his potent enemy ! '
When some old friend shall step to my bedside,
Touch my chill face, and thence shall gently slide,
But, when his next companions say :—
' How does he do ? What hopes ? ' shall turn away,
Answering only, with a lift-up hand :—
' Who can his fate withstand ? '
Then shall a gasp or two do more
Than e'er my rhetoric could before :
Persuade the world to trouble me no more—
Persuade the world to trouble me no more.

Thomas Flatman.

277

PHYLLIS, FOR SHAME

PHYLLIS, for shame ! Let us improve,
    A thousand different ways,
Those few short moments snatch'd by love
    From many tedious days.

If you want courage to despise
    The censure of the grave,
Though Love's a tyrant in your eyes,
    Your heart is but a slave.

My love is full of noble pride,
    Nor can it e'er submit,
To let that fop, Discretion, ride
    In triumph over it.

False friends I have, as well as you,
    Who daily counsel me
Fame and Ambition to pursue,
    And leave off loving thee ;

But when the least regard I show
    To fools who thus advise,
May I be dull enough to grow
    Most miserably wise !

          Charles Sackville, Earl of Dorset.

278

TO CHLORIS

AH ! Chloris, that I now could sit
    As unconcerned as when
Your infant beauty could beget
    No pleasure, nor no pain !

When I the dawn used to admire
    And praised the coming day,
I little thought the growing fire
    Must take my rest away.

Your charms in harmless childhood lay,
  Like metals in the mine :
Age from no face took more away
  Than youth concealed in thine.

But as your charms insensibly
  To their perfection prest,
Fond love as unperceived did fly,
  And in my bosom rest.

My passion with your beauty grew,
  And Cupid at my heart
Still, as his mother favoured you,
  Threw a new flaming dart.

Each gloried in their wanton part :
  To make a lover, he
Employed the utmost of his art,
  To make a beauty she !

Though now I slowly bend to love,
  Uncertain of my fate,
If your fair self my chains approve,
  I shall my freedom hate.

Lovers, like dying men, may well
  At first disordered be,
Since none alive can truly tell
  What fortune they must see.

                              Charles Sedley.

279

PHYLLIS

PHYLLIS is my only joy,
  Faithless as the winds or seas,
Sometimes cunning, sometimes coy,
  Yet she never fails to please :
      If with a frown
      I am cast down,
      Phyllis, smiling
      And beguiling,
Makes me happier than before.

Though alas ! too late I find
  Nothing can her fancy fix ;
Yet the moment she is kind
  I forgive her with her tricks,
    Which though I see,
    I can't get free :
    She deceiving,
    I believing,
What need lovers wish for more ?

Charles Sedley.

280

LOVE ENTHRONED

LOVE in fantastic triumph sate,
  Whilst bleeding hearts around him flowed,
For whom fresh pains he did create,
  And strange tyrannic power he showed.
From thy bright eyes he took his fires,
  Which round about in sport he hurled ;
But 'twas from mine he took desires
  Enough to undo the amorous world.

From me he took his sighs and tears,
  From thee his pride and cruelty ;
From me his languishment and fears,
  And every killing dart from thee.
Thus thou and I the god have armed,
  And set him up a deity,
But my poor heart alone is harmed,
  While thine the victor is, and free.

Aphra Behn.

281

OF HIS MISTRESS

AN age in her embraces past
  Would seem a winter's day,
Where life and light with envious haste
  Are torn and snatch'd away.

But, O ! how slowly minutes roll,
   When absent from her eyes,
That fed my love, which is my soul !
   It languishes and dies ;

For then, no more a soul, but shade,
   It mournfully does move,
And haunts my breast, by absence made
   The living tomb of love.
              John Wilmot, Earl of Rochester.

282

ABSENT FROM THEE

ABSENT from thee, I languish still !
   Then ask me not :—When I return ?
The straying fool 'twill plainly kill
   To wish all day, all night to mourn.

Dear, from thine arms then let me fly,
   That my fantastic mind may prove
The torments it deserves to try,
   That tears my fix'd heart from my love.

When, wearied with a world of woe,
   To thy safe bosom I retire,
Where love, and peace, and truth does flow,
   May I contented there expire !

Lest, once more wandering from that heaven,
   I fall on some base heart unblest—
Faithless to thee, false, unforgiven—
   And lose my everlasting rest !
              John Wilmot, Earl of Rochester.

283

LOVE AND LIFE

ALL my past life is mine no more,
   The flying hours are gone :
Like transitory dreams given o'er,
Whose images are kept in store
   By memory alone.

The time that is to come is not ;
   How can it then be mine?
The present moment 's all my lot,
And that, as fast as it is got,
   Phyllis, is only thine.

Then talk not of inconstancy,
   False hearts, and broken vows !
If I by miracle can be
This live-long minute true to thee,
   'Tis all that Heaven allows.

John Wilmot, Earl of Rochester.

284

UPON DRINKING IN A BOWL

VULCAN, contrive me such a cup
   As Nestor used of old !
Show all thy skill to trim it up,
   Damask it round with gold.

Make it so large that, fill'd with sack
   Up to the swelling brim,
Vast toasts on the delicious lake
   Like ships at sea may swim.

Engrave not battle on his cheek :
   With war I 've nought to do !
I 'm none of those that took Mæstrick,
   Nor Yarmouth leaguer knew.

Let it no name of planets tell,
   Fix'd stars, or constellations :
For I am no Sir Sidrophel,
   Nor none of his relations.

But carve thereon a spreading vine ;
   Then add two lovely boys ;
Their limbs in amorous folds entwine,
   The type of future joys.

Cupid and Bacchus my saints are.
   May drink and love still reign !
With wine I wash away my care,
   And then to love again.

John Wilmot, Earl of Rochester.

285

I CANNOT CHANGE

I CANNOT change, as others do,
  Though you unjustly scorn,
Since that poor swain, that sighs for you,
  For you alone was born.
No, Phyllis, no, your heart to move
  A surer way I'll try,
And, to revenge my slighted love,
  Will still love on and die.

When, kill'd with grief, Amyntas lies,
  And you to mind shall call
The sighs that now unpity'd rise,
  The tears that vainly fall,
That welcome hour, that ends this smart,
  Will then begin your pain;
For such a faithful tender heart
  Can never break in vain.

John Wilmot, Earl of Rochester.

286

TO HIS MISTRESS

WHY dost thou shade thy lovely face?   O, why
Does that eclipsing hand of thine deny
The sunshine of the Sun's enlivening eye?

Without thy light, what light remains in me?
Thou art my life: my way, my light's in thee;
I live, I move, and by thy beams I see.

Thou art my life: if thou but turn away,
My life's a thousand deaths.   Thou art my way:
Without thee, Love, I travel not but stray.

My light thou art: without thy glorious sight,
My eyes are darkened with eternal night.
My Love, thou art my way, my life, my light.

Thou art my way: I wander if thou fly.
Thou art my light: if hid, how blind am I!
Thou art my life: if thou withdraw'st, I die.

My eyes are dark and blind, I cannot see:
To whom, or whither should my darkness flee,
But to that light? and who's that light but thee?

If I have lost my path, dear lover, say,
Shall I still wander in a doubtful way?
Love, shall a lamb of Israel's sheep-fold stray?

My path is lost, my wandering steps do stray,
I cannot go, nor can I safely stay:
Whom should I seek, but thee, my path, my way?

And yet thou turn'st thy face away, and fly'st me!
And yet I sue for grace, and thou deny'st me!
Speak, art thou angry, love, or only try'st me? . . .

Thou art the pilgrim's path, the blind man's eye,
The dead man's life: on thee my hopes rely:
If I but them remove, I surely die.

Dissolve thy sunbeams, close thy wings, and stay!
See, see how I am blind, and dead, and stray,
O thou that art my life, my light, my way!

Then work thy will! If passion bid me flee,
My reason shall obey, my wings shall be
Stretched out no farther than from me to thee.

John Wilmot, Earl of Rochester.

287

MY DEAR MISTRESS

My dear mistress has a heart
  Soft as those kind looks she gave me,
When, with Love's resistless art
  And her eyes, she did enslave me;
But her constancy's so weak,
  She's so wild and apt to wander,
That my jealous heart would break,
  Should we live one day asunder.

Melting joys about her move,
  Killing pleasures, wounding blisses;
She can dress her eyes in love,
  And her lips can warm with kisses;

Angels listen when she speaks ;
  She 's my delight, all mankind's wonder ;
But my jealous heart would break,
  Should we live one day asunder.

                    John Wilmot, Earl of Rochester.

288

I DID BUT LOOK

I DID but look and love a-while,
  'Twas but for one half-hour :
Then to resist I had no will,
  And now I have no power

To sigh, and wish, is all my ease :
  Sighs, which do heat impart
Enough to melt the coldest ice,
  Yet cannot warm your heart.

O ! would your pity give my heart
  One corner of your breast,
'Twould learn of yours the winning art,
  And quickly steal the rest !

                    Thomas Otway.

· 289

FALSE THOUGH SHE BE

FALSE though she be to me and love,
  I 'll ne'er pursue revenge ;
For still the charmer I approve,
  Though I deplore her change.

In hours of bliss we oft have met :
  They could not always last,
And though the present I regret,
  I 'm grateful for the past.

                    , *William Congreve.*

290

LOVE IN HER EYES

LOVE in her eyes sits playing,
    And sheds delicious death ;
Love in her lips is straying,
    And warbling in her breath ;

Love on her breast sits panting,
    And swells with soft desire :
Nor grace, nor charm, is wanting
    To set the heart on fire.

John Gay.

291

THE DYING CHRISTIAN TO HIS SOUL

VITAL spark of heavenly flame,
Quit, O, quit this mortal frame !
Trembling, hoping, lingering, flying,
O, the pain, the bliss of dying !
Cease, fond Nature, cease thy strife,
And let me languish into life.

Hark, they whisper ! Angels say :—
'Sister spirit, come away !'
What is this absorbs me quite ?
Steals my senses, shuts my sight,
Drowns my spirit, draws my breath ?
Tell me, my soul, can this be death ?

The world recedes ; it disappears !
Heaven opens on my eyes ! my ears
    With sounds seraphic ring !
Lend, lend your wings ! I mount ! I fly !
O Grave, where is thy Victory ?
    O Death, where is thy sting ?

Alexander Pope.

R

292

SALLY IN OUR ALLEY

OF all the girls that are so smart
  There's none like pretty Sally;
She is the darling of my heart,
  And she lives in our alley.
There is no lady in the land
  Is half so sweet as Sally;
She is the darling of my heart,
  And she lives in our alley.

Her father he makes cabbage-nets,
  And through the streets does cry 'em;
Her mother she sells laces long
  To such as please to buy 'em.
But sure such folks could ne'er beget
  So sweet a girl as Sally!
She is the darling of my heart,
  And she lives in our alley.

When she is by, I leave my work,
  I love her so sincerely;
My master comes like any Turk,
  And bangs me most severely.
But let him bang his belly-full,
  I'll bear it all for Sally;
She is the darling of my heart,
  And she lives in our alley.

Of all the days that's in the week
  I dearly love but one day,
And that's the day that comes betwixt
  A Saturday and Monday;
For then I'm dressed all in my best
  To walk abroad with Sally;
She is the darling of my heart,
  And she lives in our alley.

My master carries me to church,
  And often am I blaméd
Because I leave him in the lurch
  As soon as text is naméd.
I leave the church in sermon-time,
  And slink away to Sally;
She is the darling of my heart,
  And she lives in our alley.

When Christmas comes about again,
  O, then I shall have money!
I'll hoard it up, and box it all,
  I'll give it to my honey.
I would it were ten thousand pounds,
  I'd give it all to Sally;
She is the darling of my heart,
  And she lives in our alley.

My master and the neighbours all
  Make game of me and Sally;
And, but for her, I'd better be
  A slave, and row a galley;
But when my seven long years are out,
  O, then I'll marry Sally;
O, then we'll wed, and then we'll bed,
  But not in our alley.

Henry Carey.

293

TO HER I LOVE

TELL me, thou soul of her I love,
  Ah! tell me, whither art thou fled?
To what delightful world above,
  Appointed for the happy dead?

Or dost thou free, at pleasure, roam
  And sometimes share thy lover's woe,
Where, void of thee, his cheerless home
  Can now, alas! no comfort know?

O! if thou hoverest round my walk,
  While, under every well-known tree,
I to thy fancied shadow talk,
  And every tear is full of thee:

Should then the weary eye of grief,
  Beside some sympathetic stream,
In slumber find a short relief,
  O, visit thou my soothing dream!.

James Thomson.

294

AN ODE

How sleep the brave, who sink to rest,
By all their country's wishes blest !
When Spring, with dewy fingers cold,
Returns to deck their hallow'd mould,
She there shall dress a sweeter sod
Than Fancy's feet have ever trod.

By Fairy hands their knell is rung,
By forms unseen their dirge is sung,
There Honour comes, a pilgrim gray,
To bless the turf that wraps their clay,
And Freedom shall a while repair,
To dwell a weeping hermit there.

William Collins.

295

DIRGE IN CYMBELINE

To fair Fidele's grassy tomb
  Soft maids and village hinds shall bring
Each opening sweet, of earliest bloom,
  And rifle all the breathing spring.

No wailing ghost shall dare appear
  To vex with shrieks this quiet grove,
But shepherd lads assemble here,
  And melting virgins own their love.

No wither'd witch shall here be seen,
  No goblins lead their nightly crew :
The female fays shall haunt the green,
  And dress thy grave with pearly dew.

The red-breast oft at evening hours
  Shall kindly lend his little aid,
With hoary moss and gather'd flowers,
  To deck the ground where thou art laid.

When howling winds and beating rain
  In tempests shake thy sylvan cell,
Or 'midst the chase on every plain,
  The tender thought on thee shall dwell.

Each lonely scene shall thee restore,
    For thee the tear be duly shed :
Belov'd, till life can charm no more,
    And mourn'd, till pity's self be dead.

William Collins.

296

ODE TO EVENING

IF aught of oaten stop, or pastoral song,
May hope, chaste Eve, to soothe thy modest ear,
    Like thy own solemn springs,
    Thy springs and dying gales,

O nymph reserv'd, while now the bright-hair'd Sun
Sits in yon western tent, whose cloudy skirts,
    With brede ethereal wove,
    O'erhang his wavy bed :

Now air is hush'd, save where the weak-ey'd bat
With short shrill shriek flits by on leathern wing,
    Or where the beetle winds
    His small but sullen horn,

As oft he rises 'midst the twilight path,
Against the pilgrim borne in heedless hum :
    Now teach me, maid compos'd,
    To breathe some soften'd strain,

Whose numbers, stealing through thy darkening vale,
May not unseemly with its stillness suit,
    As, musing slow, I hail
    Thy genial lov'd return !

For when thy folding-star arising shows
His paly circlet, at his warning lamp
    The fragrant Hours, and Elves
    Who slept in buds the day,

And many a Nymph who wreathes her brows with sedge,
And sheds the freshening dew, and lovelier still,
    The pensive Pleasures sweet
    Prepare thy shadowy car.

Then let me rove some wild and heathy scene,
Or find some ruin 'midst its dreary dells,
　　Whose walls more awful nod
　　By thy religious gleams !

Or, if chill blustering winds, or driving rain,
Prevent my willing feet, be mine the hut,
　　That from the mountain's side
　　Views wilds and swelling floods,

And hamlets brown, and dim-discovered spires,
And hears their simple bell, and marks o'er all
　　Thy dewy fingers draw
　　The gradual dusky veil.

While Spring shall pour his showers, as oft he wont,
And bathe thy breathing tresses, meekest Eve !
　　While Summer loves to sport
　　Beneath thy lingering light,

While sallow Autumn fills thy lap with leaves,
Or Winter, yelling through the troublous air,
　　Affrights thy shrinking train,
　　And rudely rends thy robes :

So long, regardful of thy quiet rule,
Shall Fancy, Friendship, Science, smiling Peace,
　　Thy gentlest influence own,
　　And love thy favourite name !
　　　　　　　　　　　　William Collins.

297

THE FLOWERS OF THE FOREST

I 'VE heard them lilting at our ewe-milking,
Lasses a-lilting before the dawn of day ;
But now they are moaning on ilka green loaning :—
The Flowers of the Forest are a' wede away.

At bughts in the morning nae blythe lads are scorning ;
The lasses are lanely, and dowie, and wae ;
Nae daffing, nae gabbing, but sighing and sabbing,
Ilk ane lifts her leglin, and hies her away.

In hairst, at the shearing, nae youths now are jeering:
The bandsters are lyart, and runkled, and gray.
At fair or at preaching, nae wooing, nae fleeching—
The Flowers of the Forest are a' wede away.

At e'en, in the gloaming, nae swankies are roaming
'Bout stacks wi' the lasses at bogle to play;
But ilk ane sits drearie, lamenting her dearie—
The Flowers of the Forest are a' wede away.

Dool and wae for the order sent our lads to the Border!
The English, for ance, by guile wan the day;
The Flowers of the Forest, that fought aye the foremost,
The prime of our land, lie cauld in the clay.

We'll hear nae mair lilting at our ewe-milking:
Women and bairns are heartless and wae,
Sighing and moaning on ilka green loaning:
The Flowers of the Forest are a' wede away.

Jean Elliot.

298

WHEN LOVELY WOMAN

WHEN lovely woman stoops to folly,
    And finds too late that men betray,
What charm can soothe her melancholy,
    What art can wash her guilt away?

The only art her guilt to cover,
    To hide her shame from every eye,
To give repentance to her lover,
    And wring his bosom, is—to die.

Oliver Goldsmith.

299

IF DOUGHTY DEEDS

IF doughty deeds my lady please,
    Right soon I'll mount my steed,
And strong his arm, and fast his seat,
    That bears frae me the meed.

I 'll wear thy colours in my cap,
　Thy picture at my heart ;
And he that bends not to thine eye
　Shall rue it to his smart !
　　　Then tell me how to woo thee, Love,
　　　　O, tell me how to woo thee !
　　　For thy dear sake nae care I 'll take,
　　　　Tho' ne'er another trow me.

If gay attire delight thine eye,
　I 'll dight me in array,
I 'll tend thy chamber door all night,
　And squire thee all the day.
If sweetest sounds can win thine ear,
　These sounds I 'll strive to catch :
Thy voice I 'll steal to woo thysel',
　That voice that nane can match.

But if fond love thy heart can gain,
　I never broke a vow,
Nae maiden lays her skaith to me,
　I never loved but you.
For you alone I ride the ring,
　For you I wear the blue,
For you alone I strive to sing—
　O, tell me how to woo !
　　　Then tell me how to woo thee, Love,
　　　　O, tell me how to woo thee !
　　　For thy dear sake nae care I 'll take,
　　　　Tho' ne'er another trow me.

Graham of Gartmore.

300

ON THE LOSS OF THE *ROYAL GEORGE*

TOLL for the brave !
　The brave that are no more !
All sunk beneath the wave,
　Fast by their native shore !

Eight hundred of the brave,
　Whose courage well was tried,
Had made the vessel heel,
　And laid her on her side.

A land-breeze shook the shrouds,
　And she was overset ;
Down went the *Royal George*,
　With all her crew complete.

Toll for the brave !
　Brave Kempenfelt is gone ;
His last sea-fight is fought ;
　His work of glory done.

It was not in the battle ;
　No tempest gave the shock ;
She sprang no fatal leak ;
　She ran upon no rock.

His sword was in its sheath,
　His fingers held the pen,
When Kempenfelt went down
　With twice four hundred men.

Weigh the vessel up,
　Once dreaded by our foes !
And mingle with our cup
　The tears that England owes.

Her timbers yet are sound,
　And she may float again
Full charged with England's thunder,
　And plough the distant main.

But Kempenfelt is gone,
　His victories are o'er,
And he and his eight hundred
　Shall plough the wave no more.

                                 William Cowper.

301

TO MARY

THE twentieth year is well-nigh past,
Since first our sky was overcast ;
Ah, would that this might be the last,
　　　　My Mary !

Thy spirits have a fainter flow,
I see thee daily weaker grow;
'Twas my distress that brought thee low,
　　　　　My Mary!

Thy needles, once a shining store,
For my sake restless heretofore,
Now rust disused, and shine no more,
　　　　　My Mary!

For though thou gladly wouldst fulful
The same kind office for me still,
Thy sight now seconds not thy will,
　　　　　My Mary!

But well thou playedst the housewife's part,
And all thy threads with magic art
Have wound themselves about this heart,
　　　　　My Mary!

Thy indistinct expressions seem
Like language uttered in a dream;
Yet me they charm, whate'er the theme,
　　　　　My Mary!

Thy silver locks, once auburn bright,
Are still more lovely in my sight
Than golden beams of orient light,
　　　　　My Mary!

For, could I view nor them nor thee,
What sight worth seeing could I see?
The sun would rise in vain for me,
　　　　　My Mary!

Partakers of thy sad decline,
Thy hands their little force resign,
Yet, gently prest, press gently mine,
　　　　　My Mary!

Such feebleness of limbs thou provest,
That now at every step thou movest
Upheld by two, yet still thou lovest,
　　　　　My Mary!

And still to love, though prest with ill,
In wintry age to feel no chill,
With me is to be lovely still,
　　　　　My Mary!

But ah ! by constant heed I know,
How oft the sadness that I show
Transforms thy smiles to looks of woe,
                    My Mary !

And should my future lot be cast
With much resemblance of the past,
Thy worn-out heart will break at last,
                    My Mary !

                    William Cowper.

302

THERE'S NAE LUCK ABOUT THE HOUSE

AND are ye sure the news is true?
  And are ye sure he 's weel ?
Is this a time to think of wark ?
  Ye jauds, fling by your wheel !
Is this a time to think o' wark,
  When Colin 's at the door?
Gie me my cloak ! I 'll to the quay
  And see him come ashore.

    For there 's nae luck about the house,
      There 's nae luck ava,
    There 's little pleasure in the house,
      When our gudeman's awa.

Rise up and mak' a clean fireside,
  Put on the muckle pot !
Gi'e little Kate her cotton gown,
  And Jock his Sunday coat,
And mak' their shoon as black as slaes,
  Their hose as white as snaw !
It 's a' to please my ain gudeman,
  For he 's been long awa.

There 's twa fat hens upon the bauk,
  Been fed this month and mair :
Mak' haste and thraw their necks about,
  That Colin weel may fare,
And mak' the table neat and clean,
  Gar ilka thing look braw !
It 's a' for love of my gudeman,
  For he 's been long awa.

O, gi'e me down my bigonet,
　My bishop satin gown,
For I maun tell the bailie's wife
　That Colin 's come to town.
My Sunday's shoon they maun gae on,
　My hose o' pearl blue !
'Tis a' to please my ain gudeman,
　For he 's baith leal and true.

Sae true his words, sae smooth his speech,
　His breath 's like caller air !
His very foot has music in 't,
　As he comes up the stair.
And will I see his face again ?
　And will I hear him speak ?
I 'm downright dizzy with the thought, —
　In troth, I 'm like to greet.

　　For there 's nae luck about the house,
　　　There 's nae luck ava,
　　There 's little pleasure in the house,
　　　When our gudeman 's awa.

　　　　　　　William Julius Mickle.

303

AULD ROBIN GRAY

WHEN the sheep are in the fauld, and the kye at hame,
And a' the warld to rest are gane,
The waes o' my heart fa' in showers frae my e'e,
While my gudeman lies sound by me.

Young Jamie lo'ed me weel, and sought me for his bride,
But saving a croun he had naething else beside :
To make the croun a pund, young Jamie gaed to sea,
And the croun and the pund were baith for me.

He hadna been awa a week but only twa,
When my father brak his arm, and the cow was stown awa ;
My mother she fell sick, and my Jamie at the sea—
And auld Robin Gray came a-courtin' me.

My father couldna work, and my mother couldna spin ;
I toil'd day and night, but their bread I couldna win ;
Auld Rob maintained them baith, and wi' tears in his e'e
Said :—'Jennie, for their sakes, O, marry me !'

My heart it said nay; I look'd for Jamie back;
But the wind it blew high, and the ship it was a wrack;
His ship it was a wrack . . . Why didna Jamie dee?
Or why do I live to cry Wae's me?

My father urgit sair: my mother didna speak,
But she look'd in my face till my heart was like to break:
They gi'ed him my hand, but my heart was at the sea,
Sae auld Robin Gray he was gudeman to me.

I hadna been a wife a week but only four,
When, mournfu' as I sat on the stane at the door,
I saw my Jamie's wraith, for I couldna think it he—
Till he said :—' I 'm come hame to marry thee.'

O, sair, sair did we greet, and muckle did we say;
We took but ae kiss, and I bad him gang away;
I wish that I were dead, but I 'm no like to dee,
And why was I born to say Wae's me!

I gang like a ghaist, and I carena to spin;
I daurna think on Jamie, for that wad be a sin;
But I 'll do my best a gude wife ay to be,
For auld Robin Gray, he is kind unto me.

Lady Anne Lindsay.

304

TO SPRING

O THOU with dewy locks, who lookest down
Through the clear windows of the morning, turn
Thine angel eyes upon our western isle,
Which in full choir hails thy approach, O Spring!

The hills tell each other, and the listening
Valleys hear; all our longing eyes are turned
Up to thy bright pavilions: issue forth,
And let thy holy feet visit our clime!

Come o'er the eastern hills, and let our winds
Kiss thy perfumèd garments; let us taste
Thy morn and evening breath; scatter thy pearls
Upon our lovesick land that mourns for thee!

O, deck her forth with thy fair fingers ; pour
Thy soft kisses on her bosom ; and put
Thy golden crown upon her languished head,
Whose modest tresses were bound up for thee !

William Blake.

305

HOW SWEET I ROAMED

How sweet I roamed from field to field,
   And tasted all the summer's pride,
Till I the Prince of Love beheld
   Who in the sunny beams did glide !

He showed me lilies for my hair,
   And blushing roses for my brow ;
He led me through his gardens fair
   Where all his golden pleasures grow.

With sweet May-dews my wings were wet,
   And Phœbus fired my vocal rage ;
He caught me in his silken net,
   And shut me in his golden cage.

He loves to sit and hear me sing ;
   Then, laughing, sports and plays with me ;
Then stretches out my golden wing,
   And mocks my loss of liberty.

William Blake.

306

MY SILKS AND FINE ARRAY

My silks and fine array,
   My smiles and languished air,
By love are driven away ;
   And mournful lean Despair
Brings me yew to deck my grave :
Such end true lovers have !

His face is fair as heaven
   When springing buds unfold :
O, why to him was 't given,
   Whose heart is wintry cold ?

His breast is love's all-worshipped tomb,
Where all love's pilgrims come.

Bring me an axe and spade,
  Bring me a winding-sheet;
When I my grave have made,
  Let winds and tempests beat;
Then down I'll lie, as cold as clay—
True love doth pass away!

            William Blake.

307

TO MEMORY

MEMORY, hither come,
  And tune your merry notes,
And, while upon the wind
  Your music floats,
I'll pore upon the stream
Where signing lovers dream,
And fish for fancies, as they pass
Within the watery glass.

I'll drink of the clear stream,
  And hear the linnets' song,
And there I'll lie and dream
  The day along;
And, when night comes, I'll go
To places fit for woe,
Walking along the darkened valley
With silent Melancholy.

            William Blake.

308

TO THE MUSES

WHETHER on Ida's shady brow
  Or in the chambers of the East,
The chambers of the Sun, that now
  From ancient melody have ceased

Whether in heaven ye wander fair,
　　Or the green corners of the earth,
Or the blue regions of the air
　　Where the melodious winds have birth ;

Whether on crystal rocks ye rove,
　　Beneath the bosom of the sea
Wandering in many a coral grove :
　　Fair Nine, forsaking Poetry,

How have you left the ancient love
　　That bards of old enjoyed in you !
The languid strings do scarcely move,
　　The sound is forced, the notes are few.

William Blake.

309

A SONG OF SINGING

PIPING down the valleys wild,
　　Piping songs of pleasant glee,
On a cloud I saw a child,
　　And he laughing said to me :—

' Pipe a song about a Lamb ! '
　　So I piped with merry cheer.
' Piper, pipe that song again.'
　　So I piped : he wept to hear.

' Drop thy pipe, thy happy pipe ;
　　Sing thy songs of happy cheer ! '
So I sang the same again,
　　While he wept with joy to hear.

' Piper, sit thee down and write
　　In a book, that all may read.'
So he vanished from my sight ;
　　And I plucked a hollow reed,

And I made a rural pen,
　　And I stained the water clear,
And I wrote my happy songs
　　Every child may joy to hear.

William Blake.

310

THE SICK ROSE

O ROSE, thou art sick !
 The invisible worm,
That flies in the night,
 In the howling storm,

Has found out thy bed
 Of crimson joy,
And his dark secret love
 Does thy life destroy.

William Blake.

311

THE ANGEL

I DREAMT a dream ! What can it mean?
And that I was a maiden Queen
Guarded by an Angel mild :
Witless woe was ne'er beguiled !

And I wept both night and day,
And he wiped my tears away ;
And I wept both day and night,
And hid from him my heart's delight.

So he took his wings, and fled.
Then the morn blushed rosy red ;
I dried my tears, and armed my fears
With ten thousand shields and spears.

Soon my Angel came again ;
I was armed, he came in vain ;
For the time of youth was fled,
And grey hairs were on my head.

William Blake.

312

THE TIGER

TIGER, tiger, burning bright
In the forests of the night,
What immortal hand or eye
Could frame thy fearful symmetry?

S

In what distant deeps or skies
Burnt the fire of thine eyes?
On what wings dare he aspire?
What the hand dare seize the fire?

And what shoulder and what art
Could twist the sinews of thy heart?
And, when thy heart began to beat,
What dread hand and what dread feet?

What the hammer? what the chain?
In what furnace was thy brain?
What the anvil? what dread grasp
Dare its deadly terrors clasp?

When the stars threw down their spears,
And watered heaven with their tears,
Did he smile his work to see?
Did he who made the lamb make thee?

Tiger, tiger, burning bright
In the forests of the night,
What immortal hand or eye
Dare frame thy fearful symmetry?

William Blake.

313

THE SUNFLOWER

AH ! Sunflower, weary of time,
  Who countest the steps of the sun,
Seeking after that sweet golden clime
  Where the traveller's journey is done ;

Where the Youth pined away with desire,
  And the pale virgin shrouded in snow,
Arise from their graves, and aspire
  Where my Sunflower wishes to go !

William Blake.

314

CRADLE SONG

SLEEP, sleep, beauty bright,
Dreaming in the joys of night !
Sleep, sleep ; in thy sleep
Little sorrows sit and weep.

Sweet babe, in thy face
Soft desires I can trace,
Secret joys and secret smiles,
Little pretty infant wiles.

As thy softest limbs I feel,
Smiles as of the morning steal
O'er thy cheek, and o'er thy breast
Where thy little heart doth rest.

O, the cunning wiles that creep
In thy little heart asleep!
When thy little heart doth wake,
Then the dreadful light shall break.

William Blake.

315

OF 'A' THE AIRTS

OF a' the airts the wind can blaw,
  I dearly like the west,
For there the bonie lassie lives,
  The lassie I lo'e best:
There wild woods grow, and rivers row,
  And monie a hill between,
But day and night my fancy's flight
  Is ever wi' my Jean.

I see her in the dewy flowers,
  I see her sweet and fair.
I hear her in the tunefu' birds,
  I hear her charm the air.
There's not a bonie flower that springs
  By fountain, shaw, or green,
There's not a bonie bird that sings,
  But minds me o' my Jean.

Robert Burns.

316

THE HAPPY TRIO

We are na fou, we're no that fou,
  But just a drappie in our ee:
The cock may craw, the day may daw,
  And aye we'll taste the barley bree.

O, WILLIE brew'd a peck o' maut,
  And Rob and Allan cam to see :
Three blyther hearts, that lee-lang night,
  Ye wad na find in Christendie.

Here are we met, three merry boys,
  Three merry boys, I trow, are we ;
And monie a night we 've merry been,
  And monie mae we hope to be !

It is the moon, I ken her horn,
  That 's blinkin in the lift sae hie :
She shines sae bright to wyle us hame,
  But by my sooth she 'll wait a wee !

Wha first shall rise to gang awa,
  A cuckold, coward loun is he !
Wha first beside his chair shall fa',
  He is the King among us three !

    We are na fou, we 're no that fou,
      But just a drappie in our ee ;
    The cock may craw, the day may daw,
      And aye we 'll taste the barley bree.

Robert Burns.

317

JOHN ANDERSON MY JO

JOHN ANDERSON my jo, John,
  When we were first acquent,
Your locks were like the raven,
  Your bonie brow was brent ;
But now your brow is beld, John,
  Your locks are like the snaw ;
But blessings on your frosty pow,
  John Anderson my jo.

John Anderson my jo, John,
  We clamb the hill thegither,
And monie a canty day, John,
  We 've had wi' ane anither :
Now we maun totter down, John,
  But hand and hand we 'll go,
And sleep thegither at the foot,
  John Anderson my jo,

Robert Burns.

318

O, LEEZE ME ON MY SPINNIN WHEEL

O, LEEZE me on my spinnin wheel!
O, leeze me on my rock and reel,
Frae tap to tae that cleeds me bien,
And haps me fiel and warm at e'en!
I 'll set me down and sing and spin,
While laigh descends the simmer sun,
Blest wi' content, and milk and meal—
O, leeze me on my spinnin wheel!

On ilka hand the burnies trot,
And meet below my theekit cot;
The scented birk and hawthorn white
Across the pool their arms unite,
Alike to screen the birdie's nest
And little fishes' caller rest;
The sun blinks kindly in the biel',
Where blythe I turn my spinnin wheel.

On lofty aiks the cushats wail,
And Echo cons the doolfu' tale.
The lintwhites in the hazel braes,
Delighted, rival ither's lays.
The craik amang the claver hay,
The paitrick whirring o'er the ley,
The swallow jinkin round my shiel,
Amuse me at my spinnin wheel.

Wi' sma' to sell, and less to buy,
Aboon distress, below envy,
O, wha wad leave this humble state,
For a' the pride of a' the great?
Amid the flaring, idle toys,
Amid their cumbrous, dinsome joys,
Can they the peace and pleasure feel
Of Bessy at her spinnin wheel?

Robert Burns.

319

TAM GLEN

My heart is a breaking, dear tittie,
  Some counsel unto me come len'.
To anger them a' is a pity—
  But what will I do wi' Tam Glen?

I 'm thinking, wi' sic a braw fellow,
  In poortith I might mak a fen';
What care I in riches to wallow,
  If I maunna marry Tam Glen?

There's Lowrie the laird o' Dumeller,
  'Guid-day to you,' brute! he comes ben.
He brags and he blaws o' his siller,
  But when will he dance like Tam Glen?

My minnie does constantly deave me,
  And bids me beware o' young men:
They flatter, she says, to deceive me;
  But wha can think sae o' Tam Glen?

My daddie says, gin I 'll forsake him,
  He 'll gie me guid hunder marks ten:
But, if it 's ordain'd I maun take him,
  O, wha will I get but Tam Glen?

Yestreen at the Valentines' dealing,
  My heart to my mou gied a sten:
For thrice I drew ane without failing,
  And thrice it was written, Tam Glen.

The last Halloween I was waukin
  My droukit sark-sleeve, as ye ken:
His likeness cam up the house staukin—
  And the very grey breeks o' Tam Glen!

Come counsel, dear tittie, don't tarry!
  I 'll gie you my bonie black hen,
Gif ye will advise me to marry
  The lad I lo'e dearly, Tam Glen.

Robert Burns.

320

BONIE DOON

YE flowery banks o' bonie Doon,
  How can ye blume sae fair!
How can ye chant, ye little birds,
  And I sae fu' o' care!

Thou 'lt break my heart, thou bonie bird,
   That sings upon the bough :
Thou minds me o' the happy days,
   When my fause luve was true.

Thou 'lt break my heart, thou bonie bird,
   That sings beside thy mate ;
For sae I sat, and sae I sang,
   And wist na o' my fate.

Aft hae I rov'd by bonie Doon,
   To see the woodbine twine ;
And ilka bird sang o' its luve,
   And sae did I o' mine.

Wi' lightsome heart I pu'd a rose,
   Frae aff its thorny tree ;
And my fause luver stole my rose,
   But left the thorn wi' me.

               Robert Burns.

321

GO FETCH TO ME

Go, fetch to me a pint o' wine,
   An' fill it in a silver tassie,
That I may drink before I go
   A service to my bonie lassie !
The boat rocks at the pier o' Leith,
   Fu' loud the wind blaws frae the ferry,
The ship rides by the Berwick-law,
   And I maun leave my bonie Mary.

The trumpets sound, the banners fly,
   The glittering spears are rankéd ready,
The shouts o' war are heard afar,
   The battle closes thick and bloody.
But it 's no the roar o' sea or shore
   Wad mak me langer wish to tarry,
Nor shout o' war that 's heard afar—
   It 's leaving thee, my bonie Mary !

               Robert Burns.

322

O MAY, THY MORN

O MAY, thy morn was ne'er sae sweet,
    As the mirk night o' December ;
For sparkling was the rosy wine,
    And private was the chamber ;
And dear was she I dare na name,
    But I will aye remember !

And here 's to them, that, like oursel,
    Can push about the jorum !
And here 's to them that wish us weel—
    May a' that 's guid watch o'er them !
And here 's to them we dare na tell,
    The dearest o' the quorum !

Robert Burns.

323

THE RANTIN DOG THE DADDIE O'T

O, WHA my babie-clouts will buy?
Wha will tent me when I cry?
Wha will kiss me whare I lie?—
    The rantin dog the daddie o 't !

Wha will own he did the faut?
Wha will buy the groanin maut?
Wha will tell me how to ca't?—
    The rantin dog the daddie o 't !

When I mount the creepie-chair,
Wha will sit beside me there?
Gie me Rob, I seek nae mair—
    The rantin dog the daddie o 't !

Wha will crack to me my lane?
Wha will mak me fidgin fain?
Wha will kiss me o'er again?—
    The rantin dog the daddie o 't !

Robert Burns.

324

THE GOWDEN LOCKS OF ANNA

YESTREEN I had a pint o' wine,
  A place where body saw na';
Yestreen lay on this breast o' mine
  The gowden locks of Anna.
The hungry Jew in wilderness
  Rejoicing o'er his manna
Was naething to my hinny bliss
  Upon the lips of Anna.

Ye monarchs, tak the east and west,
  Frae Indus to Savannah!
Gie me within my straining grasp
  The melting form of Anna:
There I 'll despise imperial charms,
  An Empress or Sultana,
While dying raptures in her arms
  I give and take with Anna!

Awa, thou flaunting god o' day!
  Awa, thou pale Diana!
Ilk star, gae hide thy twinkling ray,
  When I 'm to meet my Anna!
Come, in thy raven plumage, night,
  Sun, moon, and stars withdrawn a',
And bring an angel pen to write
  My transports wi' my Anna!

The kirk and state may join, and tell
  To do such things I maunna:
The kirk and state may gae to hell,
  And I 'll gae to my Anna!
She is the sunshine o' my ee,
  To live but her I canna.
Had I on earth but wishes three,
  The first should be my Anna.

                          -*Robert Burns.*

325

THE RIGS O' BARLEY

Corn rigs, an' barley rigs,
  An' corn rigs are bonie :
I 'll ne'er forget that happy night,
  Amang the rigs wi' Annie.

IT was upon a Lammas night,
  When corn rigs are bonie,
Beneath the moon's unclouded light
  I held awa to Annie.
The time flew by wi' tentless heed,
  Till, 'tween the late and early,
Wi' sma' persuasion she agreed
  To see me thro' the barley.

The sky was blue, the wind was still,
  The moon was shining clearly ;
I set her down wi' right good will,
  Amang the rigs o' barley.
I kent her heart was a' my ain ;
  I lov'd her most sincerely ;
I kiss'd her owre and owre again
  Amang the rigs o' barley.

I lock'd her in my fond embrace,
  Her heart was beating rarely :
My blessings on that happy place,
  Amang the rigs o' barley !
But, by the moon and stars so bright
  That shone that hour so clearly,
She ay shall bless that happy night
  Amang the rigs o' barley !

I hae been blythe wi' comrades dear,
  I hae been merry drinking,
I hae been joyfu' gath'rin gear,
  I hae been happy thinking :
But a' the pleasures e'er I saw,
  Tho' three times doubl'd fairly,
That happy night was worth them a',
  Amang the rigs o' barley.

Corn rigs, an' barley rigs,
  An' corn rigs are bonie:
I 'll ne'er forget that happy night,
  Amang the rigs wi' Annic.

Robert Burns.

326

GREEN GROW THE RASHES

Green grow the rashes, O!
  Green grow the rashes, O!
The sweetest hours that e'er I spend,
  Are spent amang the lasses, O!

THERE's nought but care on ev'ry han',
  In every hour that passes, O:
What signifies the life o' man,
  An' 'twere na for the lasses, O?

The warly race may riches chase,
  An' riches still may fly them, O,
An' tho' at last they catch them fast,
  Their hearts can ne'er enjoy them, O;

But gie me a canny hour at e'en,
  My arms about my dearie, O,
An' warly cares, an' warly men,
  May a' gae tapsalteeric, O!

For you sae douce, ye sneer at this,
  Ye 're nought but senseless asses, O:
The wisest man the warl' saw,
  He dearly lov'd the lasses, O!

Auld Nature swears, the lovely dears
  Her noblest work she classes, O:
Her prentice han' she tried on man,
  And then she made the lasses, O.

Green grow the rashes, O!
  Green grow the rashes, O!
The sweetest hours that e'er I spend,
  Are spent amang the lasses, O!

Robert Burns.

327

AULD LANG SYNE

For auld lang syne, my dear,
For auld lang syne,
We 'll tak a cup o' kindness yet
For auld lang syne.

SHOULD auld acquaintance be forgot,
And never brought to min'?
Should auld acquaintance be forgot,
And days o' lang syne?

We twa hae rin about the braes,
And pu'd the gowans fine;
But we 've wandered monie a weary foot
Sin auld lang syne.

We twa hae paidl't i' the burn,
Frae mornin sun till dine;
But seas between us braid hae roar'd
Sin auld lang syne.

And here 's a hand, my trusty fiere,
And gie 's a hand o' thine,
And we 'll tak a right guid-willie waught
For auld lang syne!

And surely ye 'll be your pint-stowp,
And surely I 'll be mine!
And we 'll tak a cup o' kindness yet
For auld lang syne!

For auld lang syne, my dear,
For auld lang syne,
We 'll tak a cup o' kindness yet
For auld lang syne.

Robert Burns.

328

DOES HAUGHTY GAUL INVASION THREAT

DOES haughty Gaul invasion threat?
Then let the loons beware, Sir,
There 's wooden walls upon our seas,
And volunteers on shore, Sir.

The Nith shall run to Corsincon,
　　And Criffel sink to Solway,
Ere we permit a foreign foe
　　On British ground to rally !

O, let us not like snarling tykes
　　In wrangling be divided,
Till, slap ! come in an unco loon
　　And wi' a rung decide it !
Be Britain still to Britain true,
　　Amang oursels united,
For never but by British hands
　　Maun British wrangs be righted !

The kettle o' the Kirk and State,
　　Perhaps a clout may fail in 't :
But deil a foreign tinkler loon
　　Shall ever ca' a nail in 't.
Our fathers' bluid the kettle bought,
　　And wha wad dare to spoil it,
By heaven, the sacrilegious dog
　　Shall fuel be to boil it !

The wretch that wad a tyrant own,
　　And the wretch his true-born brother,
Who would set the mob aboon the throne,
　　May they be damned together !
Who will not sing *God save the King,*
　　Shall hang as high 's the steeple ;
But while we sing *God save the King,*
　　We 'll ne'er forget the people.

Robert Burns.

329

O, MY LUVE'S LIKE A RED, RED ROSE

O, MY luve 's like a red, red rose
　　That 's newly sprung in June !
O, my luve 's like the melodie
　　That 's sweetly played in tune !

As fair art thou, my bonie lass,
  So deep in luve am I,
And I will luve thee still, my dear,
  Till a' the seas gang dry :

Till a' the seas gang dry, my dear,
  And the rocks melt wi' the sun !
I will luve thee still, my dear,
  While the sands o' life shall run.

And fare thee weel, my only luve,
  And fare thee weel awhile !
And I will come again, my luve,
  Tho' it were ten thousand mile.

Robert Burns.

330

M'PHERSON'S FAREWELL

Sae rantingly, sae wantonly,
  Sae dauntingly gaed he,
He play'd a spring and danc'd it round,
  Below the gallows tree.

FAREWELL, ye dungeons dark and strong,
  The wretch's destinie !
M'Pherson's time will not be long
  On yonder gallows tree.

O, what is death but parting breath ?
  On monie a bloody plain
I 've dar'd his face, and in this place
  I scorn him yet again !

Untie these bands from off my hands,
  And bring to me my sword,
And there 's no a man in all Scotland,
  But I 'll brave him at a word !

I 've lived a life of sturt and strife ;
  I die by treacherie :
It burns my heart I must depart,
  And not avengéd be.

Now farewell light, thou sunshine bright,
  And all beneath the sky !
May coward shame distain his name,
  The wretch that dares not die !

    Sae rantingly, sae wantonly,
      Sae dauntingly gaed he,
    He play'd a spring and danc'd it round,
      Below the gallows tree.
                          Robert Burns.

331

CHARLIE HE'S MY DARLING

    An' Charlie he's my darling,
    My darling, my darling !
    Charlie he's my darling,
    The Young Chevalier !

'TWAS on a Monday morning,
  Right early in the year,
That Charlie cam' to our town,
  The Young Chevalier !

As he was walking up the street
  The city for to view,
O, there he spied a bonie lass
  The window lookin' through.

Sae light 's he jimpéd up the stair,
  An' tirled at the pin !
An' wha sae ready as hersel
  To let the laddie in ?

He set his Jenny on his knee,
  A' in his Highland dress ;
For brawlie weel he ken'd the way
  To please a lassie best.

It 's up yon heathery mountain,
  An' down yon scroggy glen,
We daur na gang a-milking
  For Charlie an' his men !

    An' Charlie he's my darling,
    My darling, my darling !
    Charlie he's my darling,
    The Young Chevalier !

332

MARY MORISON

O MARY, at thy window be—
  It is the wish'd, the trysted hour !
Those smiles and glances let me see,
  That make the miser's treasure poor !
  How blythely wad I bide the stoure,
A weary slave frae sun to sun,
  Could I the rich reward secure,
The lovely Mary Morison !

Yestreen, when to the trembling string
  The dance gaed thro' the lighted ha',
To thee my fancy took its wing,
  I sat, but neither heard nor saw :
  Tho' this was fair, and that was braw,
And yon the toast of a' the town,
  I sigh'd, and said amang them a':—
' Ye are na Mary Morison.'

O Mary, canst thou wreck his peace,
  Wha for thy sake wad gladly die ?
Or canst thou break that heart of his,
  Whase only faut is loving thee ?
  If love for love thou wilt na gie,
At least be pity to me shown :
  A thought ungentle canna be
The thought o' Mary Morison.

Robert Burns.

333

THE FAREWELL

IT was a' for our rightfu' King
  We left fair Scotland's strand :
It was a' for our rightfu' King
  We e'er saw Irish land,
        My dear—
  We e'er saw Irish land.

Now a' is done that men can do,
  And a' is done in vain,
My love and native land farewell,
  For I maun cross the main,
      My dear—
  For I maun cross the main.

He turn'd him right and round about
  Upon the Irish shore,
And gae his bridle-reins a shake,
  With adieu for evermore,
      My dear—
  With adieu for evermore.

The sodger from the wars returns,
  The sailor frae the main ;
But I hae parted frae my love,
  Never to meet again,
      My dear—
  Never to meet again.

When day is gane, and night is come,
  And a' folk bound to sleep,
I think on him that 's far awa,
  The lee-lang night, and weep,
      My dear—
  The lee-lang night, and weep.

Robert Burns.

334

LUCY

SHE dwelt among the untrodden ways
  Beside the springs of Dove,
A Maid whom there were none to praise
  And very few to love :

A violet by a mossy stone
  Half hidden from the eye !
—Fair as a star, when only one
  Is shining in the sky.

She lived unknown, and few could know
  When Lucy ceased to be ;
But she is in her grave, and, O,
  The difference to me !

William Wordsworth.

T

335

TO THE CUCKOO

O BLITHE New-comer ! I have heard,
I hear thee and rejoice.
O Cuckoo ! shall I call thee Bird,
Or but a wandering voice ?

While I am lying on the grass
Thy twofold shout I hear :
From hill to hill it seems to pass,
At once far off and near.

Though babbling only to the Vale
Of sunshine and of flowers,
Thou bringest unto me a tale
Of visionary hours.

Thrice welcome, darling of the Spring !
Even yet thou art to me
No bird, but an invisible thing,
A voice, a mystery :

The same whom in my schoolboy days
I listened to ; that Cry
Which made me look a thousand ways
In bush, and tree, and sky.

To seek thee did I often rove
Through woods and on the green ;
And thou wert still a hope, a love—
Still longed for, never seen.

And I can listen to thee yet ;
Can lie upon the plain
And listen, till I do beget
That golden time again.

O blessed Bird ! the earth we pace
Again appears to be
An unsubstantial, faery place :
That is fit home for thee !

William Wordsworth.

336

SHE WAS A PHANTOM

SHE was a Phantom of delight
When first she gleamed upon my sight ;
A lovely Apparition, sent
To be a moment's ornament ;
Her eyes as stars of Twilight fair,
Like Twilight's, too, her dusky hair ;
But all things else about her drawn
From May-time and the cheerful Dawn ;
A dancing Shape, an Image gay,
To haunt, to startle, and way-lay.

I saw her upon nearer view,
A Spirit, yet a Woman too !
Her household motions light and free,
And steps of virgin-liberty ;
A countenance in which did meet
Sweet records, promises as sweet ;
A Creature not too bright or good
For human nature's daily food ;
For transient sorrows, simple wiles,
Praise, blame, love, kisses, tears, and smiles.

And now I see with eyes serene
The very pulse of the machine ;
A Being breathing thoughtful breath,
A traveller between life and death ;
The reason firm, the temperate will,
Endurance, foresight, strength, and skill ;
A perfect Woman, nobly planned,
To warn, to comfort, and command ;
And yet a Spirit still, and bright
With something of angelic light.

William Wordsworth.

337

ODE

THERE was a time when meadow, grove, and stream,
The earth, and every common sight,
To me did seem
Apparelled in celestial light,
The glory and the freshness of a dream.

It is not now as it hath been of yore : ·
Turn wheresoe'er I may,
By night or day,
The things which I have seen I now can see no more.

The Rainbow comes and goes,
And lovely is the Rose ;
The Moon doth with delight
Look round her when the heavens are bare ;
Waters on a starry night
Are beautiful and fair ;
The Sunshine is a glorious birth ;
But yet I know, where'er I go,
That there hath passed away a glory from the earth.

Now, while the birds thus sing a joyous song,
And while the young lambs bound
As to the tabor's sound,
To me alone there came a thought of grief :
A timely utterance gave that thought relief,
And I again am strong :
The cataracts blow their trumpets from the steep ;
No more shall grief of mine the season wrong ;
I hear the Echoes through the mountains throng,
The Winds come to me from the fields of sleep,
And all the earth is gay :
Land and Sea
Give themselves up to jollity,
And with the heart of May
Doth every Beast keep holiday ;
Thou Child of Joy,
Shout round me, let me hear thy shouts, thou happy
Shepherd-boy !

Ye blessed Creatures, I have heard the call
Ye to each other make ; I see
The heavens laugh with you in your jubilee ;
My heart is at your festival,
My head hath its coronal,
The fulness of your bliss, I feel—I feel it all,
O evil day ! if I were sullen
While Earth herself is adorning,
This sweet May-morning,
And the children are culling
On every side,
In a thousand valleys far and wide,
Fresh flowers ; while the sun shines warm,

And the Babe leaps up on his mother's arm :—
I hear, I hear, with joy I hear !
—But there 's a Tree, of many, one,
A single Field which I have looked upon,
Both of them speak of something that is gone :
The Pansy at my feet
Doth the same tale repeat :
Whither is fled the visionary gleam ?
Where is it now, the glory and the dream ?

Our birth is but a sleep and a forgetting :
The Soul that rises with us, our life's Star,
Hath had elsewhere its setting,
And cometh from afar :
Not in entire forgetfulness,
And not in utter nakedness,
But trailing clouds of glory do we come
From God, who is our home :
Heaven lies about us in our infancy !
Shades of the prison-house begin to close
Upon the growing Boy,
But He beholds the light, and whence it flows,
He sees it in his joy ;
The Youth, who daily further from the east
Must travel, still is Nature's Priest,
And by the vision splendid
Is on his way attended ;
At length the Man perceives it die away,
And fade into the light of common day.

Earth fills her lap with pleasures of her own ;
Yearnings she hath in her own natural kind,
And even with something of a Mother's mind,
And no unworthy aim,
The homely Nurse doth all she can
To make her Foster-child, her Inmate Man,
Forget the glories he hath known,
And that imperial palace whence he came.

Behold the Child among his new-born blisses,
A six years' Darling of a pigmy size !
See, where 'mid work of his own hand he lies,
Fretted by sallies of his mother's kisses,
With light upon him from his father's eyes !
See, at his feet, some little plan or chart,
Some fragment from his dream of human life,
Shaped by himself with newly-learned art ;

A wedding or a festival,
A mourning or a funeral ;
And this hath now his heart,
And unto this he frames his song :
Then will he fit his tongue
To dialogues of business, love, or strife :
But it will not be long
Ere this be thrown aside,
And with new joy and pride
The little Actor cons another part ;
Filling from time to time his ' humorous stage
With all the Persons, down to palsied Age,
That Life brings with her in her equipage ;
As if his whole vocation
Were endless imitation.

Thou, whose exterior semblance doth belie
Thy Soul's immensity ;
Thou best Philosopher, who yet dost keep
Thy heritage, thou Eye among the blind,
That, deaf and silent, read'st the eternal deep,
Haunted for ever by the eternal mind,—
Mighty Prophet ! Seer blest !
On whom those truths do rest,
Which we are toiling all our lives to find,
In darkness lost, the darkness of the grave ;
Thou, over whom thy Immortality
Broods like the Day, a Master o'er a Slave,
A Presence which is not to be put by ;
Thou little Child, yet glorious in the might
Of heaven-born freedom on thy being's height,
Why with such earnest pains dost thou provoke
The years to bring the inevitable yoke,
Thus blindly with thy blessedness at strife ?
Full soon thy Soul shall have her earthly freight,
And custom lie upon thee with a weight
Heavy as frost, and deep almost as life !

O joy ! that in our embers
Is something that doth live,
That nature yet remembers
What was so fugitive !
The thought of our past years in me doth breed
Perpetual benediction : not indeed
For that which is most worthy to be blest ;
Delight and liberty, the simple creed
Of Childhood, whether busy or at rest,

With new-fledged hope still fluttering in his breast—
Not for these I raise
The song of thanks and praise;
But for those obstinate questionings
Of sense and outward things,
Fallings from us, vanishings,
Blank misgivings of a Creature
Moving about in worlds not realised,
High instincts before which our mortal Nature
Did tremble like a guilty thing surprised:
But for those first affections,
Those shadowy recollections,
Which, be they what they may,
Are yet the fountain light of all our day,
Are yet a master light of all our seeing,
Uphold us, cherish, and have power to make
Our noisy years seem moments in the being
Of the eternal Silence: truths that wake
To perish never,
Which neither listlessness nor mad endeavour,
Nor Man nor Boy,
Nor all that is at enmity with joy,
Can utterly abolish or destroy!
Hence in a season of calm weather,
Though inland far we be,
Our Souls have sight of that immortal sea
Which brought us hither,
Can in a moment travel thither,
And see the Children sport upon the shore,
And hear the mighty waters rolling evermore

Then sing, ye Birds, sing, sing a joyous song!
And let the young Lambs bound
As to the tabor's sound!
We in thought will join your throng,
Ye that pipe and ye that play,
Ye that through your hearts to-day
Feel the gladness of the May!
What though the radiance which was once so bright
Be now for ever taken from my sight,
Though nothing can bring back the hour
Of splendour in the grass, of glory in the flower;
We will grieve not, rather find
Strength in what remains behind;
In the primal sympathy
Which having been must ever be;
In the soothing thoughts that spring

Out of human suffering;
In the faith that looks through death,
In years that bring the philosophic mind.

And O ye Fountains, Meadows, Hills, and Groves,
Forebode not any severing of our loves !
Yet in my heart of hearts I feel your might ;
I only have relinquished one delight
To live beneath your more habitual sway.
I love the Brooks, which down their channels fret,
Even more than when I tripped lightly as they :
The innocent brightness of a new-born Day
Is lovely yet ;
The Clouds that gather round the setting sun
Do take a sober colouring from an eye
That hath kept watch o'er man's mortality ;
Another race hath been, and other palms are won.
Thanks to the human heart by which we live,
Thanks to its tenderness, its joys, and fears,
To me the meanest flower that blows can give
Thoughts that do often lie too deep for tears.

William Wordsworth.

338

HUNTING SONG

Waken, lords and ladies gay,
On the mountain dawns the day,
All the jolly chase is here,
With hawk, and horse, and hunting spear !
Hounds are in their couples yelling,
Hawks are whistling, horns are knelling,
Merrily, merrily, mingle they :—
' Waken, lords and ladies gay.'

Waken, lords and ladies gay,
The mist has left the mountain grey,
Springlets in the dawn are steaming,
Diamonds on the brake are gleaming :
And foresters have busy been,
To track the buck in thicket green ;
Now we come to chant our lay :—
' Waken, lords and ladies gay.'

Waken, lords and ladies gay,
To the greenwood haste away ;
We can show you where he lies,
Fleet of foot, and tall of size ;
We can show the marks he made,
When 'gainst the oak his antlers fray'd ;
You shall see him brought to bay—
Waken, lords and ladies gay.

Louder, louder, chant the lay,
Waken, lords and ladies gay !
Tell them youth, and mirth, and glee,
Run a course as well as we.
Time, stern huntsman ! who can baulk,
Stanch as hound, and fleet as hawk :
Think of this, and rise with day,
Gentle lords and ladies gay.

Sir Walter Scott.

339

PIBROCH OF DONALD DHU

PIBROCH of Donuil Dhu,
   Pibroch of Donuil,
Wake thy wild voice anew,
   Summon Clan-Conuil.
Come away, come away,
   Hark to the summons !
Come in your war array,
   Gentles and commons.

Come from deep glen, and
   From mountain so rocky,
The war-pipe and pennon
   Are at Inverlochy.
Come, every hill-plaid
   And true heart that wears one,
Come, every steel blade
   And strong hand that bears one.

Leave untended the herd,
   The flock without shelter ;
Leave the corpse uninterr'd,
   The bride at the altar ;

Leave the deer, leave the steer,
　Leave nets and barges :
Come with your fighting gear,
　Broadswords and targes.

Come as the winds come,
　When forests are rended,
Come as the waves come,
　When navies are stranded :
Faster come, faster come,
　Faster and faster,
Chief, vassal, page and groom,
　Tenant and master !

Fast they come, fast they come ;
　See how they gather !
Wide waves the eagle plume,
　Blended with heather.
Cast your plaids, draw your blades,
　Forward, each man, set !
Pibroch of Donuil Dhu,
　Knell for the onset !

Sir Walter Scott.

340

PROUD MAISIE

PROUD Maisie is in the wood,
　Walking so early ;
Sweet Robin sits on the bush,
　Singing so rarely.

' Tell me, thou bonny bird,
　When shall I marry me ? '—
' When six braw gentlemen
　Kirkward shall carry ye.'

' Who makes the bridal bed,
　Birdie, say truly ? '—
' The grey-headed sexton
　That delves the grave duly.

' The glow-worm o'er grave and stone
　Shall light thee steady ;
The owl from the steeple sing :—
　" Welcome, proud lady ! " '

Sir Walter Scott.

341

CORONACH

HE is gone on the mountain,
  He is lost to the forest,
Like a summer-dried fountain,
  When our need was the sorest.
The font, reappearing,
  From the rain-drops shall borrow,
But to us comes no cheering,
  To Duncan no morrow !

The hand of the reaper
  Takes the ears that are hoary,
But the voice of the weeper
  Wails manhood in glory.
The autumn winds rushing
  Waft the leaves that are serest,
But our flower was in flushing,
  When blighting was nearest.

Fleet foot on the correi,
  Sage counsel in cumber,
Red hand in the foray,
  How sound is thy slumber !
Like the dew on the mountain,
  Like the foam on the river,
Like the bubble on the fountain,
  Thou art gone, and for ever.

                              Sir Walter Scott.

342

BRIGNALL BANKS

O, BRIGNALL banks are wild and fair,
  And Greta woods are green,
And you may gather garlands there,
  Would grace a summer queen ;
And as I rode by Dalton Hall,
  Beneath the turrets high,
A Maiden on the castle wall
  Was singing merrily :—

'O, Brignall banks are fresh and fair,
  And Greta woods are green !
I'd rather rove with Edmund there
  Than reign our English Queen.'—

'If, Maiden, thou wouldst wend with me
  To leave both tower and town,
Thou first must guess what life lead we,
  That dwell by dale and down?
And if thou canst that riddle read,
  As read full well you may,
Then to the greenwood shalt thou speed
  As blithe as Queen of May.'—

Yet sung she :—'Brignall banks are fair,
  And Greta woods are green !
I'd rather rove with Edmund there
  Than reign our English Queen.

'I read you, by your bugle horn
  And by your palfrey good,
I read you for a ranger sworn,
  To keep the king's greenwood.'—
'A Ranger, lady, winds his horn,
  And 'tis at peep of light ;
His blast is heard at merry morn,
  And mine at dead of night.'—

Yet sung she :—'Brignall banks are fair,
  And Greta woods are gay ;
I would I were with Edmund there
  To reign his Queen of May !

'With burnish'd brand and musketoon
  So gallantly you come,
I read you for a bold Dragoon,
  That lists the tuck of drum.'—
'I list no more the tuck of drum,
  No more the trumpet hear ;
But when the beetle sounds his hum,
  My comrades take the spear.

'And, O ! though Brignall banks be fair,
  And Greta woods be gay,
Yet mickle must the maiden dare,
  Would reign my Queen of May !

'Maiden! a nameless life I lead,
  A nameless death I'll die!
The fiend, whose lantern lights the mead,
  Were better mate than I!
And when I'm with my comrades met,
  Beneath the greenwood bough,
What once we were we all forget,
  Nor think what we are now.'

Yet Brignall banks are fresh and fair,
  And Greta woods are green,
And you may gather garlands there
  Would grace a summer queen.

Sir Walter Scott.

343

WHERE SHALL THE LOVER REST

WHERE shall the lover rest,
  Whom the fates sever
From his true maiden's breast,
  Parted for ever?
Where through groves deep and high
  Sounds the far billow,
Where early violets die
  Under the willow.

Eleu loro!   Soft shall be his pillow!

There through the summer day
  Cool streams are laving;
There, while the tempest's sway,
  Scarce are boughs waving;
There thy rest shalt thou take,
  Parted for ever,
Never again to wake,
  Never, O never!

Eleu loro!   Never, O never!

Where shall the traitor rest,
  He, the deceiver,
Who could win maiden's breast,
  Ruin, and leave her?

In the lost battle,
  Borne down by the flying,
Where mingles war's rattle
  With groans of the dying.

Eleu loro!   There shall he be lying !

Her wing shall the eagle flap
  O'er the false-hearted ;
His warm blood the wolf shall lap,
  Ere life be parted ;
Shame and dishonour sit
  By his grave ever ;
Blessing shall hallow it,—
  Never, O never !

Eleu loro!   Never, O never !

Sir Walter Scott.

344

TIME

' WHY sitt'st thou by that ruin'd hall,
  Thou aged carle so stern and grey ?
Dost thou its former pride recall,
  Or ponder how it passed away ! '—

' Know'st thou not me ? ' the Deep Voice cried,
  ' So long enjoy'd, so oft misused—
Alternate, in thy fickle pride,
  Desired, neglected, and accused ?

' Before my breath, like blazing flax,
  Man and his marvels pass away,
And changing empires wane and wax,
  Are founded, flourish, and decay !

' Redeem mine hours—the space is brief—
  While in my glass the sand-grains shiver,
And measureless thy joy or grief,
  When TIME and thou shall part for ever ! '

Sir Walter Scott.

345

DONALD CAIRD

Donald Caird's come again!
Donald Caird's come again!
Tell the news in brugh and glen,
Donald Caird's come again!

DONALD CAIRD can lilt and sing,
Blithely dance the Highland fling,
Drink till the gudeman be blind,
Fleech till the gudewife be kind,
Houp a leglin, clout a pan,
Or crack a pow wi' ony man:
Tell the news in brugh and glen,
Donald Caird's come again.

Donald Caird's come again!
Donald Caird's come again!
Tell the news in brugh and glen,
Donald Caird's come again.

Donald Caird can wire a maukin,
Kens the wiles o' dun-deer staukin',
Leisters kipper, makes a shift
To shoot a muir-fowl in the drift.
Water-bailiffs, rangers, keepers,
He can wauk when they are sleepers.
Not for bountith or reward
Daur ye mell wi' Donald Caird!

Donald Caird's come again!
Donald Caird's come again!
Gar the bagpipes hum amain,
Donald Caird's come again.

Donald Caird can drink a gill
Fast as hostler-wife can fill;
Ilka ane that sells gude liquor
Kens how Donald bends a bicker;
When he's fou he's stout and saucy,
Keeps the cantle o' the cawsey;
Hieland chief and Lawland laird
Maun gie room to Donald Caird!

Donald Caird's come again !
Donald Caird's come again !
Tell the news in brugh and glen,
Donald Caird's come again.

Steek the amrie, lock the kist,
Else some gear may weel be mis't ;
Donald Caird finds orra things
Where Allan Gregor fand the tings :
Dunts of kebbuck, taits o' woo,
Whiles a hen and whiles a sow,
Webs or duds frae hedge or yard—
'Ware the wuddie, Donald Caird !

Donald Caird's come again !
Donald Caird's come again !
Dinna let the Shirra ken
Donald Caird's come again !

On Donald Caird the doom was stern,
Craig to tether, legs to airn ;
But Donald Caird, wi' mickle study,
Caught the gift to cheat the wuddie :
Rings of airn, and bolts of steel,
Fell like ice frae hand and heel !
Watch the sheep in fauld and glen,
Donald Caird's come again !

Donald Caird's come again !
Donald Caird's come again !
Dinna let the Justice ken
Donald Caird's come again.

Sir Walter Scott.

346

SONG

AH ! County Guy, the hour is nigh :
    The sun has left the lea,
The orange flower perfumes the bower,
    The breeze is on the sea,
The lark, his lay who thrill'd all day,
    Sits hush'd his partner nigh :
Breeze, bird, and flower, confess the hour,
    But where is County Guy ?—

The village maid steals through the shade
  Her shepherd's suit to hear ;
To beauty shy, by lattice high,
  Sings high-born Cavalier ;
The star of Love, all stars above,
  Now reigns o'er earth and sky,
And high and low the influence know—
  But where is County Guy?

Sir Walter Scott.

347

BONNY DUNDEE

To the Lords of Convention 'twas Claver'se who spoke :—
' Ere the King's crown shall fall there are crowns to be broke,
So let each Cavalier, who loves honour and me,
Come follow the bonnet of Bonny Dundee.

  ' Come fill up my cup, come fill up my can,
  Come saddle your horses, and call up your men ;
  Come open the West Port, and let me gang free,
  And it 's room for the bonnets of Bonny Dundee !'

Dundee he is mounted, he rides up the street ;
The bells are rung backward, the drums they are beat ;
But the Provost, douce man, said :—' Just e'en let him be !
The Gude Town is weel quit of that Deil of Dundee.'

As he rode down the sanctified bends of the Bow,
Ilk carline was flyting and shaking her pow ;
But the young plants of grace they look'd couthie and slee,
Thinking :—Luck to thy bonnet, thou Bonny Dundee !

With sour-featured Whigs the Grassmarket was cramm'd,
As if half the West had set tryst to be hang'd ;
There was spite in each look, there was fear in each e'e,
As they watch'd for the bonnets of Bonny Dundee.

These cowls of Kilmarnock had spits, and had spears
And lang-hafted gullies to kill Cavaliers ;
But they shrunk to close-heads, and the causeway was free
At the toss of the bonnet of Bonny Dundee.

He spurr'd to the foot of the proud Castle rock,
And with the gay Gordon he gallantly spoke :—
' Let Mons Meg and her marrows speak twa words, or three,
For the love of the bonnet of Bonny Dundee.'

U

The Gordon demands of him, Which way he goes ?
'Where'er shall direct me the shade of Montrose !
Your Grace in short space shall hear tidings of me,
Or that low lies the bonnet of Bonny Dundee.

'There are hills beyond Pentland, and lands beyond Forth,
If there's lords in the Lowlands, there's chiefs in the North ;
There are wild Duniwassals three thousand times three,
Will cry *hoigh!* for the bonnet of Bonny Dundee.

'There's brass on the target of barken'd bull-hide,
There's steel in the scabbard that dangles beside :
The brass shall be burnish'd, the steel shall flash free,
At a toss of the bonnet of Bonny Dundee.

'Away to the hills, to the caves, to the rocks—
Ere I own an usurper, I'll couch with the fox ;
And tremble, false Whigs, in the midst of your glee—
You have not seen the last of my bonnet and me !'

He waved his proud hand, and the trumpets were blown,
The kettle-drums clash'd, and the horsemen rode on,
Till on Ravelston's cliffs and on Clermiston's lee
Died away the wild war-notes of Bonny Dundee.

Come fill up my cup, come fill up my can,
Come saddle the horses and call up the men,
Come open your gates, and let me gae free,
For it's up with the bonnets of Bonny Dundee !

Sir Walter Scott.

348

KUBLA KHAN

In Xanadu did Kubla Khan
A stately pleasure-dome decree :
Where Alph, the sacred river, ran
Through caverns measureless to man
   Down to a sunless sea.
So twice five miles of fertile ground
With walls and towers were girdled round :
And there were gardens bright with sinuous rills
Where blossomed many an incense-bearing tree ;
And here were forests ancient as the hills,
Enfolding sunny spots of greenery.

But O ! that deep romantic chasm which slanted
Down the green hill athwart a cedarn cover !
A savage place ! as holy and enchanted
As e'er beneath a waning moon was haunted
By woman wailing for her demon-lover !
And from this chasm, with ceaseless turmoil seething,
As if this Earth in fast thick pants were breathing,
A mighty fountain momently was forced :
Amid whose swift half-intermitted burst
Huge fragments vaulted like rebounding hail,
Or chaffy grain beneath the thresher's flail :
And mid these dancing rocks at once and ever
It flung up momently the sacred river.
Five miles meandering with a mazy motion
Through wood and dale the sacred river ran,
Then reached the caverns measureless to man,
And sank in tumult to a lifeless ocean :
And 'mid this tumult Kubla heard from far
Ancestral voices prophesying war !

    The shadow of the dome of pleasure
    Floated midway on the waves,
    Where was heard the mingled measure
    From the fountain and the caves.
It was a miracle of rare device,
A sunny pleasure-dome with caves of ice !
    A damsel with a dulcimer
    In a vision once I saw :
    It was an Abyssinian maid,
    And on her dulcimer she played,
    Singing of Mount Abora.
    Could I revive within me
    Her symphony and song,
    To such a deep delight 'twould win me
That with music loud and long,
I would build that dome in air,
That sunny dome ! those caves of ice !
And all who heard should see them there,
And all should cry, Beware ! Beware !
His flashing eyes, his floating hair !
Weave a circle round him thrice,
And close your eyes with holy dread,
For he on honey-dew hath fed,
And drunk the milk of Paradise.

Samuel Taylor Coleridge.

349

GLYCINE'S SONG

A sunny shaft did I behold,
  From sky to earth it slanted;
And poised therein a bird so bold—
  Sweet bird, thou wert enchanted!

He sank, he rose, he twinkled, he trolled
  Within that shaft of sunny mist:
His eyes of fire, his beak of gold,
  All else of amethyst!

And thus he sang:—'Adieu! adieu!
  Love's dreams prove seldom true.
    The blossoms they
    Make no delay,

The sparkling dewdrops will not stay!
    Sweet month of May,
      We must away,
        Far, far away!
          To-day! to-day!'

Samuel Taylor Coleridge.

350

SONGLETS

I

Pleasure! why thus desert the heart
  In its spring-tide?
I could have seen her, I could part,
  And but have sigh'd!
O'er every youthful charm to stray,
  To gaze, to touch—
Pleasure! why take so much away,
  Or give so much?

II

I held her hand, the pledge of bliss,
  Her hand that trembled and withdrew;
She bent her head before my kiss—
  My heart was sure that hers was true.

Now I have told her I must part,
  She shakes my hand, she bids adieu,   -
Nor shuns the kiss—Alas, my heart !
  Hers never was the heart for you.

III

Mild is the parting year, and sweet
  The odour of the falling spray ;
Life passes on more rudely fleet,
  And balmless is its closing day.
I wait its close, I court its gloom,
  But mourn that never must there fall
Or on my breast or on my tomb
  The tear that would have sooth'd it all.

IV

No, my own love of other years !
  No, it must never be.
Much rests with you that yet endears,
  Alas ! but what with me ?
Could those bright years o'er me revolve
  So gay, o'er you so fair,
The pearl of life we would dissolve,
  And each the cup might share.
You show that truth can ne'er decay,
  Whatever fate befalls ;
I, that the myrtle and the bay
  Shoot fresh on ruin'd walls.

                              Walter Savage Landor.

351

ROSE AYLMER

Ah, what avails the sceptred race !
  Ah, what the form divine !
What every virtue, every grace !
  Rose Aylmer, all were thine.
Rose Aylmer, whom these wakeful eyes
  May weep, but never see,
A night of memories and sighs
  I consecrate to thee.

                              Walter Savage Landor.

352

THE MAID'S LAMENT

I LOVED him not; and yet now he is gone
    I feel I am alone.
I checked him while he spoke; yet could he speak,
    Alas! I would not check.
For reasons not to love him once I sought,
    And wearied all my thought
To vex myself and him; I now would give
    My love, could he but live
Who lately lived for me, and when he found
    'Twas vain, in holy ground
He hid his face amid the shades of death.
    I waste for him my breath
Who wasted his for me; but mine returns,
    And this lorn bosom burns
With stifling heat, heaving it up in sleep,
    And waking me to weep
Tears that had melted his soft heart; for years
    Wept he as bitter tears.
'Merciful God!' such was his latest prayer,
    'These may she never share!'
Quieter is his breath, his breast more cold
    Than daisies in the mould,
Where children spell, athwart the churchyard gate,
    His name, and life's brief date.
Pray for him, gentle souls, whoe'er you be,
    And, O, pray too for me!

Walter Savage Landor.

353

TWENTY YEARS HENCE

TWENTY years hence my eyes may grow
If not quite dim, yet rather so,
Yet yours from others they shall know
        Twenty years hence.

Twenty years hence, though it may hap
That I be called to take a nap
In a cool cell where thunder clap
        Was never heard:

There breathe but o'er my arch of grass,
A not too sadly sighed ' Alas ! '
And I shall catch, ere you can pass,
   That wingéd word.
     Walter Savage Landor.

354

THE OLD FAMILIAR FACES

I HAVE had playmates, I have had companions,
In my days of childhood, in my joyful school-days ;
All, all are gone, the old familiar faces.

I have been laughing, I have been carousing,
Drinking late, sitting late, with my bosom cronies ;
All, all are gone, the old familiar faces.

I loved a love once, fairest among women ;
Closed are her doors on me, I must not see her—
All, all are gone, the old familiar faces.

I have a friend, a kinder friend has no man ;
Like an ingrate, I left my friend abruptly,
Left him, to muse on the old familiar faces.

Ghost-like I paced round the haunts of my childhood,
Earth seemed a desert I was bound to traverse,
Seeking to find the old familiar faces.

Friend of my bosom, thou more than a brother,
Why wert not thou born in my father's dwelling ?
So might we talk of the old familiar faces—

How some they have died, and some they have left me,
And some are taken from me ; all are departed ;
All, all are gone, the old familiar faces.
     Charles Lamb.

355

YE MARINERS OF ENGLAND

 YE Mariners of England,
 That guard our native seas,
 Whose flag has braved a thousand years
 The battle and the breeze,

Your glorious standard launch again
To match another foe,
And sweep through the deep,
While the stormy winds do blow !
While the battle rages loud and long,
And the stormy winds do blow.

The spirits of your fathers
Shall start from every wave,
For the deck it was their field of fame,
And Ocean was their grave.
Where Blake and mighty Nelson fell
Your manly hearts shall glow,
As ye sweep through the deep,
While the stormy winds do blow !
While the battle rages loud and long,
And the stormy winds do blow.

Britannia needs no bulwarks,
No towers along the steep :
Her march is o'er the mountain-waves,
Her home is on the deep.
With thunders from her native oak
She quells the floods below,
As they roar on the shore,
When the stormy winds do blow !
When the battle rages loud and long,
And the stormy winds do blow.

The meteor flag of England
Shall yet terrific burn,
Till danger's troubled night depart,
And the star of peace return.
Then, then, ye ocean warriors,
Our song and feast shall flow
To the fame of your name,
When the storm has ceased to blow !
When the fiery fight is heard no more,
And the storm has ceased to blow.

Thomas Campbell.

356

THE BATTLE OF THE BALTIC

OF Nelson and the North
Sing the glorious day's renown,

When to battle fierce came forth
All the might of Denmark's crown,
And her arms along the deep proudly shone !
By each gun the lighted brand
In a bold determined hand,
And the Prince of all the land
Led them on.

Like leviathans afloat,
Lay their bulwarks on the brine ;
While the sign of battle flew
On the lofty British line :
It was ten of April morn by the chime :
As they drifted on their path,
There was silence deep as death ;
And the boldest held his breath,
For a time.

But the might of England flushed
To anticipate the scene,
And her van the fleeter rushed
O'er the deadly space between.
'Hearts of oak !' our captains cried ; when each gun
From its adamantine lips
Spread a death-shade round the ships,
Like the hurricane eclipse
Of the sun.

Again ! again ! again !
And the havoc did not slack,
Till a feeble cheer the Dane
To our cheering sent us back ;—
Their shots along the deep slowly boom :—
Then ceased—and all is wail,
As they strike the shattered sail,
Or in conflagration pale
Light the gloom. . . .

Now joy, Old England, raise
For the tidings of thy might,
By the festal cities' blaze,
Whilst the wine-cup shines in light !
And yet, amidst that joy and uproar,
Let us think of them that sleep
Full many a fathom deep
By thy wild and stormy steep,
Elsinore !

Thomas Campbell.

357

WHEN HE, WHO ADORES THEE

WHEN he, who adores thee, has left but the name
　Of his fault and his sorrows behind,
O ! say wilt thou weep, when they darken the fame
　Of a life that for thee was resign'd ?
Yes, weep, and however my foes may condemn,
　Thy tears shall efface thy decree ;
For Heaven can witness, though guilty to them,
　I have been but too faithful to thee.

With thee were the dreams of my earliest love ;
　Every thought of my reason was thine ;
In my last humble prayer to the Spirit above
　Thy name shall be mingled with mine.
O ! blest are the lovers and friends who shall live
　The days of thy glory to see ;
But the next dearest blessing that Heaven can give
　Is the pride of thus dying for thee.

Thomas Moore.

358

THE LEGACY

WHEN in death I shall calmly recline,
　O, bear my heart to my mistress dear !
Tell her it liv'd upon smiles and wine
　Of the brightest hue, while it linger'd here ;
Bid her not shed one tear of sorrow
　To sully a heart so brilliant and light,
But balmy drops of the red grape borrow
　To bathe the relic from morn till night.

When the light of my song is o'er,
　Then take my harp to your ancient hall ;
Hang it up at that friendly door,
　Where weary travellers love to call ;
Then if some bard, who roams forsaken,
　Revive its soft note in passing along,
O ! let one thought of its master waken
　Your warmest smile for the child of song.

Keep this cup, which is now o'erflowing,
  To grace your revel, when I'm at rest :
Never, O ! never its balm bestowing
  On lips that beauty hath seldom blest ;
But when some warm devoted lover
  To her he adores shall bathe its brim,
Then, then my spirit around shall hover,
  And hallow each drop that foams for him.

Thomas Moore.

359

THE IRISH PEASANT TO HIS MISTRESS

THROUGH grief and through danger thy smile hath cheer'd my
    way,
Till hope seemed to bud from each thorn that round me lay ;
The darker our fortune, the brighter our pure love burn'd,
Till shame into glory, till fear into zeal was turn'd ;
Yes, slave as I was, in thy arms my spirit felt free,
And bless'd even the sorrows that made me more dear to thee.

Thy rival was honour'd, while thou wert wrong'd and scorn'd ;
Thy crown was of briers, while gold her brows adorn'd ;
She woo'd me to temples, whilst thou lay'st hid in caves ;
Her friends were all masters, while thine, alas ! were slaves ;
Yet cold in the earth, at thy feet, I would rather be
Than wed what I lov'd not, or turn one thought from thee.

They slander thee sorely, who say thy vows are frail—
Hadst thou been a false one, thy cheek had look'd less pale !
They say, too, so long thou hast worn those lingering chains,
That deep in thy heart they have printed their servile stains :
O ! foul is the slander—no chain could that soul subdue—
Where shineth *thy* spirit, there liberty shineth too !

Thomas Moore.

360

SHE IS FAR FROM THE LAND

SHE is far from the land where her young hero sleeps,
  And lovers are round her, sighing :
But coldly she turns from their gaze, and weeps,
  For her heart in his grave is lying.

She sings the wild song of her dear native plains,
   Every note which he lov'd awaking ;—
Ah ! little they think, who delight in her strains,
   How the heart of the minstrel is breaking.

He had liv'd for his love, for his country he died,
   They were all that to life had entwin'd him ;
Nor soon shall the tears of his country be dried,
   Nor long will his love stay behind him.

O ! make her a grave where the sunbeams rest,
   When they promise a glorious morrow :
They 'll shine o'er her sleep, like a smile from the West
   From her own lov'd island of sorrow.

Thomas Moore.

361

AND DOTH NOT A MEETING LIKE THIS

AND doth not a meeting like this make amends
   For all the long years I 've been wand'ring away—
To see thus around me my youth's early friends
   As smiling and kind as in that happy day ?
Though haply o'er some of your brows, as o'er mine,
   The snow-fall of time may be stealing—what then ?
Like alps in the sunset, thus lighted by wine
   We 'll wear the gay tinge of youth's roses again.

What soften'd remembrances come o'er the heart,
   In gazing on those we 've been lost to so long !
The sorrows, the joys, of which once they were part,
   Still round them, like visions of yesterday, throng.
As letters some hand hath invisibly trac'd,
   When held to the flame will steal out on the sight,
So many a feeling, that long seem'd effac'd,
   The warmth of a moment like this brings to light.

And thus, as in memory's bark we shall glide,
   To visit the scenes of our boyhood anew,
Though oft we may see, looking down on the tide,
   The wreck of full many a hope shining through ;
Yet still, as in fancy we point to the flowers,
   That once made a garden of all the gay shore,
Deceiv'd for a moment, we 'll think them still ours,
   And breathe the fresh air of life's morning once more.

So brief our existence, a glimpse, at the most,
  Is all we can have of the few we hold dear,
And oft even joy is unheeded and lost,
  For want of some heart, that could echo it, near.
Ah, well may we hope, when this short life is gone,
  To meet in some world of more permanent bliss,
For a smile, or a grasp of the hand, hast'ning on,
  Is all we enjoy of each other in this !

But, come—the more rare such delights to the heart,
  The more we should welcome, and bless them the more !
They 're ours when we meet—they are lost when we part,
  Like birds that bring summer, and fly when 'tis o'er.
Thus circling the cup, hand in hand, ere we drink,
  Let Sympathy pledge us, thro' pleasure, thro' pain,
That, fast as a feeling but touches one link,
  Her magic shall send it direct thro' the chain !

Thomas Moore.

362

BATTLE SONG

DAY, like our souls, is fiercely dark :
    What then ? 'Tis day !
We sleep no more ; the cock crows—hark !
    To arms ! away !
They come ! they come ! the knell is rung
    Of us or them ;
Wide o'er their march the pomp is flung
    Of gold and gem.
What collared hound of lawless sway,
    To famine dear—
What pensioned slave of Attila,
    Leads in the rear ?
Come they from Scythian wilds afar,
    Our blood to spill ?
Wear they the livery of the Czar ?
    They do his will.
Nor tasselled silk, nor epaulette,
    Nor plume, nor torse—
No splendour gilds, all sternly met,
    Our foot and horse.
But, dark and still, we inly glow,
    Condensed in ire !
Strike, tawdry slaves, and ye shall know
    Our gloom is fire.

In vain your pomp, ye evil powers,
    Insults the land ;
Wrongs, vengeance, and the cause are ours,
    And God's right hand !
Madmen ! they trample into snakes
    The wormy clod !
Like fire beneath their feet awakes
    The sword of God !
Behind, before, above, below,
    They rouse the brave ;
Where'er they go, they make a foe,
    Or find a grave.

Ebenezer Elliot.

363

PLAINT

DARK, deep, and cold the current flows
Unto the sea where no wind blows,
Seeking the land which no one knows.

O'er its sad gloom still comes and goes
The mingled wail of friends and foes,
Borne to the land which no one knows.

Why shrieks for help yon wretch, who goes
With millions, from a world of woes,
Unto the land which no one knows?

Though myriads go with him who goes,
Alone he goes where no wind blows,
Unto the land which no one knows.

For all must go where no wind blows,
And none can go for him who goes,
None, none return whence no one knows.

Yet why should he who shrieking goes
With millions, from a world of woes,
Reunion seek with it or those?

Alone with God, where no wind blows,
And Death, his shadow—doomed, he goes :
That God is there the shadow shows.

O shoreless Deep, where no wind blows !
And, thou, O Land which no one knows—
That God is All, His shadow shows !

Ebenezer Elliot.

364

THE MEN OF GOTHAM

SEAMEN three ! What men be ye?
Gotham's three wise men we be.
Whither in your bowl so free?
To rake the moon from out the sea.
The bowl goes trim.   The moon doth shine.
And our ballast is old wine—
And your ballast is old wine.

Who art thou, so fast adrift?
I am he they call Old Care.
Here on board we will thee lift.
No : I may not enter there.
Wherefore so ?   'Tis Jove's decree,
In a bowl Care may not be—
In a bowl Care may not be.

Fear ye not the waves that roll?
No : in charmèd bowl we swim.
What the charm that floats the bowl?
Water may not pass the brim.
The bowl goes trim.   The moon doth shine.
And our ballast is old wine—
And your ballast is old wine.

Thomas L. Peacock.

365

THE GRAVE OF LOVE

I DUG beneath the cypress shade
    What well might seem an elfin's grave,
And every pledge in earth I laid,
    That erst thy false affection gave.

I pressed them down the sod beneath ;
   I placed one mossy stone above ;
And twined the rose's fading wreath
   Around the sepulchre of love.

Frail as thy love, the flowers were dead
   Ere yet the evening sun was set :
But years shall see the cypress spread,
   Immutable as my regret.
                              Thomas L. Peacock.

366

BONNIE LADY ANN

THERE's kames o' hinney 'tween my luve's lips,
   An' gowd amang her hair ;
Her breasts are lapt in a holie veil,
   Nae mortal een keek there:
What lips dare kiss, or what hand dare touch,
   Or what arm o' luve dare span,
The hinney lips, the creamy loof,
   Or the waist o' Lady Ann !

She kisses the lips o' her bonnie red rose,
   Wat wi' the blobs o' dew ;
But nae gentle lip, nor simple lip,
   Maun touch her lady mou ;
But a broider'd belt wi' a buckle o' gowd
   Her jimpy waist maun span—
O, she's an armfu' fit for heaven,
   My bonnie Lady Ann !

Her bower casement is latticed wi' flowers
   Tied up wi' silver thread,
An' comely sits she in the midst
   Men's longing een to feed.
She waves the ringlets frae her cheek
   Wi' her milky, milky han',
An' her cheeks seem touch'd wi' the finger o' God,
   My bonnie Lady Ann !

The morning cloud is tassel'd wi' gowd,
   Like my luve's broider'd cap ;
An' on the mantle which my love wears
   Are monie a gowden drap ;

Her bonnie eebree 's a holie arch
  Cast by no earthlie han' ;
An' the breath o' God 's atween the lips
  O' my bonnie Lady Ann !

I am her father's gardener lad,
  An' poor, poor is my fa' ;
My auld mither gets my wee, wee fee,
  Wi' fatherless bairnies twa :
My Lady comes, my Lady gaes
  Wi' a fou and kindly han'—
O, the blessing o' God maun mix wi' my luve,
  An' fa' on' Lady Ann !

Allan Cunningham.

367

HAME, HAME, HAME

HAME, hame, hame, hame fain wad I be,
O, hame, hame, hame, to my ain countrie !

When the flower is i' the bud and the leaf is on the tree,
The larks shall sing me hame in my ain countrie.
Hame, hame, hame, hame fain wad I be,
O, hame, hame, hame, to my ain countrie !

The green leaf o' loyaltie 's begun for to fa',
The bonnie white rose it is withering an' a' ;
But I 'll water 't wi' the blude of usurping tyrannie,
An' green it will grow in my ain countrie.

O, there 's naught frae ruin my country can save
But the keys o' kind heaven to open the grave :
That a' the noble martyrs wha died for loyaltie,
May rise again and fight for their ain countrie.

The great are now gane, a' wha ventured to save,
The new grass is springing on the top o' their graves ;
But the sun thro' the mirk blinks blythe in my ee,
' I 'll shine on ye yet in yere ain countrie.'

Hame, hame, hame, hame fain wad I be,
Hame, hame, hame, to my ain countrie !

Allan Cunningham.

X

368

THE CASTLED CRAG OF DRACHENFELS

THE castled crag of Drachenfels
Frowns o'er the wide and winding Rhine,
Whose breast of waters broadly swells
Between the banks which bear the vine,
And hills all rich with blossom'd trees,
And fields which promise corn and wine,
And scatter'd cities crowning these,
Whose far white walls along them shine,
Have strew'd a scene, which I should see
With double joy wert thou with me.

And peasant girls, with deep blue eyes,
And hands which offer early flowers,
Walk smiling o'er this paradise ;
Above, the frequent feudal towers
Through green leaves lift their walls of gray,
And many a rock which steeply lowers,
And noble arch in proud decay,
Look o'er this vale of vintage-bowers ;
But one thing want these banks of Rhine,—
Thy gentle hand to clasp in mine !

I send the lilies given to me ;
Though long before thy hand they touch,
I know that they must wither'd be,
But yet reject them not as such ;
For I have cherish'd them as dear,
Because they yet may meet thine eye,
And guide thy soul to mine even here,
When thou behold'st them drooping nigh,
And know'st them gather'd by the Rhine,
And offer'd from my heart to thine !

The river nobly foams and flows,
The charm of this enchanted ground,
And all its thousand turns disclose
Some fresher beauty varying round :
The haughtiest breast its wish might bound
Through life to dwell delighted here ;
Nor could on earth a spot be found
To nature and to me so dear,
Could thy dear eyes in following mine
Still sweeten more these banks of Rhine !

Byron.

369

SHE WALKS IN BEAUTY

SHE walks in beauty, like the night
  Of cloudless climes and starry skies,
And all that's best of dark and bright
  Meet in her aspect and her eyes:
Thus mellow'd to that tender light
  Which heaven to gaudy day denies.

One shade the more, one ray the less,
  Had half-impair'd the nameless grace,
Which waves in every raven tress,
  Or softly lightens o'er her face,
Where thoughts serenely sweet express,
  How pure, how dear their dwelling-place.

And on that cheek, and o'er that brow,
  So soft, so calm, yet eloquent,
The smiles that win, the tints that glow,
  But tell of days in goodness spent,
A mind at peace with all below,
  A heart whose love is innocent!

Byron.

370

FARE THEE WELL

FARE thee well! and if for ever,
  Still for ever, fare thee well!
Even though unforgiving, never
  'Gainst thee shall my heart rebel.

Would that breast were bared before thee
  Where thy head so oft hath lain,
While that placid sleep came o'er thee
  Which thou ne'er canst know again!

Would that breast, by thee glanced over
  Every inmost thought could show!
Then thou wouldst at last discover
  'Twas not well to spurn it so.

Though the world for this commend thee—
　　Though it smile upon the blow,
Even its praises must offend thee,
　　Founded on another's woe:

Though my many faults defaced me,
　　Could no other arm be found,
Than the one which once embraced me,
　　To inflict a cureless wound?

Yet, O, yet thyself deceive not!
　　Love may sink by slow decay,
But by sudden wrench, believe not,
　　Hearts can thus be torn away.

Still thine own its life retaineth—
　　Still must mine, though bleeding, beat;
And the undying thought which paineth
　　Is—that we no more may meet!

There are words of deeper sorrow
　　Than the wail above the dead:
Both shall live, but every morrow
　　Wake us from a widow'd bed.

And when thou wouldst solace gather,
　　When our child's first accents flow,
Wilt thou teach her to say:—'Father!'
　　Though his care she must forego?

When her little hands shall press thee,
　　When her lip to thine is press'd,
Think of him whose prayer shall bless thee,
　　Think of him thy love had bless'd!

Should her lineaments resemble
　　Those thou never more may'st see,
Then thy heart will softly tremble
　　With a pulse yet true to me.

All my faults perchance thou knowest,
　　All my madness none can know;
All my hopes, where'er thou goest,
　　Wither, yet with thee they go.

Every feeling hath been shaken:
　　Pride, which not a world could bow,
Bows to thee—by thee forsaken,
　　Even my soul forsakes me now.

But 'tis done—all words are idle—
 Words from me are vainer still ;
But the thoughts we cannot bridle
 Force their way without the will.—

Fare thee well !—thus disunited,
 Torn from every nearer tie,
Sear'd in heart, and lone, and blighted,
 More than this I scarce can die.

                                    Byron.

371

STANZAS TO AUGUSTA

Though the day of my destiny's over,
 And the star of my fate hath declined,
Thy soft heart refused to discover
 The faults which so many could find ;
Though thy soul with my grief was acquainted,
 It shrunk not to share it with me,
And the love, which my spirit hath painted,
 It never hath found but in thee.

Then, when nature around me is smiling
 The last smile which answers to mine,
I do not believe it beguiling,
 Because it reminds me of thine ;
And when winds are at war with the ocean,
 As the breasts I believed in with me,
If their billows excite an emotion,
 It is that they bear me from thee.

Though the rock of my last hope is shiver'd,
 And its fragments are sunk in the wave,
Though I feel that my soul is deliver'd
 To pain—it shall not be its slave !
There is many a pang to pursue me :
 They may crush, but they shall not contemn,
They may torture, but shall not subdue me—
 'Tis of thee that I think—not of them !

Though human, thou didst not deceive me,
 Though woman, thou didst not forsake,
Though loved, thou forborest to grieve me,
 Though slander'd, thou never couldst shake :

Though trusted, thou didst not disclaim me,
  Though parted, it was not to fly,
Though watchful, 'twas not to defame me,
  Nor, mute, that the world might belie.

Yet I blame not the world, nor despise it,
  Nor the war of the many with one—
If my soul was not fitted to prize it,
  'Twas folly not sooner to shun :
And if dearly that error hath cost me,
  And more than I once could foresee,
I have found that, whatever it lost me,
  It could not deprive me of thee.

From the wreck of the past, which hath perish'd,
  Thus much I at least may recall :
It hath taught me that what I most cherish'd
  Deserved to be dearest of all :
In the desert a fountain is springing,
  In the wide waste there still is a tree,
And a bird in the solitude singing
  Which speaks to my spirit of thee.

                                       Byron.

372

WHEN WE TWO PARTED

WHEN we two parted
  In silence and tears,
Half broken-hearted
  To sever for years,
Pale grew thy cheek and cold,
  Colder thy kiss ;
Truly that hour foretold
  Sorrow to this.

The dew of the morning
  Sunk chill on my brow—
It felt like the warning
  Of what I feel now.
Thy vows are all broken,
  And light is thy fame ;
I hear thy name spoken,
  And share in its shame

They name thee before me,
  A knell to mine ear ;
A shudder comes o'er me—
  Why wert thou so dear?
They know not I knew thee,
  Who knew thee too well :—
Long, long shall I rue thee
  Too deeply to tell !

In secret we met—
  In silence I grieve,
That thy heart could forget, ,
  Thy spirit deceive.
If I should meet thee
  After long years,
How should I greet thee?—
  With silence and tears.

Byron.

373

AND THOU ART DEAD

AND thou art dead, as young and fair,
  As aught of mortal birth !
And form so soft, and charms so rare,
  Too soon return'd to Earth !
Though Earth received them in her bed,
And o'er the spot the crowd may tread
  In carelessness or mirth,
There is an eye which could not brook
A moment on that grave to look.

I will not ask where thou liest low,
  Nor gaze upon the spot ;
There flowers or weeds at will may grow,
  So I behold them not :
It is enough for me to prove
That what I loved, and long must love,
  Like common earth can rot ;
To me there needs no stone to tell
'Tis nothing, that I loved so well.

Yet did I love thee to the last
  As fervently as thou,
Who didst not change through all the past,
  And canst not alter now.

The love where Death has set his seal,
Nor age can chill, nor rival steal,
  Nor falsehood disavow :
And, what were worse, thou canst not see
Or wrong, or change, or fault in me.

The better days of life were ours ;
  The worst can be but mine :
The sun that cheers, the storm that lowers,
  Shall never more be thine.
The silence of that dreamless sleep
I envy now too much to weep ;
  Nor need I to repine
That all those charms have pass'd away
I might have watch'd through long decay.

The flower in ripen'd bloom unmatch'd
  Must fall the earliest prey ;
Though by no hand untimely snatch'd,
  The leaves must drop away :
And yet it were a greater grief
To watch it withering, leaf by leaf,
  Than see it pluck'd to-day ;
Since earthly eye but ill can bear
To trace the change to foul from fair.

I know not if I could have borne
  To see thy beauties fade ;
The night that follow'd such a morn
  Had worn a deeper shade :
Thy day without a cloud hath pass'd
And thou wert lovely to the last :
  Extinguish'd, not decay'd—
As stars that shoot along the sky
Shine brightest as they fall from high.

As once I wept, if I could weep,
  My tears might well be shed
To think I was not near to keep
  One vigil o'er thy bed :
To gaze, how fondly ! on thy face,
To fold thee in a faint embrace,
  Uphold thy drooping head,
And show that love, however vain,
Nor thou nor I can feel again.

Yet how much less it were to gain,
   Though thou hast left me free,
The loveliest things that still remain
   Than thus remember thee !
The all of thine that cannot die
Through dark and dread Eternity
   Returns again to me,
And more that buried love endears
Than aught, except its living years.

                              Byron.

374

THERE 'S NOT A JOY THE WORLD CAN GIVE

THERE 's not a joy the world can give like that it takes away!
When the glow of early thought declines in feeling's dull decay,
'Tis not on youth's smooth cheek the blush alone, which fades so
    fast,
But the tender bloom of heart is gone, ere youth itself be past.

Then the few, whose spirits float above the wreck of happiness,
Are driven o'er the shoals of guilt or ocean of excess:
The magnet of their course is gone, or only points in vain
The shore to which their shiver'd sail shall never stretch again.

Then the mortal coldness of the soul like death itself comes down ;
It cannot feel for others' woes, it dare not dream its own ;
That heavy chill has frozen o'er the fountain of our tears,
And though the eye may sparkle still, 'tis where the ice appears.

Though wit may flash from fluent lips, and mirth distract the
    breast,
Through midnight hours that yield no more their former hope of
    rest ;
'Tis but as ivy-leaves around the ruin'd turret wreath,
All green and wildly fresh without but worn and grey beneath.

O, could I feel as I have felt,—or be what I have been,
Or weep as I could once have wept, o'er many a vanish'd scene !
As springs in deserts found seem sweet, all brackish though they be,
So midst the withered waste of life those tears would flow to me.

                                Byron.

375

THERE BE NONE OF BEAUTY'S DAUGHTERS

THERE be none of Beauty's daughters
   With a magic like thee;
And like music on the waters
   Is thy sweet voice to me:
When, as if its sound were causing
The charmed ocean's pausing,
The waves lie still and gleaming,
And the lull'd winds seem dreaming.

And the midnight moon is weaving
   Her bright chain o'er the deep,
Whose breast is gently heaving,
   As an infant's asleep:
So the spirit bows before thee,
To listen and adore thee,
With a full but soft emotion,
Like the swell of summer's ocean.

Byron.

376

MY BOAT IS ON THE SHORE

MY boat is on the shore,
   And my bark is on the sea;
But, before I go, Tom Moore,
   Here's a double health to thee!

Here's a sigh to those who love me,
   And a smile to those who hate;
And, whatever sky's above me,
   Here's a heart for every fate.

Though the ocean roar around me,
   Yet it still shall bear me on;
Though a desert should surround me,
   It hath springs that may be won.

Were't the last drop in the well,
   As I gasped upon the brink,
Ere my fainting spirit fell,
   'Tis to thee that I would drink.

With that water, as this wine,
  The libation I would pour
Should be :—' Peace with thine and mine,
  And a health to thee, Tom Moore !'

                            Byron.

377

SO, WE LL GO NO MORE A ROVING

So, we'll go no more a roving
  So late into the night,
Though the heart be still as loving,
  And the moon be still as bright.

For the sword outwears its sheath,
  And the soul wears out the breast,
And the heart must pause to breathe,
  And love itself have rest.   ·

Though the night was made for loving,
  And the day returns too soon,
Yet we'll go no more a roving
  By the light of the moon.

                            Byron.

378

O, TALK NOT TO ME

O, TALK not to me of a name great in story !
The days of our youth are the days of our glory,
And the myrtle and ivy of sweet two-and-twenty
Are worth all your laurels, though ever so plenty.

What are garlands and crowns to the brow that is wrinkled?
'Tis but as a dead-flower with May-dew besprinkled.
Then away with all such from the head that is hoary !
What care I for the wreaths that can only give glory?

O Fame !—if I e'er took delight in thy praises,
'Twas less for the sake of thy high sounding phrases,
Than to see the bright eyes of the dear one discover
She thought that I was not unworthy to love her.

There chiefly I sought thee, there only I found thee ;
Her glance was the best of the rays that surround thee ;
When it sparkled o'er aught that was bright in my story,
I knew it was love, and I felt it was glory.

Byron.

379

THE ISLES OF GREECE

THE isles of Greece, the isles of Greece !
  Where burning Sappho loved and sung,
Where grew the arts of war and peace,
  Where Delos rose, and Phœbus sprung !
Eternal summer gilds them yet,
But all, except their sun, is set.

The Scian and the Teian muse,
  The hero's harp, the lover's lute,
Have found the fame your shores refuse ;
  Their place of birth alone is mute
To sounds which echo further west
Than your sires' ' Islands of the Blest.'

The mountains look on Marathon—
  And Marathon looks on the sea ;
And musing there an hour alone,
  I dream'd that Greece might still be free ;
For, standing on the Persian's grave,
I could not deem myself a slave.

A king sate on the rocky brow
  Which looks o'er sea-born Salamis ;
And ships, by thousands, lay below,
  And men in nations—all were his !
He counted them at break of day—
And when the sun set, where were they ?

And where are they ? and where art thou,
  My country ? On thy voiceless shore
The heroic lay is tuneless now—
  The heroic bosom beats no more !
And must thy lyre, so long divine,
Degenerate into hands like mine ?

'Tis something, in the dearth of fame,
   Though link'd among a fetter'd race,
To feel at least a patriot's shame,
   Even as I sing, suffuse my face;
For what is left the poet here?
For Greeks a blush—for Greece a tear.

Must we but weep o'er days more blest?
   Must we but blush?   Our fathers bled.
Earth! render back from out thy breast
   A remnant of our Spartan dead!
Of the three hundred grant but three
To make a new Thermopylæ!

What, silent still? and silent all?
   Ah! no;—the voices of the dead
Sound like a distant torrent's fall,
   And answer:—' Let one living head,
But one, arise—we come, we come!'
'Tis but the living who are dumb.

In vain—in vain!   Strike other chords,
   Fill high the cup with Samian wine!
Leave battles to the Turkish hordes,
   And shed the blood of Scio's vine!
Hark! rising to the ignoble call—
How answers each bold Bacchanal!

You have the Pyrrhic dance as yet—
   Where is the Pyrrhic phalanx gone?
Of two such lessons, why forget
   The nobler and the manlier one?
You have the letters Cadmus gave—
Think ye, he meant them for a slave?

Fill high the bowl with Samian wine!
   We will not think of themes like these!
It made Anacreon's song divine:
   He served—but served Polycrates—
A tyrant; but our masters then
Were still, at least, our countrymen.

The tyrant of the Chersonese
   Was freedom's best and bravest friend;
That tyrant was Miltiades!
   O! that the present hour would lend
Another despot of the kind!
Such chains as his were sure to bind.

Fill high the bowl with Samian wine !
  On Suli's rock and Parga's shore
Exists the remnant of a line
  Such as the Doric mothers bore ;
And there, perhaps, some seed is sown,
The Heracleidan blood might own.

Trust not for freedom to the Franks—
  They have a king who buys and sells !
In native swords, and native ranks,
  The only hope of courage dwells ;
But Turkish force and Latin fraud
Would break your shield, however broad.

Fill high the bowl with Samian wine !
  Our virgins dance beneath the shade—
I see their glorious black eyes shine ;
  But, gazing on each glowing maid,
My own the burning tear-drop laves,
To think such breasts must suckle slaves.

Place me on Sunium's marbled steep,
  Where nothing, save the waves and I,
May hear our mutual murmurs sweep :
  There, swan-like, let me sing and die.
A land of slaves shall ne'er be mine—
Dash down yon cup of Samian wine !

                                            Byron.

380

'ON THIS DAY I COMPLETE MY THIRTY-SIXTH YEAR'

'Tis time this heart should be unmoved,
  Since others it hath ceased to move :
Yet, though I cannot be beloved,
    Still let me love !

My days are in the yellow leaf ;
  The flowers and fruits of love are gone ;
The worm, the canker, and the grief
    Are mine alone !

The fire that on my bosom preys
  Is lone as some volcanic isle ;
No torch is kindled at its blaze—
    A funeral pile.

The hope, the fear, the jealous care,
  The exalted portion of the pain
And power of love, I cannot share,
        But wear the chain.

But 'tis not thus—and 'tis not here—
  Such thoughts should shake my soul, nor now,
Where glory decks the hero's bier,
        Or binds his brow.

The sword, the banner, and the field,
  Glory and Greece, around me see !
The Spartan, borne upon his shield,
        Was not more free.

Awake ! (not Greece—she is awake !)
  Awake, my spirit !   Think through whom
Thy life-blood tracks its parent lake,
        And then strike home !

Tread those reviving passions down,
  Unworthy manhood !—Unto thee
Indifferent should the smile or frown
        Of beauty be.

If thou regret'st thy youth, why live ?
  The land of honourable death
Is here :—up to the field, and give
        Away thy breath !

Seek out—less often sought than found—
  A soldier's grave, for thee the best ;
Then look around, and choose thy ground,
        And take thy rest.

                                        Byron.

381

ODE TO THE WEST WIND

I

O WILD West Wind, thou breath of Autumn's being,
Thou, from whose unseen presence the leaves dead
Are driven, like ghosts from an enchanter fleeing

Yellow, and black, and pale, and hectic red,
Pestilence-stricken multitudes : O thou,
Who chariotest to their dark wintry bed

The wingéd seeds, where they lie cold and low,
Each like a corpse within its grave, until
Thine azure sister of the spring shall blow

Her clarion o'er the dreaming earth, and fill
(Driving sweet buds like flocks to feed in air)
With living hues and odours plain and hill :

Wild Spirit, which art moving every where,
Destroyer and preserver, hear, O, hear !

II

Thou on whose stream, 'mid the steep sky's commotion,
Loose clouds, like earth's decaying leaves, are shed,
Shook from the tangled boughs of Heaven and Ocean,

Angels of rain and lightning : there are spread
On the blue surface of thine airy surge,
Like the bright hair uplifted from the head

Of some fierce Mænad, even from the dim verge
Of the horizon to the zenith's height,
The locks of the approaching storm.　Thou dirge

Of the dying year, to which this closing night
Will be the dome of a vast sepulchre,
Vaulted with all thy congregated might

Of vapours, from whose solid atmosphere
Black rain, and fire, and hail will burst : O, hear !

III

Thou who didst waken from his summer dreams
The blue Mediterranean, where he lay,
Lulled by the coil of his crystàlline streams,

Beside a pumice isle in Baiæ's bay,
And saw in sleep old palaces and towers
Quivering within the wave's intenser day,

All overgrown with azure moss and flowers
So sweet, the sense faints picturing them !　Thou
For whose path the Atlantic's level powers

Cleave themselves into chasms, while far below
The sea-blooms and the oozy woods, which wear
The sapless foliage of the ocean, know

Thy voice, and suddenly grow grey with fear,
And tremble and despoil themselves: O, hear! ‿

IV

If I were a dead leaf thou mightest bear ;
If I were a swift cloud to fly with thee ;
A wave to pant beneath thy power, and share

The impulse of thy strength, only less free
Than thou, O uncontrollable !   If even
I were as in my boyhood, and could be

The comrade of thy wanderings over heaven,
As then, when to outstrip thy skiey speed
Scarce seemed a vision : I would ne'er have striven

As thus with thee in prayer in my sore need !
O ! lift me as a wave, a leaf, a cloud !
I fall upon the thorns of life ! I bleed !

A heavy weight of hours has chained and bowed
One too like thee : tameless, and swift, and proud.

V

Make me thy lyre, even as the forest is :
What if my leaves are falling like its own !
The tumult of thy mighty harmonies

Will take from both a deep, autumnal tone,
Sweet though in sadness.   Be thou, spirit fierce,
My spirit !   Be thou me, impetuous one !

Drive my dead thoughts over the universe
Like withered leaves to quicken a new birth !
And, by the incantation of this verse,

Scatter, as from an unextinguished hearth
Ashes and sparks, my words among mankind !
Be through my lips to unawakened earth

The trumpet of a prophecy ! O wind,
If Winter comes, can Spring be far behind?

Percy Bysshe Shelley.

Y

382

THE CLOUD

I BRING fresh showers for the thirsting flowers
　　　From the seas and the streams.
I bear light shade for the leaves when laid
　　　In their noon-day dreams.
From my wings are shaken the dews that waken
　　　The sweet buds every one,
When rocked to rest on their mother's breast,
　　　As she dances about the sun.
I wield the flail of the lashing hail,
　　　And whiten the green plains under,
And then again I dissolve it in rain,
　　　And laugh as I pass in thunder.

I sift the snow on the mountains below,
　　　And their great pines groan aghast ;
And all the night 'tis my pillow white,
　　　While I sleep in the arms of the blast
Sublime on the towers of my skiey bowers,
　　　Lightning my pilot sits ;
In a cavern under is fettered the thunder,—
　　　It struggles and howls at fits.
Over earth and ocean, with gentle motion,
　　　This pilot is guiding me,
Lured by the love of the genii that move
　　　In the depths of the purple sea ;
Over the rills, and the crags, and the hills,
　　　Over the lakes and the plains,
Wherever he dream, under mountain or stream,
　　　The Spirit he loves remains ;
And I all the while bask in heaven's blue smile,
　　　Whilst he is dissolving in rains.

The sanguine sunrise, with his meteor eyes
　　　And his burning plumes outspread,
Leaps on the back of my sailing rack,
　　　When the morning star shines dead,
As on the jag of a mountain crag,
　　　Which an earthquake rocks and swings,
An eagle alit one moment may sit
　　　In the light of its golden wings ;
And when sunset may breathe, from the lit sea beneath,
　　　Its ardours of rest and of love,

And the crimson pall of eve may fall
    From the depth of heaven above,
With wings folded I rest on mine airy nest
    As still as a brooding dove.

That orbéd maiden with white fire laden,
    Whom mortals call the moon,
Glides glimmering o'er my fleece-like floor
    By the midnight breezes strewn ;
And wherever the beat of her unseen feet,
    Which only the angels hear,
May have broken the woof of my tent's thin roof,
    The stars peep behind her and peer ;
And I laugh to see them whirl and flee
    Like a swarm of golden bees,
When I widen the rent in my wind-built tent,
    Till the calm rivers, lakes, and seas,
Like strips of the sky fallen through me on high,
    Are each paved with the moon and these.

I bind the sun's throne with a burning zone,
    And the moon's with a girdle of pearl.
The volcanoes are dim, and the stars reel and swim,
    When the whirlwinds my banner unfurl.
From cape to cape, with a bridge-like shape,
    Over a torrent sea,
Sunbeam-proof, I hang like a roof—
    The mountains its columns be.
The triumphal arch, through which I march
    With hurricane, fire, and snow,
When the powers of the air are chained to my chair,
    Is the million-coloured bow :
The sphere-fire above its soft colours wove,
    While the moist earth was laughing below.

I am the daughter of earth and water
    And the nursling of the sky.
I pass through the pores of the ocean and shores :
    I change, but I cannot die.
For after the rain when, with never a stain,
    The pavilion of heaven is bare,
And the winds and sunbeams with their convex gleams
    Build up the blue dome of air,
I silently laugh at my own cenotaph,
    And out of the caverns of rain,
Like a child from the womb, like a ghost from the tomb,
    I arise and unbuild it again.

        :   *Percy Bysshe Shelley.*

383

ASTRÆA REDUX

THE world's great age begins anew,
  The golden years return,
The earth doth like a snake renew
  Her winter weeds outworn:
Heaven smiles, and faiths and empires gleam
Like wrecks of a dissolving dream.

A brighter Hellas rears its mountains
  From waves serener far;
A new Peneus rolls his fountains
  Against the morning-star;
Where fairer Tempes bloom, there sleep
Young Cyclads on a sunnier deep.

A loftier Argo cleaves the main,
  Fraught with a later prize;
Another Orpheus sings again,
  And loves, and weeps, and dies;
A new Ulysses leaves once more
Calypso for his native shore.

O, write no more the tale of Troy,
  If earth Death's scroll must be!
Nor mix with Laian rage the joy
  Which dawns upon the free,
Although a subtler Sphinx renew
Riddles of death Thebes never knew!

Another Athens shall arise,
  And to remoter time
Bequeath, like sunset to the skies,
  The splendour of its prime,
And leave, if naught so bright may live,
All earth can take or Heaven can give.

Saturn and Love their long repose
  Shall burst, more bright and good
Than all who fell, than One who rose,
  Than many unsubdued:

Not gold, not blood, their altar dowers,
But votive tears and symbol flowers.

O, cease ! must hate and death return ?
  Cease ! must men kill and die ?
Cease ! drain not to its dregs the urn
  Of bitter prophecy.
The world is weary of the past—
O, might it die or rest at last !

                    Percy Bysshe Shelley.

384

THE SONG OF PAN

FROM the forests and highlands
We come, we come !
From the river-girt islands
Where loud waves are dumb,
Listening to my sweet pipings !
The wind in the reeds and the rushes,
The bees on the bells of thyme,
The birds on the myrtle bushes,
The cicale above in the lime,
And the lizards below in the grass,
Were as silent as ever old Tmolus was,
Listening to my sweet pipings.

Liquid Peneus was flowing,
And all dark Tempe lay
In Pelion's shadow, outgrowing
The light of the dying day,
Speeded by my sweet pipings.
The Sileni, and Sylvans, and Fauns,
And the nymphs of the woods and waves,
To the edge of the moist river-lawns
And the brink of the dewy caves,
And all that did then attend and follow,
Were silent with love, as you now, Apollo,
With envy of my sweet pipings.

I sang of the dancing stars,
I sang of the dædal Earth,
And of Heaven, and the Giant Wars,
And Love, and Death, and Birth—
And then I changed my pipings:
Singing how down the vale of Menalus
I pursued a maiden and clasped a reed!
Gods and men, we are all deluded thus:
It breaks in our bosom, and then we bleed:
All wept, as I think both ye now would,
If envy or age had not frozen your blood,
At the sorrow of my sweet pipings.

Percy Bysshe Shelley.

385

THE INDIAN SERENADE

I ARISE from dreams of thee
In the first sweet sleep of night,
When the winds are breathing low,
And the stars are shining bright:
I arise from dreams of thee,
And a spirit in my feet
Hath led me—who knows how!
To thy chamber window, Sweet!

The wandering airs they faint
On the dark, the silent stream—
And the champak's odours fail
Like sweet thoughts in a dream;
The nightingale's complaint,
It dies upon her heart;—
As I must on thine,
O belovéd as thou art!

O, lift me from the grass!
I die! I faint! I fail!
Let thy love in kisses rain
On my lips and eyelids pale.
My cheek is cold and white, alas!
My heart beats loud and fast—
O, press it to thine own again,
Where it will break at last!

Percy Bysshe Shelley.

386

RARELY, RARELY, COMEST THOU

RARELY, rarely comest thou,
    Spirit of Delight !
Wherefore hast thou left me now
    Many a day and night ?
Many a weary night and day
'Tis since thou art fled away.

How shall ever one like me
    Win thee back again ?
With the joyous and the free
    Thou wilt scoff at pain.
Spirit false ! thou hast forgot
All but those who need thee not.

As a lizard with the shade
    Of a trembling leaf,
Thou with sorrow art dismayed ;
    Even the sighs of grief
Reproach thee, that thou art not near,
And reproach thou wilt not hear.

Let me set my mournful ditty
    To a merry measure :
Thou wilt never come for pity,
    Thou wilt come for pleasure ;
Pity then will cut away
Those cruel wings, and thou wilt stay.

I love all that thou lovest,
    Spirit of Delight !
The fresh Earth in new leaves dressed,
    And the starry night,
Autumn evening, and the morn
When the golden mists are born.

I love snow, and all the forms
    Of the radiant frost ;
I love waves, and winds, and storms—
    Everything almost
Which is Nature's, and may be
Untainted by man's misery.

I love tranquil solitude,
  And such society
As is quiet, wise, and good ;
  Between thee and me
What difference ?—But thou dost possess
The things I seek, not love them less.

I love Love—though he has wings,
  And like light can flee ;
But above all other things,
  Spirit, I love thee—
Thou art love and life !   O, come,
Make once more my heart thy home !

Percy Bysshe Shelley.

387

I FEAR THY KISSES

I FEAR thy kisses, gentle maiden,
  Thou needest not fear mine :
My spirit is too deeply laden
  Ever to burthen thine.

I fear thy mien, thy tones, thy motion,
  Thou needest not fear mine :
Innocent is the heart's devotion
  With which I worship thine.

Percy Bysshe Shelley.

388

TO NIGHT

SWIFTLY walk o'er the western wave,
Spirit of Night !
Out of the misty eastern cave,
Where all the long and lone daylight,
Thou wovest dreams of joy and fear,
Which make thee terrible and dear—
Swift be thy flight !

Wrap thy form in a mantle grey,
Star-inwrought !
Blind with thine hair the eyes of Day

Kiss her until she be wearied out,
Then wander o'er city, and sea, and land,
Touching all with thine opiate wand—
Come, long sought!

When I arose and saw the dawn,
I sighed for thee;
When light rode high, and the dew was gone,
And noon lay heavy on flower and tree,
And the weary Day turned to his rest,
Lingering like an unloved guest,
I sighed for thee.

Thy brother Death came, and cried:—
'Wouldst thou me?'
Thy sweet child Sleep, the filmy-eyed,
Murmured like a noon-tide bee:—
'Shall I nestle near thy side?
Wouldst thou me?'—And I replied:—
No, not thee!

Death will come when thou art dead,
Soon, too soon!
Sleep will come when thou art fled.
Of neither would I ask the boon
I ask of thee, belovéd Night—
Swift be thine approaching flight,
Come soon, soon!

Percy Bysshe Shelley.

389

FROM THE ARABIC: AN IMITATION

My faint spirit was sitting in the light
    Of thy looks, my love;
It panted for thee like the hind at noon
    For the brooks, my love.
Thy barb whose hoofs outspeed the tempest's flight
    Bore thee far from me;
My heart, for my weak feet were weary soon,
    Did companion thee.

Ah! fleeter far than fleetest storm or steed,
    Or the death they bear,
The heart which tender thought clothes like a dove
    With the wings of care;

In the battle, in the darkness, in the need,
　　Shall mine cling to thee,
Nor claim one smile for all the comfort, love,
　　It may bring to thee.

Percy Bysshe Shelley.

390

SONG

MUSIC, when soft voices die,
Vibrates in the memory ;
Odours, when sweet violets sicken,
Live within the sense they quicken ;
Rose-leaves, when the rose is dead,
Are heaped for the belovéd's bed :
And so thy thoughts, when thou art gone,
Love itself shall slumber on.

Percy Bysshe Shelley.

391

LAMENT

O WORLD ! O life ! O time !
On whose last steps I climb,
　　Trembling at that where I had stood before,
When will return the glory of your prime ?
　　No more—O, never more !

Out of the day and night
A joy has taken flight :
　　Fresh spring, and summer, and winter hoar,
Move my faint heart with grief, but with delight
　　No more—O, never more !

Percy Bysshe Shelley.

392

A BRIDAL SONG

THE golden gates of Sleep unbar,
　　Where Strength and Beauty, met together,
Kindle their image, like a star
　　In a sea of glassy weather.

Night, with all thy stars look down—
　Darkness, weep thy holiest dew—
Never smiled the inconstant moon
　　　On a pair so true !
Let eyes not see their own delight :
Haste, swift Hour, and thy flight
　　　Oft renew !

Fairies, sprites, and angels keep her !
　Holy stars, permit no wrong !
And return to wake the sleeper,
　　　Dawn—ere it be long !
O joy ! O fear ! what will be done
In the absence of the sun !
　　　Come along !
　　　　　　　　Percy Bysshe Shelley.

393

SONG

　WHEN the lamp is shattered,
The light in the dust lies dead ;
　When the cloud is scattered,
The rainbow's glory is shed ;
　When the lute is broken,
Sweet tones are remembered not ;
　When the lips have spoken,
Loved accents are soon forgot.

　As music and splendour
Survive not the lamp and the lute,
　The heart's echoes render
No song when the spirit is mute :
　No song but sad dirges,
Like the wind through a ruined cell,
　Or the mournful surges
That ring the dead seaman's knell.

　When hearts have once mingled,
Love first leaves the well-built nest :
　The weak one is singled
To endure what it once possessed.
　O Love ! who bewailest
The frailty of all things here,
　Why choose you the frailest
For your cradle, your home and your bier ?

Its passions will rock thee
As the storms rock the ravens on high.
  Bright reason will mock thee,
Like the sun from a wintry sky.
  ⁖From thy nest every rafter
Will rot, and thine eagle home
  Leave thee naked to laughter,
When leaves fall and cold winds come.

Percy Bysshe Shelley.

394

TO JANE

  THE keen stars were twinkling,
And the fair moon was rising among them,
      Dear Jane !
  The guitar was tinkling,
But the notes were not sweet till you sung them
      Again.

  As the moon's soft splendour
O'er the faint cold starlight of heaven
      Is thrown,
  So your voice most tender
To the strings without soul had then given
      Its own.

  The stars will awaken,
Though the moon sleep a full hour later
      To-night ;
  No leaf will be shaken,
Whilst the dews of your melody scatter
      Delight.

  Though the sound overpowers,   ·
Sing again, with your dear voice revealing
      A tone
  Of some world far from ours,
Where music and moonlight and feeling
      Are one.

Percy Bysshe Shelley.

395

HYMN TO PAN

' O THOU, whose mighty palace roof doth hang
From jagged trunks, and overshadoweth
Eternal whispers, glooms, the birth, life, death
Of unseen flowers in heavy peacefulness ;
Who lovest to see the Hamadryads dress
Their ruffled locks where meeting hazels darken ;
And through whole solemn hours dost sit, and hearken
The dreary melody of bedded reeds—
In desolate places, where dank moisture breeds
The pipy hemlock to strange overgrowth,
Bethinking thee, how melancholy loth
Thou wast to lose fair Syrinx—do thou now,
By thy love's milky brow,
By all the trembling mazes that she ran,
Hear us, great Pan !

' O thou, for whose soul-soothing quiet turtles
Passion their voices cooingly 'mong myrtles,
What time thou wanderest at eventide
Through sunny meadows, that outskirt the side
Of thine enmosséd realms : O thou, to whom
Broad-leavéd fig-trees even now foredoom
Their ripened fruitage ; yellow-girted bees
Their golden honey-combs ; our village leas
Their fairest-blossomed beans and poppied corn ;
The chuckling linnet its five young unborn,
To sing for thee ; low-creeping strawberries
Their summer coolness ; pent-up butterflies
Their freckled wings ; yea, the fresh-budding year
All its completións—be quickly near,
By every wind that nods the mountain pine,
O forester divine !

' Thou, to whom every Faun and Satyr flies
For willing service ; whether to surprise
The squatted hare while in half-sleeping fit ;
Or upward ragged precipices flit
To save poor lambkins from the eagle's maw ;
Or by mysterious enticement draw
Bewildered shepherds to their path again ;
Or to tread breathless round the frothy main,
And gather up all fancifullest shells
For thee to tumble into Naiads' cells,

And, being hidden, laugh at their out-peeping ;
Or to delight thee with fantastic leaping,
The while they pelt each other on the crown
With silvery oak-apples, and fir-cones brown—
By all the echoes that about thee ring,
Hear us, O satyr king !

'O Hearkener to the loud clapping Shears,
While ever and anon to his shorn peers
A ram goes bleating: Winder of the Horn,
When snouted wild-boars, routing tender corn,
Anger our huntsmen : Breather round our farms,
To keep off mildews, and all weather harms :
Strange Ministrant of undescribéd sounds,
That come a-swooning over hollow grounds,
And wither drearily on barren moors :
Dread Opener of the Mysterious Doors
Leading to universal knowledge—see,
Great Son of Dryope,
The many that are come to pay their vows
With leaves about their brows !

'Be still the unimaginable lodge
For solitary thinkings ; such as dodge
Conception to the very bourne of heaven,
Then leave the naked brain ! be still the leaven,
That spreading in this dull and clodded earth,
Gives it a touch ethereal—a new birth !
Be still a symbol of immensity ;
A firmament reflected in a sea ;
An element filling the space between ;
An unknown—but no more ! We humbly screen
With uplift hands our foreheads, lowly bending,
And, giving out a shout most heaven-rending,
Conjure thee to receive our humble Pæan
Upon thy Mount Lycean !'

                                        John Keats.

396

THE INDIAN LADY

I

O SORROW !
Why dost borrow
The natural hue of health, from vermeil lips ?—

To give maiden blushes
To the white rose bushes?
Or is it thy dewy hand the daisy tips?

O Sorrow!
Why dost borrow
The lustrous passion from a falcon-eye?—
To give the glow-worm light?
Or, on a moonless night,
To tinge, on syren shores, the salt sea-spry?

O Sorrow!
Why dost borrow
The mellow ditties from a mourning tongue?—
To give at evening pale
Unto the nightingale,
That thou mayest listen the cold dews among?

O Sorrow!
Why dost borrow
Heart's lightness from the merriment of May?
A lover would not tread
A cowslip on the head,
Though he should dance from eve till peep of day—
Nor any drooping flower
Held sacred for thy bower,
Wherever he may sport himself and play.

To Sorrow!
I bade good morrow,
And thought to leave her far away behind;
But cheerly, cheerly!
She loves me dearly;
She is so constant to me, and so kind:
I would deceive her,
And so leave her,
But ah! she is so constant and so kind.

II

Beneath my palm-trees, by the river side,
I sat a-weeping: in the whole world wide
There was no one to ask me why I wept—
And so I kept
Brimming the water-lily cups with tears
Cold as my fears.

Beneath my palm-trees, by the river side,
I sat a-weeping : what enamour'd bride,
Cheated by shadowy wooer from the clouds,
          But hides and shrouds
Beneath dark palm-trees by a river side?

And as I sat, over the light blue hills
There came a noise of revellers : the rills
Into the wide stream came of purple hue—
          'Twas Bacchus and his crew !
The earnest trumpet spake, and silver thrills
From kissing cymbals made a merry din—
          'Twas Bacchus and his kin !
Like to a moving vintage down they came,
Crown'd with green leaves, and faces all on flame ;
All madly dancing through the pleasant valley,
          To scare thee, Melancholy !
O then, O then, thou wast a simple name !
And I forgot thee, as the berried holly
By shepherds is forgotten, when in June,
Tall chestnuts keep away the sun and moon—
          I rush'd into the folly ! . . .

III

' Whence came ye, merry Damsels ! whence came ye,
So many, and so many, and such glee ?
Why have ye left your bowers desolate,
          Your lutes, and gentler fate ? '—
' We follow Bacchus ! Bacchus on the wing,
          A-conquering !
Bacchus, young Bacchus ! good or ill betide,
We dance before him thorough kingdoms wide :—
Come hither, lady fair, and joined be
          To our wild minstrelsy ! '

' Whence came ye, jolly Satyrs ! whence came ye,
So many, and so many, and such glee ?
Why have ye left your forest haunts ? why left
          Your nuts in oak-tree cleft ? '—
' For wine, for wine we left our kernel tree ;
For wine we left our heath, and yellow brooms,
          And cold mushrooms ;
For wine we follow Bacchus through the earth ;
Great god of breathless cups and chirping mirth !
Come hither, lady fair, and joinéd be
          To our mad minstrelsy ! '

IV

Over wide streams and mountains great we went,
And, save when Bacchus kept his ivy tent,
Onward the tiger and the leopard pants,
      With Asian elephants :
Onward these myriads—with song and dance,
With zebras striped and sleek Arabians' prance,
Web-footed alligators, crocodiles,
Bearing upon their scaly backs, in files,
Plump infant laughers mimicking the coil
Of seamen and stout galley-rowers' toil :
With toying oars and silken sails they glide,
      Nor care for wind and tide.

Mounted on panthers' furs and lions' manes,
From rear to van they scour about the plains ;
A three days' journey in a moment done ;
And always, at the rising of the sun,
About the wilds they hunt with spear and horn,
      On spleenful unicorn.

I saw Osirian Egypt kneel adown
      Before the vine-wreath crown !
I saw parch'd Abyssinia rouse and sing
      To the silver cymbals' ring !
I saw the whelming vintage hotly pierce
      Old Tartary the fierce !
The kings of Ind their jewel-sceptres vail,
And from their treasures scatter pearled hail ;
Great Brahma from his mystic heaven groans,
      And all his priesthood moans,
Before young Bacchus' eye-wink turning pale !
Into these regions came I, following him,
Sick-hearted, weary—so I took a whim
To stray away into these forests drear,
      Alone, without a peer :
And I have told thee all thou mayest hear.

V

      Young stranger !
      I 've been a ranger
In search of pleasure throughout every clime.
      Alas ! 'tis not for me :
      Bewitch'd I sure must be,
To lose in grieving all my maiden prime.
      Z

Come then, Sorrow,
Sweetest Sorrow !
Like an own babe I nurse thee on my breast :
I thought to leave thee,
And deceive thee,
But now of all the world I love thee best.

There is not one,
No, no, not one
But thee to comfort a poor lonely maid :
Thou art her mother
And her brother,
Her playmate and her wooer in the shade.'

John Keats.

397

TO THE POETS

BARDS of Passion and of Mirth,
Ye have left your souls on earth !
Have ye souls in heaven too,
Double-lived in regions new ?
Yes, and those of heaven commune
With the spheres of sun and moon ;
With the noise of fountains wondrous
And the parle of voices thund'rous ;
With the whisper of heaven's trees
And one another, in soft ease
Seated on Elysian lawns
Browsed by none but Dian's fawns ;
Underneath large blue-bells tented,
Where the daises are rose-scented,
And the rose herself has got
Perfume which on earth is not ;
Where the nightingale doth sing
Not a senseless, tranced thing,
But divine melodious truth,
Philosophic numbers smooth,
Tales and golden histories
Of heaven and its mysteries.

Thus ye live on high, and then
On the earth ye live again ;
And the souls ye left behind you
Teach us, here, the way to find you,

Where your other souls are joying,
Never slumber'd, never cloying.
Here your earth-born souls still speak
To mortals, of their little week ;
Of their sorrows and delights ;
Of their passions and their spites ;
Of their glory and their shame ;
What doth strengthen and what maim :
Thus ye teach us, every day,
Wisdom, though fled far away !

Bards of Passion and of Mirth,
Ye have left your souls on earth !
Ye have souls in heaven too,
Double-lived in regions new !

John Keats.

398

TO PSYCHE

O GODDESS ! hear these tuneless numbers, wrung
  By sweet enforcement and remembrance dear,
And pardon that thy secrets should be sung
  Even into thine own soft-conchéd ear :
Surely I dreamt to-day, or did I see
  The wingéd Psyche with awakened eyes ?
I wandered in a forest thoughtlessly,
  And, on the sudden, fainting with surprise,
Saw two fair creatures, couched side by side
  In deepest grass, beneath the whispering roof
  Of leaves and trembled blossoms, where there ran
    A brooklet, scarce espied :
'Mid hushed, cool-rooted flowers fragrant-eyed,
  Blue, silver-white, and budded Tyrian,
They lay calm-breathing on the bedded grass ;
  Their arms embracéd, and their pinions too ;
  Their lips touched not, but had not bade adieu
As if disjoinéd by soft-handed slumber,
And ready still past kisses to outnumber
  At tender eye-dawn of aurorean love :
    The wingéd boy I knew ;
  But who wast thou, O happy, happy dove ?
    His Psyche true !

O latest-born and loveliest vision far
  Of all Olympus' faded hierarchy !
Fairer than Phœbe's sapphire-regioned star
  Or Vesper, amorous glow-worm of the sky ;
Fairer than these, though temple thou hast none,
      Nor altar heaped with flowers ;
Nor Virgin-choir to make delicious moan
      Upon the midnight hours ;
No voice, no lute, no pipe, no incense sweet
  From chain-swung censer teeming ;
No shrine, no grove, no oracle, no heat
  Of pale-mouthed prophet dreaming !
O brightest ! though too late for antique vows,
  Too-too late for the fond believing lyre,
When holy were the haunted forest boughs,
  Holy the air, the water, and the fire ;
Yet even in these days so far retired
  From happy pieties, thy lucent fans,
  Fluttering among the faint Olympians,
I see, and sing, by my own eyes inspired !
  So let me be thy choir, and make a moan
      Upon the midnight hours !
Thy voice, thy lute, thy pipe, thy incense sweet
  From swinged censer teeming :
Thy shrine, thy grove, thy oracle, thy heat
  Of pale-mouth'd prophet dreaming.

Yes, I will be thy priest, and build a fane
  In some untrodden region of my mind,
Where branchéd thoughts, new-grown with pleasant pain,
  Instead of pines shall murmur in the wind :
Far, far around shall those dark-clustered trees
  Fledge the wild-ridged mountains steep by steep ;
And there by zephyrs, streams, and birds, and bees
  The moss-lain Dryads shall be lull'd to sleep ;
And in the midst of this wide quietness
A rosy sanctuary will I dress
With the wreath'd trellis of a working brain—
  With buds, and bells, and stars without a name,
With all the gardener Fancy e'er could feign,
  Who, breeding flowers, will never breed the same :
And there shall be for thee all soft delight
  That shadowy thought can win,
A bright torch, and a casement ope at night
  To let the warm Love in !

John Keats.

399

TO A NIGHTINGALE

My heart aches, and a drowsy numbness pains
  My sense, as though of hemlock I had drunk,
Or emptied some dull opiate to the drains
  One minute past, and Lethe-wards had sunk:
'Tis not through envy of thy happy lot,
  But being too happy in thy happiness,
    That thou, light-wingéd Dryad of the Trees,
      In some melodious plot
Of beechen green and shadows numberless,
  Singest of summer in full-throated ease.

O, for a draught of vintage, that hath been
  Cool'd a long age in the deep-delvéd earth,
Tasting of Flora and the country-green,
  Dance, and Provençal song, and sun-burnt mirth!
O, for a beaker full of the warm South,
  Full of the true, the blushful Hippocrene,
    With beaded bubbles winking at the brim,
      And purple-stainéd mouth,
That I might drink, and leave the world unseen,
  And with thee fade away into the forest dim!

Fade far away, dissolve, and quite forget
  What thou among the leaves hast never known:
The weariness, the fever, and the fret
  Here, where men sit and hear each other groan;
Where palsy shakes a few, sad, last grey hairs;
  Where youth grows pale, and spectre-thin, and dies;
    Where but to think is to be full of sorrow
      And leaden-eyed despairs;
Where beauty cannot keep her lustrous eyes,
  Or new Love pine at them beyond to-morrow!

Away! away! for I will fly to thee,
  Not charioted by Bacchus and his pards,
But on the viewless wing of Poesy,
  Though the dull brain perplexes and retards!
Already with thee? Tender is the night,
  And haply the Queen-Moon is on her throne,
    Cluster'd around by all her starry Fays;
      But here there is no light,
Save what from heaven is with the breezes blown
  Through verdurous glooms and winding mossy ways.

I cannot see what flowers are at my feet,
Nor what soft incense hangs upon the boughs,
But, in embalméd darkness, guess each sweet
Wherewith the seasonable month endows
The grass, the thicket, and the fruit-tree wild :
White hawthorn, and the pastoral eglantine ;
Fast-fading violets cover'd up in leaves ;
And mid-May's eldest child,
The coming musk-rose, full of dewy wine,
The murmurous haunt of flies on summer eves.

Darkling I listen ; and—for many a time
I have been half in love with easeful Death,
Call'd him soft names in many a mused rhyme,
To take into the air my quiet breath—
Now more than ever seems it rich to die,
To cease upon the midnight with no pain,
While thou art pouring forth thy soul abroad
In such an ecstasy !
Still wouldst thou sing, and I have ears in vain—
To thy high requiem become a sod.

Thou wast not born for death, immortal Bird !
No hungry generations tread thee down ;
The voice I hear this passing night was heard
In ancient days by emperor and clown :
Perhaps the self-same song that found a path
Through the sad heart of Ruth, when, sick for home,
She stood in tears amid the alien corn ;
The same that oft-times hath
Charmed magic casements, opening on the foam
Of perilous seas, in faery lands forlorn.

Forlorn ! the very word is like a bell
To toll me back from thee to my sole self.
Adieu ! the fancy cannot cheat so well
As she is famed to do, deceiving elf !
Adieu ! adieu ! thy plaintive anthem fades
Past the near meadows, over the still stream,
Up the hill-side ; and now 'tis buried deep
In the next valley-glades :
Was it a vision, or a waking dream?
Fled is that music :—do I wake or sleep?

John Keats.

400

LA BELLE DAME SANS MERCI

'O, WHAT can ail thee, knight-at-arms,
 Alone and palely loitering?
The sedge has wither'd from the lake,
 And no birds sing.

'O, what can ail thee, knight-at-arms,
 So haggard and so woe-begone?
The squirrel's granary is full,
 And the harvest's done.

'I see a lily on thy brow
 With anguish moist and fever dew,
And on thy cheeks a fading rose
 Fast withereth too.'—

'I met a lady in the meads,
 Full beautiful—a faery's child:
Her hair was long, her foot was light,
 And her eyes were wild.

'I made a garland for her head,
 And bracelets too, and fragrant zone.
She looked at me as she did love,
 And made sweet moan.

'I set her on my pacing steed,
 And nothing else saw all day long,
For sidelong would she bend, and sing
 A faery's song.

'She found me roots of relish sweet,
 And honey wild, and manna dew,
And sure in language strange she said:—
 'I love thee true!'

'She took me to her elfin grot,
 And there she wept and sigh'd full sore,
And there I shut her wild wild eyes
 With kisses four.

' And there she lulléd me asleep,
    And there I dreamed—ah ! woe betide !
The latest dream I ever dreamed
    On the cold hill's side !

' I saw pale kings and princes too,
    Pale warriors, death-pale were they all.
They cried :—' La Belle Dame sans Merci
    Hath thee in thrall ! '

' I saw their starved lips in the gloam,
    With horrid warning gapéd wide,
And I awoke and found me here
    On the cold hill's side.

' And this is why I sojourn here,
    Alone and palely loitering,
Though the sedge is wither'd from the lake,
    And no birds sing.'

                                John Keats.

401

IT WAS THE TIME OF ROSES

I

It was not in the winter
Our loving lot was cast :
It was the time of roses—
We plucked them as we passed !

II

That churlish season never frown'd
On early lovers yet !
O, no—the world was newly crown'd
With flowers, when first we met.

III

'Twas twilight, and I bade you go,
But still you held me fast :
It was the time of roses—
We plucked them as we passed.

                                Thomas Hood.

402

DREAM-PEDLARY

IF there were dreams to sell,
  What would you buy?
Some cost a passing bell ; .
  Some a light sigh
That shakes from Life's fresh crown
Only a rose-leaf down.
If there were dreams to sell,
Merry and sad to tell,
And the crier rung the bell,
  What would you buy?

A cottage lone and still,
  With bowers nigh,
Shadowy, my woes to still,
  Until I die.
Such pearl from Life's fresh crown
Fain would I shake me down.
Were dreams to have at will,
This would best heal my ill,
  This would I buy.

But there were dreams to sell
  Ill didst thou buy ;
Life is a dream, they tell,
  Waking, to die.
Dreaming, a dream to prize,
Is wishing ghosts to rise ;
  And, if I had the spell
  To call the buried well,
    Which one would I ?
                    Thomas Lovell Beddoes.

403

DIRGE

IF thou wilt ease thine heart
Of love and all its smart,
  Then sleep, dear, sleep,
And not a sorrow
  Hang any tear on your eyelashes !
  Lie still and deep,
  Sad soul, until the sea-wave washes
The rim o' the sun to-morrow ·
  In eastern sky.

But wilt thou cure thine heart
Of love and all its smart,
    Then die, dear, die !
'Tis deeper, sweeter,
  Than on a rose bank to lie dreaming
    With folded eye,
  And then alone, amid the beaming
Of love's stars, thou 'lt meet her
    In eastern sky.

        Thomas Lovell Beddoes.

404

HOW MANY TIMES

How many times do I love thee, dear?
  Tell me how many thoughts there be
    In the atmosphere
    Of a new-fall'n year,
Whose white and sable hours appear
  The latest flake of eternity :—
So many times do I love thee, dear !

How many times do I love again ?
  Tell me how many beads there are
    In a silver chain
    Of evening rain,
Unravelled from the tumbling main,
  And threading the eye of a yellow star:
So many times do I love again !

        Thomas Lovell Beddoes.

405

ULALUME

THE skies they were ashen and sober,
  The leaves they were crispéd and sere—
  The leaves they were withering and sere ;
It was night in the lonesome October
  Of my most immemorial year ;
It was hard by the dim lake of Auber,
  In the misty mid region of Weir—
It was down by the dank tarn of Auber,
  In the ghoul-haunted woodland of Weir.

Here once, through an alley Titanic
    Of cypress, I roamed with my soul—
    Of cypress, with Psyche, my Soul.
These were days when my heart was volcanic
    As the scoriac rivers that roll—
    As the lavas that restlessly roll—
Their sulphurous currents down Yaanek
    In the ultimate climes of the Pole—
That groan as they roll down Mount Yaanek
    In the realms of the Boreal Pole.

Our talk had been serious and sober,
    But our thoughts they were palsied and sere—
    Our memories were treacherous and sere—
For we knew not the month was October,
    And we marked not the night of the year
    (Ah, night of all nights in the year !)—
We noted not the dim lake of Auber
    (Though once we had journeyed down here),
Remembered not the dank tarn of Auber
    Nor the ghoul-haunted woodland of Weir.

And now, as the night was senescent
    And star-dials pointed to morn—
    As the star-dials hinted of morn—
At the end of our path a liquescent
    And nebulous lustre was born,
Out of which a miraculous crescent
    Arose with a duplicate horn—
Astarte's bediamonded crescent
    Distinct with its duplicate horn.

And I said:—' She is warmer than Dian
    She rolls through an ether of sighs—
    She revels in a region of sighs :
She has seen that the tears are not dry on
    These cheeks, where the worm never dies,
And has come past the stars of the Lion
    To point us the path to the skies—
    To the Lethean peace of the skies—
Come up, in despite of the Lion,
    To shine on us with her bright eyes—
Come up through the lair of the Lion
    With love in her luminous eyes.'

But Psyche, uplifting her finger,
　　　Said:—' Sadly this star I mistrust—
　　　Her pallor I strangely mistrust—
O, hasten !—O, let us not linger !
　　　O, fly !—let us fly !—for we must.'
In terror she spoke, letting sink her
　　　Wings until they trailed in the dust—
In agony sobbed, letting sink her
　　　　Plumes till they trailed in the dust—
　　　　Till they sorrowfully trailed in the dust.

I replied :—' This is nothing but dreaming ;
　　　Let us on by this tremulous light !
　　　Let us bathe in this crystalline light !
Its Sybilic splendour is beaming
　　　With Hope and in Beauty to-night :—
　　　See !—it flickers up the sky through the night !
Ah, we safely may trust to its gleaming,
　　　And be sure it will lead us aright—
We safely may trust to a gleaming
　　　That cannot but guide us aright,
　　　Since it flickers up to Heaven through the night.'

Thus I pacified Psyche, and kissed her,
　　　And tempted her out of her gloom—
　　　And conquered her scruples and gloom ;
And we passed to the end of the vista,
　　　But were stopped by the door of a tomb
　　　By the door of a legended tomb ;
And I said :—' What is written, sweet sister,
　　　On the door of this legended tomb ?'
　　　She replied :—' Ulalume—Ulalume—
　　　'Tis the vault of thy lost Ulalume !'

Then my heart it grew ashen and sober
　　　As the leaves that were crisped and sere—
　　　As the leaves that were withering and sere—
And I cried :—' It was surely October
　　　On this very night of last year
　　　That I journeyed—I journeyed down here—
　　　That I brought a dread burden down here !
　　　On this night of all nights in the year,
　　　Ah, what demon has tempted me here ?
Well I know, now, this dim lake of Auber,
　　　This misty mid region of Weir—
Well I know, now, this dank tarn of Auber,
　　　This ghoul-haunted woodland of Weir.'

　　　　　　　　　　　　　　　Edgar Allan Poe.

FOR ANNIE

THANK Heaven ! the crisis—
  The danger is past,
And the lingering illness
  Is over at last—
And the fever called ' Living '
  Is conquered at last.

Sadly, I know
  I am shorn of my strength,
And no muscle I move;
  As I lie at full length—
But no matter !—I feel
  I am better at length.

And I rest so composed,
  Now, in my bed,
That any beholder
  Might fancy me dead—
Might start at beholding me,
  Thinking me dead.

The moaning and groaning,
  The sighing and sobbing
Are quieted now,
  With that horrible throbbing
At heart—Ah ! that horrible,
  Horrible throbbing !

The sickness—the nausea—
  The pitiless pain—
Have ceased, with the fever
  That maddened my brain—
With the fever called ' Living '
  That burned in my brain.

And O ! of all tortures
  That torture the worst
Has abated—the terrible
  Torture of thirst
For the naphthaline river
  Of Passion accurst—
I have drunk of a water
  That quenches all thirst :—

Of a water that flows,
  With a lullaby sound,
From a spring but a very few
  Feet under ground—
From a cavern not very far
  Down under ground.

And Ah ! let it never
  Be foolishly said
That my room it is gloomy,
  And narrow my bed
For man never slept
  In a different bed—
And, to *sleep*, you must slumber
  In just such a bed.

My tantalised spirit
  Here blandly reposes,
Forgetting, or never
  Regretting its roses—
Its old agitations
  Of myrtles and roses:

For now, while so quietly
  Lying, it fancies
A holier odour
  About it, of pansies—
A rosemary odour,
  Commingled with pansies—
With rue and the beautiful
  Puritan pansies.

And so it lies happily,
  Bathing in many
A dream of the truth
  And the beauty of Annie—
Drowned in a bath
  Of the tresses of Annie.

She tenderly kissed me,
  She fondly caressed,
And then I fell gently
  To sleep on her breast—
Deeply to sleep
  From the heaven of her breast.

When the light was extinguished,
  She covered me warm,

And she prayed to the angels
  To keep me from harm—
To the queen of the angels
  To shield me from harm.

And I lie so composedly,
  Now in my bed
(Knowing her love),
  That you fancy me dead—
And I rest so contentedly,
  Now in my bed
(With her love at my breast),
  That you fancy me dead—
That you shudder to look at me,
  Thinking me dead :—

But my heart it is brighter
  Than all of the many
Stars in the sky,
  For it sparkles with Annie—
It glows with the light
  Of the love of my Annie—
With the thought of the light
  Of the eyes of my Annie.

                    Edgar Allan Poe.

407

THE HAUNTED PALACE

IN the greenest of our valleys
  By good angels tenanted,
Once a fair and stately palace—
  Radiant palace—reared its head.
In the monarch Thought's dominion,
  It stood there !
Never seraph spread a pinion
  Over fabric half so fair !

Banners yellow, glorious, golden,
  On its roof did float and flow
(This—all this—was in the olden
  Time long ago),
And every gentle air that dallied
  In that sweet day,
Along the ramparts plumed and pallid,
  A wingéd odour went away.

Wanderers in that happy valley
   Through two luminous windows saw
Spirits moving musically
   To a lute's well-tunéd law,
Round about a throne where, sitting
   (Porphyrogene !)
In state his glory well befitting,
   The ruler of the realm was seen.

And all with pearl and ruby glowing
   Was the fair palace door,
Through which came flowing, flowing, flowing
   And sparkling evermore,
A troop of Echoes, whose sweet duty
   Was but to sing,
In voices of surpassing beauty,
   The wit and wisdom of their king.

But evil things, in robes of sorrow,
   Assailed the monarch's high estate
(Ah, let us mourn !—for never morrow
   Shall dawn upon him desolate !) ;
And round about his home the glory,
   That blushed and bloomed,
Is but a dim-remembered story
   Of the old time entombed.

And travellers, now, within that valley
   Through the red-litten windows see
Vast forms, that move fantastically
   To a discordant melody,
While, like a ghastly rapid river,
   Through the pale door
A hideous throng rush out forever,
   And laugh—but smile no more.

Edgar Allan Poe.

408

ANNABEL LEE

IT was many and many a year ago,
   In a kingdom by the sea,
That a maiden there lived whom you may know
   By the name of Annabel Lee ;
And this maiden she lived with no other thought
   Than to love and be loved by me.

I was a child, and she was a child
 In this kingdom by the sea:
But we loved with a love that was more than love—
 I and my Annabel Lee—
With a love that the winged seraphs of heaven
 Coveted her and me.

And this was the reason that, long ago,
 In this kingdom by the sea,
A wind blew out of a cloud, chilling
 My beautiful Annabel Lee;
So that her high-born kinsman came
 And bore her away from me,
To shut her up in a sepulchre
 In this kingdom by the sea.

The angels, not half so happy in heaven,
 Went envying her and me!
Yes!—that was the reason (as all men know
 In this kingdom by the sea)
That the wind came out of the cloud by night,
 Chilling and killing my Annabel Lee.

But our love it was stronger by far than the love
 Of those who were older than we—
 Of many far wiser than we—
And neither the angels in heaven above
 Nor the demons down under the sea
Can ever dissever my soul from the soul
 Of the beautiful Annabel Lee:

For the moon never beams, without bringing me dreams
 Of the beautiful Annabel Lee;
And the stars never rise, but I feel the bright eyes
 Of the beautiful Annabel Lee;
And so all the night-tide I lie down by the side
Of my darling—my darling!—my life and my bride,
 In the sepulchre there by the sea,
 In her tomb by the sounding sea.

       Edgar Allan Poe.

NOTES

1-3. GEOFFREY CHAUCER (1340-1400).

1. From *The Legend of Good Women* : Text A in Professor Skeat's Third Volume of *The Complete Works of Geoffrey Chaucer* (Oxford, 1894). A formal ballade, less the envoy.

giltë=golden	*clere*=bright	*disteyne*=bedim
y-fere=together	*chere*=face	*betraysed*=betrayed
Maketh=make (*imp.*)		*soun*=sound

2. Selected from the Fifth Book of *Troilus and Criseyde*. It is, not a formal lyric but, an excerpt from a romance in verse. But it is charged with an emotion which is not of a day but of all time; its effect is absolutely lyrical; and, to this compiler at least, it makes as perfect a *liederkranz* as is in the language. Section I corresponds to Stanzas 77-79 of Professor Skeat's Edition (as above), Vol. ii.

 y-hight=called *quaint*=quenched *gye*=guide *lisse*=joy

II corresponds to Stanzas 81-3.

 onës=once : *alderlevest*=dearest of all

III corresponds to Stanzas 91-92, the first two lines of Stanza 91 being omitted.

IV corresponds to Stanzas 93-94.

 hennës=hence : *ginnë*=begin to

V corresponds to Stanzas 96-97.

sote=sweet	*stoundëmele*=from time to time
bote=benefit	*twinnëd*=parted

3. A triple roundel, as Professor Skeat notes (*Works*, as above, i. 386-7).

hem=them	*helen*=heal	*halt*=holds
stervë=starve	*y-strike*=struck	*sclat*=slate

4-6. WILLIAM DUNBAR (*c.* 1465?-1520?).

A master of metre, a rare humourist, a satirist of lasting distinction, a writer whose vocabulary amazes even now, the most considerable poet bred in Scotland between Robert Henryson and Robert Burns, Dunbar lived to see himself in print in the first volume issued by the Scottish Press (1508). My text is more or less modernised from *The Poems of William Dunbar*, edited, in Four Parts, by John Small (M.A., F.S.A. Scot.) for the Scottish Text Society (Edinburgh, 1884-90). **4.** This number consists of Stanzas i.-xiii. and Stanzas xxiv.-xxv. of Dunbar's *Lament for the Makaris* (=poets) *Quhen He Wes Seik*. For the form, that of the kyrielle (a favourite with Dunbar, who has a round dozen of examples), see Banville, *Petit Traité*:—

> Qui voudra sçavoir la pratique
> De cette reine juridique,
> Je dis que bien mise en effet
> *La Kyrielle ainsi se fait.*

The 'Monk of Bury' (Stanza xiii.) is John Lydgate.

brukle=feeble	*wickir*=willow	*lave*=rest
dansand=dancing	*tyrand*=tyrant	*Rhetors*=orators
enarmed=under arms	*stour*=battle	*Hes done petuously*
sowkand=sucking	*captain*=chief of a gar-	*devour*=Has pitifully
slee=sly	rison	devoured
sickir=secure	*tour*=tower	*Of force*=of necessity
mellee=mellay	*piscence*=puissance	*remeid*=remedy
campion=hero	*surrigians*=surgeons	*dispone*=prepare
sary=woe-begone	*Art-magicians*=wizards	

Here are Stanzas xiv.-xxiii., for whose omission I make no apology, even though they demonstrate beyond the possibility of doubting that Dunbar's *Lament* was suggested by Villon's immortal trilogy of ballades, 'Des Dames du Temps Jadis'; 'Des Seigneurs du Temps Jadis'; and 'Mesme Propos en Vieil Langage François':—

> The gude Syr Hew of Eglintoun,
> Et eik Heryot, et Wyntoun,
> He hes tane out of this cuntre;
> Timor Mortis conturbat me.

> That scorpioun fell hes done infek
> Maister Iohne Clerk, and James Afflek,
> Fra balat making et trigide;
> Timor Mortis conturbat me.

> Holland et Barbour he has berevit;
> Allace! that he nought with ws lewit
> Schir Mungo Lokert of the Le;
> Timor Mortis conturbat me.

> Clerk of Tranent eik he has tane,
> That maid the anteris of Gawane;
> Schir Gilbert Hay endit has he;
> Timor Mortis conturbat me.

> He has Blind Hary, et Sandy Traill
> Slaine with his schour of mortall haill,
> Quhilk Patrik Iohnestoun myght nought fle;
> Timor Mortis conturbat me.

> He hes reft Merseir his endite,
> That did in luf so lifly write,
> So schort, so quyk, of sentence hie;
> Timor Mortis conturbat me.

He hes tane Roull of Aberdene,
And gentill Roull of Corstorphin[e];
Two bettir fallowis did no man se;
　　Timor Mortis conturbat me.

In Dumfermelyne he has done rovne
With Maister Robert Henrisoun;
Schir Iohne the Ros enbrast hes he;
　　Timor Mortis conturbat me.

And he has now tane, last of aw,
Gud gentill Stobo et Quintyne Schaw,
Of quham all wichtis hes peté:
　　Timor Mortis conturbat me.

Gud Maister Walter Kennedy,
In poynt of dede lyis veraly,
Gret reuth it wer that so suld be;
　　Timor Mortis conturbat me.

5. The obsession of Winter, which bears so heavily on such middle-aged folk as are susceptible to external influences, has nowhere been conveyed, I think, so powerfully as here.

dirk = dark	*drumlie* = muddy	*dulē* = wretched
dulē spreit = troubled spirit	*lurk for schoir* = cower for dread	*requeir* = require
does forloir = wearies	*leif* = live	*kist* = chest
yettis = gates	*lowt* = stoop	*cowp* = cup

6. The stanza here is the ballade octave, but the rhymes change as the octave ends. In the last verse but one, as often in Burns, the strong Scots *r* gives 'world' the value of a dissyllable.

Wend thee fro = pass from thee	*ythand* = steady
Dress from desert = Forth from the waste	*ass* = ashes
graithing in thy gait = working on thy road	

7-8. JOHN SKELTON (14—?·1529).

7. The litany *In Praise of Johanna Scroope* forms part of *The Boke of Phyllyp Sparowe*. The Latin refrains are omitted. In the original, upon the line ' In beauty and virtue,' there follows this quatrain :—

　　　　Haec claritate gemina,
　　　　O gloriosa fœmina,
　　　　Memor esto verbi tui servo tuo!
　　　　Servus tuus sum ego.

Upon the recurrence of the same line :—

　　　　Hac claritate gemina,
　　　　O gloriosa fœmina,
　　　　Bonitatem fecisti cum servo tuo, domina,
　　　　Et ex præcordiis sonant præconia.

The third overword runs thus :—

　　　　Hac claritate gemina,
　　　　O gloriosa fœmina,
　　　　Defecit in salutatione tua anima mea;
　　　　Quid petis filio, mater dulcissima? babæ!

The fourth :—

> Hac claritate gemina,
> O gloriosa fœmina,
> Quomodo dilexi legem tuam, domina !
> Recedant vetera, nova sint omnia.

The fifth :—

> Hac claritate gemina,
> O gloriosa fœmina,
> Iniquos odio habui !
> Non calumnientur me superbi.

The sixth :—

> Hac claritate gemina,
> O gloriosa fœmina,
> Mirabilia testimonia tua !
> Sicut novellæ plantationes in juventute sua.

The seventh :—

> Hac claritate gemina,
> O gloriosa fœmina,
> Clamavi in toto corde, exaudi me !
> Misericordia tua magna est super me.

The eighth :—

> Hac claritate gemina,
> O gloriosa fœmina,
> Principes persecuti sunt me gratis !
> Omnibus consideratis,
> Paradisus voluptatis
> Hæc virgo est dulcissima.

The ninth and last :—

> Hac claritate gemina,
> O gloriosa fœmina !
> Requiem æternam dona eis, Domine !

clere = bright *ennewéd* = refreshed *stepe* = deep
jelofer = gillyflower *enhatched* = crossed *pastaunce* = chee
tote = glance *wood* = mad
emportured with coráge (doubtful : perhaps =) full of passion.

8. The song *In Praise of Isabel Pennell* is taken from *The Garland of Laurell* (lines 972-1002).

reflaring = odorous *jelofer* = gillyflower *nepte* = calamint

The text is that printed by Dyce in the First Volume of his Edition of *The Poetical Works of John Skelton* (London, 1843).

9. SIR THOMAS WYATT (1503-1542).

Reprinted and modernised from Mr. Arber's Reprint (London, 1870) of the Miscellany called *Songes and Sonnettes written by the ryght honorable Lorde Henry Howard, late Earle of Surrey and other* [sic]. *Apud Richardum Tottel* (1557). The title in Tottel reads :—*The louer complayneth the unkindnes of his loue.* Wyatt is rather an ingenious metrist than a poet ; but he made his mark, and even now, as here, is sometimes readable.

10-12. HENRY HOWARD, EARL OF SURREY
(1517-1546),

the true Morning Star of the English Renascence, of whom Marlowe learned the numerousness of the heroic iambic, and Shakespeare, as my No. 11 will show, the cadence and the cut, the capacity and spirit, of the English quatorzain. All three pieces are modernised from Mr. Arber's Reprint of Tottel. The original title of 10 is *A praise of his loue: wherin he reproueth them that compare their Ladies with his*; that of 12 is *Complaint of the absence of her louer being upon the sea.*

13. NICHOLAS GRIMALD (1519-1562).

The first among the *Songes Written by Nicolas Grimald*, as reprinted by Mr. Arber in his Edition of Tottel.

14-17. ALEXANDER SCOTT (1520?-158-?),

called 'the Scottish Anacreon,' was a writer of singular elegance and ease, an expert in form, at once a lyrist and a wit; but for nearly two centuries he existed only in the famous *Manuscript* compiled, (1568), in a time of pestilence, by George Bannatyne. Allan Ramsay, drawing on this *Manuscript* for his *Ever Green* (1724), quoted some Scotts as nearly as he dared—(for Scott, like all the makers, was anything but mim-mouthed)—and in 1821 the late David Laing, keen for the honour of Scotland, but shrinking, as Ramsay before him, from Scott in his integrity, published a First Edition of the *Poems*, complete, I believe, so far as numbers go, but something chastened in the matter of diction. An Edition has been done of late for the Scottish Text Society; but my text is more or less modernised from *The Bannatyne MS.* as printed (1879) at Glasgow for the Hunterian Club. 14 is No. ccxxxi. in the Hunterian Edition aforesaid. The stanza is the ballade octave—*a b, ab, b c, b c.*

hald=keep	*Nor*=than	*sall gang*=shall go
belappit=oppressed	*perigall*=privileged	*sen*=since
garth=garden-close	*laif*=rest	*saif*=save
suaif=sweet	*haif*=have	*clear of hue*=bright in colour
Do go with mine, with mind invart=Go as I go, not merely in semblance, but also in spirit.		

15. The stanza, an exceeding hard one, is a variation from that of the decasyllabic ballade: also of *ten* verses on *four* rhymes.

halesome=lusty	*loup*=leap	*Braisit*=enveloped
Fermit=confirmed	*thirlage*=servitude	*sallat*=refreshment
In blanch farm=Free of charge	*sytt*=grieve	*siching*=sighing
sussy=repine	*herd*=keep	*steer*=rudder
but=without	*corse*=body	*cure*=charge
Whilk=which	*meittand*=having fed	*syne walk*=then depart
cossis=exchange	*howp*=hope	*wathe*=danger

16. Here Scott writes with the very cadence of Christina Rossetti, and the Swinburne of a certain number in the old, *inoubliable*, epoch-making *Poems and Ballads*.

remeid=remedy	*deid*=death	*sich*=sigh
thirled=enslaved	*makand*=making	*gloir*=glory

17. A set of this number, differently staged and five stanzas long, is printed in Mr. Yeowell's Edition of Wyatt in the *Aldine Poets*, under this heading :—*The Abused Lover Admonishes the Unwary to Beware of Love*.

18. RICHARD EDWARDS (1523-1566).

18. Reprinted and modernised from *The Paradice of Dainty Deuises*: ' Containing sundry pithie precepts, learned Counsailes and excellent Inuentions: right pleasant and profitable for all estates. Deuised and written for the most parte by M. Edwardes, sometime of her Maiesties Chappell: the rest by sundry learned Gentlemen both of Honor and Worship, whose names heerafter followe. Whereunto is added sundry new Inuentions, very pleasant and delightfull. At London. Printed by Edward Allde for Edward White dwelling at the little North doore of Saint Paules Church, at the signe of the Gunne. Anno 1596.' The present piece is the Forty-Ninth *Deuise*.

19-26. ANONYMOUS.

19. From the *Royal MS.* (Appendix 58) in the British Museum. The quatrain has been printed in Professor Ewald Flügel's *Neueng-lisches Lesebuch* (Halle, 1895). **20.** From the Second Edition of Tottel's *Miscellany* (Mr. Arber's reprint). **21.** From Tottel's *Miscellany* (Arber), where it opens thus :—

> ' My youthful years are past,
> My joyful days are gone :
> My life it may not last,
> My grave and I am one.'

The first four quatrains are here omitted. **22.** This graceful lyric lacks nothing of the formal ballade, save the envoy, and the consonance of rhymes *a | a* through all three octaves. Preserved in *The Bannatyne MS.* (Part v. No. cxcii. in the Hunterian Club's impression), it was transcribed by Ramsay for *The Ever Green*, and there may very well have given Burns a hint for the metrical structure of his *Mary Morison* (p. 288).

o'erfret=adorned	*schawës*=woods	
sheen=bright	*mene*=complain	
done depaint=painted	*hyd and hue*=skin and complexion	
blinkis=catches a glimpse	*mae*=more	

23. From Mr. Arber's reprint of Tottel's *Miscellany* (1870). **24.** No. ccxx. in *The Bannatyne MS.*, as above. This fresh and joyous ditty is mentioned in *The Complaynt of Scotland* (1549), and is quoted, with an additional stanza and a tune, in *John Forbes his Songs*

and Fancies (1682), often described as the 'Aberdeen Cantus.' David
Laing inclined to ascribe it, not without reason, as I think, to Alexander
Scott, who writes, indeed, of May in the right Chaucerian spirit :—

> ' May is the moneth maist amene
> For them in Venus' service bene
> To recreate their heavy hearts :
> May causes courage from the splene,
> And everything in May revarts,' *etc.*

sheen=bright	*preluciand*=shining	*till*=into
bewis=boughs	*birth*=kind	

25. No. ccxxvi. in *The Bannatyne MS.*, as above. Attributed to
Alexander Scott by Henry Weber (who may very well have got the
idea from Sir Walter himself), and reprinted by David Laing in the
notes to his edition of that maker (1821).   Compare, in effect,
No. 15 in the present collection.

high above=uplifted	*wiss*=wish	*heill*=health	*invart*=inward
venust=delightful	*others'*=each other's	*usand*=using	*departs*=divides
glowffin=' to open the eyes at intervals in awaking from a disturbed sleep '			
remeid=remedy	*deid*=death		

26. From Mr. Arber's reprint of Tottel's *Miscellany*, as above.

27-69.

27. From *Exodus*, chap. xv.   The first eighteen verses are set
down, with the refrain of Miriam in the twenty-first verse as a *finale*.
28. From *The Second Book of Samuel*, chap. i.   The verses selected
run from the nineteenth to the twenty-seventh, inclusive. **29.** The
Twenty-Fourth Psalm of David. **30.** The Twenty-Ninth Psalm of
David.   **31.** The Forty-Second Psalm : 'to the chief musician
Maschil, for the sons of Korah.' **32.** The Forty-Seventh Psalm : 'to
the chief musician, a Psalm for the sons of Korah.' **33.** The Eighty-
Third Psalm : 'a Song or Psalm of Asaph.' **34.** The One Hundred
and Fourth Psalm. **35.** The One Hundred and Twenty-Sixth Psalm :
'a song of degrees.' **36.** The One Hundred and Thirty-Seventh
Psalm. **37.** The One Hundred and Thirty-Ninth Psalm. **38.** The
One Hundred and Forty-Eighth Psalm. **39.** The Third Chapter of
The Book of Job. The first two verses are omitted. **40.** The Reply of
Eliphaz the Temanite in the Fourth Chapter of *The Book of Job*. The
first two verses are omitted. **41.** The Ninth and Tenth Chapters of
The Book of Job, containing the Reply to Bildad. **42.** The Fourteenth
Chapter of *The Book of Job*. **43.** The Twenty-Sixth Chapter of *The
Book of Job*. The first verse is omitted. **44.** The Thirty-Eighth and
Thirty-Ninth Chapters of *The Book of Job*. **45.** The Fortieth and
Forty-First Chapters of *The Book of Job*. The first six verses of the
Fortieth Chapter are omitted. **46.** The Seventh Chapter of *The
Proverbs*. **47.** The Thirty-First Chapter of *The Proverbs*. The first
nine verses are omitted. **48.** The First Chapter of *Ecclesiastes*. The
first verse is omitted. **49.** The first eleven verses of the Ninth Chapter
of *Ecclesiastes*. **50.** The first seven verses of the Twelfth Chapter of

Ecclesiastes. **51.** The First Chapter of *The Song of Songs.* The first verse is omitted. **52.** The Second and Third Chapters of *The Song of Songs.* **53.** The Fourth Chapter of *The Song of Songs.* **54.** The Fifth Chapter of *The Song of Songs.* **55.** The Seventh Chapter of *The Song of Songs.* **56.** The Thirteenth Chapter of *The Book of the Prophet Isaiah,* with the exception of the first verse. **57.** The Fifteenth Chapter of *Isaiah* : 'the Burden of Moab.' **58.** The Twenty-Third Chapter of *Isaiah* : 'the Burden of Tyre.' **59.** The last two verses of the Thirty-Fourth Chapter of *Isaiah,* to which is added the Thirty-Fifth Chapter. **60.** From the tenth to the twentieth verse inclusive of the Thirty-Eighth Chapter of *Isaiah.* **61.** The twelve opening verses of the Fifty-Second Chapter of *Isaiah.* **62.** The Sixtieth Chapter of *Isaiah.* **63.** From the third to the twelfth verses inclusive of the Forty-Sixth Chapter of *The Book of the Prophet Jeremiah.* **64.** The First Chapter of *The Lamentations of Jeremiah.* **65.** The Seventh Chapter of *The Book of the Prophet Ezekiel.* The first verse and half the second are omitted. **66.** The Nineteenth Chapter of *Ezekiel.* The first verse and two words of the second omitted. **67.** The Second Chapter of *Joel,* to the end of the eleventh verse. **68.** From the fourth to the ninth verse of *Amos,* his Fifth Chapter. **69.** The Third Chapter of *Habakkuk,* being his prayer upon Shigionoth. The first verse is deleted, as are the final direction 'to the chief singer on stringed instruments.'

70. GEORGE GASCOIGNE (153-?-1577).

The *Lullaby* is reprinted from the volume entitled *A Hundreth sundrie Flowres bounde vp in one small Poesie* : 'Gathered partely (by translation) in the fyne outlandish Gardins of Euripides, Ouid, Petrarke, Ariosto, and others: and partly by inuention, out of our owne fruitefull Orchardes in Englande: Yelding sundrie sweete savours of Tragical, Comical, and Morall Discourses, bothe pleasaunt and profitable to the well smelling noses of learned Readers.' The book, imprinted at London 'for Richarde Smith,' is anonymous and without date ; but it is referred to 1572. Gascoigne's share in its composition is avowed by the Printer's confession (p. 344):—'I will now deliver unto you so many more of Master Gascoignes Poems as have come to my hands, who hath never been dayntie of his doings, and therfore I conceale not his name.' There is good reason to believe that *The deuises of sundrie Gentlemen,* of which the *Lullaby* forms part, are all the work of Gascoigne himself.

71-72. ALEXANDER MONTGOMERIE (154-?-1610 ?).

The text of both examples is partly modernised from Dr. Cranstoun's Edition of *The Poems of Alexander Montgomerie,* printed at Edinburgh for the Scottish Text Society in 1887. The title of **71** is *He bids adeu to his Maistress* (*Miscellaneous Poems,* xxxix.). The stanza is that of Montgomerie's long allegory *The Cherry and the Slae,* and his charming *Banks of Helicon;* and, as he everywhere approves himself a metrist of extraordinary skill, there is no reason to doubt the tradition which ascribes its invention to him.

hant into=enter   *but*=without   *weinds*=try   *maik*=mate

72. The title in Dr. Cranstoun is *The night is neir Gone.*

Now shroudẽs the shaws=Now the woods clothe themselves		
skails=clear, empty	*blonkẽs*=white horses	*brays*=neigh
lowes=flames	*gowans*=daisies	*pairty*=partner
rone=rowan berry	*grone*=bell	*tynds*=horns
hurchons=hedgehogs	*maiks*=mates	*dichts*=scours
hairs=hares	*stoned steed*=stallion	*cramps*=prances
fone=foes	*freikes*=warriors	*wicht*=strong
lamps=gallops	*flitts*=slips	*groomẽs*=riders
trone=throne		

73-75. NICHOLAS BRETON (1542-1626?).

73. Under the heading, *A Sweet Lullaby,* these verses from *The Arbour of Amorous Devices* (1593-4) are attributed to Nicholas Breton by Mr. A. H. Bullen in his *Poems, Chiefly Lyrical, from Romances and Prose-Tracts of the Elizabethan Age* (London, 1890). **74.** Reprinted from the aforesaid collection. **75.** Mr. Bullen states that this piece of Breton's, 'originally published in 1591,' is 'from Michael Este's *Madrigals of Three, Four and Five Parts,* 1604.' It is here given as in Bullen's *Lyrics from the Song-Books of the Elizabethan Age* (London, 1889).

76-77. EDMUND SPENSER (1552-1599).

76. This sumptuous and majestic pageant of pure lyrism is re-printed from the Fifth Volume of the Aldine Edition of *The Poetical Works of Edmund Spenser* (London, 1866). Such forms as 'theyr' and 'rayse' are spelled modernwise. **77.** The original title is:— *Prothalamion: or a Spousall Verse, made by Edm. Spenser.* 'In honour of the double marriage of the two Honorable and vertuous Ladies, the Ladie Elizabeth, and the Ladie Katherine Somerset, Daughters to the Right Honorable the Earle of Worcester, and espoused to the two worthie Gentlemen, M. Henry Gilford and M. William Peter, Esquyers.' The text is taken from the Aldine Edition (as above).

78-79. SIR WALTER RALEIGH (1552-1618).

From Dr. Hannah's Edition of *The Poems of Sir Walter Raleigh, Collected and Authenticated with those of Sir Henry Wotton and other Courtly Poets from 1540 to 1650* (London, 1875). The current spelling, 'Raleigh,' is retained, though, in fact, it does not appear that Sir Walter ever used it.

80. ANTHONY MUNDAY (1553-1633).

Reprinted from the Second Edition of *England's Helicon, or The Muses Harmony*, printed for Richard More in London, and 'sould at his Shop in S. Dunstanes Church-yard. 1614.' The First Edition dates from 1600. The verses *To Colin Clout* are assigned to 'Shepheard Tonie,' otherwise Anthony Munday, or, as some think, for no good reason, Anthony Copley.

81-88. SIR PHILIP SIDNEY (1554-1586).

81. The Fourth Song in *Astrophel and Stella*, reprinted and modernised from Dr. Grosart's Edition of *The Complete Poems of Sir Philip Sidney* (London, 1877). **82.** The Seventy-Seventh Sonnet in *Astrophel and Stella*. **83.** The Thirty-First Sonnet in *Astrophel and Stella*. **84.** The Thirty-Third Sonnet in *Astrophel and Stella*. **85.** Reprinted from that section of Dr. Grosart's Second Volume entitled *Pansies from Penshurst and Wilton*. The song is set *To the tune of 'Wilhelmus van Nassau.'* **86.** No. xlix. in Dr. Grosart's Reprint of the Poems from *The Countess of Pembroke's Arcadia* (vol. ii.). The closing stanza is omitted. **87.** No. xii. of the section *Sidera* in Dr. Grosart's Second Volume. **88.** The One Hundred and Tenth Sonnet in *Astrophel and Stella*.

89. JOHN LYLY (1554-1606).

The Spring's Welcome, as Mr. Bullen styles it in his *Lyrics from the Dramatists of the Elizabethan Age* (London, 1889), occurs in *Alexander and Campaspe*. It is to be noted that 'Lyly's songs are not found in the original editions of his plays.'

90-92. THOMAS LODGE (1556?-1625).

These numbers are reprinted from Mr. A. H. Bullen's *Poems, Chiefly Lyrical, from Romances and Prose-Tracts of the Elizabethan Age: with Chosen Poems of Nicholas Breton* (London, 1890).

93. GEORGE PEELE (1558?-1592?).

From *Polyhymnia* (1590), and here given, with one slight change, after Mr. Bullen's text in the *Lyrics from the Dramatists of the Elizabethan Age* (London, 1889).

94-96. ROBERT GREENE (1560?-1592).

94. Doron's Description of Samela in *Menaphon* (Vol. vi. of Dr. Grosart's Reprint of *The Complete Works in Prose and Verse of*

Robert Greene, M.A. For private circulation only). 95. Sephestia's Song to her Child in *Menaphon.* 96. *The Shepheards Wiues Song* in *The Mourning Garment* (Grosart, *Works,* Vol. ix. *ut supra.*)

97. ROBERT SOUTHWELL (1560-1595).

First given in *Saint Peter's Complaint, Newly Augmented with other Poems*: undated but ascribed to 1596. Here reprinted from Dr. Grosart's Edition, in the Fuller Worthies' Library, of *The Complete Works of Robert Southwell,* S.J. (privately printed in 1872.)

98-99. SAMUEL DANIEL (1562-1619).

98. A sequence of three sonnets (Nos. xxxiv.-xxxvi.) from *Delia and Rosamund* (1594), reprinted by Mr. Arber in Vol. iii. of *An English Garner.* The intention is plainly lyrical, as the 'true begetter' is plainly Ronsard. A fourth, completing the cycle, is omitted, as of less merit than its compeers. 99. The song of the First Chorus in *Hymen's Triumph* (Act v. sc. 1).

100-102. MICHAEL DRAYTON (1563-1616).

100. The Forty-Third number in *Idea*: 'In Sixty-Three Sonnets, by Michael Drayton, Esquire.' (London, 1619.) 101. *From Poems Lyrick and Pastorall.* (London, N.D.) The Sixty-First Number in *Idea* (as above).

103-104. CHRISTOPHER MARLOWE (1564-1593), AND SIR WALTER RALEIGH (1552-1618).

103. Incompletely given in *The Passionate Pilgrim* (1599), this number is presented at length in *England's Helicon,* with Marlowe's name attached to it. Walton cites it in *The Complete Angler* (1653) as 'that smooth song which was made by Kit Marlowe, now at least fifty years ago.' 104. Partly printed, like the companion-piece, in *The Passionate Pilgrim,* and fully set forth in *England's Helicon,* over the signature 'Ignoto.' Walton denotes it as 'made by Sir Walter Raleigh in his younger days.'

105-127. WILLIAM SHAKESPEARE (1564-1616).

105. From *Love's Labour's Lost* (Act iv. sc. 3). 106. From *The Two Gentlemen of Verona* (Act iv. sc. 2). 107. From *Love's Labour's Lost* (Act v. sc. 2). 108. The first stanza is sung by Amiens, the second by the chorus, in the Forest of Arden in *As You Like It* (Act ii. sc. 5). 109. Amiens his song in *As You Like It* (Act ii. sc. 7). 110. The Boy's song in *Measure for Measure* (Act iv. sc. 1). 111. From *Cymbeline* (Act ii. sc. 3). 112. Sung by Guiderius and Arviragus in *Cymbeline* (Act iv. sc. 2). 113-114. Ariel in *The Tempest* (Act i.

sc. 2; and Act v. sc. 1). **115-127.** The Twenty-Ninth; Thirtieth; Fifty-Third; Seventy-First; Seventy-Third; Ninetieth; Ninety-Seventh; Hundred and Second; Hundred and Fourth; Hundred and Ninth; Hundred and Sixteenth; and Hundred and Forty-Sixth of Shakespeare's *Sonnets.*

128. RICHARD ROWLANDS *alias* 'VERSTEGEN (1565-1630?).

The grandson of Theodore Roland Verstegen, a Dutchman, whose family was expatriated *c.* 1500, Richard Rowlands was born in the shadow of the Tower of London, and partly educated at Christ Church, Oxford, which, being an ardent Catholic, and as such declining to take the tests, he left without a degree. Antiquary, polemist, poet, and translator, as occasion served—(he knew Anglo-Saxon, wrote Latin, and was master of several living languages, German included, besides his own)—he was a zealous champion of his Church against Elizabeth—(his *Theatrum Crudelitatum Hereticarum,* Antwerp, 1587, was translated into French, and went through three editions in its original form)—he published (1601) his *Odes in Imitation of the Seaven Penitential Psalms*; 'with sundry other Poemes and ditties tending to devotion and Pietie,' and from *Our Blessed Ladies Lullaby,* one of the numbers contained therein (pp. 50-54), the lyric treated in this Note is excerpted. I took it from the enlarged Edition of *The Golden Treasury* (1890), where it is printed anonymously, and referred to a collection dated 1620; but I am indebted to Mr. Palgrave for the information—(he had it not himself, he tells me, till his own volume was stereotyped, and correction was, of course, impossible)—which has enabled me to set it in its right perspective as a piece of pure Elizabethanism. Mr. Orby Shipley, I may add, has reprinted all the twenty-four stanzas of *Our Blessed Ladies Lullaby,* in his *Carmina Mariana* (London, 1893).

129-135. THOMAS CAMPION (1567-1640).

Campion, a most curious metrist, is, with so much else that is sweet and good in Elizabethan verse, Mr. A. H. Bullen's find; and these numbers are reprinted from his delightful *Lyrics from Elizabethan Song-Books,* an anthology which shows, on every page, how high was the lyric average of the 'spacious times' which bred it. **129** appears in Campion and Rosseter's *Book of Airs* (1601). **130.** First given in Campion's *Third Book of Airs* (*c.* 1617). **132.** From Campion's *Fourth Book of Airs* (*c.* 1617). **133.** From Campion's *Third Book of Airs* (*c.* 1617). **134.** From Campion and Rosseter's *Book of Airs* (1601). **135.** From *Two Bookes of Ayres. The First Contayning Diuine and Morall Songs.* . . . To be sung to the Lute and Viols, in two, three, and foure Parts; or by one Voyce to an Instrument,' reprinted in Mr. Bullen's edition of *The Works of Dr. Thomas Campion* (London, 1889). In my first selection from Campion I included that very graceful thing, *Follow thy Fair Sun*, from *The Book of Airs*. Afterwards I withdrew it. Now, repenting me of its exclusion, I am minded to give it here :—

FOLLOW THY FAIR SUN

FOLLOW thy fair sun, unhappy shadow!
 Though thou be black as night,
 And she made all of light,
Yet follow thy fair sun, unhappy shadow!

Follow her, whose light thy light depriveth!
 Though here thou liv'st disgraced,
 And she in heaven is placed,
Yet follow her whose light the world reviveth!

Follow those pure beams, whose beauty burneth!
 That so have scorched thee
 As thou still black must be
Till her kind beams thy black to brightness turneth.

Follow her, while yet her glory shineth!
 There comes a luckless night
 That will dim all her light;
And this the black unhappy shade divineth.

Follow still, since so thy fates ordained!
 The sun must have his shade,
 Till both at once do fade,
The sun still proved, the shadow still disdained.'

136-137. THOMAS NASHE (1567-1600).

136. Reprinted, after Mr. Bullen, from *Summer's Last Will and Testament* (1600). **137.** Reprinted after the text in Mr. Bullen's *Lyrics from the Dramatists of the Elizabethan Age* (London, 1889).

138. SIR HENRY WOTTON (1568-1639).

From Dr. Hannah's Edition of *The Poems of Sir Walter Raleigh, Collected and Authenticated with those of Sir Henry Wotton and other Courtly Poets from 1540 to 1650* (London, 1875). The song, set to music, was printed in Este's *Sixth Set of Ayres* in 1624.

139-152. ANONYMOUS.

139-140. Reprinted from *The Phœnix Nest* (1593), according to the text in the Second Volume of T. Park's *Heliconia* (London, 1815). **141-142.** From the Second Volume of *Davison's Poetical Rhapsody* (Mr. Bullen's reprint, London, 1891). **143.** From John Dowland's *Third and Last Book of Songs or Airs* (1603). The text is that in Mr. Bullen's *Lyrics from the Song-Books of the Elizabethan Age* (London, 1889). **144.** Given by Mr. Bullen (as above) from Robert Jones's *Second Book of Songs and Airs* (1601). **145.** Cited from John Dowland's *Second Book of Songs or Airs* (1600) by Mr. Bullen;

above). **146.** From John Wilbye's *Madrigals* (1598). (Bullen, as above.) **147.** From Robert Jones's *Second Book of Songs and Airs* (1601). (Bullen, as above.) **148.** From John Dowland's *First Book of Songs or Airs* (1597). (Bullen, as above.) **149.** From John Wilbye's *Second Set of Madrigals* (1609). **150.** From Thomas Ford's *Music of Sundry Kinds* (1607), as Mr. Bullen notes. **151.** From John Wilbye's *Second Set of Madrigals* (1609). **152.** From Thomas Bateson's *First Set of English Madrigals* (1604). (Bullen, as above.)

153-162. BEN JONSON (1573-1637).

153. From *Cynthia's Revels* (Act v. sc. 3). The text of the Jonson lyrics is taken from Gifford's Edition, re-edited by Lieutenant-Colonel Francis Cunningham (London, 1871). **154.** The fourth of the 'ten lyric pieces' in 'celebration of Charis.' The verses, as they stand, appeared in *Underwoods* (1640): the Second and Third Stanzas were printed earlier (1631) in *The Devil Is an Ass*, first played in 1616. **155.** The Sixth Song in *The Forest*. **156.** The Seventh Song in *The Forest*, written, if we may believe the *Conversations with Drummond*, as 'a penance to approve it [the thesis] in verse,' by command of Lady Pembroke. **157.** The Ninth Song in *The Forest*, and perhaps the best known of Jonson's lyrics. Cumberland, with much indignation, expresses his surprise 'to find our learned poet, Ben Jonson, had been poaching in an obscure collection of love-letters, written by the sophist Philostratus in a very rhapsodical stile,' &c. The song is, in fact, the most exquisite piece of selection and arrangement in the whole range of English verse. **158.** Hedon's song in *Cynthia's Revels* (Act iv. sc. 1). **159.** The Seventh Number in the *Underwoods* series, where the full title runs—*Begging Another, on Colour of Mending the Former*. **160.** The Third in the *Underwoods* series (2nd section). **161.** From *The Hue and Cry after Cupid*, a masque with nuptial songs 'celebrating the happy marriage of John, Lord Ramsay, Viscount Hadington, with the Lady Elizabeth Ratcliffe, daughter to the Right Honourable Earl of Sussex.' **162.** The Second in the *Underwoods* series (2nd section).

163-165. JOHN DONNE (1573-1631).

From Dr. Grosart's Edition of *The Complete Poems of John Donne, D.D.*, printed for private circulation in 1872-1873.

166. RICHARD BARNFIELD (1574-1637).

From Barnfield's *Poems: in Divers Humors*: 'Printed by G. S. for Iohn Iaggard, and are to be solde at his shoppe neere Temple-barre, at the Signe of the Hand and Starre' (1598). I follow, with certain differences, Dr. Grosart's Edition of the *Complete Poems*, printed for the Roxburghe Club (London, 1876).

167. JOSEPH HALL (1574-1656).

From *The Shaking of the Olive Tree*, issued posthumously in 1660.

168. ANONYMOUS.

From Walter Porter's *Madrigals and Airs* (1632), quoted in Mr. Bullen's *Lyrics from the Song-Books of the Elizabethan Age* (as above).

169-170. THOMAS DEKKER (1575-1640).

From *The Pleasant Comedy of Patient Grissell* (1603), by Dekker, Chettle and Haughton; but Mr. Bullen, from whose *Lyrics of the Elizabethan Dramatists* I reprint, adds :—'Doubtless the songs are by Dekker.'

171-172. THOMAS HEYWOOD (157-?-16—?).

171. From *The Fair Maid of the Exchange* (1607). 172. From *The Rape of Lucrece* (1608). Reprinted, like its predecessor, from Mr. Bullen's *Lyrics of the Elizabethan Dramatists* (as above).

173-180. JOHN FLETCHER (1579-1625).

173. From *The Maid's Tragedy* (Act ii. sc. 1). 174. Sung by the Boy in *The Captain* (Act iii. sc. 4). 175. From *The Captain* (Act iv. sc. 5). The song was conveyed by Thomas Killigrew (1612-1683), and appears in *Thomaso, or The Wanderer* (Part I. Act ii. sc. 3). 176-177. From *Valentinian* (Act ii. sc. 5), where it is sung upon the entry of Chilax, Lucina, Claudia and Marcellina. 178. Leandro's song in *The Spanish Curate* (Act ii. sc. 4), the subject of the play being derived from Céspedes y Meneses his *Gerardo*, Englished by Leonard Digges. 179. From *The Two Noble Kinsmen* (Act. i. sc. 1). There are who think that, at least, the songs in this play are Shakespeare's. 180. Sung by the Passionate Lord in *The Nice Valour* (Act iii. sc. 3). The text is Mr. Bullen's (as above).

181. PHILIP MASSINGER (1584-1639).

Eudocia's song in *The Emperor of the East* (Act v. sc. 3).

182. FRANCIS BEAUMONT (1585-1613).

From Dyce's Reprint of the *Poems* (Beaumont and Fletcher, *Works*, vol. xi. p. 497).

183-184. WILLIAM DRUMMOND (1585-1649).

Reprinted from *The Poetical Works of William Drummond of Hawthornden*, as edited by William B. Turnbull (London, 1856).

185. GILES FLETCHER (1588-1623).

The Song of the Enchantress, inserted between the Fifty-Ninth and Sixtieth Stanzas of *Christ's Victorie on Earth*, reprinted in Dr. Grosart's edition of *The Complete Poems of Giles Fletcher, B.D.* (London, 1876).

186. JOHN FORD (1586-1640).

This dirge from *The Broken Heart* (Act v. sc. 3) is sung by the chorus at Calantha's order :—

> 'Command the voices
> Which wait at th' altar now to sing the song
> I fitted for my end.'

187-188. WILLIAM BROWNE (1588-1644).

From *The Poems of William Browne of Tavistock:* edited by Gordon Goodwin, with an Introduction by A. H. Bullen (London, 1894); with certain readings from Chalmers's version in the *English Poets* (1818).

189-192. THOMAS CAREW (1589-1639).

From *The Poems and Masque of Thomas Carew*, 'Gentleman of the Privy-Chamber to King Charles I., and Cup-bearer to His Majesty.' Edited by Joseph Woodfall Ebsworth (London, 1893).

193. FRANCIS QUARLES (1592-1664).

From the Fifth Book of the *Emblemes* as given in Dr. Grosart's Edition of *The Complete Works in Prose and Verse of Francis Quarles*. The four last stanzas are omitted.

194. PETER HAUSTED (159-?-1645).

From *The Rival Friends* (Act iv. sc. 15). A. H. Bullen (as above).

195-198. GEORGE HERBERT (1593-1634).

From *The Temple. Sacred Poems and Private Ejaculations*, printed at Cambridge by Buck and Daniel in 1633.

199-221. ROBERT HERRICK (1594-1674).

The text followed is Mr. Pollard's:—*The Hesperides and Noble Numbers*, published by Messrs. Lawrence and Bullen (London, 1891). The three and twenty little masterpieces of which my selection from this unique lyrist is composed, are all from the *Hesperides*, and are numbered as follows:—53, 94, 132, 160, 178, 201, 205, 208, 216, 227, 238, 257, 262, 267, 274, 316, 413, 442, 447, 497, 582, 621, 665. The list is a long one, truly; but I think it will be found that not a single number could be spared.

222-223. JAMES SHIRLEY (1596-1661).

222. Reprinted from Mr. Bullen's *Lyrics from the Dramatists of the Elizabethan Age.* The song occurs in *The Imposture* (Act ii. sc. 2). 223. Cited by Mr. Bullen (as above) from the Third Scene (the play is not divided into Acts) of *The Contention of Ajax and Ulysses*, where it is given to Calchas, this, says Oldys, is 'the fine song which old Bowman used to sing to King Charles, and which he has often sung to me.'

224. JOHN WEBSTER (15—?-16—?).

The dirge from *The Duchess of Malfi* (Act iv. sc. 2).

225. JASPER MAYNE (1604-1672). ｀

From *The Amorous Warre* (Act iv. sc. 5), where the song is put into the mouths of 'Two Amazons.' The play exists with a title-page dated 1648, but is mostly found bound up with *The City Match*, reprinted in 1658—'both long since written by J. M. of Ch. Ch. in Oxon.'

226-228. SIR WILLIAM DAVENANT (1605-1668).

From the *Poems on Several Occasions, Never before Printed*, given in Herringman's folio, 'at the sign of the Blew Anchor,' dated 1673. In the original the title of 227 is 'The Soldier Going to the Field.' 228 is Viola's song in *The Law against Lovers* (Act iii. sc. 1).

229. WILLIAM HABINGTON (1605-1654).

From Mr. Arber's reprint of *Castara* (1870).

230-231. EDMUND WALLER (1605-1687).

From Robert Bell's Edition of the *Poetical Works of Edmund Waller* (London, 1854). Waller wrote little that is worth remembering, and nothing that is remembered save these two numbers. But he respected his art, and generally wrote well.

232-235. SIR JOHN SUCKLING (1608-1642).

From *The Works of Sir John Suckling, containing all his Poems,
Love-Verses, Songs, Letters, and his Tragedies and Comedies.* Never
before printed in one volume. (London, 1696.) I wish I could quote,
and quote in all its ripe yet elegant completeness, the unrivalled
Ballad of a Wedding. But it is outside the scheme of this book.

236-244. JOHN MILTON (1608-1674).

236-238. From *Poems: English and Latin, with a Few in Italian
and Greek.* Reprinted in vol. ii. of Professor Masson's Edition of
Milton's *Poetical Works* (London, 1874). 239-241. From *Comus.*
Milton's *Poetical Works*, vol. ii. of Masson's Edition. 242. *Lycidas*
is reprinted entire from Masson. 243. A Song from *Comus.* As
above, from Vol. ii. of Masson's Edition. 244. Part of a Chorus
(ll. 1268-1286) from *Samson Agonistes.*

245. WILLIAM CARTWRIGHT (1615-1643).

Reprinted from the verses at the end of the volume entitled
*Comedies, Tragi-Comedies, with other Poems, by Mr. William Cart-
wright, late Student of Christ-Church in Oxford, and Proctor of the
University* :—' The Ayres and Songs set by Mr. Henry Lawes, servant
to His late Majesty in His Publick and Private Musick.' (London,
1651.) 'My son Cartwright writes like a man.' Thus Ben Jonson.
He knew what he was talking about ; yet one cannot read his son
without a certain sense of disappointment.

246. THOMAS JORDAN (1612?-1685).

From the *Roxburghe Ballads.* But Jordan was City Poet in his
day, and the piece is given in *London's Triumph* (London, 1675),
and in Mr. Ebsworth's *Bagford Ballads* ii. 722-4). The Stanzas here
selected are the First, Second, Third—(which has been lavishly, but
not excessively, praised by Mr. Swinburne)—and Seventh. A coarser
set (arranged, no doubt, by the ingenious Tom D'Urfey) appears in
Wit and Mirth (1619), and is found in many eighteenth century
song-books, and some original asperities of rhythm and expression
have got rubbed away in the course of its descent down the stream
of years ; while the refrain survives unto this day in the burden of an
American thieves' song :—

> 'O, where will be the culls of the bing
>   A hundred stretches hence?
> The bene morts that sweetly sing,
>   A hundred stretches hence :—

and in a proverb dear to the British Workman :—'What's the odds
in a hundred years after?' In the Third Stanza 'bit' (=' piece') is

still a cant name for a girl ; while 'hogo' (Fr. *haut goût*) was, when the song was written, good enough fashionable slang for 'a taste,' or 'a savoury morsel.'

247. JAMES GRAHAM, MARQUESS OF MONTROSE
(1612-1650).

The First, Second, and Fifth Stanzas from the Roxburghe Collection in the British Museum (iii., p. 579), entitled *A Proper New Ballad to the Tune of 'I'll never Love thee mare,'* and best known as 'Montrose's Lines.' There is not much doubt that Montrose wrote them.

248-250. RICHARD CRASHAW (1615-1652).

From Mr. Turnbull's Edition of *The Complete Works of Richard Crashaw* in the 'Library of Old Authors.' (London, 1858.)

251-253. RICHARD LOVELACE (1618-1658).

From '*Lucasta. The Poems of Richard Lovelace.*' In Two Parts. The First comprising those published by himself; the Second, his posthumous poems.' (Chiswick, 1818.)

254. ABRAHAM COWLEY (1618-1668).

From the Third Book of *Davideis* as given in *The Works of Mr. Abraham Cowley : consisting of those which were formerly Printed, and those which he Design'd for the Press.* 'New Published out of the Author's Original Copies with *The Cutter of Coleman-Street.*' (London, 1700.)

255. ALEXANDER BROME (1620-1666).

The seventeenth in order of the *Songs and other Poems.* By Alex. Brome, Gent. (London, 1668.)

256-257. ANDREW MARVELL (1621-1678).

Reprinted from the First Volume of Dr. Grosart's Edition, in the Fuller Worthies' Library, of *The Complete Works in Verse and Prose of Andrew Marvell, M.P.* (1872).

258-262. HENRY VAUGHAN (1621-1695).

From Mr. Lyte's edition of *Silex Scintillans, etc. Sacred Poems and Pious Ejaculations.* By Henry Vaughan, 'Silurist.' (London, 1883.)

263-266. ANONYMOUS.

263. From the *Percy Folio MS.* (1650). Sets are found in *The Tea-Table Miscellany* (1724), i. 179-80, and the *Orpheus Caledonius* (1733) i. 71-73. In both the last line runs thus:—'For a maid again I'll never be'; and the latter includes this very superfluous stanza:—

> 'When Cockle-shells turn siller Bells,
> And Muscles grow on every Tree,
> When Frost and Snaw shall warm us a',
> Then shall my Love prove true to me.'

waly waly = out and alas	*syne* = afterwards	*siller* = silver
bow'd = bent	*cramasie* = crimson	*aik* = oak
kame = comb	*burn* = brook	*busk* = adorn
brae = hillside	*lichtly* = scorn	

264. With slight verbal changes, from Walter Scott's *Minstrelsy of the Scottish Border* (Kelso, 1802). The verses given in the text are the Second Part of the ballad. The First Part—'the production of a different and inferior bard,' the Editor thinks—begins thus:—

> 'O! sweetest sweet, and fairest fair,
> Of birth and worth beyond compare,
> Thou art the causer of my care,
> Since first I lovéd thee.'

265. From the Third Volume of Scott's *Minstrelsy of the Scottish Border*.

corbies = ravens	*mane* = moan	*wat* = know
gang = go	*fail-dyke* = fence of turfs	*een* = eyes
kens = knows	*hause-bane* = breast-bone	*theek* = thatch
ae = one	*the tane* = the one	

266. This is Mr. F. T. Palgrave's redaction of the ballad from the text of divers sets, done for *The Golden Treasury*. I am indebted to him for permission to reproduce it here.

hecht = promised	*gin* = if	*twined* = bereft
lavrock = lark	*haughs* = riverside meadows	*marrow* = spouse
lee-lang = livelong	*ilka* = every	

By way of contrast I subjoin the set sent, with other fragments of folk-song current in the West, by Robert Burns (1787) to W. Tytler of Woodhouselee, and printed in Cromek's *Scottish Songs* (1810). Burns, who had not then begun to vamp songs for Johnson's *Museum*, protested to his correspondent that he 'counted it sacrilege' to lay improving hands on 'the shattered wrecks of these venerable old compositions.' But, I think, the first quatrain is plainly his own:—

> 'Nae birdies sang the mirky hour
> Among the braes o' Yarrow,
> But slumbered on the dewy boughs
> To wait the waukening morrow.
>
> "Where shall I gang, my ain true love,
> Where shall I gang to hide me;
> For weel ye ken, i' yere father's bow'r
> It wad be death to find me."

"O, go you to yon tavern house,
    An' there count owre your lawin,
An' if I be a woman true
    I'll meet you in the dawin."

O, he's gone to yon tavern house
    An' counted owre his lawin,
When in there cam three armèd men
    To meet him in the dawin.

O, woe be unto woman's wit,
    It has beguilèd many !
She promisèd to come hersel',
    But she sent three men to slay me !

   .   .   .   .   .   .

Get up, get up, now sister Ann,
    I fear we've wrought you sorrow ;
Get up, ye'll find your true love slain
    Among the banks of Yarrow.

She sought him east, she sought him west,
    She sought him braid and narrow,
Till in the clintin of a craig
    She found him drown'd in Yarrow.

She's ta'en three links of her yellow hair,
    That hung down lang and yellow,
And she's tied it about sweet Willie's waist,
    An' drawn him out of Yarrow.

   .   .   .   .   .   .

I made my love a suit of clothes,
    I clad him all in tartan,
But ere the morning sun arose
    He was a' bluid to the gartan.

For yet another of many sets see Allan Ramsay, *The Tea-Table Miscellany*, ii. 114; and Thomson, *Orpheus Caledonius*, ii. 110. Hamilton of Bangour's descant on the same theme is of extreme interest—as the most notable experiment in cadence done in the first half of the eighteenth century : a period when scarce any one could be stately but in rigid iambics, and when the anapest (speaking generally, for it, too, had its moments) was given over to the service of Bacchus and the expression of the Abstract Buck.

267. ANONYMOUS.

From the first *Westminster Drollery* (1671), where it appears as *A Song at the Duke's House*. Mr. Ebsworth, from whose Reprint of the *Drolleries* (1875) it is taken, notes that a vastly inferior set (lacking the Second and Third Octaves, too) appears, to an air by Henry Lawes, in Playford's *Select Ayres and Dialogues* (1659). The full title of the collection, which begins with the pleasant, affectionate ditty ascribed to Charles II.:—

'I pass all my Hours in a shady old Grove,
And I live not the Day that I see not my Love :—

runs thus:—*Westminster Drollery; or, A Choice Collection of the Newest Songs and Poems Both at Court and Theaters.* ' By a Person of Quality. With Additions. London : Printed for *H. Brome* at the *Gun* in *St. Paul's Church Yard* near the *West End.* MD/CLXXI.'

268. THOMAS STANLEY (1625-1678).

From *Poems and Translations. By Thomas Stanley, Esquire.* ' Printed for the Author, and his Friends.' (London, 1647.)

269-273. JOHN DRYDEN (1631-1700).

The Dryden pieces are few in number for the simple reason that the lyrics of this master rhythmist, this rare artist in cadence, whether or not he wrote ' to please a ribald King and Court,' are often too gross in sentiment and too lewd in effect for quotation. The present selection is reprinted from Walter Scott's edition of *The Works of John Dryden.* (Edinburgh, 1821.) **269.** The *Song for Saint Cecilia's Day* is given in vol. xi. **270** is likewise reprinted from vol. xi. **271.** From *Cleomenes* (Act ii. sc. 2). **272.** Damilcar's song from *Tyrannic Love; or, The Royal Martyr* (Act iv. sc. 1). **273.** From *Secret Love; or, The Maiden Queen* (Act iv. sc. 2).

274. THOMAS BETTERTON (1635-1710).

From *The Prophetess; or, The History of Diocletian.* (London, 1716.) Founded on Beaumont and Fletcher's play, remodelled, ' with alterations and additions, after the manner of an Opera by Betterton.' Purcell wrote the music for it in 1690-1. The song, which may be fairly described as at the worst a capital imitation of Dryden, occurs in Act iii. sc. 3.

275-276. THOMAS FLATMAN (16—?-17—?).

From *Poems and Songs. By Thomas Flatman.* (London, 1674.)

277. CHARLES SACKVILLE, EARL OF DORSET (1637-1706).

From the first volume of *The Works of Celebrated Authors, of Whose Writings there are but small Remains.* (London, 1750.) Herein Dorset figures with Roscommon, Halifax, and Garth.

278-279. SIR CHARLES SEDLEY (1639-1701).

278. Victoria's song from *The Mulberry Garden* (Act iii. sc. 1), given in the Second Volume of *The Works of the Honourable Sir Charles Sedley, Bart., in Prose and Verse.* (London, 1722.) **279.** From the *Poems on Several Occasions* in Sedley's First Volume (as above). (London, 1722.)

280. APHRA BEHN (1642-1689).

Reprinted from *Poems upon Several Occasions: with a Voyage to the Island of Love.* By Mrs. A. Behn. (London, 1684.) The title of the song in this Edition is *Love Arm'd.*

281-287. JOHN WILMOT, EARL OF ROCHESTER (1647-1680).

281-285. From *Poems, &c., on Several Occasions: with Valentinian; a Tragedy.* Written by the Right Honourable John, late Earl of Rochester. (London, 1696.) The original form of 281 consists of nine stanzas; the first three are here selected. **286.** Reprinted, save for the omission of certain stanzas, from *The Works of the Right Honourable the Earls of Rochester and Roscommon.* 'With some Memoirs of the Earl of Rochester's Life by Monsieur St. Evremont. In a letter to the Dutchess of Mazarine.' The Third Edition. (London, 1709.) **287.** Reprinted from the 1696 edition of *Poems, &c., on Several Occasions: with Valentinian; a Tragedy* (as above).

288. THOMAS OTWAY (1651-1685).

Under the style of *The Inchantment*, this song figures among *Poems by Mr. Thomas Otway* in *A Supplement to the Works of the Most Celebrated Minor Poets.* (London, 1750.)

289. WILLIAM CONGREVE (1670-1729).

From the *Poems on Several Occasions* in the second volume of *The Works of Mr. William Congreve.* (London, 1719.)

290. JOHN GAY (1688-1732).

Acis's song from the first act of *Acis and Galatea*: 'An English Pastoral Opera. In three Acts. As it is Perform'd at the New Theatre in the Hay-Market; Set to Musick by Mr. Handel.' (London, 1733.)

291. ALEXANDER POPE (1688-1744).

From Elwin and Courthope's Edition of Pope's *Works* (vol. iv.). The first draft of *The Dying Christian to his Soul* was printed as early as 1730 in Lewis's *Miscellany*:—

'Vital spark of heavenly flame,
Dost thou quit this mortal frame?
Trembling, hoping, lingering, flying,
Oh the pain, the bliss of dying;
Cease, fond nature, cease thy strife,
Let me languish into life.

My swimming eyes are sick of light,
The lessening world forsakes my sight,
A damp creeps cold o'er every part,
Nor moves my pulse, nor heaves my heart,
The hovering soul is on the wing,
Where, mighty Death ? oh, where's thy sting ?

I hear around soft music play,
And angels beckon me away !
Calm as forgiven hermits rest,
I'll sleep, or infants at the breast ;
Till the last trumpet rends the ground,
Then wake with pleasure at the sound.'

This version of Hadrian's *Animula vagula, blandula* was rejected
for that in the text, which appeared in 1736.

292. HENRY CAREY (169-?-1742).

From *Poems on Several Occasions.* By Henry Carey. (London,
1729.) The earlier Editions (of 1713 and 1720) contain neither *Sally
in our Alley* nor *Namby-Pamby.*

293. JAMES THOMSON (1700-1748).

From the First Volume of the quarto: *Works of James Thomson,
with his last Corrections and Improvements.* (London, 1762.)

294-296. WILLIAM COLLINS (1721-1757).

From Langhorne's Edition of *The Poetical Works of Mr. William
Collins : with Memoirs of the Author ; and Observations on his Genius
and Writings.* (London, 1765.)

297. JEAN ELLIOT (1727-1805).

From Scott's *Minstrelsy of the Scottish Border* (as above).

ilka = each	*loaning* = field road	*wede* = taken
bughts = folds	*daffing* = larking	*leglin* = milk-pail
dowie = drooping	*hairst* = harvest	*bandsters* = binders
lyart = faded	*runkled* = wrinkled	*fleeching* = wheedling
swankies = strapping	*bogle* = bogey	*ilka ane* = each one
youngsters	*Dool and wae* = sorrow and woe	*wae* = miserable
loaning = a grassy road by a field- or meadow-side		

298. OLIVER GOLDSMITH (1728-1774).

Olivia's song, from the Fifth Chapter of *The Vicar of Wakefield.*
(London, 1766.)

299. ROBERT GRAHAM, OF GARTMORE (1735-1797).

From Scott's *Minstrelsy of the Scottish Border.* (Kelso, 1802.) Sir Walter wrote that these stanzas 'are averred to be of the age of Charles I.' They are also (as in the *Dictionary of National Biography*) ascribed to Robert Graham (afterwards Cunninghame-Graham), M.P. for Stirlingshire in 1794-6 ; and in effect, the flavour of them is neo-romantic enough to justify the ascription.

300-301. WILLIAM COWPER (1731-1800).

From the third volume of *Poems.* 'By William Cowper, of the Inner Temple, Esq.' (London, 1815.)

302. WILLIAM JULIUS MICKLE (1734-1788)
OR JEAN ADAMS (1710-1765).

'About the year 1771 or '72 it came first on the streets as a ballad, and I suppose the composition of the song was not much anterior to that period.' Thus Burns of this delightful thing, which is claimed for both Mickle and a certain Jean Adams, once a teacher at Craw-ford's Dyke, near Greenock, who published a volume of verse, and died (1765) in Glasgow Town Hospital.

jauds=jades	*gudeman*=husband	*slaes*=sloes
bauk=beam	*thraw*=wring	*ilka*=*every*
braw=nice	*bigonet*=a linen coif	*bishop*='a bustle,
maun gae=must go	*caller*=fresh	a *tournure*'

303. LADY ANNE LINDSAY (1750-1825).

Reprinted, with slight variations, from Sir Walter Scott's text—'the first authentic edition'—prepared for, and dedicated to, the Bannatyne Club (July 1828).

kye=kine	*gudeman*=husband	*win*=earn
wraith=ghost	*sair*=sorely	*greet*=weep
muckle=much	*ae*=one	*gang*=go

304-314. WILLIAM BLAKE (1757-1827).

304-308. From *Poetical Sketches.* (London, 1783.) 309. Entitled *Introduction* in the *Songs of Innocence.* (London, 1789.) 310-314. From the *Songs of Experience.* (London, 1794.) Gilchrist, in his *Life of William Blake*, gives a version of *The Tiger*, with small variants from the original. The second version is given by Mr. W. M. Rossetti (pp. 120-121) in his edition of *The Poetical Works of William Blake, Lyrical and Miscellaneous.* (London, 1874.)

315·333. ROBERT BURNS (1759-1796).

315. Many of Burns's songs are only parcel-Burns—are Burns, that is, *plus* some one else (forgotten). But this sincere and charming lyric—(which is very often sung in Scotland, as it is printed in Mr. Palgrave's *Golden Treasury of Songs and Lyrics* (1893), with additions by absurd Scotsmen)—is, so far as I know, undoubted and unquestioned.

airts=points (of the compass)   *row*=roll   *shaw*=wood

316. This admirable extravaganza is pure Burns likewise.

fou=drunk	*drappie in our ee*=droplet in our eye	
daw=dawn	*bree*=brew	*lee-lang*=live-long
Christendie=Christendom	*blinkin*=shining	*lift*=welkin
hie=high	*wyle*=coax	*a wee*=a little
gang awa=go away		

317. As it stands, this is all Burns, except the first and last lines of the stanza, which date from the sixteenth century, and are used to excellent purpose in a song (not fit for modern print) 'found in *The Masque* (London, 1768), and other song-books' (*The Centenary Burns*, iii. 249, Edinburgh, 1896).

jo=sweetheart	*acquent*=acquainted	*brent*=straight
beld=bald	*pow*=pate	*canty*=jolly

318. Suggested by an old song, but none the less an excellent example of Burns at his best and happiest.

leeze me on=commend me to		*cleeds*=clothes
bien=well	*haps*=wraps	*fiel*=comfortably
laigh=low	*ilka*=every	*burnies*=brooklets
theekit=thatched	*birk*=birch	*caller*=cool
biel=shelter	*aiks*=oaks	*lintwhites*=linnets
ither's=each other's	*craik*=corncrake	*paitrick*=partridge
ley=pasture	*jinkin*=dodging	*aboon*=above
a'=all		

319. Right Burns, this.

tittie=sister	*len*=lend	*braw*=fine
poortith=poverty	*mak a fen*=make a shift	*minnie*=mother
blaws o' his siller=vapours about his money		*waukin*=lying awake to
deave=deafen	*sten*=leap	watch
droukit=drenched		

320. Burns and none else. It exists in three sets, of which this is the second and the best. The more popular version was spoiled by being bombasted with inexpressive adjectives to make it fit a tune. **321.** Burns, who was scrupulous in the matter of ascriptions, declared the first quatrain—(the best of the song)—to be traditional; but thus far we have only his word for it.

tassie=cup

322. This also is very Burns:—it is held to refer to Sylvander's last (victorious) meeting with Clarinda (6th December 1791). **323.** Pure Burns:—'I composed this song pretty early in life,' he says, 'and

sent it to a young girl'—(Armour or Paton)—'a very particular
acquaintance of mine, who was at that time under a cloud.'

babie-clouts=baby-clothes   *tent*=heed   *faut*=fault
groanin=a lying-in   *groanin maut*=ale for the gossips
creepie-chair=the stool of repentance   *crack*=talk
my lane=alone   *fidgin-fain*=tingling with fondness

324. This, too, is Burns's own ; and he thought it one of his best.

yestreen=yester-night   *gie*=give   *ilk*=each   *canna*=cannot
gae=go   *kirk*=church   *but*=without

325. All Burns except the two first lines of the chorus. It appeared
in the Kilmarnock Edition (1786), and is therefore very early work.

rigs=ridges   *tentless*=careless   *gear*=money

326. Suggested by a blackguard old song preserved, together with
another set attributed to Burns, in the 'unique and interesting garland
called *The Merry Muses of Scotland* (*c.* 1800), probably—almost certainly—collected by Burns himself' (*The Centenary Burns*, as above,
i. 415, 1896) :—

> 'Green grows the rashes, O,
> Green grows the rashes, O,
> The feather bed is no sae saft,' etc.

canny=quiet   *gang tapsalteerie*=go topsy-turvy.
war'ly=worldly   *douce*=prudent

327. Burns asserted of this famous song that he 'took it down from
an old man's singing.' For the older sets on which it is certainly
founded, see *The Centenary Burns* (as above) iii. 407-410.

rin=run   *paidl't*=paddled   *dine*=noon
braes=hills   *burn*=brook   *waucht*=draught
gowans=daisies   *guid-willie*=friendly   *fiere*=partner

328. Pure Burns, this one.

loons=rascals   *unco*=stranger   *rung*=cudgel
clout=patch   *tinkler*=tinker   *ca'*=drive

329. An arrangement, first and last, of fancies and expressions current in popular song long before Burns wrote. For his origins see
The Centenary Burns (as above), iii. 402-406. His result is not
incomparable to Ben Jonson's in *Drink to Me Only*, as to which see
ante, p. 384, Note to No. 157. 330. Suggested, and more, by an old
broadside ballad, *The Last Words of James Mackpherson, Murderer*,
which ends thus :—

> 'Thus wantonly and rantingly
> I am resolved to die ;
> And with undaunted courage I
> Will mount this fatal tree.'

spring=a dance tune : *sturt*=trouble

331. This, like *Kenmure's On and Awa*, is probably referable to a
Jacobite original ; but none has ever been discovered.

sae=so   *jimpèd*=jumped   *scroggy*=scrubby
brawly weel=finely well   *tirled*=rasped

332. Pure Burns, again, and very early work, though it remained unpublished till 1800 (Currie). For the stanza, see *ante*, p. 376, Note to No. 22.

> *trysted*=appointed   *stoure*=dust, turmoil   *canna*=cannot

333. The third stanza is the last of the broadside ballad of *Mally Stewart*, which begins thus :—

> 'The cold winter is past and gone,
> And now comes on the spring,
> And I am one of the King's lifeguards,
> And must go fight for my King,
> My dear—
> I must go fight for my King':—

a copy of which, dating as early as 1745-6, was communicated to the editors of *The Centenary Burns* (iii. 433-436) by the Rev. J. W. Ebsworth. The rest is Burns.

334-337. WILLIAM WORDSWORTH (1770-1850).

334. *Poems Founded on the Affections*, No. VIII. **335.** *Poems of the Imagination*, No. I. **336.** *Poems of the Imagination*, No. VIII. **337.** 'Intimations of Immortality from Recollections of Early Childhood.'

338-347. SIR WALTER SCOTT (1771-1832).

The Scott numbers are reprinted from *The Poetical Works* of Sir Walter, edited by Lockhart and published by Cadell (Edinburgh) in 1848. **338.** This *Hunting Song* is said to have been 'first published in the continuation of Strutt's Queenhoo Hall, 1808, inserted in the *Edinburgh Annual Register* of the same year, and set to a Welsh air in *Thomson's Select Melodies*, vol. iii., 1817.' **339.** Written, Lockhart notes, 'for Campbell's *Albyn's Anthology*, 1816. It may also be seen, set to music, in Thomson's Collection, 1830.' **340.** This wonderful lyric, wherein Romance is taken in the act as nowhere else in song, is from *The Heart of Midlothian* (Chapter xl.). **341.** From *The Lady of the Lake* (Canto iii.). **342.** From *Rokeby* (Canto iii.). **343.** From *Marmion* (Canto iii.). **344.** From *The Antiquary* (Chapter x.). **345.** 'Written for *Albyn's Anthology*, vol. ii., 1818, and set to music in Mr. Thomson's Collection, in 1822.'—(Lockhart.)

Caird=tinker
Fleech=wheedle
leglin=milk-pail
maukin=hare
Ilka=every
cantle o' the cawsey= middle of the pavement
kist=chest
Dunts o' kebbuck=pieces of cheese
Whiles=now
Craig to tether=neck to halter

lilt=carol
gudewife=wife
clout=mend
leisters kipper = spears salmon
bends a bicker=trolls a bowl
steek=shut
gear=property
webs or duds=sheets or clothes
airn=iron

gudeman=husband
houp=hoop
pan=pot
pow=pate
hostler-wife=hostess
fou=drunk
amrie=cupboard
orra=odd
taits o' woo=portions of wool
wuddie=gallows

346. From *Quentin Durward* (Chapter iv.). 347. In his *Journal* (December 22, 1825) Sir Walter writes :—'The air of *Bonny Dundee* running in my head to-day, I wrote a few verses to it before dinner, taking the keynote from the story of Clavers leaving the Scottish Convention of Estates in 1688-89. I wonder if they are good?'

douce=prudent	*ilk carline*=each beldam	*flyting*=scolding
couthie=pleasant	*set tryst*=made an appointment	*gullies*=knives
cowls of Kilmarnock=broad bonnets		*marrows*=comrades

348-349. SAMUEL TAYLOR COLERIDGE (1772-1834).

The text is that published in Mr. Ashe's Aldine Edition. (London, 1885.) Glycine's song is from *Zapolya* (1817).

350-353. WALTER SAVAGE LANDOR (1775-1864).

350. The songlets under this number are given separately (Nos. x., lxv., lxxv., clxxvi.) in the *Miscellaneous Poems*, which form the Eighth Volume of Landor's *Works and Life*. (London, 1876.) 351. This is numbered cii. in the *Miscellaneous Poems* just noted. 352. *The Maid's Lament* is found in *The Citation of William Shakespeare* (*Works*, vol. ii., pp. 483-484). 353. This song is numbered lviii. in the *Miscellaneous Poems* aforesaid.

354. CHARLES LAMB (1775-1834).

From *The Poetical Works of Charles Lamb*. (London, 1836.)

355-356. THOMAS CAMPBELL (1777-1844).

From the Aldine Edition of *Thomas Campbell's Poetical Works*. (London, 1875.) 355. This noble ballad is imitated from an ancient broadside :—

> 'You Gentlemen of England,
>   That lives at home at ease,
> Full little do you think upon
>   The dangers of the seas,' etc. :—

from which, moreover, Campbell borrowed his refrain :—

> 'When the stormy winds do blow.'

And this again is given by Mr. Ebsworth (*Roxburghe Ballads*, vi. 432-3) as 'altered from Martin Parker,' whose original, to the tune of *Saylors for My Money*, is printed in the same Volume (797), and begins thus :—

> 'Countrie men of England, who live at home at ease
> And little think what dangers are incident o' the seas,
> Give ear unto the Saylor who unto you will shew
> His case, his case,
>   *How ere the Winds doth blow.*

Certain stanzas are omitted from 356 as tending to bathos, and ruining the effect of a singularly fine and stirring piece of verse.

357-361. THOMAS MOORE (1779-1850).

These five pieces are taken from the *Irish Melodies* as given in the *Poetical Works of Thomas Moore.* (London, 1840-41.)

362-363. EBENEZER ELLIOTT (1781-1849).

From *The Poetical Works of Ebenezer Elliott* edited by his son Edwin Elliott, Rector of St. John's, Antigua. (London, 1876.)

364-365. THOMAS LOVE PEACOCK (1785-1866).

364. The catch sung by Mr. Hilary and the Reverend Mr. Larynx in *Nightmare Abbey*: from Dr. Garnett's Edition. (London, 1891.) 365. From the third volume of Cole's Edition of Peacock's *Works*. (London, 1875.) The Table of Contents refers the song to 1806; in the text (p. 50) it is said to be 'written after 1806.'

366-367. ALLAN CUNNINGHAM (1785-1842).

From *Poems and Songs* by Allan Cunningham. With an Introduction, Glossary, and Notes by Peter Cunningham. (London, 1847.) Both were forged by 'honest Allan' (who never could refuse a chance of appearing to vie with Burns in the manipulation, or even the manufacture, of traditional material) for Cromek's *Remains of Nithsdale and Galloway Song* (1810).

366.
kames o' hinney=honey-combs		*een*=eyes
keek=peep	*loof*=palm	*jimpy*=slender
armfu'=spouse	*eebree*=eyebrow	*fa'*=lot
fee=hire	*bairnies*=small children	*fou*=full

367.
mirk=black cloud : *blinks*=shines

368-380. BYRON (1788-1824).

My selection is printed from *The Works of Lord Byron* (1837), the First Complete Edition, undertaken by Murray, it would seem, at the urgent instancing of Sir Walter Scott, and 'respectfully inscribed' 'To the Right Honourable Sir Robert Peel, Bart., etc. etc. etc.,' as being a 'Collective Edition of the Works of His "School and Form Fellow"' at Harrow. 368. From the Third *Harold* (1817); addressed to Augusta Leigh. 369. No. 1 of the *Hebrew Melodies* (January, 1815). 370. Addressed to Lady Byron, and published, together with *A Sketch from Private Life*:—Born in a garret, in a kitchen bred :— in *The Champion* of Sunday, April 14, 1816, and in *The Morning Chronicle* two days after. In the former print—(which says, by the way, that 'though not sold, they have been distributed by his respectable publisher, Mr. Murray')—the verses are dated March 17, 1816; in the latter, March 30 of the same year. 371. Addressed to Augusta Leigh, under date of July 24, 1816. 372. Written in 1808. 373. Dated 1812, and published (1812) in the Second Edition of

Childe Harold, i. and ii., under this device :—'Heu, quanto minus est cum reliquis versari, quam tui meminisse.'   374. Dated 1815, and suggested, directly or indirectly, by the death of Byron's old school-mate, the Duke of Dorset (killed by a fall from his horse), these 'Stanzas for Music,' which the writer describes as 'the *truest*, though the most melancholy, I ever wrote,' were sent to Moore for Power (publisher of the *Irish Melodies*), who brought them out 'with very beautiful music by Sir John Stevenson.'   375. Not dated, but apparently written in 1815.   376. 'This should have been written fifteen moons ago; the first stanza was.'   Thus Byron to Moore under date of 10th July 1817, so that this brave, affectionate lyric—(surely its Second Stanza embodies as good and sound a philosophy of life as protestant could desire?)—was meant as the writer's farewell ere he went into exile in the April of 1816.   377. Written at Venice, in 1817, when, 'although I did not dissipate much upon the whole, yet I found the sword wearing out the scabbard, though I have but just turned the corner of twenty-nine.'   378. Dated November 1821; 'com-posed . . . on the road from Florence to Pisa'; and addressed to Mme. Guiccioli.   379. From the Third *Juan* (1821).   380. Dated 'Missolonghi, Jan. 22, 1824.'

381-394. PERCY BYSSHE SHELLEY (1792-1822).

These examples of the art and genius of the master-lyrist of our race are reprinted from the Aldine Edition.   381-382. The *Ode to the West Wind* and *The Cloud* appear among the miscellaneous poems issued with *Prometheus Unbound* (1820).   383. The final chorus in *Hellas* (1822).   384. First given in the *Posthumous Poems* (1824).   385. First printed in 1822, in the Second Number of *The Liberal*, under the style and title of *Song, Written for an Indian Air*.   386-393. From the *Posthumous Poems* (as above).   394. The first title, when the poem appeared in *The Athenæum* of November 17, 1832, was :—*An Ariette for Music.   To a Lady Singing to her Accompaniment on the Guitar.*

395-400. JOHN KEATS (1795-1821).

In the case of the selections from Keats, the Aldine text, edited by Lord Houghton, is adopted.   395. The *Hymn to Pan* is from the First Book of *Endymion* (1818).   396. From the Fourth Book of *Endymion*.   At the close of the second section I have ventured to omit a stanza of the original, because it examples all Keats's defects, and embitters the perfect sweetness by which it is surrounded.   For the pedant's sake I give it here :—

> ' Within his car, aloft, young Bacchus stood,
>   Trifling his ivy-dart, in dancing mood,
>   With sidelong laughing ;
>   And little rills of crimson wine imbrued
>   His plump white arms, and shoulders, enough white
>   For Venus' pearly bite ;
>   And near him rode Silenus on his ass,
>   Pelted with flowers as he on did pass
>   Tipsily quaffing.'

2 C

401. THOMAS HOOD (1799-1845).

From the First Volume of *The Poetical Works of Thomas Hood.*
(London, 1856.)

402-404. THOMAS LOVELL BEDDOES (1803-1849).

These pieces are reprinted from Pickering's edition of *The Poems,
Posthumous and Collected, of Thomas Lovell Beddoes.* (London, 1851.)
Two stanzas of *Dream-Pedlary* (402) are omitted from the text :—

> ' If there are ghosts to raise,
>   What shall I call,
> Out of hell's murky maze,
>   Heaven's blue pall ?
> Raise my loved long-lost boy—
> To lead me to his joy.
>   There are no ghosts to raise ;
>   Out of death lead no ways ;
>   Vain is the call.
>
> Know'st thou not ghosts to sue ?
>   No love thou hast.
> Else lie as I will do,
>   And breathe thy last.
> So out of Life's fresh crown
> Fall like a rose-leaf down.
>   Thus are the ghosts to wooe ;
>   Thus are all dreams made true ;
>   Ever to last ! '

The *Dirge* is from *Death's Jest-Book ; or, The Fool's Tragedy* (Act ii.
sc. 1). 404. From *Torrismond* (Act i. sc. 3).

405-408. EDGAR ALLAN POE (1809-1849).

From Mr. Andrew Lang's edition of *The Poems of Edgar Allan Poe.*
(London, 1881.)

AUTHORS

FIRST LINES

2 C 2

Printed by T. and A. Constable, Printers to Her Majesty
at the Edinburgh University Press